She's Mine

Tammy Doherty

Books by Tammy Doherty

Celtic Cross

Sometimes you have to forget who you are to become who you should be.

Christian Historical Romance set in 1880s Colorado

Claddaugh

Leigh Latham chose money over love, turning her back on family and friends. When the dream becomes a nightmare, can she hope to find forgiveness?

Christian Historical Romance set in late 1800s Colorado

Celtic Knot

Murder, kidnapping, counterfeiting—all in a day's work for Kyle Lachapelle

Christian Historical Romance set in 1890s Colorado

About the Author

Tammy Doherty lives in a small town in central Massachusetts, eerily similar to Naultag. When not writing, she grows and sells perennials with her husband and two children. A veterinary technician by training, Tammy now also works for a veterinary distribution company. Her days are filled with family, animals, plants, and writing. Connect with Tammy on Facebook at www.facebook.com/TammyDohertyAuthor or follow her on Twitter: @tdinishowen

A Mystique of NaultagNovel

She's Mine

Tammy Doherty

She's Mine
Tammy Doherty
Copyright 2014 Tammy Doherty

Cover designed and created by Tiffany M. Doherty

ISBN-13: 978-1505284461

ISBN-10: 1505284465

So do not fear, for I am with you; do not be dismayed, for I am your God. I will strengthen you and help you; I will uphold you with my righteous right hand.

Isaiah 41:10

ONE

The house looks abandoned. Like me.

Caitlin stared at the ranch style house with its fieldstone siding. Jumbled and irregular, like her life. The only continuity died along with Gram. Hard to believe only a year had passed. Yews along the front sported spiked punk hairstyles. Dark, blank windows shunned the warm afternoon sunlight.

At least poison ivy hadn't swallowed the house whole like the barn across the street.

Hope remained.

Taking a deep breath, she pushed the car door open. Head up, shoulders squared, face the memories. Pray for a new beginning in an old, familiar setting. A door banged shut in the distance. Fear prickled the back of Caitlin's neck as she spun around. Pent up breath rushed from her lungs. It was only Mr. Henderson. The elderly man stood beside an equally elderly truck across the street.

"Hi, Mr. Henderson."

The old man grinned, returned her wave. Nice, normal, nothing to fear.

Inside, the house was quiet. She inhaled the faint odor of Murphy's Oil soap, Gram's favorite cleaner. Her aunts must've used it when they cleaned out the house. Memories flooded her mind. Doing homework at the kitchen table while Gram made supper. Reading alongside Gram in the evening. Birthdays, holidays, every day with Gram.

Mom driving away, leaving me behind as if I was nothing more than a piece of furniture. Except Mom came back for the furniture.

Now here she was again, once more unwanted.

That wasn't fair. The city of Lynn had laid off a number of teachers. Nothing personal. It still stung. She sighed. Look on the bright side, now she could move back into the only real home she'd ever known. Rent free.

Dark rectangular patches showed where family pictures once hung. Empty closets, bare walls, unadorned windows. Nothing remained of the past. It, too, had deserted her.

Had even God abandoned her?

A deep rumble drew her to the kitchen window. Grandpa's old Ferguson tractor backed out of the shed with a stranger at the wheel. She glanced up and down the street but saw no sign of Mr. Henderson. Unbelievable! This guy must've waited until Mr. Henderson left before helping

himself to the equipment. Still, hadn't he noticed her car? He really had nerve. A tremor of indignation surged through her.

Grandpa used to let her ride with him on the tractor as he worked in the fields. She'd sit on his lap, grasping the wheel and sometimes even steer the tractor. She couldn't reach the pedals, so Grandpa controlled the speed. Even now, nearly eighteen years after his death, Caitlin remembered feeling safe and loved with Grandpa's arms encircling her. She couldn't just stand by and let this thief take those memories, as well.

Whirling, she stormed out of the house, dress swirling around her knees. If this guy thought he'd get away with stealing a vintage piece of equipment, he was in for a big surprise.

Halfway across the street she faltered. What if he had a gun?

Ridiculous. No one would carjack a sixty-year-old tractor. Even at full throttle, she could outrun the antique. She charged toward the shed.

The odor of gasoline washed over her. Mr. Bold-as-you-please had backed the Ferguson around to the far side of the building. She rounded the corner and crashed head-on into the stranger.

He grunted.

She stumbled backward and tripped on a rock.

The tractor thief grasped her arms, saving her from falling.

She sucked in a sharp breath as fear wrapped numbing tendrils around her mind. What was she thinking, coming out here to confront this guy? Tall, broad shoulders and strong arms... she couldn't defend herself against him. Forget the gun. He just might be more dangerous without it. His fingers were like a fiery brand on her chilled skin.

"Whoa, where's the fire?" A hint of concern mixed with his humorous tone.

She pulled away, looking up into blue-gray eyes the color of Boston Harbor on a hazy day. He raised an eyebrow, head tilted to meet her gaze. Unruly blond curls topped a sun-bronzed face. He didn't look menacing, especially when his lips curled into a slow grin.

Why had she come out here? Oh, yeah…

"Don't think you'll get away with this." She looked at her arm. A muted cry escaped her lips. "You got grease all over me."

"I'm sorry." He pulled a rag from his back pocket. "I was trying to save you from falling."

"Oh, like it's my fault."

He swiped at the offending smudge.

"Stop that!" She stepped back. "You'll get it on my dress." She narrowed her eyes, hoping to look tougher than she felt.

"So why were you racing out here?" He tucked the rag back into his pocket.

"Don't act innocent. I'm not letting you steal that tractor."

He laughed. "And just who are you to stop me?"

She put her hands on her hips, as if he was an insolent student. A car raced into the driveway beside them, stirring up dust. Caitlin coughed, waving her hands to dissipate the cloud. She recognized the driver as Mr. Henderson's younger son, Randy. Her adversary folded his arms over his chest, glaring at the car.

"Hey, Caitlin, how are ya?" Randy called as he strolled across the dusty driveway. "I see you've met my cousin Sean."

"You're late," Sean growled.

Randy grinned but otherwise ignored him.

Caitlin's gaze went back to the man she'd just accused of being a thief. "You're Randy's cousin? So that makes you Mr. Henderson's nephew?"

The corner of Sean's mouth lifted slightly. "Guilty as charged."

"I'm sorry. I didn't know who you were." She backed away a few steps. "I thought you were stealing my grandfather's tractor."

Sean's smirk inched higher up his cheeks. The effect was disarming. "I'm no thief. Besides, the tractor doesn't belong to your grandfather."

"It most certainly does…er, I mean, it did. Now it belongs to—"

"Me," Randy interrupted. "I bought it from your grandmother two years ago."

Gram sold the tractor? She must've needed money. Caitlin's cheeks burned. She should have been here to help, instead of being too wrapped up in her own life. She was no better than her parents. Shame warmed her cheeks as she stared at her toes. Bad enough jumping to the rash conclusion that Sean was stealing. She'd also shown both men how she'd let Gram down. She backed away a few more steps and snuck a peek at Sean. His eyes crinkled with humor, lips curved in a heart-stopping grin.

Why did the man standing before her suddenly seem more threatening now that she knew he wasn't a thief?

* * *

Sean Taggart watched Caitlin stomp back across the street. Straight, stiff spine, head held high. Her sandals made a slapping sound on the pavement then quieted when she reached the lawn. The black grease smudge on her arm showed clearly even from this distance. He regretted getting her dirty, especially since it upset her so much. But he hadn't come close to ruining her pretty dress.

Wearing sandals dusted with sparkling rhinestones and soft coral nail polish on her toenails and fingernails, she looked like she'd just stepped out of a magazine. Even her honey brown hair was perfectly styled, with a blue headband that matched her dress. Like she belonged lounging on the deck of a yacht or sipping iced tea brought to her by servants. She didn't belong in the middle of nowhere, which was pretty much the exact map location for Naultag, Massachusetts.

"There goes the ice princess." Randy stared at Caitlin's retreating form. "She never dressed like that back in school. Not that it mattered."

Sean raised an eyebrow. "I don't remember her." He wouldn't forget a girl like Caitlin. He hadn't been that clueless in high school.

"She transferred in the year after you graduated. 'Sides, she wasn't into the social scene." Randy continued staring, although Caitlin was no longer in sight. "She was a nerd, back then. Sure has changed."

Sean tried to picture the woman he'd just encountered as a nerd. Impossible. Today's Caitlin was poised, confident—almost arrogant—down right attractive. To look at any way.

"She wouldn't go out with you, huh?"

Randy shrugged. "She wasn't normal. President of the math club and in the chess club. Pretty girl like her should've gone out with at least a few of the guys who asked."

"She didn't date anyone?"

"Nope, 'cept maybe Scott Bartlett. They were always together, even when Bartlett started dating Janelle. They've always had a strange relationship. A *Three's Company* kind of thing, know what I mean."

Knowing Randy, he wasn't talking about a guy living platonically with two women. Sean frowned. An indecent implication.

"I'm telling you, Caitlin Harrington acted like she was better than all of us." Randy shook his head. "Maybe she thought being Jack Harrington's daughter made her special."

"*The* Jack Harrington?"

"Yeah, the guy who owns the chain of sporting goods stores. He was a local celebrity for a while when he played major league baseball."

"I know who he was, and is." Anyone around here interested in baseball knew about Jack Harrington.

"And Caitlin is his little princess." Randy snorted. "Weird that he never came to any school functions, though. And she hated it whenever anyone asked her about Jack."

Maybe Randy just thought she was a princess. Sometimes insecure, quiet people got mistakenly labeled as being snobbish. Not that she seemed the least bit shy or insecure. Didn't matter, either way. They'd only just met and Sean didn't know her. He certainly wasn't about to pass judgment on her personality. But the last thing he needed in his life was another princess. Especially not one as beautiful as Caitlin.

He shook his head, as if that could dispel thoughts of Caitlin Harrington. "You ready to start working?"

"What's your rush? We've got all week."

Sean crossed his arms over his chest, leaning back as he eyeballed Randy. "We still need to get that culvert in up at the campground. Preferably before it rains."

Randy swung up into the tractor seat. "You should've done that last fall."

"I had other things to worry about back then."

"Yeah, I remember. Uncle Pat's heart attack scared my folks half to death."

Sean's gut clenched. Even now, seven months later, fear coursed through his veins when he thought about Dad's heart attack. He'd always pictured his father as a rugged, hardworking man. Seeing him in the hospital bed, frail and elderly, looking like the pillows might swallow him whole, was a shock.

"Your folks should just retire for real."

"Probably." Sean focused on the disc harrows behind the tractor. Although he'd taken over running the family campground five years ago, Dad still entrenched himself in the work. Sean liked having him around, liked that both his parents were part of running the business. On the other hand, Dad would be seventy this year. He was fond of quoting a favorite song by saying he was old enough to know better but still too young to care. Sean might have to work harder at persuading them to stay in retirement year round.

"If I owned a condo in Florida, I'd stay there and never come back to this hick town."

"We don't all hate Naultag as much as you do, Randy. Some of us even like it here."

Randy *hmphed*. He swatted at a cloud of mayflies. "Maybe if you got married they would retire and stay in Florida."

The thought had gnawed at Sean for months. Marrying just might be enough to convince them their job was done. His life was perfect—then Dad's heart attack changed everything. It wasn't enough to work hard, invest smart and give back to the community whenever possible. Now he had to find a wife so his parents could retire. Not like he didn't want to get married. He'd love to one day have a marriage as perfect as his parents' was. Finding Ms. Right on his own hadn't worked out, though, and so far the Lord hadn't seen fit to bring the right woman into his life.

"Face it, Tag, you're the kind of guy who should be married and raising a family." Randy stood with his arms crossed, grinning. "You aren't getting any younger."

"Thirty-two is not old." Sean would love to plow that smirk under like the weeds in the field. *Lord, please give me patience.*

"You need to get passionate about something besides work."

"I like my work." Sean's jaw flexed. He controlled his life, not anyone else. He took a couple long strides toward the tractor shed. "Let it be, Randy. I don't need a guilt trip from you."

Behind him, the Ferguson's engine grumbled to life. Sean focused on work and put aside thoughts of marriage, passion and Caitlin Harrington.

TWO

Caitlin pulled the door open, letting in the bright morning sunshine. Fluttering paper caught her eye—a note taped to the wood frame. Handwritten in bold black marker, the words sent a chill down her spine.

You don't belong here.

Someone had lurked outside her front door and she hadn't even heard. When had this note been left? Her gaze swept the surrounding area.

No one in sight.

She darted back inside, closed the door and threw the deadbolt. Who would leave such an ominous message? In the last ten years she hadn't been home long enough to have made any enemies. And she hadn't had time to antagonize anyone since arriving yesterday afternoon.

Except Sean Taggart.

The words were written in a careful, precise style. Hard to say if the author was a man or a woman. It was possible Sean Taggart wrote the note. But why? He seemed more amused than offended by her accusation yesterday. His wide grin flashed in her memory. A warm tingle tickled her belly as she recalled the feel of his strong arms catching her, saving her from a fall.

On the other hand, as Charlie Henderson's nephew, he had almost as much claim on this farm as she did. The Henderson family had been using the land since before Grandpa died. Sean might not want her here, no matter how friendly he'd acted. Besides, a man wasn't always what he seemed. She'd learned that the hard way.

Maybe it was a joke. A sick, twisted joke. Randy Henderson was capable of such perverted humor. In high school, he was the king of tired, clichéd pick-up lines. It would be like him to say something along the lines of, "You don't belong here, you belong with me."

A new current of fear jolted Caitlin's nerves. She examined

the note again, checking for the second half of the sentiment. The back of the paper was blank. Her last conversation with Adam echoed in her mind. "Stay with me, Caitlin," Adam had said. "We belong together." Could he have written the note?

No, she left him in Lynn. Adam had no reason to follow her here. Then again, he'd had no reason to sit in his car, parked across the street from her condo, all night Saturday. She'd made clear her lack of feelings for him. She moved two weeks early for that very reason, to put space between them.

The note couldn't be from Adam.

A knock vibrated the door at her back. She squelched a yelp and peered out the door sidelight. Janelle Bartlett met her gaze and made a face, crossing her eyes and sticking out her tongue. Caitlin let out a pent up breath, smiling as she opened the door.

"What's with the deadbolt? This isn't the city, you know, and it's broad daylight."

Caitlin suppressed a groan. She should've known Janelle would recognize the sound of the deadbolt unlocking. She crunched the note into a ball, hiding it in her hand. Janelle was her best friend but sometimes she went all mother hen. No need to give her a reason.

"Come in, Janelle." She stepped back to let the other woman pass. "I guess some habits will take awhile to break. Besides, even in Naultag it's a good idea to lock the door at night."

"You were here all night? Why didn't you call? You said you were driving out this morning." Janelle paused in the entryway, eyebrows drawn together with concern.

"No, I said I'd meet you here this morning."

"Where'd you sleep?"

"I camped out in the living room. It was fun." *Liar.* She had lain awake half the night, listening to the assorted groans and creaks of the house. At last the incessant *peep-peep-peep* of the spring peepers lulled her to sleep.

"Yeah, right, fun." Janelle shook her head and resumed walking toward the kitchen. "I brought coffee." She held up a large cardboard container with the Dunkin Donuts BOX O' JOE logo on the side.

"You're an angel." Caitlin kissed Janelle's cheek then took the container and set it on the breakfast bar. Janelle chuckled. A moment of quiet followed as they poured cups of coffee.

"When do you expect the movers to arrive?" Janelle asked.

"Uncle Rick said the truck would leave around eight, so it should get here about ten or ten thirty." It was handy that her godfather owned the moving company. He'd been more than willing to juggle schedules to accommodate Caitlin.

"That gives us a little less than two hours. We need to figure out where everything is going to go." Janelle set her coffee cup down, her gaze sweeping the room with focused intensity.

Caitlin chuckled. "There's not much to plan for, just my bedroom set and the home office stuff. The living room furniture belonged to my roommate and stayed with the condo."

"Ooh, I know a great furniture store in Spencer. We'll go shopping later today, after the movers leave. I'm sure you'll need curtains, too. And an area rug for the living room."

"Whoa, please keep in mind that I'm not rich. My student loans eat up most of my non-existent income."

Janelle waved a dismissive hand. "The school is paying you a nice salary. You can afford to splurge a little."

"I don't get paid until school starts in the fall. It would be nice to have some money for food between now and then."

"You could ask your father for help."

"No." Caitlin set her cup down hard enough to splash coffee onto the counter. "His help comes with strings attached. I'm not going to live my life the way he wants."

A soft knock at the front door saved them from an argument. Caitlin walked down the hall, expecting to see Janelle's husband, Scott, on the other side of the door. Instead, Mr. and Mrs. Henderson stood on the top step.

"Welcome home, Caitlin." Mrs. Henderson held out a plate of cookies. "We're happy you've moved back into Sophie's house."

Caitlin opened the screen door, eyeing the cookies. "Come in, please. Would you like some coffee?"

Mr. Henderson caught his wife's elbow. "We can't stay. We're babysitting grandkids today. Remember, Charlotte?"

Mrs. Henderson's frown melted. "Oh, I'd nearly forgotten. But I did want to be sure you're settling in okay. Do you need anything?"

"I'm all set, thank you."

"Well, you enjoy these cookies. Will we see you at church on Sunday?"

"I'll be there." Caitlin took the proffered plate. "Are these oatmeal raisin? They're my favorite."

"It's Sophie's famous recipe."

The cookies gave off a warm, fresh baked aroma. Caitlin inhaled, closing her eyes as memories flooded her mind. The smell of vanilla and melting butter, the sweet taste of brown sugar, heat radiating into the kitchen as Gram opened the oven. Caitlin's throat tightened.

"If there's anything we can do to help, be sure to call."

Caitlin opened her eyes and smiled. "Thank you, Mrs. Henderson. I'll be fine."

Mr. Henderson looked like he doubted her confidence. "I told the boys to look out for you. Don't be afraid to ask for help."

He pointed over his shoulder toward the field across the street. Randy backed the old Ferguson out of the tractor shed. Sean hefted a bag of corn seed from the back of a blue F150 truck and walked toward the building, the heavy bag draped over one forearm. He made carrying it look as easy as toting a pile of laundered towels. Even from this distance Caitlin admired the way his muscles rippled beneath his t-shirt.

"I'll keep it in mind. Thanks again for the cookies and the warm welcome." She watched the elderly pair make their way back to their car parked at the edge of the road.

"There's a couple of eligible bachelors." Janelle startled Caitlin.

She turned. Janelle nodded her chin to indicate the men across the street. Caitlin frowned. "Oh please, I'm not stupid enough to get involved with Randy Henderson."

"Okay, then how about Sean Taggart?"

Right, date the guy she'd accused of being a thief.

Sunlight shimmered in Sean's fair hair. She thought about his ocean blue eyes, the warmth of his touch. The idea of going out with Sean held definite appeal. Except for the high probability of getting hurt.

"Ooh, unless you're already involved with someone?" Janelle grasped her arm, excitement lighting her eyes. "A few times you mentioned going out. Are you seeing someone?"

"No." Caitlin pried Janelle's fingers off her arm. "I went out a few times with a friend. We weren't dating and I'm not involved with him."

She walked down the hall, plate of cookies in hand. Janelle trotted along behind her.

"Come on, Cait, why won't you just admit you were dating?"

"Because I wasn't." She turned in the kitchen doorway. "We went out for coffee after Bible study. And a couple times we met for lunch. But that was all."

Why had Adam thought they were more than just friends? She'd even tried to fix him up with Tracy, one of the other women in Bible study. Tracy thought Adam was Mr. Tall Dark and Handsome, said his subtle Southern drawl reminded her of a country music singer. He was too metropolitan for Caitlin's taste, with his perfect hair and tailored clothing. Even in jeans and a tee shirt, she couldn't imagine him ever hefting bags of grain or driving a greasy old tractor.

She fixed Janelle with a stare. "I am not looking for a husband."

"So? That doesn't mean you can't have a little fun." Janelle plunked her hands on her hips. "Going out to dinner or to a movie doesn't mean you have to marry the guy."

"Guys expect things." Adam sure had. He'd expected much more. She didn't want to talk about that fiasco. Instead, she lifted the plate of cookies. "Let's save these for Scott. He'll love them."

Janelle shook her head. "You need someone other than my husband to give cookies to."

* * *

Sean watched Caitlin Harrington and Janelle Bartlett come out of the house, their laughter carrying on the breeze. Randy's implication yesterday flashed in his memory: Caitlin and Scott Bartlett were always together, in a weird love triangle. If Caitlin was still involved in a romantic affair with Scott Bartlett, his wife didn't seem to care. Or maybe Janelle didn't know. Sean shook his head. When had he become such a busybody?

The disc blades and depth wheel on the row crop planter still needed adjusting. Sean focused on the task. Randy had already performed annual maintenance on the equipment. His cousin was a self-proclaimed boozing womanizer, but when it came to equipment he was a no-nonsense, born mechanic.

After the adjustments were complete Sean checked the chains. Satisfied, he stood slowly and arched his back, stretching cramped muscles before glancing into the seed boxes. He fished out some bits of paper and string and tossed it into the trash barrel, wiped his hands clean with a rag from his back pocket then grabbed a can of soda from the cooler.

"So what's the plan?" Randy ambled over and grabbed a soda. He chugged the drink, belched then grinned when Sean frowned. "Lighten up. You're like an old biddy, worrying about manners and etiquette. You gotta get out more, live a little."

"I have a perfectly nice life, thank you."

"Perfectly *bo-ring*." Randy dragged out the last word. "What you need is the love of a good woman."

Sean groaned. "Don't start that again. You sound like my mother."

"What's the problem, still hung up on Melissa?"

"No." Sean clenched his fists at his side. He was over Melissa. Way over her. So over her there was no way he'd risk falling for another conniving, money hungry, controlling…He took a slow, deep breath.

Randy dropped an arm around his shoulder. "The women around here aren't hideous. I oughtta know. Why can't you give one a try?"

"You make it sound like test driving a car." Sean flung Randy's arm away.

Randy lifted his shoulders in a lazy shrug. "What can I say, chicks dig me." He stared across the street for a long minute. "If you just like spinning your wheels, maybe you should try dating Caitlin Harrington. If Bartlett will let you."

Sean followed Randy's nod. Scott Bartlett's truck pulled into the yard across the street. He shook his head, shaking off Randy's ridiculous accusation. If Bartlett were over there alone with Caitlin, maybe he'd believe there was something illicit going on. Instead, Janelle was spending time with Caitlin and it was normal for her husband to show up at some point.

What Caitlin did with her life was none of his business.

So how come he was still interested?

* * *

"That's my grandmother's bedroom," Caitlin hissed, pointing to the master bedroom.

"Not any more, Cait," Janelle reasoned.

"I can't sleep in there. It would be…disrespectful."

"Don't you think she'd want you to have the biggest

bedroom? And it has its own bath."

Scott looked from one woman to the other and shook his head. "So where are we putting the bed, ladies?"

Behind him, the moving company men leaned on the headboard of Caitlin's bed set, waiting. Caitlin bit the inside of her lip. She should've made up her mind before the movers arrived.

The last time she'd visited, Gram had been bedridden. Two weeks later she died. The room held ghosts, phantoms of memories both good and bad. Still, the larger room would be nice. And not having to stumble down the hall at night to the bathroom. Janelle was right. She should take the master bedroom as her own.

She sighed. Stepping back to allow the men to pass, she indicated the room at the end of the hall. "Put it in the master bedroom."

"I'm glad you came to your senses." Janelle embraced her. "Scott can move the dresser,"

"No," Caitlin reached another uncomfortable decision. "Leave the dresser. I'll use it."

The bedroom set was the last of Caitlin's belongings to come off the moving van. After signing the necessary paperwork, Caitlin surveyed her new home. Boxes stacked in the living room oddly gave the space a lived-in feel.

Janelle opened one of the boxes labeled kitchen stuff. She pulled out the coffee maker, a smile lighting her face. "Now you'll be all set for the morning."

"Good thing I went grocery shopping yesterday." Caitlin searched for bed sheets. Janelle had organized the boxes, grouping them by room. The ones labeled "bedroom stuff" had been shoved toward the hall. Caitlin smiled.

"Thanks for helping today." She hefted a box. "It's nice having someone here who knows exactly what I need."

"I'm always happy to help." Janelle placed books on the shelf in the living room. "We have a small problem with my plans, though. The afternoon is almost half over. We don't have time to go shopping today."

"We can go tomorrow. That gives us the whole day."

"I was hoping you'd say that." Janelle put the last book on a shelf. She moved to the stack of boxes destined for the bedroom, lifted one and accompanied Caitlin. "How about supper at our house tonight?"

"Hmmm," Caitlin feigned deep contemplation. "Janelle's home cooking or that scrumptious microwave lasagna I had been planning? What to do?"

"It's settled, then. Supper at our house," Scott answered for her. "You'd probably burn the lasagna even though it's prepackage and precooked."

"Geez, burn one teakettle and this is the reputation I get." Caitlin laughed.

Scott stepped to the hall. "I'll leave you two to work on putting all the little things in their proper places. Think I'll take a walk over to talk to Tag about Saturday."

"Who's Tag?" Caitlin asked.

"Sean Taggart," Scott answered.

"You know Sean Taggart?" A strange flutter tickled inside Caitlin's ribcage. "Is he a friend of yours?"

Scott paused, turning to answer. "I know Tag. We're both on the fire department, but we don't hang out or anything."

"Oh, he must be like his cousin, then."

"Randy?" Humor raised Scott's voice an octave. "No, he's nothing like Randy. Tag is an okay guy, just in case you're worried about him working across the street."

His long stride took him quickly out of the house. As soon as the screen door banged shut, Caitlin turned to Janelle.

"Why does Scott need to talk to Sean Taggart? What's happening on Saturday?"

Janelle busied herself putting away clothing. "The Asparagus Festival is scheduled for Saturday, if the weather cooperates. I think Scott wants to ask Sean to help set up the stage for the bands."

"What's the Asparagus Festival?"

"I forgot to tell you about it. You weren't supposed to be here for two more weeks, so it didn't occur to me."

"That doesn't tell me what it is."

"About three years ago, the Historical Society wanted to do something to celebrate spring. We also wanted it to have some connection to our local heritage." Janelle waved her hands as she spoke. "It turns out the man credited with bringing asparagus to this country, Diederik Leertouwer, lived around here at the end of his life. So we decided to commemorate this bit of history with the Spring Asparagus and Flower Heritage Festival."

"Sounds like fun." Caitlin hadn't been to a country fair in years. "And you were planning to tell me when? Because I'm sure you'll need someone to keep an eye on the twins." Adorable six-year-olds Connor and Cody Bartlett got into everything. She loved their insatiable curiosity. They showed her the world in a whole new light.

Janelle smiled. "I would've remembered before Saturday."

Caitlin went back to making the bed.

"You seem awfully curious about Sean Taggart." Janelle stood in front of the dresser, the clothing in her hands seemingly forgotten. Caitlin smoothed the already smooth sheet, debating whether or not to confess what happened yesterday.

"Well, like Scott suggested, I just wondered since he's working all around my house."

Janelle raised an eyebrow. "It doesn't have anything to do with Sean being a hunk?"

Heat flamed Caitlin's cheeks. She'd never call someone a hunk. Not out loud, anyway. "I didn't say that."

"Yeah, but you thought it, didn't you?"

THREE

"I can't believe there's a Harrington Sports here."

Caitlin glared at the store, tucked into the corner of the shopping plaza, untouched by other buildings. Like her father, who'd always held himself apart from his family. And now Jack expected her to welcome him into her life with open arms. Uh-uh, no way.

"We don't have to go in here," Janelle said. "The boys want new baseball gloves for their birthday, but I can come back."

"No, it's okay." Caitlin stepped up to the door, opening it for her friend. "It's not like my father will be here."

Baseball equipment and paraphernalia dominated the center of the store. Well, it was that time of year. Caitlin trailed behind Janelle, glancing at the shelves of sports gear. Baseball bats, gloves, batting helmets, and a whole aisle of cleats. A sign in the shoe aisle assured customers more sizes were available. A display held posters, mostly of Red Sox players but there were a few other ball clubs represented as well.

One wall prominently displayed a team photo of the Red Sox after winning the World Series in 2004, breaking the eighty-six year long "Curse." Autographs were scrawled along the edges of the picture. Glossy photographs of the team after winning the World Series in 2007 and 2013 hung on the wall behind the cash register. Jack Harrington had many connections, especially in the Red Sox baseball franchise. He'd played professional baseball for ten years. According to Jack, he would've been a hall of famer if a shoulder injury hadn't taken him out of action.

Trips to Sox games as a girl, ugh. Every time her brother, James, chanted, "Yankees suck!" she'd wanted to scream, "Baseball sucks!" But figuring out RBI's had been her first foray into the world of math. And she'd been hooked ever since.

"Hi, Marci." Janelle's voice drew Caitlin back to the present. "Has Jason outgrown his cleats again?"

"You know how boys grow."

"Oh, Caitlin, you know Marci Coffey, don't you?" Janelle pulled Caitlin forward, introducing her to the petite blonde woman standing in the shoe aisle. "Marci is married to Eric."

"We've met." Marci frowned. "You're taking Cindy Abbott's position at the junior high school."

Janelle spoke before Caitlin could respond. "It was my understanding Cindy Abbott retired. It's not like Caitlin stole her job."

Marci smiled, but her eyes remained cold. "I'm sorry. I didn't mean to imply anything like that. We hoped for a replacement capable of filling Mrs. Abbott's shoes." Her gaze traveled from Caitlin's face to her painted toes and back again. "Cindy's sensible, no-frills philosophy will be missed."

Caitlin glanced down. Sixty-two year old Cindy Abbott probably didn't wear sandals adorned with sparkling rhinestones. So what? Caitlin wouldn't be wearing them to school. Besides, she bought them at WalMart, in keeping with her no-frills budget. Still, a diplomatic response would be best.

"I'm looking forward to school in the fall."

Marci huffed. "I need to be going now. It was nice seeing you, Janelle." She clasped a shoebox to her chest and hurried away.

"Wow, she doesn't like you." Janelle turned to Caitlin. "What'd you do to her?"

Caitlin shrugged. "She's never been friendly toward me. When she came to calling hours for Gram, she spoke with both my aunts, my mother and Uncle Paul but ignored me completely."

Janelle absently picked up a catcher's mitt. "Eric is still nice to you, though, right? It wouldn't be good to be on the bad side of the police department."

"I'm not a criminal, Janelle." Caitlin grinned at the idea. "Anyway, Eric is just one officer of fifteen. He isn't even the chief, so I'm not worried about being in the good graces of the police department. And Eric is always nice to me."

* * *

"My sweet Caitlin," Gram whispered. "Do you know how much joy you brought to my life?"

Caitlin smiled. "I wasn't always a joy." She watched each shallow breath Gram took.

Gram's hazel eyes brightened, the only sign of life in her fading form. "You were a trial some days, to be sure. But always a blessing."

Caitlin grasped her grandmother's hand, throat tight with emotion. "I love you, Gram," she whispered.

"I love you, too, sweetheart." Gram squeezed her hand. "I want you to remember that God loves you more than I ever could."

"Gramma, please don't go." Caitlin felt like she was five years old again. Tears rolled down her face. She held tighter to Gram's hand. "Don't leave me here alone."

"You're never alone, Caitlin. The Lord is always with you."

Caitlin woke with a start, remembering Gram's last words. The dark, empty house reminded her of the days following that conversation. Gram's death left a void in her life.

Most of the time Caitlin believed in God's love, but it was hard when she considered the painful experiences of her life. If God loved her so much, why had He allowed her to be hurt? Once, she thought being raised by her grandmother made bearable the pain of being abandoned by her parents after their divorce. Then the Lord took Gram from her—just as she faced losing her job. She found another job but she'd never be able to replace Gram.

"Lord, I know in my heart that you love me but my head says you'll abandon me like everyone else. Please help me be strong. Help me know you'll always be with me."

The old kitchen clock ticked. The sound should be familiar, comforting but instead it underlined the loneliness of the house. Her loneliness.

She pushed up on her elbows. Water dripped off the eaves outside. Thick dark clouds padded the sky, blocking the sun. A dull ache lurked just behind her eyes, a migraine waiting to pounce. Caitlin glanced at the clock then dropped back onto her pillows. Nearly eight-thirty. She never slept this late. That explained the headache. On the way to the shower, she paused long enough to swallow two Excedrin Migraine tablets. The hot shower jets tingled her skin like acupuncture therapy. She stood under the stream until the water grew cold.

After a bowl of cereal and a big mug of coffee, her headache had faded. She pulled on a wool fisherman knit sweater and headed outside. Clouds plowed into the eastern horizon. The sun concentrated on burning through the patchy edge of the cloudbank. The weather was decent enough for a walk.

Caitlin meandered through the yard. The rain-drenched grass soaked her feet just as if she walked along the edge of the surf. The breeze smelled clean with a touch of freshly turned soil. No hint of fishy smell, and the birds chirruping softly in the background were a far cry from the raucous chatter of seagulls. Back in Lynn, she had shared a condo on the second floor of a restored Victorian. Two blocks from Lynn Shore Drive, the air always carried the scent of the ocean. She had enjoyed walking along the shoreline, watching birds diving into the whitecaps, marveling at how small the cargo ships and oil tankers out on the harbor appeared. At night, lights reflected on the bay like a galaxy of stars.

Naultag was a world apart. Woodland interspersed with houses. Birds hopped across the lawn, waiting patiently for the early worm. Her home now—a sixty-year-old, ranch style house, two blocks from an overgrown millpond, which rarely sported whitecaps. Waterskiing boats on nearby Lake Naultag really were small. At night, light ribboned over the lake like party streamers.

Caitlin inhaled, savoring the damp warmth as the sun dried the landscape. Though she'd miss much about Lynn, this was home. It felt good to be back, like walking into Gram's loving embrace at the end of a long school day.

In front, between the house and the big dairy barn, the patch where Gram had kept a vegetable garden lay bare. Caitlin pictured the rectangle surrounded by bright yellow marigolds. "These flowers ward off rabbits and deer," Gram had instructed. They had little effect on the rabbits, and deer never came into the front yard anyway. Still, Gram insisted on planting the marigolds every spring. Caitlin made up her mind to plant her own vegetable garden, complete with marigolds. And she'd work on the flowerbeds in back as well.

Remembering her long walks along the Lynn shoreline, Caitlin set out to get reacquainted with the neighborhood. She headed west, down Brickyard Road. At the far end was the clay pit pond where she'd learned to ice skate as a child. "It's very important to tie your laces tightly, honey," her father's advice echoed from the past. "Here, let Daddy do it for you." He could usually be counted on to be around if any type of sport was involved.

Another memory slammed into the first, extinguishing the kindling warmth. "Quit bawling, Caitlin. You don't see James crying just because he fell on the ice." Her father had smiled at her brother, then turned back to her and scowled. "I swear, trying to teach you anything is a waste of time."

The breeze tugged at Caitlin's hair but didn't stir the water. She tossed a rock into the pond. The ripples vanished quickly, the surface once more a dark mirror. If only she could sink the memories of her past so easily.

The peninsula where she stood divided the pond into two unequal halves. On the right, the obsidian surface remained smooth and placid. To the left, tussocks of scruffy grass and twisted shrubs convoluted the shoreline. Several gnawed-off trees bobbed in the water, waiting for beavers to haul them to the dam blocking the outlet of the pond.

Maybe that was her problem. Time should flow like a river. Bitter memories and old grudges clogged life's natural current, holding her back. The still waters behind the emotional dam were safe but stagnant. She needed to break the barrier. But would she drown in the rushing torrent?

A great blue heron stood like a flamingo lawn statue at the shallow edge across from Caitlin, unconcerned by her presence. A peaceful scene. "Lord, how can I find such peace?" She closed her eyes and soaked up the warmth of the sun. Her thoughts drifted once more to living in Lynn and walking along the shoreline.

Two days before leaving, she'd spent the afternoon with Adam. She'd worn this same sweater. Adam had traced the cable knit pattern along her arm as they talked. At the time she hadn't thought much of the action. Now she shuddered remembering the caress. Often his hand rested over hers as they sipped coffee after Bible study and discussed the verses they had read. It seemed harmless, a gesture between friends. She never reciprocated, hadn't ever so much as brushed a hand over his hair. But Adam had been laying the groundwork for the relationship he hoped they would have. He wasn't satisfied with just being friends.

That's what came of romantic notions.

Sean Taggart, now, he seemed like a nice guy. How could she be sure, though? Adam had also seemed nice. Oh how wrong she'd been. The back of Caitlin's neck prickled with unease. Glancing around, she saw nothing but a squirrel. She laughed. Just passed the trees on the far side of the pond, cars hummed by regularly, a reminder of the nearness of civilization. She turned and headed home.

She was almost back to the house when a short siren blast made her jump and spin around. One of the town police cruisers rolled slowly behind her. The officer called out the open window. "Hey, Caitlin! Good to see you back home."

She squinted and then smiled. "Eric, how are you?"

He pulled over and stopped the cruiser. "I'm well, thanks. You're all moved in, huh? Things going okay?"

"I'm adjusting."

"If you have any problems, just call me." Eric gazed out the front windshield. "You're kinda set apart from the neighbors. Do you have an alarm system?"

"Alarm system, in Naultag?" She chuckled. "And I thought *I* was being paranoid by keeping the deadbolt locked all the time."

"There are a lot of new people in town, Caitlin. I'm not saying they're criminals, but many of 'em have money and that attracts burglars." He held her eye for a moment before grinning. "Just keep the doors locked. And call me if you have any concerns."

"Thanks, Eric." Caitlin glanced at the cornfield. No Sean there today. "Do you know Sean Taggart?"

"Sure, everyone knows Tag. Why do you ask?"

"I hadn't met him before." She chewed the inside of her lip. What would she say if Eric wanted to know why she was asking about Sean?

"You're one of the few who doesn't know Tag. He's a member of the fire department, coaches little league, is active in his church."

"So he's a nice guy?"

Eric shrugged, looking forward again. "I never had any trouble with him. Why're you asking me? You should ask your friend Scott."

"I already did, and he said about the same thing as you. I just figured since you're a cop, you'd know better. Scott just thinks he knows everything."

Eric chuckled then nodded his chin toward her house. "You've got company."

A Verizon phone truck pulled into the driveway. Caitlin stepped away from the cruiser. "I better get home. They're installing a phone in the house."

The telephone company technician waited beside his truck as she approached. He was an inch or two taller than her with an average build, much like Adam. Dark hair combed neatly. Just like Adam's. Alarm jolted through her. She hesitated, looked around for

Eric, for anyone else.

Stop being paranoid. Caitlin drew in a deep breath and continued toward the Verizon truck. When she got closer, the technician stepped forward to meet her. He squinted at his clipboard then pulled it closer to his face. His eyes met hers and he smiled.

"Forgot my reading glasses at home this morning. Are you Caitlin Harrington?" He waited for her to nod. "Says here you want phone lines run to additional rooms?"

He was much older than Adam. Nervous tension uncoiled in her stomach. She smiled and led the way into the house. At the door she paused while the technician continued inside. Her gaze swept the surrounding area. No one in sight.

So why did she feel like someone watched her?

* * *

The phone rang. Caitlin rushed to answer, eager to connect with the outside world.

"You're all set, Ms. Harrington," the Verizon technician said.

As soon as the call ended, Caitlin lifted the receiver again. She should call Mom, like a good daughter. She dialed Janelle instead.

"Hey, the phone works," Caitlin exclaimed when Janelle answered.

"Great, now Scott can stop worrying about you."

"I hope not."

"He's *my* husband, Cait. He should worry about me."

"Oh, Janelle, you know he does. All the time. But we've been friends so long, and we are cousins, more like siblings sometimes."

"You're giving him gray hair. That's my job." Janelle snickered. "Of course, the boys are making him lose his hair."

Scott bald—Caitlin laughed. "All right, he can stop worrying about me."

When the call ended, Caitlin stared at the telephone. She should call her parents. Mom would want to know why Caitlin moved two weeks early. Her gaze wandered to the clock. At this time in the afternoon her mother was probably still at work. If Caitlin called now, she could avoid confrontation. Leaving a message would only put off the inevitable. At least she'd have the rest of the day to prepare for the inquisition.

She lifted the receiver and dialed.

A husky male voice answered. "Hello?"

Caitlin hesitated. Had she dialed wrong? "May I speak with

Irene Baxter?"

"She ain't here."

"Who is this?"

"Gary. Who's this?"

Caitlin closed her eyes. Gary, Mom's latest boyfriend. "This is Caitlin."

"Oh, hi Caitlin. Irene's at work."

"What are you doing there?" She'd only met Gary once. He seemed okay, but she was a terrible judge of character.

"I was sleeping till you called. I work nights, ya know, gotta sleep during the day."

Caitlin rolled her eyes. "Why aren't you sleeping in your own apartment?"

Gary chuckled. "Ain't talked to your ma in a while, have ya? This *is* my apartment."

Living together, great. It was too much to hope they might've gotten married first. She clamped her mouth shut. *Lord, please give me patience.*

"Want me to give Irene a message?"

He sounded more alert than when he had first answered, but she doubted he'd write down her message. And she didn't want to discuss any of it with him. "Just tell her I called."

Why was life so complicated?

She stared at the phone, trying to work up courage to call her father. He wouldn't ask why she moved early. He'd question—again—the wisdom of moving at all. They'd get into another discussion about the merits of living close to Boston. A job wasn't good enough reason to move. If she tried harder, waited a little longer, something better and more suitable would come along. If she'd be more social, she'd find a suitable husband who would care for her so she didn't have to work.

She started to dial her father's home number. With her luck, Linda would answer. At least Jack and Linda *were* married, despite the fact Linda was twenty years younger than Jack. Linda was always overly cheerful, like she was trying to be friends but only for Jack's sake.

Should she call his office instead? It didn't matter. Either way was bound to be wrong.

FOUR

Caitlin's breath came out in white puffs. She rubbed her hands together for warmth and eyed the early morning sky. A ribbon of blue showed on the western horizon but the sun remained shrouded in clouds low in the east. The weather forecast called for mostly sunny skies. Hopefully it would warm up as well.

"There's Coach Tag." Connor pointed across the field then turned to tug at Scott's sleeve. "Can we go say hi, Dad?"

"Please," Cody took up the plea. Scott laughed at his sons.

"Go on." He shooed them away and turned toward Caitlin and Janelle. "I have to talk to Tag, anyway."

Caitlin watched him saunter across the grass, long strides eating the distance in unhurried speed. Sean Taggart stood on the back of his truck, hand shielding his eyes as he gazed across the field. From this distance, Caitlin couldn't read his expression but saw a flash of white as he smiled. Connor and Cody reached the truck just ahead of Scott.

Sean hopped down and crouched to the boys' eye level. The twins waved their arms as they spoke. Sean laughed, ruffled both their hair and rose to full height. Caitlin watched, fascinated by his affection toward the boys and their adoration of him. Then Scott moved, blocking her view of Sean.

"He *is* good looking, isn't he?"

"Janelle!" Caitlin made a pretense of swatting at her friend. "You're married."

"But not blind." Janelle's cheeks rounded with a grin. "More to the point, I know you think he's good looking. Why can't you just admit it?"

Caitlin turned away and started walking. Warmth crept over her face. No use denying the accusation. Janelle could see the proof. Saying it out loud felt like taking an irrevocable step into an inconsistent multivariable linear system. No solution possible. Physics made her head ache. She preferred a nice algebraic formula.

Romance, love and marriage—and divorce— had no clean,

easily solved equations.

They approached the food serving area, a large pavilion tent with rectangular tables down each side. Two women Caitlin didn't recognize told Janelle they were going to get more supplies. Caitlin helped Janelle carry a six-foot long table over to set up along one end of the tent.

"Come on, Caitlin," Janelle needled. "Just say the words. No harm done."

"I'm not interested."

Janelle pursed her lips in a soft frown. After a moment she spoke. "You can admire a flower without picking it, right? Well, this is just like that. Saying a man is good-looking doesn't mean you have to marry him, or even go out on a date."

The table legs snapped into place with a loud pop. Caitlin glared at Janelle then threw her arms up in frustration.

"Fine, he's good-looking. Very good-looking."

"Who, me?" Scott's voice startled Caitlin.

She closed her eyes as her shoulders sagged. This was the other reason she avoided making such embarrassing statements out loud. When she opened her eyes, Scott stood beside Janelle, grinning. Caitlin forced a smile of her own.

"We weren't talking about you." Janelle shooed him away. "Caitlin, let's go help bring stuff over from the church."

"Can you take the boys?" Scott asked. "When we get things set up, they can help me put the stage together."

"I'll watch them." Caitlin looked to where the twins flanked Sean as he set up a large gas grill. "If you can tear them away, that is."

"Boys," Scott called. "Go with Aunt Caitlin."

They grumbled. Sean waggled a wrench at them. "If you can't obey your parents, you can't play on my team."

Connor shuffled toward Caitlin, head down, feet kicking blades of grass. Cody resisted a moment longer then followed his brother. Caitlin's gaze went from the boys to Sean, who had already returned to connecting the gas tank. She frowned. The twins liked him, more than her, and he didn't even notice.

In the church kitchen, food preparations were well underway. Large stockpots filled the six-burner stove, tended by a couple of ladies from the congregation. Margie Swenson oversaw a group of teens wrapping vegetables in aluminum foil. Stepping closer, Caitlin spotted asparagus spears and an assortment of seasonings.

"We'll steam the asparagus on the grill and then it gets rolled into a sandwich wrap." Margie placed the silver bundles in a box.

"These need to go out." Marci Coffey tapped a pile of red and white checked tablecloths. "And that box of paper plates. Somewhere there's a box of cups and plastic utensils."

Marci turned and her gaze rested on Caitlin. Her lips pressed into a tight, thin line as her eyes narrowed. "You don't belong here."

The icy hiss plunged into Caitlin's veins. A chill trickled down her spine. She shivered. *You don't belong here.* They were the same words as the anonymous note left Tuesday morning.

"Nonsense, Marci," Margie Swenson interjected. "We can use all the help we can get. The more the merrier."

Marci's stiff lips twisted into a tense smile. "Of course Caitlin is welcome to help. I only meant the children shouldn't be in here."

"They came with me—to help." Caitlin reached past Marci and lifted the stack of tablecloths. She divided it and gave half to Connor and half to Cody. "You boys carry these. I'll get this box."

Could Marci Coffey hate her enough to leave that note? Probably just a coincidence. Marci didn't want her back in Naultag but there was no logical reason why she'd go to the bother of leaving an anonymous note. Marci wasn't shy about sharing her feelings.

Outside, the sun burned a hole in the clouds. The blue ribbon on the western horizon had grown. Caitlin trudged behind the twins. The box of paper plates wasn't heavy, just bulky. Suddenly, Eric was beside her.

"Here, let me carry that." He took the box. "I overheard Marci. Don't let her get to you. She doesn't like change and new faces. Eventually, she'll adjust."

"Oh." Caitlin nodded, keeping her focus straight ahead. "Is that all it is?"

"Well," Eric paused. They were near the food pavilion now and the boys ran on ahead. "She found out about the salary the school offered you. She's a little upset that you're getting paid as much as teachers who have been here much longer."

She did have six years of experience and a master's degree. In Lynn she'd made much more per year. The higher salary would make things easier, help pay off her student loans quicker. But goodwill was more valuable, especially in a small town like this.

"You're worth the money, Caitlin."

A warm sense of welcome and friendship filled her. Marci might stir up trouble, but at least Caitlin's friends wanted her here in Naultag.

Eric set the box on a table. He stared down the length of the town common, though he didn't seem to notice the activity of vendors setting up display booths. He sighed and ducked his head before speaking again. "I gotta confess, Caitlin. I lied when I said Marci doesn't like new faces. It's more than that."

He looked up, his gaze meeting hers. "Lately she's been irrational, complaining all the time. I work too much, my paycheck's too small, the kids are always whining. She hates everything about her life."

"I'm sorry to hear that." Did that excuse Marci's behavior? She'd been pleasant to Janelle. But then, like Marci, Janelle had been married since graduating high school, and she had two rambunctious kids. Maybe Marci thought Janelle was dissatisfied with life, too.

"Frankly, I'm worried about her," Eric continued. "I suggested counseling. Maybe therapy will bring back the woman I married."

Poor Eric. Caitlin placed a hand on his arm. "I hope things get better. Marci shouldn't go through life being miserable. And you deserve happiness, too."

The radio clipped to Eric's belt squawked. The words sounded blurred and staticky, but apparently Eric understood them.

"Gotta go. They need someone directing traffic down at Howard Street. See ya' around."

She watched him head across the grass. No wonder Marci was being so nasty toward her. She probably envied everything about Caitlin's life. Single, no one to tie her down, no demanding kids— and she'd just landed the perfect job.

"Aunt Caitlin," Connor tugged on her sweatshirt. "Can we go help Dad now?"

She pulled her thoughts back to the moment and looked down at the boys' eager faces. "We can go check on him."

"Yay!" They raced away without waiting to see if she followed.

The raised wooden stage was close to completion. Scott lay flat on his back, tackled by his sons. Sean sat nearby, watching the scene and grinning. Caitlin stopped beside the stage, crossed her arms and cleared her throat.

"I thought you were coming to *help* your father." She used her stern teacher voice.

Scott pushed the boys aside and sat up. "Uh-oh, guys, Aunt Caitlin's mad."

Cody jumped up, brushed himself off and stood at attention. "We're sorry, Aunt Caitlin."

Connor led the way for most of their adventures but Cody was the diplomat. Looking into his earnest expression, Caitlin couldn't hold the scowl. She chuckled and crossed the stage to hug him.

"I'm just teasing, Cody."

The boy wrapped his arms around her and held the hug for a long moment. Then Connor hugged her, too. She loved the way their little boy tough guy exterior melted at a whim. If only they could stay this sensitive and bold forever. Unfortunately, they'd grow up too soon and then her Prince Charmings would be gone.

"Why the long face?" Scott ducked his head to peer at her.

Caitlin released the boys and looked up at Scott. "Just wishing they could stay this adorable for the rest of their lives."

"Of course they will. They'll be just like their old man."

"Oh, conceited and full of themselves?"

Scott laughed. "It's only conceit when it's not true." He opened his arms wide, encompassing the stage. "Look at the fantastic job I did."

"Ahem," Sean Taggart cleared his throat. "I did some of the work."

"Oh, right. And the boys are gonna finish." Scott grabbed a hammer and returned to the area where boards needed to be nailed into place.

"I'll go see about breakfast." Sean turned to Caitlin. "Would you like to come help me? Or are you a carpenter, too?"

"I'm no carpenter." She turned to look at the food area. "What's for breakfast?"

Sean stepped off the stage and waited for Caitlin to follow. He matched his strides to hers. Caitlin rammed her hands into the pockets of her sweatshirt and studied the wet stripes left on her canvas sneakers as she walked through the morning dew. If only Janelle hadn't forced her to admit Sean was handsome. Now it was all she could think about.

"…sandwiches."

Oops, he'd been talking and she hadn't heard a word. "I'm sorry, what were you saying?"

"I said Janelle brought homemade biscuits. We're going to fry up some eggs and sausage patties and make sandwiches."

Though she tried hard not to, Caitlin glanced up as he spoke. He wasn't looking at her, which was a relief. He pointed to the large gas grill.

"You're cooking eggs on the grill?" The question blurted out before she could think.

Sean chuckled. "There's a griddle on the side. But if I wanted to, there's no reason why eggs couldn't be cooked in a pan right on the grill."

Of course. She felt like smacking her forehead and using one of her students' favorite expressions, *du-uh*. He must think her a complete idiot. She clamped her mouth shut, determined not to make any more stupid comments.

Caitlin paused to help Janelle staple the tablecloth edges, preventing them from blowing off during the day. Sean didn't seem to care that she'd stopped. He continued ambling to the behemoth grill. She snuck frequent peeks at him, until Scott and the boys joined them in the food pavilion.

"Momma, come see us climb a tree!" Connor tugged at Janelle's hand.

She met Caitlin's gaze and rolled her eyes. "As if they don't climb trees at home." Janelle pretended to make the boys drag her away.

"You, too, Dad." Cody grasped Scott's hand and pulled.

People continued going to and from the church, bringing supplies and foodstuffs. A row of coolers now filled the space beneath one table. Caitlin finished tacking down the last tablecloth and stood staring across the town common. All along the edges of the field, merchants set up tents and canopies. A low-pitched buzz hovered on the edge of hearing as people milled about in the open center of the field. Off to her right, a bright splash of color pulled Caitlin's attention to a display of flowering plants. Next to that a tent had been draped with gauzy curtains and jewels dangling from the edges sparkled in the morning sun. A wind chime tinkled in the breeze. On the other side of the common another plant seller set up beside a canopy bearing a sign advertising "The World's Best Fudge." Obviously the asparagus and flower heritage theme received wide interpretation.

Out of the corner of her eye, Caitlin saw Sean walk away from the grill. She turned to watch him for a moment. Rebellious curls at the nape of his neck waved in the breeze. The same wind rippled the t-shirt which clung to his wide shoulders and was tucked neatly into faded denim jeans. He wiped his hands on a towel then set it down on the table to open a package of paper plates. As he pulled at the plastic wrapper, muscles in his forearm bunched and bulged.

You can admire a flower without picking it, right? Sean was the most attractive 'flower' Caitlin had ever admired. She sighed. "Curse you, Janelle Bartlett."

"Did you say something?" Sean started to turn in her direction.

"I'm just muttering." Caitlin looked away. Her cheeks felt sunburned. To her relief, Sean didn't question the lame excuse.

She returned to watching the growing crowd. About thirty feet away, a large tent displayed local artwork. Two paintings stood sentinel beside the entry. As Caitlin studied the splash of colors on the canvas, a man came around from behind the tent. He stopped next to the painting on the right and looked directly at her. His grin lifted the corners of his lips without warming his expression.

Adam.

Caitlin gulped air. He *had* followed her. She backed rapidly away from the table until colliding with the grill. Her arms windmilled. She flung one hand down for support.

Adam disappeared. A dark haired older gentleman now stood in the space he had occupied. Had she imagined him?

Then pain seared into her palm.

FIVE

A piercing shriek ripped through Sean. He whirled, seeking the source.

Caitlin was backed against the grill, one hand on a sizzling sausage patty. Flames flared and leapt in a hungry dance around her arm. Tongues of fire licked upward, toward her face. She pulled her arm away. Not soon enough. Wisps of smoke curled from the baggy sleeve of her sweatshirt as a thin tendril of flame took hold. Another cry escaped her lips.

Visions of third degree burns bubbling and distorting Caitlin's graceful arms snatched the breath from Sean's lungs. But only for a second before years of experience and training took over. He grabbed a towel and raced to Caitlin. The cloth wrapped around her arm smothered the burning shirt. With his free hand Sean pushed the grill lid closed.

Caitlin remained still. She didn't try to pull away from him.

"What were you thinking?" His voice went up an octave with anger and fear. Taking advantage of her apparent calm, he took a moment to shut off the gas burners. "If I hadn't been here, your sweatshirt could've burned and melted to your skin. Do you realize how dangerous fire can be?"

He turned back to Caitlin. She was not calm. Eyes wide. The soft suntan was gone from her face along with any other color. She appeared to be in shock. Or scared. Well, she should be frightened. Fire was nothing to play around with.

"You need to be more careful around the grill." He shouldn't be so harsh with her, but the image of Caitlin engulfed in flames kept playing in his mind's eye.

"I...I..." She took a deep breath. Her pupils constricted to normal size. "I was startled."

Something inside him softened. "Let's take a look at the damage."

He unwrapped the towel and turned Caitlin's hand palm up.

The bottom half of the sweatshirt sleeve was badly singed but at least it hadn't fused to her skin. A large reddened patch showed where her hand had rested on the hot sausage patty.

"Stay here," he ordered.

One of the coolers contained bottles of water, to be sold as beverages later in the day. Sean grabbed several and returned to Caitlin. She looked around as if searching for someone. He cracked open one of the water bottles and poured it in a slow, steady stream over the burn.

Caitlin jerked her arm back. "That's cold."

"Good." He kept a firm grip on her wrist and put light pressure on the burn. "Does that hurt?"

She winced and pushed at him with her other hand. Confirmation enough. He continued pouring water over her hand for several minutes. He pressed the last, half-full bottle into her good hand.

"Drink this while I get the first aid kit."

The cabinet under the grill contained a small first aid kit from which Sean extracted a gauze roll and medical tape. He was wrapping Caitlin's hand when Scott returned.

"I heard you scream. What happened?"

An explanation would be nice. Why does an otherwise rational adult woman suddenly back into a burning gas grill? Sean glanced at her face, which had returned to a healthy pink. Her eyes shifted to Scott. Tears glistened, threatening to spill.

"I saw...he was ..." She shook her head then continued in a whisper. "I'm not sure."

Sean finished bandaging her hand. He fingered the burned sleeve. Unless she turned it into a sleeveless pullover, the garment was ruined. Caitlin dropped her gaze and saw the damage.

"It's ruined." She sniffed as a tear broke free. "Gram bought this."

"Aw, don't start crying, Cait." Scott held out pleading hands. "The important thing is you weren't seriously injured." He could've saved his breath. Tears dripped off Caitlin's chin as she looked up.

"I must be seeing things. Imagining monsters that aren't there." She tried to cover her face but the water bottle got in the way.

Sean eased the bottle from her hand. What monsters did she see that weren't really there? Deep inside an emotion bloomed, one he'd never experienced before. All at once he wanted to protect Caitlin, vanquish her demons.

Or at least stop her tears.

Scott pulled Caitlin into an embrace. She rested her forehead against his chest and cried while Scott rubbed her back, saying nothing.

A pang of jealousy slapped at the tenderness in Sean's heart. He wanted do something, anything, to stop her crying and bring back her bright, warm smile. But even though Sean had come to her rescue, Caitlin turned to Scott for comfort.

* * *

Caitlin slipped into the sanctuary of the two hundred year old church and sat in the first pew. Everything looked the same as it had ten years ago when she worshipped here with Gram. A Bible lay on the padded bench seat, the top edge of last Sunday's bulletin sticking out of it. She removed the bulletin and studied the front page. Squiggly lines wavered across the paper.

Had even her sanity abandoned her? Adam couldn't be here, it was just someone who looked like Adam. She was under a lot of stress with moving and getting ready to start a new job. Finding out Mom was shacking up with her latest. Another confrontation with her father loomed on the horizon. Plus she still wasn't sleeping well.

It was the stress, not insanity. She hadn't seen Adam.

The lines on the page resolved into an image of Jesus. Below, the words of Matthew 28:20 were written in bold letters: "I am with you always, to the very end of the age." She looked up and focused on the stained glass window behind the choir loft.

"Are you, Lord? Always with me, I mean. Sometimes it's hard to believe."

If He'd kept her safe, she wouldn't have touched the grill. She studied the gauze-wrapped hand resting on her lap. She'd been caught up in her own world, not thinking about God. Her actions stemmed from fear of Adam, not from anything the Lord did or did not do. Yet when the fire flared, the flames danced all around her arm without causing serious harm.

"And I should be grateful, I suppose, that Sean Taggart was there to provide first aid." She stared at the portrait of Jesus hanging at the altar, waiting for Him to respond. After several minutes of silence, she relented and smiled. Yes, she should be thankful for all the times Jesus stepped in and saved her from herself. A sense of peace filled her.

After the incident with the grill, Caitlin had been assigned to watch Connor and Cody. An easy task that didn't require the use of her injured hand. Pony rides, petting zoo and a maze constructed of hay bales kept them occupied. Just before noon, Janelle's parents arrived and took over childcare duties. Which left Caitlin with nothing to do.

Outside, the Asparagus and Flower Heritage Festival was in full swing. The community fair atmosphere had lost its charm for Caitlin. She'd been banned from helping at the food pavilion. The historical society ladies didn't want to further injure her hand. Perhaps she would go out and stroll one more time around the common and then head home.

She left the sanctuary and crossed the library, pausing at the door. On the other side, hushed voices caught her attention.

"I'm telling you, Janelle, Caitlin Harrington can't be trusted." Marci Coffey's voice dripped with accusation. "I did some background checking when she applied for the teaching job. The people at her school all thought she was strange."

True. Caitlin didn't socialize with her coworkers, and most of them treated her like she was an alien.

"I think something was going on with her and a married man, and that's why she left." Marci paused, probably for dramatic emphasis. "She's got her sights set on another married man here in Naultag. Maybe more than one. That's why she came back."

"Don't be ridiculous." Janelle chuckled. "Caitlin got laid off along with dozens of teachers. And she came home because our school gave her a new job."

At least Janelle didn't believe she'd committed adultery.

"But look at the way she is with men. I mean, she's wearing your husband's sweatshirt."

Scott had lent Caitlin his sweatshirt after seeing the damage to hers. It drooped from her shoulders and the arms were too long. She'd accepted it because it had still been cold at the time of the incident. She should've taken it off and left it with Janelle when it warmed up outside.

"And another thing," Marci continued. "I didn't say anything at the time because you had enough to worry about. Back when you were pregnant with the twins a rumor went around about

Caitlin and your husband."

Janelle laughed, but it sounded hesitant, doubtful. *She couldn't honestly believe anything illicit had ever happened between Scott and I. Could she?*

"They've been friends since they were five, Marci. There's nothing going on between them, not then and not now."

"I'm just trying to warn you. Caitlin Harrington can't be trusted."

One set of footsteps crossed the carpet. A sliver of sunlight slid into the room where Caitlin hid. She peeked through the narrow gap between the door and jamb. Janelle started across the foyer, responding to Marci's last accusation.

"I trust my husband."

SIX

Caitlin held her breath, waiting for the two women to leave. The wide band of light streaming under the door narrowed and disappeared. They were gone. She let her breath out and sagged against the wall. Janelle's parting words reverberated in her mind: *I trust my husband.*

But not her best friend?

Slowly, Caitlin unzipped the sweatshirt and slid it off her shoulders. It smelled of fresh cut lumber, like Scott. Goose bumps prickled her arms. Maybe she was too close to him. It had seemed so wonderful when her two best friends got married. It hadn't ever occurred to her that she needed to stop being friends with Scott.

To keep Janelle's friendship, she had to let go of Scott's. If she remained friendly with him, she would lose Janelle. There wasn't a fair choice.

She found Margie Swenson alone in the kitchen. The older woman looked up as Caitlin approached, giving her a warm smile. "Have you had any asparagus chowder?" Margie asked. "I'm just bringing out the last pot."

"Yes, it was delicious." Caitlin hesitated a moment. "Could you do me a favor? Something's come up and I need to leave. Would you mind giving this to Janelle Bartlett?"

Margie accepted the proffered sweatshirt. "Oh dear, I hope it's nothing serious. Of course I'll be happy to take this to Janelle. Is it your hand? Can I do anything more for you?"

"No, I'll be all right." Caitlin cradled the bandaged hand, ashamed to let Margie believe a lie. What else could she say? "I just want to get away from the crowd."

"I understand." The older woman patted her arm. "It must have been very traumatic. You just go on home and rest a bit. I'll let Janelle know."

"Thank you."

Margie hefted the stockpot and headed for the door. "Could you get the lights for me?"

When Caitlin crossed the room and flicked the lights off, she noticed the door to the lower level was open and the lights were on. Downstairs, something rattled.

"Hello? Is anyone down there?"

No one responded. Still, better to make sure no kids were hiding in the basement. She descended the steep stairs to the room where she'd had Sunday school as a kid. Movement caught her eye. On the far side of the room, the door leading to the storeroom below the sanctuary swung slowly, bumping a paint can. Caitlin moved closer. Someone had propped the door open, probably to get the pavilion tent out of storage. With all the activity of the festival, it had been forgotten. She checked her watch. At least four hours remained before the tent came back to the basement.

Lifting the paint can, Caitlin glanced around the cavernous space. Bare bulbs glowed from the ceiling, casting intersecting circles of light that didn't quite reach the corners. Steel shelving lined the wall to her right. She set the can on the second section, next to some others.

Footsteps scuffed in the doorway. Caitlin turned in time to see the door begin to close. Marci Coffey met her gaze.

"You aren't welcome here," Marci said. "Go away."

Caitlin rushed the door but not fast enough. The door *snicked* closed as her left hand grasped the doorknob. Pain knifed through her palm, sucking the breath from her lungs. She yanked her arm away, cradling the injured hand, and stumbled back a few steps. She collided with the shelving. Something fell, grazing her temple.

The lights went out.

* * *

All the vendors were gone when Sean returned to the festival. He drove onto the common and backed up to the food pavilion. Volunteers loaded the tables onto a nearby trailer. He spotted the Bartletts and waved to get Scott's attention. Together they easily lifted the gas grill into the bed of Sean's truck.

"Can you help us with the tent, Sean?" Janelle asked when the grill was secured.

"Sure." He swept his gaze around the group of volunteers. "Is Caitlin around? I brought her some burn cream."

Janelle shook her head. "No, she went home hours ago."

Disappointment washed over him. He had hoped to see Caitlin again, maybe have a chance to make up for turning his back and walking away this morning.

"Are you sure?" Scott stared across the field. "Her car is still in the same spot over in the church parking lot."

"That's strange." Janelle frowned. "I haven't seen her all afternoon."

"Did she say anything before leaving?" Scott asked. "Maybe she got sidetracked."

"She said something had come up and she was going home." Janelle pushed a hair behind her ears. It bobbed back. "Margie thought Caitlin needed to rest after her traumatic morning."

"She likes spending time with the boys. How traumatic could that have been?" Scott's brow scrunched.

"I'm sure Margie meant the hand burning incident." Sean chuckled.

If Caitlin went home, maybe he could swing over there later and bring her the burn cream. That way, he'd have her undivided attention. To explain how to take care of her injury.

"Do you think Caitlin needed to rest?" Scott tossed the question over his shoulder as he ambled to a nearby cooler.

Janelle shook her head. She picked at her sleeve. "We weren't letting her help in the food pavilion. I...I think maybe she was bored."

Scott lifted a folded gray sweatshirt and waved it. "Janelle, don't you think maybe Cait left because she was upset? You know how easily she gets offended."

Janelle stared at the ground, one hand still picking at her sleeve. Without making eye contact, the couple maintained a non-verbal standoff. Sean looked back at Scott. Obviously they both understood Caitlin on a deep level. A desire to understand what made Caitlin tick itched inside Sean.

At last, Scott sighed. "What exactly did she say to you?"

Janelle exhaled loudly. "Nothing. She gave the sweatshirt to Margie Swenson and asked her to pass on the message about going home."

Scott set the sweatshirt back down in a deliberate, slow act. He stared into the distance. "Where did Margie see her?"

"In the church kitchen."

"Great, Cait in a kitchen." Scott snorted a halfhearted chuckle and patted Janelle's arm. "I'm sure she's fine. She probably got a ride home from someone."

"Maybe." Janelle's lips wobbled in an attempt to smile. "I just feel bad about banning her from helping. Not much of a friend, am I?"

"You meant well." Scott turned away, dialing his cell phone. After a moment, he disconnected. "No answer at her house."

"Doesn't she have a cell phone?" Sean asked.

Scott shook his head. "Nope. She hates 'em." He shrugged when Sean raised an eyebrow. "I've never been able to figure Cait out and she's too pigheaded to listen to reason."

Something inside Sean did a happy jig. Scott didn't know Caitlin that well after all. Sean turned away before Bartlett could see his grin. In any case, they still needed to find Caitlin.

"We've got to put the tent away." Sean indicated the pile of poles and canvas waiting to be put into its box. "Why don't we check the church, see if maybe she's just been hanging out over there?"

"Good idea." Scott rammed the tent components into the box.

Sean joined him, his thoughts on Caitlin. He should be worried about being interested in another beautiful woman from a wealthy family. Caitlin wasn't Melissa, he needed to accept that reality. Besides, being nice didn't mean he had to date her. Not that what he wanted mattered. Even though he had rescued her, Caitlin had turned to Scott for comfort. His earlier joy turned to an unaccustomed twinge of jealousy.

When they brought the tent across the street, the church bustled with activity. Pots and pans had been scrubbed clean and were now being put away. The banquet tables were brought into Fellowship Hall and set up for tomorrow morning. Sean and Scott carried the pavilion tent box through the kitchen. Marci Coffey opened the door to the stairs for them, flicking the light switch as they went past.

"Janelle," Scott called over his shoulder, "check if anyone has seen Caitlin."

* * *

Someone tapped on the window. A muffled voice called her name. Caitlin scrambled to hide behind the lawn tractor. Adam was angry, he mustn't find her. The bulkhead rasped open.

"I know you're in there." He drawled in soft, pretended niceness. "Come out now, Caitlin."

Caitlin jerked awake. Her heart thumped heavy, erratic beats. It was just a dream, just a dream. After a minute or two, her heart slowed to normal pace. Light slanted through the one window, a shining trapezoid in the gloom. The brightness grew dim as sunset approached. How many hours had she been sitting here?

"Where are you now, Lord?" she whispered to the shadows.

No one was coming for her. No one cared.

She wasn't welcome here.

A new sound teased at the edge of her hearing. Voices. She scrambled away from the door. A thin band of light showed at the bottom of the threshold. It intersected with a glowing vertical line. The triangle grew as the door opened.

Ceiling lights blazed. Caitlin blinked, covering her eyes until they adjusted. A long rectangular box with legs eased into the room. Air whooshed from Caitlin's lungs. People had come. Not for her, but she was free any way. A sound halfway between a laugh and a sob escaped her.

The box dropped, accompanied by a grunt from the doorway. Sean Taggart scowled.

"What are you doing down here?" He sounded irritated, as if she'd disturbed his plans.

Oh, just having a little pity party for myself. So glad you could join me. Caitlin clamped her lips to keep the words from slipping out. Sarcasm was uncalled for. She should be grateful just to get out of here.

Scott charged into the room. "Caitlin? You had us worried."

At least someone cared. Why did it have to be Scott? He approached wearing his big brother face and she knew a bear hug was coming. Now Janelle was sure to think the worst. She sidestepped, putting boxes between them. Unfortunately, that brought her closer to Sean.

Sean leaned forward to peer into her face. "Have you been crying? Is that why you're hiding?"

Hours ago, when pounding on the door brought no help, Caitlin had given in to tears. Surely her eyes weren't puffy still. Although, they did sting and felt bloodshot. So what of it? Anyone would've been upset in the same situation. She raised her chin, meeting Sean's scrutiny, silently daring him to challenge her right to cry.

"I have not been hiding. I've been locked in here for hours, trapped in the dark."

His eyebrows scrunched. One side of his mouth quirked downward in a half frown. "How could you be trapped? The door wasn't even locked. Oh, I get it. You're afraid of the dark."

"I am not." Heat flared in her cheeks. "The door was locked."

Sean threw a glance over his shoulder. "Did I unlock the door before we came in?"

"No," Scott answered.

"So you see the door was not locked. Maybe you were…confused…" He reached for her forehead. "Did you hit your head?"

Caitlin jerked to the side, avoiding his hand. "Something fell off the shelf, but it's just a scratch. And it did not cause me to be confused. The door was locked."

"Cait, the door wasn't locked." Scott stretched out an inviting hand. "Maybe you got hit harder than you realize. Let me take a look."

"No, I'm fine." She scooted further from him. "I just want to go home. At least no one there thinks I'm crazy."

Sean snorted. Caitlin glared at him. A slow grin pushed up the edge of his mouth. The humor rode right up to crinkle the corners of his eyes. He leaned in close and spoke softly. "Your house is empty, Caitlin." He held her gaze, smile deepening.

Yeah, the house was empty. No one to think she was confused. No one to accuse her of stealing husbands. She peeked at Scott. And no one's husband would be there to feed the rumors. She turned back to meet Sean's sympathetic eyes.

"I don't need your pity." Speaking slowly helped keep her temper reined in. "I did not imagine the door to be locked. I was not confused. The darkness did not make me cry."

Sean shook his head slowly. He pointed to the open doorway. "The only way that door locks is with a barrel bolt. It can't accidentally lock and it can't unlock itself. It must've gotten stuck and you simply thought it was locked."

"I know it was locked because I saw who…" Accusing Marci Coffey wouldn't help matters. Especially since Marci had been so public about her dislike of Caitlin. Sean would assume Caitlin was being petty, accusing Marci of a malicious act. Scott had moved to her side. He grasped her arm, forcing her to look at him. One glance and she knew she could never say who had locked the door.

He'd start a small war going after Marci for retribution. Scott had no concept of what "turn the other cheek" meant. Admittedly, Caitlin struggled with the thought of forgiving Marci but she'd work it out privately, without causing more harm.

"Who locked the door, Caitlin?" Scott's voice was low like the far off rumble of a thunderstorm. He touched the tender spot on her temple and lightning flashed in his eyes.

"You have to stop." Caitlin pulled out of his grip. "Stop protecting me. Stop worrying about me."

"If I don't take care of you, who will?"

"I am not a helpless, defenseless little girl. I can take care of myself." She stared him straight in the eye, making sure he got the message. "I. Don't. Need. You."

Scrambling over the tent box, she bolted from the room. Hundreds of tiny daggers stabbed at her insides. Blood rushed through her head in a deafening roar. Scott had been her friend for over twenty years. She'd just put the first nail in the coffin of their friendship.

Janelle stood at the bottom of the stairs. Caitlin avoided her gaze. It would take time to accept her choice. When Janelle reached out for her, Caitlin shrugged off the gesture. She didn't pause in the kitchen. Behind her, footsteps pounded up the steps. She didn't care. She had to make Scott stop caring about her, even if it meant being cruel in the process. It was for the best in the end.

Outside, the sun slid behind a bank of dark clouds on the western horizon. The air smelled of the coming rain. The breeze turned gusty, rushing through the trees with a calming susurration. Caitlin paused. She closed her eyes, drawing deep and slow breaths. Her blood pressure lowered, her heartbeat returned to normal.

"You shouldn't drive home alone."

Her blood pressure skyrocketed. She spun around to confront Sean Taggart. "I am perfectly capable of driving home alone. I do not need you, or any man, to take care of me."

Sean backed up a step. His eyes narrowed and he pointed to her bandaged hand. "I do have some experience with burns. You need to be careful with that hand."

She glanced down. After grabbing the doorknob when Marci locked her in the basement, Caitlin had learned her lesson and refrained from using that hand. The filmy gauze wrap was grimy. It should be changed. Did she have a first aid kit? On the way home she'd stop and buy some bandaging supplies.

"Look, if you're too stubborn to let one of us drive you home, at least let me help with your hand." His expression softened.

She had no intention of trusting him. Still, a firefighter likely had more experience with burns than she did. At a minimum, she could find out how he intended to help.

"I brought you some burn cream. It's in my truck." He pointed to the blue Ford parked in front of the church. "If I promise not to abduct you, will you walk with me over that way?"

"I never thought you'd abduct me." Caitlin smiled. Sean could be quite charming. If she wasn't careful, he would convince her to let him drive her home.

Sean opened the first aid kit on the passenger seat. He turned, holding a pair of bandage scissors. He snapped them open and closed in a menacing manner, a big grin belying his maniacal laugh. A stronger gust of wind assaulted them. Caitlin shivered and rubbed her bare arms. She regretted returning Scott's sweatshirt. No, better this way even if she was cold. If only she could hang on to that thought, wrap it around her shoulders as protection from the wind.

"I can't cut that bandage off if you're trembling like a leaf." Sean reached behind the seat, pulled out a dark blue, cotton duck canvas jacket and placed it over her shoulders.

The coat smelled of pine needles and earth. A dark smudge of grease adorned the right sleeve. Caitlin wanted to protest that she could handle the cold as well as Sean but the thermal lined coat was warm and comfortable. Besides, Sean wore a long sleeve shirt so it wasn't like she was being a wimp.

After slicing the gauze along the back of her hand, Sean removed the bandage. He produced a gray and blue tube of ointment and smeared it across her palm. Caitlin focused on her throbbing hand. Sean maintained a firm grip on her wrist. As the cool cream relieved the burned palm, the warmth from his fingers grew more noticeable.

With her free hand, Caitlin pulled the jacket closed, snuggling into its quilted lining. Sean was being nice right now but that didn't mean he'd stay that way. Remember Adam, all friendly and nice until their last day together. She raised her eyes enough to watch Sean's profile as he gently applied a new bandage. Try as she might, Caitlin couldn't make herself fear Sean. At least, she wasn't afraid that he would hurt her physically. She averted her gaze before he looked at her. She *was* scared of what he might do to her heart.

"The important thing is to prevent infection," Sean explained, "and that's what this cream is for. You should apply it once or twice a day until the burn heals."

"Are you a doctor?" Her hand rested in the cradle of his left hand.

"No, just a guy with loads of experience getting burned." He wrapped the gauze with a feather-light touch. Almost like a caress.

Caitlin dragged her gaze up from her hand to his face. Oh yes, these feelings fluttering around inside her were very frightening. She needed something to focus on, a distraction. Think of a constant, unchangeable math formula. That should keep her mind off Sean. *Things equal to equal things are equal to each other.* She loved the confused expression on her students' faces whenever she told them that one.

"Be sure to use a Telfa pad whenever you wrap your hand." Sean dropped the burn cream, a few rolls of gauze and a handful of Telfa pads into a plastic shopping bag.

"You don't have to give me all that. I can stop at the store on my way home."

"I have plenty. If you feel guilty, you can replace them later." He put the bag into her good hand then pulled his jacket around her like a cocoon. "You really shouldn't drive."

"Please," she wiggled loose from his grip and slid out of the jacket. "I'm not helpless."

"You burned your hand, chased after the Bartlett twins, and spent the last few hours stuck in an unlocked basement. Don't you think you're a little tired? Maybe exhausted enough to be bleary or even sleepy behind the wheel?"

Ah, yes, things equal to equal things...Scott and Sean—and her father. She narrowed her eyes. "You mean my overwrought female brain can't handle any more stimuli."

"I don't care if you're a man, woman or Martian. You convinced yourself that door was locked and you were trapped. Obviously your brain isn't working the way it normally should."

"My brain is working just fine. I know the door was locked. I saw who did it."

"And who was that?"

Caitlin shifted her gaze away from his. "I don't want to cause trouble."

Sean snorted. He leaned down to capture her gaze once more. "What about this morning? Weren't you imagining something when you bumped into the grill?"

Caitlin crushed her teeth together. No way would she say another word and give him more ammunition to store up for a later argument. Not that there'd be a later. She planned to avoid him and thus avoid future discussions.

When she turned to go, Sean caught her arm and pulled her back around to face him.

"Look, I'm not trying to be harsh. I've responded to enough car accidents caused by drivers who thought they had it all under control. Prying people out of mangled, burning vehicles is not pleasant. I'd hate to see something like that happen to you."

Why did all the men in her life feel they needed to control her every action?

SEVEN

The Henderson family took up two full rows of pews in the center section of Naultag Chapel. Sean slid into his customary seat behind them as the prelude music concluded. He glanced at the bulletin, noted the Scripture for today's message and opened his Bible to bookmark the page. A flash of color and movement caught his attention.

Caitlin Harrington walked down the aisle on the far side of the sanctuary. She sat in the pew her grandmother had traditionally occupied. Today, Caitlin wore a sweater that clung to her curves and a long skirt covered her shapely legs. A light jacket draped over her left arm, hiding her injured hand. Did she have trouble with the bandage this morning? Maybe after service he'd offer to help.

He forced his gaze away from Caitlin and focused on the stained glass window behind the choir loft. This was a house of God, he needed to stop obsessing over a woman. A very beautiful woman. Who just might be crazy. Or at the very least, slightly disturbed. He slanted another glance at her. She didn't look insane. But what other explanation could there be for her actions yesterday? Why wouldn't she say who had locked the door? He didn't buy her lame excuse about not wanting to cause trouble.

The congregation rose for praise and worship songs. Sean focused on the lyrics, pushing aside thoughts of Caitlin. He succeeded until Pastor Don came to the podium.

"I'd like to welcome Caitlin Harrington back to our church family." Pastor Don swept an arm out to indicate where Caitlin sat. "As many of you will recall, Caitlin is the granddaughter of Sophie Baxter, our beloved sister who went home to the Lord last year. We're glad to see you here, Caitlin."

Pastor Don wore an expectant expression. Sean turned to see Caitlin's reaction. Some people relished the attention when put into the spotlight by the minister. Caitlin's rosy cheeks showed discomfort, as if she was upset at having been pointed out. Even so, she stood and acknowledged the welcome.

"Thank you, Pastor Don." Her voice carried clearly through

the church. "I'm happy to be back home in Naultag. I look forward to seeing old family friends and making new acquaintances."

A graceful, tactful speech. Events of the day before ran through Sean's mind. Scott Bartlett had been her friend for many years, yet Caitlin spurned his attempts to help and comfort her in the church basement. Odd behavior for someone eager to connect with friends.

Pastor Don smiled and nodded. "Let's turn our attention to prayer concerns in the bulletin." The minister listed off several names, explaining each person's needs. He asked for any other prayer requests. Marci Coffey stood.

"Could we please pray for Caitlin Harrington?" She glanced toward Caitlin. "Yesterday, in a careless accident, she badly burned her hand."

Sean's eyes narrowed as he considered the request. Marci's smile was much too smug. He felt sure that bit about carelessness was a deliberate slam. Why would Marci be so catty? He glanced at Caitlin. She stared straight ahead, her face crimson. In embarrassment or anger, he couldn't tell. Someone else made another prayer request and attention shifted away from Caitlin.

After service, Sean followed the other parishioners into Fellowship Hall. What used to be coffee hour had morphed into a weekly luncheon. Volunteers provided foods ranging from cookies to chili—a great opportunity to get a good, home-cooked meal. Something he missed during the winters with his parents in Florida. He heaped a plate with food, leaving a generous donation in the basket, and headed for the tables.

"Sean, I'd hoped to run into you." Marci Coffey blocked his path. "I wanted to be sure you're planning to attend the special meeting Tuesday night."

Sean raised an eyebrow. Of course he'd be there, but what did it matter to Marci?

"As the wife of a public safety officer, I'm trying to do my best to raise awareness of issues affecting both the police and fire departments."

"I'll be at the meeting but I'm already aware of the issues we face."

Marci leaned toward him to whisper her next comment. "There are some interesting reasons why the school superintendent is opposed to spending money on a new fire truck."

Ah, gossip. Marci's stock in trade. He frowned. *Not very charitable, Taggart.* Marci did some part-time work as a file clerk in the town offices. Maybe she heard something important, factual and not gossip. He eyed the food cooling on his plate and sighed. Marci took his silence as encouragement to continue.

"You know they hired several new teachers, don't you?" When Sean nodded she continued. "Well, one of them is costing the school fifteen grand more than the others."

"I'm sure there's a good explanation. Maybe that teacher has more experience."

"She's costing them ten grand more than their allotted salary budget." Marci brought her chin down as if to say *so there.* "That's why Arlene Millis is fighting the new truck. She can't afford to lose any money from the school budget. And the last thing she wants is for people to know it's because of her inept hiring practices."

"Don't be so quick to judge Arlene. I'm sure she had good reasons. Replacing the LaFrance has nothing to do with the school budget anyway. It'll be a debt exclusion."

"The school is going to need an increased budget next year. Without the fire truck debt, people might not notice. But everyone is looking closely at department budgets these days, especially if taxes go up."

The bowl of chili, which supported his plate of food, grew hot in Sean's hand. His stomach rumbled. With luck, Marci would notice and leave him alone. Or she could ramble on about town finances, as long as she let him eat while she did it. For a fleeting moment, he pitied Eric Coffey. While Marci's insight on the school budget was interesting, it just couldn't compete with food.

"I'll be at the meeting, Marci. Now if you'll excuse me, my food is getting cold."

* * *

Getting in and out of church without being noticed was just a pipe dream. Not that Caitlin didn't like the church members. They meant well. Most of them. But after the harrowing week she'd just been through, she wanted to worship and learn about the word of God without the hassle of questions.

Pastor Don's welcome had given her a pleasant, warm feeling. Then Marci made sure everyone knew about the grill accident, with the added implication of carelessness. No one would believe Caitlin now if she accused Marci of locking her in the basement. Not when Marci had been kind enough to offer prayer for her healing.

Then she saw Sean talking with Marci. Now she couldn't say anything to him against Marci. Even if he didn't think she was being petty, it would only be a matter of time before he told Scott. The fallout from that was more than Caitlin wanted to contemplate.

What she really wanted was to leave. Pastor Don had detained her long enough after service for Margie Swenson to catch her. The older woman expressed concern about yesterday afternoon. Caitlin didn't want to lie, but no one believed the truth anyway. Though touching, the interest irritated Caitlin. People wanted to know what happened. When she wouldn't elaborate, they moved on.

"Are you sure you don't need anything?" Charlotte Henderson interrupted her thoughts. At least Charlotte's concern seemed genuine.

"Thank you, no. The burn isn't that bad."

"You be sure to let us know if there's anything we can do to help."

"I'm fine, really." Caitlin waved her injured hand to emphasize her statement.

"Whoa, careful with that hand." Sean grabbed her wrist.

Caitlin swallowed an involuntary yelp. She pivoted to face him. He grinned.

"Remember what happened the last time you waved your arms around."

"Sean, be nice now." Charlotte patted his arm.

"You know me, Aunt Charlotte. Always nice."

Charlotte gave Caitlin a motherly smile and walked away to chat with someone else.

Caitlin stared at Sean's fingers circling her arm in a firm grip. A snappy retort died on her tongue, overpowered by a growing sense of fear. Ice flooded her veins. In a flash, heat roared over her. She tugged against his hold and staggered back when he relinquished without struggle. Sean grabbed her arm again, this time preventing her from falling. She stared at the floor, willing her breathing to return to normal. *Sean is not Adam, Sean is not Adam.* Her eyes clenched against unwanted images and memories.

She tried to pry loose from Adam's grip on her wrist. Instead, his other arm went around her like a steel band, pulling her close, trapping her hands. "We have something special—"

"Caitlin?" Sean's voice dragged her out of the nightmare. He tilted his head, bending to catch her gaze. Creases puckered his brow, forming a V. "Maybe you should sit down."

He guided her to a chair. People had noticed the commotion. They watched from around the room, looking like they knew she was crazy. She was beginning to think so herself.

"I have to go." She tried to pull away from Sean but his grip tightened.

"Oh, no, not this time. I'm not letting you drive when you're obviously upset." With his free hand, he pressed down on her shoulder.

Resistance lasted only a moment until her knees buckled and she sank onto the seat. He hooked another nearby chair with a foot, pulled it closer, and sat. He took her injured hand, turning it palm up, and cradled it in his. Heat seeped through the bandage. Not the electric heat of panic but pleasant warmth. She closed her eyes, leaning back to enjoy the comfort of his hand holding hers.

"How's the burn today?" Sean's voice was as gentle as his hand. He touched her palm and the peace shattered. Caitlin emitted a short shriek as she jerked and sat up straight. One more time she pulled away. He let her go.

"You didn't have to poke it so hard." She tucked her hand close against her.

"I barely touched you." Sean met her gaze with a knowing expression. "Do you have blisters today?"

Caitlin nodded.

"If it's any consolation, the pain is a good sign. Means the burn didn't go deep enough to damage nerve endings." His lopsided grin faded. "I was wrong yesterday. Should've insisted you see a doctor. You definitely need to have that looked at."

The pain in her hand subsided to a dull ache. Sean's tenderness had numbed her senses. Now she remembered why she wanted to avoid him. He wasn't Adam, but he was just like her father. Domineering, overbearing and controlling.

"I don't need you to tell me whether or not to see a doctor. I'm a grown woman." She rose, grateful her legs remained steady. "I appreciate your kindness, but you don't have to worry about me."

Back straight, chin up, a smile pasted on her face, Caitlin left the church. Never would she admit to Sean that she'd already decided to seek medical attention for her hand. He'd take it as proof of his superiority.

* * *

The answering machine beeped a greeting when Caitlin got home. Ignoring it, she turned to lock the door before shuffling down the hall. She went first to the bathroom, setting the bag from the pharmacy on the counter. The pharmacist had suggested a non-childproof cap for her Vicodin prescription. As she popped the lid off with one hand, Caitlin said a prayer of thanks. Her hand throbbed pain in rhythm with her pulse.

Seeing a doctor had been the right thing to do. But sometimes getting better meant feeling a whole lot worse first. She put a pill in her mouth and washed it down with a glass of water. At least she wouldn't have to change the bandage on her hand until tomorrow. And thanks to McDonald's, she didn't have to worry about cooking supper. The bed looked inviting, even though it was only a little after five. She changed into sweatpants and a t-shirt, tossing the skirt and sweater onto the chair in the corner. In the morning she'd deal with them. She fluffed up the pillows, made sure her book was close and crawled into bed.

The answering machine beeped.

Maybe putting the phone and answering machine on her nightstand hadn't been such a good idea. It seemed smart at the time, having the phone nearby in case of a nighttime emergency. Ignoring the incessant beep was out of the question. Tomorrow she'd turn off the audio notification.

She pushed the button to retrieve messages.

"Caitlin, I'm worried about you." Janelle didn't bother identifying herself. "Scott said I should give you time, but I can't wait. Are you mad at me? I'm sorry about not letting you help at the food pavilion. Please forgive me." There was a second of silence. "I just realized what time it is. You're probably at church. I'll call back later."

The next message played.

"Caitlin, it's your mother. I'm returning your call." *Nice, Mom. I called two nights ago.* "Well, Gary and I are going out. I'll call you again later."

Right, later when you don't have more important things in your life. Later, when Gary's at work and you're bored. *We'll do it later, Caitlin. Not now, Caitlin. Mommy's busy, Caitlin.* She should be used to it by now, but it still hurt.

Another message from Janelle followed. "Cait, is everything okay? You haven't called. Please don't stay mad at me."

The phone rang as the message ended. Caitlin's eyelids closed. Why wouldn't the noise stop? She could unplug the phone but that defeated the purpose of having it by her bed. The caller ID screen on the handset showed Scott Bartlett. *Janelle will just keep calling if I don't answer.* She lifted the receiver.

"Where have you been?" Janelle asked. "I went over at three and you weren't home. You've been gone all day. Are you okay? Is anything wrong?"

"Slow down." Caitlin eased her head onto the pillow, eyes closed. She smiled. Silence really was golden. It glowed around the edges of her eyelids like dawn peeking around the window shades.

"Cait, are you still there?"

Oh, yeah, Janelle. "Sorry, I can't talk right now. Too sleepy…"

"Wait! Don't hang up. Caitlin? Are you there? Is something wrong?"

"I went to the doctor." Caitlin rubbed her eyes but couldn't stifle a yawn. "She gave me some pain pills and they're making me tired. I'll talk to you tomorrow. Promise."

She hung up and snuggled into the bed, glad to let sleep take control. The phone rang again. Now who? Probably Mom. She wasn't up to dealing with her mother right now. Let the machine get it.

"Hi, Caitlin, this is Sean…Taggart."

Oh, yeah, the answering machine was set for call screening. Something else to fix.

"Saw your car in the yard. Hope you're resting. Kind of a rough weekend for you." After a few seconds of quiet, he cleared his throat and continued. "I'm sorry if I upset you today at church. I just wanted to be sure you're okay."

Aw, that's sweet. Maybe she was wrong about him being an arrogant jerk.

EIGHT

The note was taped to her front door, just as before. *Remember where you belong. Jealousy enrages. No mercy will be shown when I take revenge.* Fear sent an icy current down Caitlin's spine, radiating out to her fingertips. She stepped back inside, locking the door.

No one was out there. Not now. Sometime during the night, while she slept unaware, the vicious note had been placed on the heavy wooden door, inside the screen door. Who hated her so much? Marci Coffey? Maybe, but Marci didn't seem like the type to leave notes. She worked in more devious ways. Besides, Marci had no reason to be jealous.

Janelle, warning her to stay away from Scott? Twelve years of friendship and not one sign of jealousy. Until Saturday. Yet, Janelle hadn't said she didn't trust her. Caitlin had assumed the implication.

This note resembled the first one. Thick black marker, bold handwriting. The question of where she belonged.

Adam. *"Stay with me Caitlin. We belong together."*

It hadn't been her imagination playing tricks on Saturday. He was here. Why? She told him she wasn't interested. Made it quite clear. And though he knew she was moving, she'd never told him to where. Had she?

Tears dripped onto the paper. *Get a grip, Caitlin. Call Eric.* He'll know what to do. A police presence should scare off Adam. Just like in Lynn, when her roommate had called the police to complain about Adam sitting out front in his car, all night.

The trembling inside stilled as she looked up Eric's number. He'd do something to help. She hesitated. What if Marci answered? Maybe Caitlin should call him at the police station since it was official business. Asking for Eric might start a rumor. If Marci found out, she'd have fuel for her anger, even if it was imagined fuel. Talking to someone else and saying she suspected Marci...wouldn't that get Eric in trouble? Telling a complete stranger about Adam was out of the question. She hadn't even been able to bring herself to talk with Janelle about the incident.

Caitlin set the cordless phone down on the desk. She couldn't call anyone. *Lord, how could you let this happen? I thought you're supposed to watch over me and keep me safe?*

* * *

Sean stared at the weather report on television. Eighty percent chance of rain today. *Twenty percent chance of Caitlin wanting to see me again.* Worse if she realized he'd followed her yesterday, even if it was only as far as the emergency room entrance.

Did the doctor prescribe something for her pain? He could call, offer to help change her bandage. What was the worst that could happen?

This was the worst. Caitlin stuck in his thoughts. She wasn't the first woman he found attractive. Although, since breaking up with Melissa there hadn't been anyone serious.

Beautiful, flawless Melissa. She wore her wealth with charm and grace, exuding sophistication. And she'd chosen Sean to be at her side. All he had to do was let Melissa mold him into her vision of perfection. She picked out his suits, introduced him to the right people, planned his future. She had painted an exquisite picture in his dreams. But that's all it had been, a dream. When he had refused to turn the campground into house lots, her anger boiled over.

"Do you know how much that real estate is worth? I deserve that money." Her face had bloomed red beneath layers of makeup as her voice rose. "After all I've done. You were just a dumb hick when we met. Now look at you. Mingling with the *crème de la crème*. Dining at the poshest restaurants. A position with one of the best firms on Wall Street. I made you who you are today. You owe me."

Melissa used her father's money and name to get what she wanted but it wasn't enough. She needed a husband who could support her opulent way of life. She only saw him as a tool for maintaining her bank account. She was in love with his earning potential. And she was his stepping-stone. He'd been attracted to her family's money. Her prestige. Her lifestyle. They used one another. The only difference, Melissa did it consciously. Sean had fooled himself into believing he was in love.

Why was he letting a woman monopolize his thoughts and dreams again?

Caitlin was beautiful, but it went beyond that. She didn't

flaunt her father's wealth and fame. The farm could be sold off as building lots for a great deal of money. Instead, she'd moved into the house, keeping it in the family. She looked comfortable and at ease here in Naultag. Like she belonged.

She had backbone and nerve but got scared of imaginary monsters. She didn't want anyone's help, yet managed to get stuck in an unlocked basement. When she interacted with the Bartlett twins she'd let down the bristly facade. Warmth infused her voice, reflected in her eyes.

Who was crazier—a woman who sees imaginary monsters or the man who wanted to vanquish them for her?

* * *

Caitlin stared at the ringing phone. Was God calling with an answer to prayer? The pain medication was really messing with her mind. She lifted the receiver.

"Hi, Caitlin, this is Sean."

His message last night mentioned that he drove by her house. Was he spying on her? "How'd you get this number?"

"Uh, I called information. Are you supposed to be unlisted?"

"No." It wouldn't do any good. The only people she wanted to hide from knew where to find her anyway. She closed her eyes and drew in a long breath. *Sean is not Adam.* Sean apologized for upsetting her. Adam would never have done that.

"Actually, I'm glad you called."

"Really?" He sound surprised, as if he'd expected her to hang up on him.

"The cream you gave me, could I give it to Charlotte Henderson to give back to you?"

"Oh, yeah, I guess that would work. Are you sure you don't need it?"

"I have a brand new tube from the pharmacy. I'll send a replacement for the gauze bandaging, too."

"Did the doctor give you anything for pain?"

"Yes. And I don't need your advice about taking medication."

"I wasn't going to offer any." An awkward silence crackled on the line. "Well, I just called to see if you were okay. Do you need anything?"

"I'm fine. Thank you." Caitlin glanced at the note. They had butted heads. Even so, Sean seemed like a nice guy. Except for his patronizing, chauvinistic tendencies. Certainly he had no reason to be jealous. The notes must be from Adam.

"I could swing by and pick up that stuff, if you really want to return it."

Say yes! Then tell him about Adam. He could call Eric for help and Marci wouldn't have reason to hate her more. *Right, what'll really happen is he'll think I'm certifiably insane.* If he believed her story about seeing Adam on Saturday, he'd question why she hadn't called the police herself. She'd have to tell him about Marci, who was one of his friends. He'd never believe Caitlin. And she definitely couldn't talk to him about what happened with Adam in Lynn.

"No, you don't need to come here. I'll drive over to the Henderson's." She slumped in the chair. The memory of Sean's hand gently cradling hers sent a warm rush through her. It would've been nice to have someone to lean on. Someone with broad, strong shoulders who could carry the weight of her worries.

"You really shouldn't drive until your hand heals. Or at least not until you can touch it without causing pain."

"I can drive just fine. And what would you know about the pain in my hand?"

He cleared his throat. She got the distinct impression he was smiling. Okay, so he'd seen her reaction yesterday.

"I've been burned a few times." At least he didn't laugh. "Plus, I've seen people with some pretty bad burns. Experience is a good teacher."

Oh, that's right, he's a firefighter. Well, she could be just as tough. If he could get burned and chuckle about it, so could she. "I can take care of myself. Thank you, anyway."

* * *

Sean snapped the cell phone closed and clipped it to his waistband. He trudged to the barn, muttering under his breath as he rolled the door open. *Call her. Offer to help. What's the worst that could happen?* Caitlin wanted nothing to do with him, huh? What a loser, chasing after her like a lovesick little boy. Well, no more. He had a campground to run, employees to supervise, grass to mow. A T-ball team to coach. The new fire training schedule to plan.

No more obsessing. No matter how beautiful she was. Let her vulnerable bravery impress some other guy. She could vanquish her own demons.

He was done with thinking about Caitlin Harrington.

NINE

Why couldn't she stop thinking about Sean Taggart?

Caitlin rolled over and eyed the alarm clock. Three minutes until it buzzed. She'd been awake for almost fifteen. Bad enough that Sean had popped into her thoughts throughout the day yesterday. But dreaming about him? That was too much. She shut off the alarm clock.

With her left hand.

Pain streaked along her fingers. She whimpered and pulled her hand close. It still hurt but not as much as when Sean poked it on Sunday. Already the blisters were healing. The doctor said the burn would be much better in a week to ten days. Caitlin had doubted that at the time, but now it looked like a possibility. Maybe life would start to improve.

After dressing, Caitlin went to the front entry, nerves churning her gut. She opened the door wide and stepped outside. No note. Surly gray clouds mounded in the western sky, advancing eastward. More rain on the way, but it wasn't here yet. There should be time for a walk after breakfast.

Gossamer drizzle caressed her face with its silky mist at the start of her walk. A blue pickup truck slowed as it came around the corner then drove by the house. Caitlin stopped and blinked several times. The truck was real, but it wasn't Sean's.

Her hand throbbed. She unclenched her fist. That man thought he knew best about everything. He'd probably decided she was a crazy woman, making up imaginary foes. It didn't matter. She wasn't interested in his opinion. Whether he found her attractive or thought her insane held no relevance in her life. Men were only interested in women they could control. And once a man had a woman under control, he moved on, leaving her tethered to a fantasy. Not Caitlin. She wouldn't be duped into marrying a controlling, egotistical chauvinist like her father. She'd learned from her mother's mistakes, even if Mom hadn't.

The driveway gravel crunched underfoot. It would be nice to talk to Janelle about all this. Then again, she was the one who got

Caitlin focused on how handsome Sean was. Still, Janelle was her best friend. They could laugh about it was and in the end Caitlin would feel better. At least, that's how they would've talked in the past. Before she knew Janelle had doubts about Caitlin's relationship with Scott. Before Marci locked her in the church basement.

The drizzle coalesced into rain. A cold drop rolled off the windbreaker collar and streaked an icy trail down her spine. Caitlin shivered and pulled up the hood. If she didn't talk to Janelle soon, they wouldn't have a friendship. She walked briskly to the Bartlett's house. Janelle opened the door before Caitlin could knock.

"Why are you walking in the rain? Without an umbrella." She took Caitlin's windbreaker, looking closely at the U. S. Navy logo. "Nice jacket. Did James give it to you?"

Caitlin nodded. "It was a Christmas gift from him and Debbie last year. It would've been perfect if the drizzle hadn't changed to a downpour."

After hanging the dripping jacket, Janelle led Caitlin upstairs and poured two cups of coffee, adding milk to each. She motioned to the sugar on the table.

"Sorry I haven't called back." Caitlin stared into the coffee whirlpool her spoon created.

"I figured you're still mad at me for not letting you help with the food concessions."

"I was never angry about that." Caitlin followed Janelle to the table. What was the best way to confront Janelle about what Marci had said? *If she really doesn't trust me, she wouldn't be so concerned about me being mad at her.*

"So if you weren't upset, why'd you tell Margie you were going home?"

The edge of the coffee mug rolled smoothly under Caitlin's thumb. The coral nail polish needed touching up along the top of her nails. Janelle would love to do that. Caitlin sighed.

"I heard you talking with Marci," she whispered.

"About wha—oh, that." Janelle set her mug on the table. "That woman has some issues. I'm not sure what her problem with you is, but she was way out of line Saturday."

Caitlin locked gazes with Janelle. "Do you trust *me?*"

"Of course, why wouldn't I?"

"You told Marci that you trust Scott but you didn't say you

trust me."

Janelle laughed. A little bit of dread drained away from Caitlin. Things couldn't be too bad between them if Janelle laughed like that.

"The idea of you having an affair with any man, married or not, is preposterous. It never occurred to me that I'd have to say I trust you."

"Then why'd you defend Scott?" Were they having marital problems? Caught up in her own troubles, Caitlin hadn't stopped to think about her friends.

It was Janelle's turn to be uncomfortable. She swirled the coffee in her cup, taking a minute before answering. "I know Scott loves me, and I don't really think he would have an affair with another woman. But sometimes…" Janelle lifted one shoulder as she met Caitlin's gaze. "It's silly, really. He spends more time with work than at home. Then he comes home and his first words are 'how long until supper?' not, 'hi honey, how was your day?' He spends weekends with the boys. Then there's the fire department. And can't forget sports. Ask him who won the game three weeks ago and he'll give you the score and all the details. But ask him what I said three hours ago and he won't remember."

"Wow, I thought you two had a good marriage." Caitlin had never heard Scott gripe about Janelle and until today, Janelle had never complained about him.

"We do have a good marriage." Janelle waved a hand as if dismissing her earlier words. "We still go out, just the two of us, once or twice a month. He even remembers my birthday. Sometimes, for no reason at all, he brings me flowers. But once in a while it would be nice for him to say he loves me."

"So you have doubts about Scott?"

"No, not really." Janelle shook her head. "When Marci told me there were rumors about you and Scott, I didn't think they were true. It was just a reminder that he takes me for granted. And maybe I take him for granted, too."

"Another reason I don't ever want to get married."

Janelle put a hand on her arm. "All that stuff I just said about Scott? It works the same with friendships. If I hadn't excluded you from helping, you wouldn't have been in the frame of mind to be hurt by what you overheard."

Caitlin looked down. Janelle's wedding band gleamed, the

polished gold reflecting light from overhead. If marriage was like friendship, there was hope. The few friends she had were good, loyal, trustworthy people. Maybe her parents' marriage was horrible because they had lacked friendship. And Mom hardly got to know a guy before she moved in with him. Or in Gary's case, let him move in with her.

"You just need to meet the right man." Janelle patted her arm before getting up to pour more coffee. "How's your hand?"

"Much better." Caitlin shook her head when Janelle offered a refill. "I went to the emergency room on Sunday. The doctor gave me a prescription for Vicodin. That's why I was so loopy when you called Sunday night."

"I understand completely." Janelle flashed a grin. "Is the pain what made you go to the hospital?"

"Partly, and also because a couple of big blisters appeared." She wrinkled her nose. "I debated going to the emergency room or waiting until Monday for a regular appointment."

"What decided it for you?"

Caitlin set her bandaged hand in the other, looking at the fresh gauze wrap but seeing her hand resting in Sean's. For a brief moment on Sunday, she'd trusted him completely and without reserve. It had felt good thinking she could rely on someone, lean on his strength when she was weak. Then he'd touched her palm, and she'd accused him of hurting her on purpose.

"Cait?"

She shook her head, looking up to meet Janelle's concern. "After church, Sean convinced me to go to the doctor right away."

"You talked to him at church? That's wonderful. I had a feeling you'd like him."

"I don't like him." Heat flared in her cheeks. "He poked my hand. How could I like someone that insensitive?"

"Sean, insensitive? I've never met a more caring person."

"He's full of himself. Controlling. Chauvinistic. Just like my father."

Janelle shook her head. "What is it with you and your father, anyway? Jack seems nice. I've never seen him act like a chauvinist."

Where to begin? Caitlin knew Janelle's parents. Nice, loving people who doted on their daughter and grandchildren. How could Janelle understand what it was like growing up with parents whose hate for each other left no room to love their children?

"Most of my childhood, my father wasn't around. When he was, he did nothing but criticize and belittle everything about my mother, and me. I was never good enough for him, but James could do no wrong. I wanted to join the Little League, because maybe then he'd approve. Jack told me girls weren't meant to play baseball and I should stick to dolls." She wrinkled her nose. "I never played with dolls."

"So your dad wasn't the greatest. I still don't see how Sean is anything like him."

"Sean Taggart is patronizing. He treated me as if I'm foolish, getting burned on the grill. Like it wasn't an accident. Then he believed I was brainless enough to be stuck in an unlocked room." She took a deep breath, let it out slowly. "He even implied that I wasn't capable of driving without crashing."

"Scott was worried about you driving with only one hand."

"Exactly," she brought her chin down to emphasize the point. "He's a control freak, too."

"No, he cares about you. Maybe Sean was just concerned."

"He thinks I imagined being locked in the basement. Do you believe that, too?"

"No and neither does Scott. But why won't you tell us who locked the door?"

"If I tell Scott, what do you think he's going to do?" Caitlin waited as the realization washed over Janelle. "He doesn't do forgive and forget. I don't want to be the cause of trouble."

"You can tell me. I won't go looking for revenge."

She shook her head. "You'd have to lie to Scott."

"How about Sean? You could tell him, and then he'd know you aren't crazy."

"Why would he believe me? I can't point a finger at someone in this community and expect there won't be repercussions. It's best the whole thing gets forgotten."

Janelle held her gaze. Caitlin resisted the urge to turn away. Janelle needed to know she was serious about letting go of the incident. At last Janelle shook her head. "Okay, I'll forget about it. For now."

Caitlin let out a pent-up breath. She was right to put the basement incident behind her. But Janelle was right about something, too. Sean wasn't Jack Harrington.

TEN

"It seems to me, Chief, the truck you want to buy has all sorts of bells and whistles we just don't need." Arlene Millis stood to challenge Fire Chief Darren Sminski. Several people gathered for the special town meeting agreed with her sentiment.

Sean groaned. The school superintendent and fire chief had a lifelong feud. No one knew what it was about —at least, they weren't saying. Probably something stupid like a messed up prom date forty years ago. But why did Arlene have to take it out on the fire department?

Darren didn't back down. He never did. "The town's ISO rating is in peril if we cannot adequately provide fire protection. And homeowners' insurance rates will go up. We need this truck, with these *bells and whistles.*"

The debate volleyed back and forth between them. Intelligent discussion. Sean relaxed. Arlene's arguments actually helped get more information to the townspeople.

Then Marci Coffey stood and directed a question at Arlene. "Are you opposed to the new fire engine because the school will be drastically over budget in the coming year?"

Ah, here it comes, Marci's top secret bombshell. Sean turned to get a better view of both women.

"School finances have nothing to do with my concerns." Arlene faced Marci.

"Isn't it true, salaries for the new teachers are higher than originally planned?"

A hush settled on the auditorium. Arlene smiled and glanced around the room before replying. "Yes, that is correct. However, the salary budget was not set in stone. We were prepared for the increase. All of our teachers are paid in accordance with their training and experience."

"Experience?" Marci's voice went up in pitch. "Your new eighth grade math teacher only has experience teaching fifth grade."

The auditorium erupted with people talking all at the same time. Town moderator Mike Fitzpatrick thwacked his gavel several times.

Arlene's voice rose above the buzz. "Ms. Harrington is more than qualified for the position."

"She ought to be with what you're paying her." Marci's gaze swept the room. "And what about the impropriety that led to her being fired?"

"I don't know what you're talking about."

"Because you failed to properly look into the matter." Marci looked smug. "You hired her just because she's Jack Harrington's daughter."

"Mrs. Coffey, that's enough." Mike banged the gavel again. "This is neither the time nor the place for this discussion."

"People have a right to know."

Marci obviously had it out for Caitlin, but was there any real basis for these allegations? Arlene didn't deny the higher salary, that part must be true. The impropriety, though? Sean recalled Randy's suggestion about Caitlin and Scott Bartlett but after watching their interactions last Saturday, he seriously doubted anything illicit had ever occurred. Scott and Caitlin treated each other exactly the same way Randy and his next oldest sister, Jenn, behaved with each other.

Jack Harrington's little princess, Randy had also said. Did Caitlin use her father's name and reputation to get the teaching job? And why had Caitlin lost her previous job? Maybe she didn't care about the kids or teaching math, she just cared about getting a better paycheck.

Quiet descended, starting in the back of the room and moving forward like a wave. Something had the effect Mike's gavel lacked. Sean twisted in his seat. Officer Eric Coffey, in uniform, strode down the aisle. He stopped at the row where Marci stood, her mouth open as if to say more.

"You're disrupting the meeting." Eric's voice stayed even and calm. Professionally cold. "I think it best you leave now." He gestured toward the door and stepped back to allow his wife to precede him out of the auditorium.

Mike Fitzpatrick cleared his throat, breaking the silence. "Yes, well, are there any other questions?"

People shifted in their seats. A few glanced at the door where the Coffeys had exited. Arlene Millis shook her head when Mike pointed to her. Sean had heard enough. Time to get out and go home.

He couldn't shake Marci's comments. Arlene wasn't stupid. Surely she'd checked Caitlin's references and knew what salary was appropriate. Or perhaps Caitlin felt she was worth more and had demanded a higher salary. Maybe for her it wasn't about the kids, it was about the money. No wonder she didn't want anything to do with him. He was just a poor hick from the boonies, nothing to be gained from him. She wasn't any different from Melissa after all.

* * *

A clear blue sky greeted Wednesday morning. After three days of rain, the piercing radiance of the sun blinded Caitlin. She stood on the front step, eyes closed, absorbing the warmth. Although the temperature hovered in the forties it was expected to get up to sixty this afternoon. By the weekend, the weatherman said, it would be in the eighties. Summertime weather for the Memorial Day weekend.

Caitlin ambled around the yard. The house was clean, all the furniture moved and boxes unpacked. No more feud with best friend to settle. Nothing to worry about. Although, Janelle had phoned last night about the special town meeting and Marci's outburst.

"I'm not going to think about that. I'm just going to enjoy the beautiful morning." Caitlin stopped and inspected the prospective vegetable garden. Scott had offered to till the patch. The muddy earth would take time to dry. In a few days, she should be able to start planting.

Songbirds made a racket in the field behind the house. Shrill chirps of sparrows mixed with the rich warble of a purple finch. Caitlin strolled to the dilapidated fence surrounding what used to be the horse pasture. A blue jay perched on the gatepost, a sawed-off telephone pole still sturdy after thirty years in the ground. The bird scolded her sharply. She turned away and it flew off with an indignant flutter.

Remembering long trail rides with Gram brought a smile. The pasture gate hung open, its hinges rusted so it no longer moved. The morning dew soaked her canvas deck shoes as Caitlin walked toward the barn. It sagged in the middle, like an old, swaybacked horse. The end near the road showed recent repairs—Mr.

Henderson used that section for storage. The horse stalls had been at the far end. A worn path still led along the side of the building. Footprints showed in the mud. Someone had traipsed the length of the barn recently. Maybe Mr. Henderson had examined the rest of the building for possible expanded storage capacity.

The massive barn door rolled open with a deep, thunderous rumble. A prickly sensation tingled down the back of Caitlin's neck. What if the footprints weren't Mr. Henderson's? A person could easily hide inside the unused portion of the barn. She hesitated, glancing around. There was no one in sight. With a shake, she dismissed the feeling. No more notes had appeared since Monday morning. She doubted, now, that Adam had anything to do with them. Marci Coffey most likely left the notes. Clearly she disliked Caitlin enough to do almost anything to drive her out of town. Why else would she resort to false allegations that could easily be disproved?

"Not gonna think about that." She held her hand up in a *stop* gesture.

The interior of the barn gaped like an ominous black hole. Swooping from above, barn swallows zoomed into the morning sunshine while less timid sparrows followed Caitlin inside. Mice skittered across the concrete floor. Spider webs draped from the ceiling and across most of the open space.

"*Eww.*" Caitlin shivered, as if a spider crawled down her spine. She started to turn around, but the stalls lured her on. She let herself get caught up in the memories. Gram taught her to ride and how to properly care for the horses. As a child it was sheer delight; as a teen, blissful escapism.

A shadow fell across the floor, marring the morning light streaming through the open door. For a moment, fear chilled her skin. Someone was watching her, following her. The footprints weren't Mr. Henderson's. She searched for a weapon and frowned—not even an old pitchfork. Trying to look brave, she faced the intruder.

Sean Taggart stood outside the building. Her breath whooshed out in relief. He looked as attractive as always. She took a step toward him. Her smile faltered. Was it the shadows, or was Sean scowling at her?

"Oh, it's just you." He turned to leave.

"Wait," Caitlin called. She rushed through the door. "What do you mean, it's just me?"

Sean stopped, shrugging his shoulders without turning around. "I heard the door open and figured kids were sneaking in here."

"Isn't it a school day? Why would kids go in our barn?"

"To do drugs or have sex." Sean turned, his scowl deepened. "For a school teacher you don't know much about kids."

Anger flashed hot over her cheeks. "I hadn't realized the disciplinary problems we had in the city are prevalent here in the country as well."

"Our kids face the same problems."

"I hope there aren't gangs out here in the sticks." She tried to infuse the comment with humor but his ice blue eyes put a chill on the mood.

He crossed his arms over his chest. "Oh, us hicks have come a long way in the world. We even have computers out here in the boonies."

"I was trying to be funny." She crossed her arms, mimicking him. The action caused a twinge of pain in her hand. She sucked in a sharp breath and bit the inside of her lip.

Sean's expression softened and he took a step toward her. "How's the hand?"

"Better, thank you." Her belly flip-flopped. Watching him approach, she remembered how it felt when he'd cradled her hand in his. He extended his arm, as if to take her hand again, but quickly pulled back.

"Sorry, I just remembered you don't need my help." He turned and walked toward the street. "Don't worry, I'll be too busy working to offer any more help."

After Janelle finally convinced her that Sean was one of the nicest men on earth, here he was being, well, mean. Not malicious but certainly callous. What did she do to him?

Besides being snippy about his help earlier this week.

Was he that sensitive about her calling Naultag *the sticks*?

The town meeting. Caitlin's stomach churned. Sean must've been there. She'd seen him chatting with Marci, too, at church. Apparently he believed Marci's hateful lies. Tears stung her eyes. She blinked them away. He'd been caring and considerate all weekend and she thanked him by being curt, even rude. Maybe she deserved this cold shoulder treatment.

She watched him walk away. The dew darkened the bottom edge of his faded jeans and turned his boots a deep brown. A gray shirt stretched over his broad shoulders. He'd pushed up the long sleeves, giving a glimpse of muscled forearms. Each ground-swallowing stride carried him closer to his truck, parked on the other side of the street. Further from her.

Somehow she needed to convince Sean that all of Marci's accusations were lies. She hurried after him.

"What are you doing here anyway?"

Without slowing Sean replied, "Uncle Charlie asked me to check the corn."

"It hasn't sprouted yet, you know." *Come on, Sean, stop and talk to me.*

He turned and cocked one eyebrow. "Is that your considered opinion? I thought your valuable expertise was in teaching math? "

His sarcastic tone paled in comparison to the piercing condemnation in his gaze. Oh, so it was the teaching experience thing he had a problem with. She glanced away, a perverse relief washing over her. At least he didn't think she'd had an affair with a married man.

"You're right, I don't know anything about farming." She looked up. He'd crossed his arms again. A muscle flexed in his jaw. "I just wondered how you can check corn that hasn't sprouted."

"I'm looking for washout. Or maybe you thought I was spying on you?"

It had crossed her mind. But that wasn't important because now she had his attention. Just keep him talking and find a way to convince him to…what, believe in her? Well, at the very least she wanted his good humor back.

"You said you'd be too busy working. Don't you work for Mr. Henderson?"

"No, I own High Peak Campground, on the other side of town. I just help Uncle Charlie now and then." Sean crossed the street and stopped beside his truck.

No, no, no, he couldn't leave. Not yet. She'd pushed him away for a week only to discover she liked the nice Sean. Better than this callous, sarcastic Sean anyway. She scuffed the toe of her shoe in the sand at the edge of the road.

"I'm sorry about being curt with you on Monday."

His eyebrow arched again.

"And Sunday. And Saturday. But you have to give me a little leeway with Saturday. Anyone would be crabby after a day like I had."

Sean opened the truck door. "Be honest, Caitlin. You don't want anything to do with me. That's why you were rude." He slid into the driver's seat, put the truck into gear then drove away without looking back.

* * *

Caitlin sat on the deck, staring across the expanse of lawn. One year ago, life was much simpler. She had just lost her teaching job, true. But no one was leaving nasty notes on her door. Marci Coffey wasn't spreading cruel lies about her. Adam was someone she'd just met.

A car horn tooted, yanking her out of her introspection. Her father unfolded himself from the Jaguar parked out front. Great, perfect timing as always. Pasting a smile on her face, Caitlin stepped out to greet him.

"Caitlin, you look great." His hands stayed hidden in the pockets of his dress pants. "Life in the country must agree with you."

"Thank you." She answered dutifully, letting the sweatshirt sleeve slip down to cover the bandage on her left hand. "This is where I've always felt at home."

She held his gaze, waiting for the usual excuses. Jack surprised her with a wan smile and silence. He turned away, moving to look out over the front yard. She studied his profile. Dark pants, designer shirt, light brown hair with no hint of gray. He still looked like the arrogant, imperious, superficial man she grew up with.

Jack strolled to the edge of the garden. "If memory serves, your grandmother always planted flowers around her vegetable garden." His gaze swept over the land. At last, he gestured to the house. "Well, how about you show me around the house?"

Caitlin led him up the front steps. He held the door open for her. Usually he made such gentlemanly gestures only in public, where it looked good. The house interior was dim after the bright afternoon sun. She crossed the living room to switch on a table lamp beside the armchair. A multi-colored rag rug covered the center of the hardwood floor. In addition to the armchair, a Mission style sofa and one side table occupied the room. Books lined half the built-in shelves along one wall.

"Much less cluttered than your place in Lynn." Jack delivered his assessment with a nod of approval. "It's nice. Looks like you— simple yet sophisticated."

A wave of delighted pleasure washed over her. She tamped it down. Jack knew nothing about who she was. He'd argued against her moving back to Naultag, though at the last minute he'd offered to help pay for moving expenses. If he really understood her, he'd realize that this was where she belonged. This was home.

Jack sauntered to the hall. He stood looking down its length for several minutes before shaking his head and turning to Caitlin. "Seems like a million years since I've been in this house."

Caitlin walked away. He had never visited while she lived here with Gram. Part of her wanted to scream about the past, confront him and force him to admit what a horrible father he'd been. The other part yearned for another compliment, a sign of his approval. Praise from Jack came at long intervals. It could be years before she heard another kind word from him.

"Are you going to offer your old man a cup of coffee?"

There it was, the autocratic attitude. And here she was, obediently pouring a cup, desperate to get it right for once. He took it from her and found a place at the breakfast bar. She sat on the opposite side of the counter, diagonally across from him. He stared into his mug.

"I spoke with James last week." He smiled. James was the favorite, even after he ran off and joined the Navy. "Chief Petty Officer James Harrington. Has a nice ring to it."

Nicer than math teacher Caitlin Harrington? She put the cup to her mouth, hiding a frown and drowning the bitter words that wanted to come out.

"He seems in good spirits, considering how long he's been at sea."

"He'll be back before Debbie's due date. That's what he's focusing on."

"I hope the Navy doesn't disappoint him." He fiddled with his cup. "Speaking of due dates, Linda and I are having a baby."

Caitlin froze for a moment. Then a wave of nausea roiled her gut. She must not have heard him right. How could he start another family after deserting the first one?

"So that's why you complimented the living room. You just wanted to soften the blow." She sucked in a breath and held it.

Never in her life had she dared speak to him like this.

"I meant what I said. You've done a nice job decorating in here."

Having crossed the threshold, Caitlin plunged into belligerence. "How can you say it looks like me? You don't know anything about me."

"You're my daughter." Bright splotches of red colored Jack's face. "I know more about you than you could imagine."

"I'd have to imagine, since you were never around."

"I'll admit your mother and I made mistakes when we were young. I've learned from the past, Caitlin. I wasn't a good father when you were growing up, but I'm trying to make up for it now as best I can." He stood and came around the bar. He reached for her hands. "I never meant to hurt—what happened to your hand?"

She let him take the injured hand. He held it in a firm grip. It didn't hurt but she also didn't feel the sensation of warmth and security as when Sean had cradled her hand. With a gentle tug, she broke free from her father's hold. It wasn't Jack's place to comfort her.

"There was an accident and I got burned on a gas grill."

"When did this happen? Are you okay?" Jack reached for her hand again.

Caitlin pulled back. *Oh, no, you don't get to comfort me. Only someone who was there can do that. Someone who reacted quickly enough to keep my clothes from catching fire.* Sean had more than earned the right to care about how her hand healed. Too bad she'd turned him against her.

"I'm fine. I went to the doctor and got medicine."

"What doctor did you see? I want you to see my doctor, just to be safe. You don't want an unsightly scar."

"I don't need to see another doctor. It's nothing."

"Nothing? You're burned enough for a bandage, that's not nothing. What exactly happened?" He put his hands on his hips and frowned. "You have to pay attention when using a grill, Caitlin. You're too easily distracted. If other things were going on, you should've let someone else take care of the grill. Fire isn't something to play around with."

She ground her teeth, biting back anger and hurt. She thought he was changing, that maybe he did love her and could be as proud of her as he was of James. But he was the same man who haunted her unhappy memories.

"I can take care of myself."

He threw his hands up. "You always were independent and stubborn." An unexpected smile creased his face. "The independence you get from me. The stubborn must be from your mother's side. Ah, well, no one's perfect. At least I gave you some of my good genetics."

She narrowed her eyes. Could she really be the offspring of someone so conceited? Jack chuckled and rubbed her arm.

"Will you tell your mother about the baby for me? She's still not talking to me, but I don't want her to hear it through the grapevine. You know how irrational she gets about things like that."

He turned and walked toward the door. "The baby is due in November," he spoke over his shoulder. "You'll finally be a big sister."

He left. Caitlin closed the door and leaned against it. Wonderful, in the middle again. Once more Jack was running out on his responsibilities and leaving her to deal with the consequences. He didn't want to put up with Mom's tirade yet had no qualms about making Caitlin deal with the inevitable melodrama.

Now her father was starting a new family. Just what she wanted, to become a big sister at twenty-eight. He'd probably be Daddy of the Year for this baby.

"It's not right," she indulged in self-pity. "I should be the one getting married and having babies."

So do it. Caitlin glanced over her shoulder, half expecting someone to be standing behind her. No one was there, the house was empty. She went back to the kitchen to wash the coffee cups. The voice sounded in her head again. *Stop being such a coward and give love a chance.*

Give heartache a chance was more like it.

There is no fear in love. Perfect love drives out fear.

Caitlin frowned. But what if she failed to find *perfect* love?

ELEVEN

Traffic on route 146 was light at this time of day in the middle of the week. Sean nudged the accelerator. When the Accord reached 60, he set the cruise control and settled back in the seat. Less than an hour to T.F. Green Airport.

A familiar four-beat rhythm caught his attention and he turned up the radio. "Cold As Ice" by Foreigner cranked out of the stereo speakers. He tapped the steering wheel in time to the music. Ah, this could be Caitlin's theme song. She wouldn't take advice, at least not from him. The way she shut him out, like slamming a door. And digging for gold...oh, yeah, she was just another money loving, self-absorbed princess.

This morning, though, she'd been more approachable. Followed him, kept stopping him as if she didn't want him to leave. He snorted—she even tried joking with him. There was a moment when he had almost taken her hand between his. She looked so vulnerable, chewing on her lip, hazel eyes wide, hopeful. Had she wanted him to hold her hand?

Last Saturday flashed in his memory. Caitlin's pale, fear-stricken face. Eyes full of trust as he tended her wounded hand. The way her lower lip trembled just before she cried. He'd wanted to pull her into his arms, hold her, comfort her. Promise to keep her safe. Bring back her smile.

He smacked the steering wheel, accidentally tooting the horn. No, he would not be drawn in by a pretty face. Every time he tried being friendly, she turned his words against him. Today he was downright rude and she apologized for being curt. How was he supposed to know which attitude to expect from her?

Caitlin was like a late-night fire—you saw the flames but the full extent was hard to judge and there was a high risk of getting burned.

Focus, that's what he needed to do. Keep his mind on the task at hand, picking up Mom and Dad. And figure out some way to convince them to stay in Florida. He liked having Mom around to cook and Dad was always good company. But they should relax, enjoy their retirement. If only Mom didn't have her heart set on seeing him married.

Memories of last summer careened into his mind. "Margie's niece is visiting next week." Mom always made these kind of casual off-handed statements, as if he wouldn't know what was about to follow. "Why don't you take her out to dinner, Sean dear?" He could say no, and usually did—at first. In the end, though, he'd be on a date. Let's see, counting Margie's niece, Mom had set him up with four women in three months. And tried to get him to go out with Shirley Russo's granddaughter this winter.

Okay, get his parents to retire for real without getting sucked into Mom's matchmaking schemes. Should be a piece of cake. He snorted and steered the car around short-term parking until reaching the gate for lot D. Despite fresh landscaping, the area looked like a jungle of concrete, metal and glass. He'd be glad to get back to green trees and rolling countryside.

The car chirruped when Sean set the alarm. He smiled. Nobody set their car alarm in Naultag. Back home, no one worried about leaving the car or house unlocked. A person could even leave windows open with no fear. Well, except...he looked up at the clear blue sky. Nope, rain wasn't a concern today. Crossing the parking lot Sean entered the steel-and-glass-fronted terminal. Inside, light flooded the building, giving it a welcoming feel even with increased security presence.

"Sean!" Mom waved and hurried over, leaving Dad at the baggage claim carousel. Cradling his face in her hands, she pulled him down and planted a kiss on his forehead.

Sean wrapped his arms around Mom's plump frame. He kissed her cheek then led her back to the carousel. "Have you been waiting long?"

Dad shook his hand. "Just got in, your timing is perfect."

"Ooh, there are our bags." Mom grabbed Sean's arm as she pointed.

Sean took charge of their suitcases, loading them onto a cart. Dad waited with Mom at the curbside while Sean brought the car around. Then he held the door open for his mother. Dad got into the front passenger seat.

"How'd the meeting go last night?" Dad asked. "Think there'll be any problems getting the new truck?"

Ah, the meeting. He'd been trying not to think about that. Marci's little bombshell was nothing more than gossip and the last thing he wanted to do was spread rumors. Still, his parents would hear about it all at some point.

"Arlene Millis had some objections, as expected."

"Of course." Dad nodded. "Just personal, you think?"

Sean shrugged. "Probably. There are some rumors going around about the school being over budget with teacher salaries."

"Nothing ever changes," Mom said. "What else is going on in town?"

"Well, Sophie Baxter's granddaughter moved into her house."

Now why'd he go and blurt that out? There must be at least a dozen other things he could've told Mom. But no, he brought the conversation around to Caitlin. That woman was going to drive him insane.

"Little Caitlin has come back?" Mom asked.

"You know Caitlin?" Sean glanced into the rearview mirror.

"Of course." Mom smiled wistfully. "I remember when she was a little girl and Sophie brought her to church for the first time. A perfect little lady, she was."

"I'm surprised you don't remember her, son," Dad said. "She spent just about every summer with Sophie and Peter."

"Guess I was too involved with sports."

"Remember when she came to stay?" Mom spoke to Dad now. "After the divorce she was a different child. Quiet, reserved."

"You were in college then," Dad added. "I wonder why she's moved back now."

"She's teaching here in the fall."

"Oh, how wonderful." Mom scooted forward, leaning close to his shoulder. "Did she mention her mother?"

"No, nothing about either of her parents."

Mom shook her head. "No, I suppose she wouldn't. Sophie mentioned they didn't have a good relationship. Irene's had a difficult time since the divorce. I do hope she's well."

His parents began chatting about Florida and the retirement community where they lived. Sean listened without commenting. Dad said something that made Mom blush and chastise him. Dad grinned and winked at Sean. After almost forty years of marriage his parents were still in love. That's what Sean wanted, someday, but the prospect looked pretty dim.

At last he drove up High Peak Road and pulled into the driveway between the white colonial farmhouse and large red barn. Classic New England color scheme. Just what people expected to see, perfect for the campground. He parked in front of the barn.

"We should invite her to dinner," Mom announced at the end of a conversation about their Florida neighbor.

"Myrtle? Isn't it a bit far for her to come?" Sean asked.

Slapping his arm lightly, Mom clarified, "Don't be silly. I mean Caitlin of course."

"Oh, of course." Sean rolled his eyes. "I'm not sure she'd come."

"Why ever not?" Mom leaned forward.

Because she's cold, uncaring and doesn't want anything to do with the world. Even if that weren't true, he'd been so rude this morning she'd have to be insane to accept a dinner invitation. Then again, he had doubts about her sanity. Better to keep those thoughts to himself.

* * *

Breakfast the next morning reminded Sean why it was great having his parents around. Especially Mom. "You know what would go great on these pancakes?"

Mom pointed. "Syrup's in the microwave."

"Blueberry pancakes with warm maple syrup and thick slices of bacon. I've died and gone to heaven."

Dad looked at his plate. "Where's my bacon?"

"You're on a low sodium diet," Mom reminded.

"Blasted doctors."

Mom set a small plate beside him. "Lucky for you, your son loves you enough to buy some low sodium bacon."

"Thanks, Sean." Dad ate a slice. "What's on tap for today?"

"I got the new culvert finished. We should be able to use the lower end of Raccoon Trail now. Those sites need clearing."

"I'll work on that."

"I've got to go over the water and electric lines down there."

"Sounds like we've got the day planned." Dad drained his coffee. "And you Margaret?"

"Shopping. You did a decent job, Sean, but there's plenty you overlooked."

He shrugged. "Sorry, I have no idea what you use to make all those wonderful meals."

"You should by now." Mom turned, waving a spatula in admonishment. "And do you know what I could use around here?"

"Help in the kitchen?" Sean and Dad spoke in unison.

"A daughter-in-law."

Sean groaned. "Come on, Mom, you just got here. Give it a week or two before you start in on me getting married." He gave her what he hoped was a charming smile.

She held her frown only a minute. "Get out of here, you incorrigible child."

Laughing, Sean followed his father out to work.

As it turned out, Sean had to dig up the water pipes in the lower end of the campground. Finding the break in the line wasn't as easy as it should've been because the ground was too saturated from all the rain. After trenching the entire length of the road, he located the problem. A joint in the pipe had let go.

Late in the afternoon Sean traipsed back toward the house. His shirt clung to him with a mixture of sweat and dirt. Grease from the backhoe covered his hands. Good thing Caitlin wasn't here—he'd probably smear it all over her arm and make her angry at him again. He stomped across the porch, knocking muck out of his boot treads. Inside, he took the boots off. Formerly white socks outlined his feet in dingy brown. Better take them off, too. And get to the shower before Mom complained about all the dirt he'd tracked in.

Dad sat at the kitchen table reading *The Naultag Weekly*. Sean paused as the headline caught his eye: ARE OUR TEACHERS QUALIFIED? Great. Rumors and gossip passing as news. He shouldn't be surprised. Tilting his head, he tried to read the article. Even squinting, the words were too small.

"You see this?" Dad shook the paper. Of course Sean hadn't seen it. The paper came while he was out working. "Don't they have better things to do with their time than harass young people who only want to come here and teach our children?"

Sean groaned. Harass. So the reporter went after Caitlin. Before or after Sean treated her rudely? He scrubbed a hand through his hair then remembered the grease. Geez, he couldn't do anything right these days.

"That poor girl." Dad shook his head. "You should've told us about Marci's accusations."

"What's wrong?" Mom came up the basement stairs, a bowl of potatoes in her hands.

"Caitlin Harrington." Dad pointed to the paper. "They're accusing her of lying to get a higher salary, and that's the nice part."

"What are you talking about?"

Sean gave them a brief version of Marci's outburst on Tuesday night.

"That's ridiculous." Mom shook a potato as she spoke. "Sophie raised that girl practically her whole life. Caitlin has better moral fiber than to be involved in any impropriety."

"To be fair, Margaret, we haven't seen Caitlin in years. She hadn't been home to visit Sophie until the end. We don't know what kind of person she became after college."

"Patrick Taggart! You aren't suggesting we believe this newspaper article?"

Dad patted her arm, while also pushing the potato she wielded out of his face. "No, dear, what I'm saying is that we shouldn't form any opinion until we know the facts."

Something twisted in Sean's gut as he thought about the way he'd reacted. He let someone else make up his mind. That was wrong. Even criminals got to defend themselves. Caitlin deserved a chance.

Mom *tch-tched.* "Now we really must invite Caitlin to dinner. She needs to know not everyone in Naultag believes in rumors and gossip."

Sean picked up the paper and scanned the article. The front page recapped what he already knew. He turned to the continuation inside to see if Caitlin had made a statement.

At the time of printing, this reporter has been unable to reach Ms. Harrington for comment. However, TNW has verified that Ms. Harrington was one of a large number of teachers let go due to a budget crisis. A spokesperson for the City of Lynn school department also confirmed that Ms. Harrington maintained an exemplary work ethic. No complaints or allegations of impropriety have been lodged against Ms. Harrington in the past.

"Well?" Dad's voice cut into Sean's concentration. He glanced up. Dad stared at him, one eyebrow raised. Obviously he'd missed something while reading. What were his parents expecting from him now?

"Well what?" He folded the paper.

"You should call Caitlin and invite her to dinner." Mom

answered while Dad continued to hold Sean's gaze.

"Me?" He cleared his throat. "You're the ones who want to welcome her. Besides, Caitlin wants nothing to do with me."

Way to go, moron. Now you'll have to explain.

"What did you do to her?" Mom crossed her arms and glared.

"Nothing. I just...nothing. I didn't do anything."

A slow grin bloomed on Dad's face. "She was a pretty girl if memory serves."

"What she looks like has nothing to do with this conversation. She made it perfectly clear she's not interested in me. End of story."

Mom smiled now, too. She turned away and began washing the potatoes. "So you've chatted quite a bit with her, then?"

"Not really." He inched toward the door.

Mom laughed. "Relax, Sean. I want a daughter-in-law but I'm not going to force you to marry someone you don't like." She glanced over her shoulder. "But we still want to invite her to dinner one evening soon."

Why hadn't he made a run for the shower when he had the chance?

TWELVE

"Mrs. Taggart, something's come up and I can't make it to dinner tonight." Caitlin breathed in deeply and exhaled slowly, calming her nerves.

"Oh, dear, I hope it's nothing serious." The motherly concern in Mrs. Taggart's voice nearly overwhelmed Caitlin's composure.

"Nothing life threatening or anything like that." She hesitated. Surely someone as kind as Mrs. Taggart would understand. "It's just, well, my car has a flat tire and—"

"Is that all? Don't you worry about a flat tire. Sean would be more than happy to come down and pick you up. He can even change the tire for you while he's there."

"I couldn't ask him to do that."

"You didn't ask, we offered. Sean can be there in about twenty minutes, unless you need more time."

"Twenty minutes is fine." She'd discovered the flat tire when she was about to leave. As she set the phone down a quiver of *something* tingled her senses. Excitement or apprehension? She hadn't seen Sean since last Wednesday, except from a distance. After church she'd left without socializing. The twins pointed him out at the parade yesterday but Sean seemed to be avoiding her as much as she'd wanted to avoid him earlier. When she accepted the dinner invitation from his parents she hadn't realized he'd be there as well. Now he was on the way over. Which Sean would show up, friendly, considerate Sean or bristly, aloof Sean?

The sound of a car door closing startled her. Only a few minutes had passed since talking to Mrs. Taggart—too soon for Sean to be here. Caitlin moved toward the window. *Please don't be Jack.* Her father had been irate when he learned of Marci's accusations and the newspaper article. "We'll sue her for slander," he proclaimed in his last phone call. If only there'd been a way to keep him from finding out. It would be just like Jack to show up unannounced, as usual, to demand she do what he knew was best.

Letting Jack handle the situation would be like throwing gasoline on a fire.

A glance out the sidelight beside the front door put Caitlin's worry to rest. A police cruiser, not Jack's Jaguar, sat behind her car in the driveway. She flung open the heavy wooden door and stepped outside just as Eric Coffey reached the steps.

"Eric, this is a pleasant surprise." Caitlin moved down the stairs to stand beside him.

"I was driving by and, uh, wanted to check that you're okay." He stared at the ground, scuffing a boot in the gravel and raising his eyes to meet hers before continuing. "I mean, after Marci's outburst last week. I should've come by sooner but..."

"You don't have to apologize, Eric." She placed a hand on his arm. "For whatever reason, Marci doesn't like me but you aren't responsible for her actions. Besides, at least now everyone is focused on my work experience and they'll all realize I *am* qualified for the position."

"You're just being nice. Like you always are." His smile revealed his relief. Grasping her hand, he gave it a brief squeeze before letting go. "For what it's worth, I think you did a good thing putting in an appearance at the parade yesterday. Riding with the Bartletts in Rescue 1 showed everyone you aren't ashamed of anything and you're a civic minded citizen."

"Helping Cody and Connor toss candy to all the kids couldn't hurt my status with the students, either." She shared a laugh with Eric.

"Hey, I just remembered you're supposed to be having dinner with the Taggarts. That's tonight, isn't it?"

"How do you know about that?"

He stared off into the distance and stroked his chin. "I have my sources." Then he met her gaze and a wide grin raised his lips. "In this case, I overheard Mr. and Mrs. Taggart inviting you. Don't let me keep you."

Caitlin shook her head and pointed at her car. "I had planned to leave now but I didn't count on a flat tire."

Eric glanced at her car. "That's not a problem. I'll change that tire and get you on your way in not time."

"No, no," Caitlin protested. "You'll get your uniform all dirty. Besides, Sean Taggart is on his way to pick me up."

A frown creased Eric's expression. "Well, at least I can fix that

TAMMY DOHERTY

flat so you'll be set to drive tomorrow." He moved to the car, opening the driver's door and reaching in to pop the trunk latch. "And don't worry about my uniform. Helping is just part of my job."

"You're paid to protect the public, keep us safe from law breakers. Not be a car repairman."

"Protect *and* serve, Caitlin." He flashed a grin as he hefted the spare tire. "This is the serve part."

It wasn't her idea of what the police department should be doing but then again, she'd been living in the city for the last ten years. This was just another example of how country living differed from life in the city. As she watched Eric fit the handle into the jack and position it under the car, gratitude for friends and the neighborly attitude of small town residents pushed away earlier worries. Then Eric looked closely at the offending tire and sucked in a sharp breath.

"What's wrong?" Had he hurt himself somehow? She stepped forward, mentally reviewing where she'd left all the first aid supplies.

"Did you notice anyone around here this afternoon?" He looked up but his hand rested on the valve stem sticking out of the wheel rim.

She shook her head. "No, why?"

He sighed. "It looks like someone jammed a small pebble into the stem, depressing the valve and letting all the air out of your tire. They replaced the cap but too loose, which is why I noticed."

Caitlin leaned closer to see what he indicated. "There's no possibility of that being accidental?"

"Not likely." He stood, brushing dust from his slacks. "Have you had any problems? Phone calls, messages, anything suspicious? Could be related to the meeting last week."

A sick feeling curdled Caitlin's stomach. Actually, since the town meeting she'd had very little in the way of problems. Not even a note on the front door. Maybe the person leaving the notes had decided to get her attention in another way. A flat tire was annoying but hardly life threatening. Still, it left her with that uncomfortable feeling of being watched.

Caitlin met Eric's gaze. Concern etched his face and darkened his brown eyes. She took a deep breath, nodding and stepping away from Eric. The time had come to tell him. "A note got left on my door. I figured it was someone who didn't want me coming back to teach in Naultag."

He nodded. "You thought it was Marci and you didn't want to say anything to me."

She stared at the ground. It was unlikely that Marci had messed with her tires. The odds were in favor of the notes being unrelated to this incident. So why was she reluctant to tell Eric about all the notes? Because she didn't want to tell him about Adam. She couldn't talk about what happened that last night in Lynn, certainly not with Eric. At some point she'd tell Janelle— they shared everything, kept no secrets. But Eric was right, the notes likely were Marci's doing and this inconvenience with the tire was probably just a kid pranking a school teacher.

"I don't know why she dislikes you so much, Caitlin." Eric's voice snapped her out of her contemplation. "I think she's jealous. You're young, single, just landed a fantastic job. Basically, in Marci's eyes, you have the perfect life. After the meeting last week, we had a long talk. I convinced her to spend the summer down on the Cape. Her folks have a cottage in Dennis. She and her sister have been making plans. Marci's really excited. I don't think you'll have any more trouble from her."

Caitlin let out a long breath. "That's a relief. And I'm happy she's got something to look forward to."

Eric turned back to the car. "I guess this could've been some kid's idea of a joke. I'll change the tire for you. Plus I'll talk to the chief about sending a patrol car by here regularly to watch out for anyone out of place. A few days of that should discourage the town troublemakers."

* * *

Sean would be more than happy to pick you up. Mom's words echoed in his head. Sean ground his teeth. He'd been happy watching the sports recap on the news. Trekking across town to help a woman who'd made it clear she didn't need his help wasn't on his list of happy things. Mom and Dad always helped neighbors and friends and expected him to do the same. They wouldn't understand or appreciate his frustration regarding Caitlin. He didn't understand it himself.

He took a shortcut across town, barreling down a pitted dirt road as if rushing to a fire. One advantage of driving a four-wheel drive vehicle—no road in town posed a problem for him. The half-dozen grain bags in back kept the truck from bouncing too much.

Keep his wits tonight, that was the goal. Find out if Marci's rumors held any truth. His parents would be pleasant and cordial to an old friend's granddaughter. Sean would find out if Caitlin cared only about money. A pretty face, and equally attractive figure, would not distract him.

By the time he approached the Baxter farm, Sean's pulse had steadied. He rounded the last corner and spotted the police cruiser parked behind Caitlin's gray Hyundai. Had something more than just a flat tire occurred? He raced into the driveway, skidding to a halt beside the cruiser.

Caitlin opened the door before he could knock. His gaze swept over her. She looked fine. Really *fine*. He swallowed.

"Are you okay?" He gestured behind him. "Saw the cruiser..." His words died in the warmth of Caitlin's smile.

"Nothing's wrong." She stood back, swinging the door wider to let him enter. "After I talked to your mother, Eric happened by. He stopped and offered to help."

Sean followed Caitlin into the living room area. Eric Coffey sat on the sofa, legs stretched out, arms draped across the back of the seat. Quite at ease. He held Sean's gaze as the corner of his mouth twitched upward.

"Good thing for you, Tag. Save you from getting those fancy clothes all dirty."

Sean glanced down at his polo shirt and khakis then speared Coffey with his gaze. "Well, at least you're doing some kind of work in that uniform, even if it is just changing a tire."

Eric *hmphed*. After a few seconds, he snickered then his smile turned to a frown. "Unfortunately the lug nuts are seized."

Sean crossed his arms. "Just need to hit 'em with a hammer."

"Cait doesn't have one. I'll get the car towed to the garage tomorrow." Eric's frown deepened. He stood and fished a business card out of his wallet. "Here's my cell number, Cait, in case you need anything." He stepped toward the door. "I better get back to work now."

"Thanks, Eric." Caitlin hugged him. "You're a sweetie."

"I mean it. Anytime, anything, just call me."

Meaning Sean wasn't reliable? When had he ever not taken good care of a date? "I'll take good care of her, Eric. No need for the police to get involved."

Caitlin's gaze collided with his and a soft flush crept across her cheeks. She turned back to Eric. "Thank you both but I'm capable of taking care of myself." Unlike past times when she'd rejected his help, a brilliant smile softened this rebuff.

As Caitlin walked Eric outside, Sean looked around the room. Books filled the middle of the floor to ceiling shelving along one wall. Below them, DVD's marched in a neat line. *White Christmas* stood beside *Operation Petticoat,* and *Chitty Chitty Bang Bang* joined the *Lord of the Rings* trilogy.

The wall clock above a small writing desk had math equations where the hourly numbers should be. A notebook computer claimed the desktop. Beside it rested a coffee mug with numbers and symbols scrawled all over it. He recognized Pi. His stomach grumbled.

Two framed prints broke up the otherwise empty east wall. One was a series of random spiral patterns, like frost on an early morning window except full of muted color. The second print seemed to be a magnified flame-orange leaf, the serrated edges brilliant green against the black background. Sean stepped closer to read the caption printed at the bottom. "Mathematics reveals her secrets only to those who approach her with pure love for her own beauty. – Archimedes"

"I love that picture."

Caitlin's voice startled Sean. He spun around. She studied the artwork as if they were masterpieces in The Louvre. Turning back, he scrutinized the patterns once more. His gift for financial management gave him an appreciation for math yet he'd never thought of it in terms of artistic or even beautiful.

"It's called fractal art," Caitlin stated. "Some students like numbers and bare facts, others are drawn to the patterns. I try to share both to inspire, if not love for, at least enjoyment of math."

She sighed and turned away, moving to the chair where she picked up a sweater. Words seemed to have abandoned Sean. He swept his gaze around the room again, numbed by all the mathematical nick-knacks. If she was a phony, she put on a good show. Maybe it was about the kids and teaching, not about the money. Caitlin should let the reporter from The Naultag Weekly interview her here, in this room. One look would convince anyone she was serious about her job. Though a curious person might wonder about the odd collection of DVDs and books.

"*In Harm's Way* and *Lord of the Rings?*" He pointed to the shelf and raised an eyebrow.

Caitlin shrugged, her lips making a slight curve upwards. "My brother joined the Navy when I was thirteen. Naval stuff is a big part of my family. And I like Tolkien. See, I have the books, too."

And the entire C.S. Lewis *Narnia* series as well as some other books Sean didn't recognize but they looked to be similar fantasy-type novels. No romance books or chick-flicks. Didn't all women love *Twilight?* Caitlin wasn't like other women, apparently. Especially not like any he'd dated in the past.

On the way to his truck, they passed Caitlin's car. Sean paused to give the flat tire a cursory inspection. Perhaps Marci was wrong about Caitlin merely wanting more money. The other implication still dangled out there, the accusation of impropriety. Yes, the official in Lynn said there'd never been any hint of impropriety on Caitlin's behalf, but maybe Marci's feathers were ruffled by something closer to home.

"You seem pretty friendly with Eric Coffey." He kept his focus on the tire as he spoke.

"Eric and I have been friends since high school."

"Like you and Scott Bartlett?"

A very unfeminine snort response surprised Sean. He slanted a glance up but Caitlin was staring across the fields, in the direction of Bartlett's house. Her lips curled softly. Was Randy right, did they have some sort of weird love triangle? Caitlin shifted, turning her focus back to him.

"The first time we met, I ordered Scott off my grandpa's property. He didn't leave, of course. He never does what I tell him to do." She shook her head. "He'd probably say the same thing about me, though."

The scene at the Asparagus Festival played through his mind: Scott comforting Caitlin. There was a bond, a connection between them. Sean toyed with the valve stem on the tire. Anything to avoid seeing Caitlin's expression. She loved Scott Bartlett, a married man. Marci was right.

"He's my cousin, you know."

She might just as well have shot him with a CO_2 fire extinguisher. His thoughts froze, his mind numb. "Cousin?"

"Well, kind of a cousin. His uncle married my great aunt so we're not actually blood relatives but our families always considered us to be cousins. Since James joined the Navy, though, Scott acts more like he's my brother."

Sean focused on the flat tire, fighting the smile that wanted to break out. Just because Caitlin really was a qualified, dedicated teacher and wasn't having an illicit affair didn't make her someone he would want to have a relationship with. She'd made it clear she wanted nothing to do with him. And there was the whole locked in an unlocked basement thing that brought her sanity into question. Plus, Bartlett was Caitlin's cousin which didn't explain Eric Coffey's weird behavior earlier. Kind of possessive. *Or maybe that was all me, being jealous or something.* He sighed.

"So you and Eric have been friends since high school." Sean didn't look up as he spoke, carefully treading through his thoughts. "Bet that makes interesting dinner conversation at his house."

"What?"

Sean let his gaze slide to Caitlin's face as he mimicked Eric Coffey's voice. "Guess what I did today, dear. Stopped to help your mortal enemy, Caitlin Harrington. Please pass the potatoes."

Caitlin stared, her expression blank for a moment. Then a grin lit up her eyes as laughter erupted. "You have a way with words. Besides, I don't think people have mortal enemies in the real world."

Standing, Sean brushed dust off his hands. "Oh, I don't know. Marci sure acts like you're her mortal enemy."

"Yeah, I don't know what's up with that. I guess she resents what she thinks is my perfect life. No kids, no hubby, no worries."

Didn't sound like Caitlin thought her life was so perfect. Well, she certainly had worries. Specifically ones brought on by Marci Coffey. And Sean hadn't helped with the way he'd treated Caitlin last week after the town meeting. What a jerk. He could be kind this evening, maybe make up for earlier bad behavior. That was it, though, no letting himself be attracted to her.

He placed a hand on the small of her back, guiding her toward his truck. The frisson of awareness that tingled all the way up his arm gave away reality. He was already attracted to Caitlin. All he could do is fight it growing stronger. He'd been devastated by the break up with Melissa. Caitlin seemed so perfect, surely she'd break his heart beyond recovery if he let himself fall in love. He pulled his hand away as if she were a flame. Thankfully they'd reached his truck. Opening the door gave a good reason for breaking contact.

There was a folded tarp on the floor of the passenger side, topped by the spool of line for the weed whacker. His earmuffs had slid almost off the passenger seat followed closely by the loppers, pruning saw and heavy-duty work gloves. Sean stepped in front of Caitlin and tossed the tools and trimmer line behind the seat.

"Sorry about the truck." He brushed away a few leaves. She'd have to put her feet on the tarp, it wouldn't fit behind the seat without hampering the seatbelt.

"No need to apologize." Caitlin hopped into the truck as if she rode in one every day. "I like trucks. And yours smells like fresh cut grass."

"That's the work gloves and it's actually Mom's forsythia, which I brutally hacked this afternoon."

"Why, what did the shrub do to you?" One side of her lips curved. Smart, dedicated, a great sense of humor...no one could be this perfect.

Sean grinned back, shut her door and trotted around to the driver's side. As he turned the key in the ignition, Pink Floyd's "Another Brick In The Wall II" lyrics exploded out of the radio speakers. Not the ideal song to have playing while driving with a school teacher. He slapped the button to shut it off.

"Don't turn off the radio on my account." Humor sparked in her expression. "I do like music. And I promise there's no dark sarcasm in my classroom."

Shame flamed up his neck. Yeah, he was guilty of judging Caitlin unfairly as a teacher, partly because of Marci but mostly because of her treatment of him. Still, thinking back on something she'd said last week, the events at the Asparagus Festival were enough to make anyone cranky. Why she lashed out at Bartlett, Sean didn't understand, but being angry with everyone trying to smother her with what they thought was consideration probably was understandable. He, for one, preferred to be left alone after a rough fire scene — especially if he'd been injured. Taking a deep breath first, he met Caitlin's smile with one of his own.

"So what kind of music do you like?"

"Well, when I'm grading papers or working on course prep, I listen to Classical music. You know, Beethoven, Mozart, those guys." The twinkle in her eyes said she figured he didn't know what Classical music was. Sean groaned; he knew full well. Caitlin gave a short laugh. "Relax, it's your truck. And you weren't even planning to give me a ride tonight. Listen to what you enjoy."

He studied her for a long moment. "First the truck and now you'll listen to Rock even though you don't enjoy it. You're too polite."

"I'm always polite." When Sean quirked an eyebrow, her smile faltered then came back full blast. "Okay, maybe not always, but I try."

He couldn't help but match her expression. She did seem to be trying to be polite today. Downright friendly, in fact. Least he could do was find a compromise on the music front. He turned the radio back on and pushed one of the preset buttons. A signature Alan Jackson song rolled out of the speakers. A quick glimpse in Caitlin's direction told Sean he'd made a good choice.

* * *

Dinner was pleasant. Sean's parents knew most of Caitlin's family. Her mother was usually an uncomfortable subject but with Mr. and Mrs. Taggart, Caitlin was able to talk easily, completely relaxed. Mrs. Taggart seemed to understand that the relationship Caitlin had with her parents was shaky at best. It was refreshing chatting without fear of being judged. Sean said very little during the meal though he wasn't quiet as if unhappy with her presence. In fact, he smiled at her frequently, like he just wanted her to know she was welcome in their home.

After the meal, Mrs. Taggart shooed Sean and Caitlin out onto the porch to enjoy dessert. They sat in the matching Adirondack chairs, silently enjoying strawberry shortcake. Caitlin stared into the black night, remembering Mr. Taggart's descriptions of the campground. Three nights without a phone or television had left her with a healthy appreciation for civilization. She could do without television so long as she had a good book but it was still pleasant to have a connection of some kind with the outside world. According to Sean's dad, they had a lot of what they called "seasonals" - people who came every weekend and sometimes for several weeks on end. Surely there must be some sort of cable television hook-up, along with electricity and water. Roughing it possibly wasn't as rustic as it used to be.

Smoke from the chimney drifted across the end of the porch, disappearing into the evening shadows. Caitlin inhaled deeply.

"Mmm, apple wood. I love that smell." Returning her attention to Sean, she risked bringing up what might be a tender subject. For her, anyway. "Your mother and father are wonderful. Must be nice, having a family like that."

"I gather there's still tension between your parents?"

"My mother never forgave my father."

"For what?"

She stared into the darkness. "He was playing major league ball when they married."

"Played for the Red Sox." Admiration glowed in Sean's face and words.

"Ah, another Jack Harrington fan." Her voice dripped disdain.

"He does sponsor my T-ball team. I gather you are not one of his fans?"

"He had enough adoring female fans. One less won't hurt his reputation."

Sean nodded. "Ah, I see. That's what your mother won't forgive him for, right? Jack adored his fans as much as they adored him."

"That's a polite way of putting it." She fought a frown. "He moved on with his life, and she didn't."

"She never remarried?"

Caitlin paused, taking several slow breaths before responding. How could Sean possibly understand? His parents were obviously still very much in love, their every action revealing respect not only for each other but for their son as well. Anything she said about either of her parents was bound to come out sounding bitter. She settled for shaking her head. Sean said nothing yet his gaze was soft, kind, inviting her to open up.

"Thankfully she's never married any of the losers she's hooked up with over the years." What in the world made her say that? She'd just decided not to get into it with Sean. Maybe if she elaborated a little. "My mother has exceptionally poor judgment when it comes to the men she falls for."

Oh, yeah, that made it all sound so much better. *Smooth, Caitlin.* Sure enough, Sean raised an eyebrow as if questioning her own judgment.

"And you lump your father into that category, too?"

Caitlin sighed. Might as well finish her thought. "Jack Harrington doesn't care about anything but himself."

"Sounds like that might be your mother talking."

"You have no idea what it was like, going through that

divorce. And afterwards, when neither of my parents wanted me. That's why they dumped me on my grandmother. Jack was too busy with his new sport stores and Mom went looking for the next Mr. Right."

There. Now she wouldn't have to worry about being friendly to Sean or whether or not he was kind to her. After this conversation, he wouldn't want anything to do with such a bitter, whiny and childish woman.

THIRTEEN

"Caitlin, how are you?" Margaret Taggart greeted her at the front of the church. "Would you like to sit with us, dear?"

Caitlin glanced over the older woman's shoulder. Patrick sat in the customary Taggart pew, alone. Where was Sean? Sitting with a man's parents in church might be seen as a commitment. Then again, not accepting a friendly invitation would send a message as well.

Margaret placed a hand on her arm. "We would enjoy your company. Sean isn't here this morning and I always feel his absence strongly. You would bring me comfort."

Caitlin smiled softly. "How could I refuse such a request?"

Patrick stood when she scooted into their pew and waited until she sat before returning to his seat. The organ prelude announced the beginning of service. Hush settled over the congregation. After announcements, everyone stood to sing Praise and Worship songs. Caitlin focused on the words projected onto the wall beside the choir loft.

A quiet exclamation from Margaret pulled her attention that way. Sean leaned down and kissed his mother's cheek. His gaze met Caitlin's and smile lines erupted around his eyes. Her stomach lurched. He stood straight, faced forward and started singing.

Words blurred and jumbled. She squinted and stopped singing. Better to wait for the next song than to try catching up with this one. The next one was as difficult to keep up with. Whoever chose today's songs had picked the longest and most complicated ones.

Pastor Don came forward. Caitlin wasn't listening anymore, instead slanting a peek at Sean. He wore a t-shirt and jeans. Odd for a man who dressed up for dinner. He leaned back in the pew, giving her a view of his profile. His head turned and she yanked her gaze forward once more.

She hadn't seen Sean since Wednesday when he fixed her tire.

He'd come early in the morning, while she was still having her first cup of coffee. Declining a cup for himself, he had set to work immediately on the tire. To her chagrin, Scott dropped by during the proceedings, but thankfully didn't come inside to question her about Sean. Later in the day, Sean returned with the repaired tire and made the swap. He did talk with her then, briefly, apologizing for not having more time. Said things were busy at the campground and he needed to get ready for another full weekend. Probably he just wanted to avoid spending time with someone who was always either being rude to him or complaining about her parents. And crazy, couldn't forget crazy. After all, he still believed she had been stuck in an unlocked basement.

The pastoral prayer ended. In the brief lull while the choir prepared to sing, Margaret whispered to Sean, "I didn't expect you."

"It was a false alarm."

He leaned forward to grab a hymnal. Caitlin recognized his shirt—navy blue with a Maltese cross on the left breast and the words *Naultag Fire Department* across the back. Scott often wore one just like it. Sean had been called out to a fire.

She managed to focus on the sermon. Soon service was over and parishioners headed for Fellowship Hall. Caitlin allowed Margaret and Patrick to guide her along with them.

"Charlotte would like to talk to you, Caitlin." Margaret steered her to where Charlotte Henderson stood talking with Margie Swenson.

"Oh, Caitlin, I'm glad you're here." Charlotte said. "I wanted to ask if you'd consider teaching Sunday school this fall."

Teach Sunday school on top of starting a new job? "I'm not sure—"

"You don't need to give me an answer today. Just promise you'll give it thought and prayer before you decide."

"Okay, I'll do that."

Charlotte moved off to round up grandchildren. Caitlin massaged her temples. She needed a cup of coffee. Turning, she spotted Sean talking with Marci Coffey. With his back to her, he couldn't know she watched. Marci saw her, though.

"You did your best to humiliate Arlene in public, Marci. The woman has some pride. I'm sure she wants to save face," Sean said.

Marci met Caitlin's gaze, a catty smile twitching on her lips.

"Don't you think it's possible Arlene can't back down on the salary issue because the teacher in question won't change her contract?"

Sean sighed. He pointed a carrot stick at Marci. "Caitlin cares more about teaching kids than money. I don't know what your problem is with her, but she's not the evil witch you'd like us all to believe."

Warmth percolated through Caitlin. He believed in her. She met Marci's hard gaze and smiled. Marci broke eye contact.

"Do you have any idea the reputation she had in Lynn?"

Sean crunched the carrot. Caitlin turned away. Whatever followed that question was bound to be unpleasant. She found a place to sit at an unoccupied table and dropped her head into her hands.

Sean defended her as a teacher. Why wasn't she thrilled? Because Marci's preposterous stories about her sordid lifestyle in Lynn would outbalance the equation. The lies made Janelle stop and think before dismissing them. Sean barely knew her, of course he'd believe Marci.

"You look like you could use a cup of coffee." Sean sat down beside her and slid a steaming Styrofoam cup toward her. "Cream, no sugar, right?"

He remembered how she liked her coffee. A trill of pleasure shot through her. She looked up, meeting his gaze, sinking into the amazing warmth of his eyes. He rocked the chair back, sipping his own coffee.

"Wow, Marci Coffey does not like you." He shook his head. "If she could figure out a way to do it, I think she'd lock you away where no one would ever find you."

Caitlin dropped her gaze quickly. The coffee burned a little when she took a gulp. At least it kept the truth from blurting out. She startled as Sean sat up abruptly, the legs of his chair hitting the floor with a metallic-edged thud. Coffee spilled onto the tablecloth. Sean leaned forward, ducking to make eye contact with her again.

"That's who locked you in the church basement." His eyes narrowed, mouth tightened in a hard line.

She pulled back. What would he do?

Sean straightened, staring across the room at Marci. "Your reluctance to tell is understandable, I guess. She's got pull in this town, mainly because of her husband. And her willingness to spread rumors like jam on toast."

"I don't want to cause trouble for Eric." Caitlin held Sean's gaze. "It's important for me to forgive and forget. To show I'm not who she says I am and to set an example for her."

"Very admirable." Dimples gouged his cheeks. "We'll just keep an eye on her. To be sure she doesn't try anything more drastic and dangerous."

Getting locked in the basement was drastic. He had a valid point, though. More important, Sean believed Caitlin, not Marci. And apparently wasn't avoiding her or at least was willing to spend time with her in the future.

* * *

The corn in Uncle Charlie's field was a few inches tall already. So was the grass around Caitlin's house, which was why Aunt Charlotte had called Sean, asking him stop by and offer to mow the lawn. A flash of yellow caught his eye. Caitlin had planted a neat border of sunny marigolds around the vegetable garden. He smiled. She was a country girl at heart.

Opening the truck door, he heard Caitlin complain about stupid machines. The sound came from around the side of the house. Going around the corner he spotted the open garage door, yawning black. Her voice carried clearly—she was irritated. Peering inside, he got a fine view of her back. She kicked a tire on the lawn tractor, muttering incoherently.

"Caitlin?"

With a startled yelp, she spun around. She released the sharp intake of breath in loud relief, sniffling and swiping a hand across her eyes.

Sean stepped inside the garage, concerned. "Something wrong?"

"I hate this thing." She sniffled again.

"Hate? That's a rather strong emotion."

"I suppose you're going to tell me hate is a sin."

"Well, there is that. What I would suggest is that if you're going to feel so passionately about something it should at least be animate."

She flushed, humor tugging at her lips.

"What seems to be the problem?"

"It won't start. And before you ask, yes, I put gas in it."

He eyeballed the tractor. A Cub Cadet, probably purchased by her grandfather at least twenty years ago, it looked to have been in storage for years. The tractor itself showed its age, with faded yellow paint chipped in strategic places around the front. The mower deck was spotlessly clean, only a few rust spots hinting that it, too, was decades old.

"When was the last time anyone used this?" he asked.

"Must've been sometime last month. The lawn had been mowed when I got here."

"That was Randy's doing. Well, on orders from his father."

"Oh. I thought Uncle Paul or Uncle Steve did it."

He lifted the hood to get a look at the engine. "The mouse nest doesn't bode well."

"Yuk." Caitlin made a face, turning away as he cleared out the nest. "Will it work now?"

"I don't think so." One finger lifted a broken wire. "This is for the ignition. Needs a new spark plug, too. In fact, a general overhaul would be a good idea to find out what else is wrong. A new mower might be easier."

"Grampa always took such good care of this tractor."

"Like all his equipment." Sean smiled. "But he's been dead almost fifteen years. Sophie hired kids to mow the lawn and I'm sure they didn't winterize the tractor properly. Plus it's been sitting unused for over a year."

"Can you do that overhaul thing? Or do you know who could?" Her eyes pleaded with him to help. A warm thrill passed through him. She wasn't pushing him away, declining his offers of assistance.

"Randy would be your best bet. He's as good as any equipment place. He'll tell you honestly if it's worth fixing."

"Randy? Are you sure?"

"He's not a screw-off, that's mostly a front."

"Why? Never mind," she held up a hand stopping him. "I don't want to delve into Randy's psyche. If you trust him, I'll trust you."

"Thank you." Another rush of pleasure went through him. "In the meantime maybe we should let Uncle Charlie hay the lawn."

"It's not that bad!"

He laughed at her indignation. "No, not quite, but the big mower can do the job quickly. I'll try to come by tomorrow."

"You? Don't you have enough to do at the campground?"

"Tuesdays are generally quiet. Dad can deal with anything that comes up during the few hours I'd be here."

"I'll pay you of course."

"Of course you won't."

"Why not?"

"For one thing, when my parents found out I'd be in big trouble." She probably thought he was being a momma's boy. Just to be safe, he added one more argument. "What would Scott say if he found out I took money for doing you a favor?" Her grimace was answer enough. "I get on pretty well with Scott and since I often have to rely on him to watch my back in a burning building, I'd like to continue getting along with him."

"Okay, you win." She narrowed her eyes, studying him. "You seem to have a knack for showing up at the right moment."

"Call me the cavalry." Her frown was not the reaction he hoped for. "Just dumb luck?"

"Mmm, probably that." She smiled. "Have you eaten yet?"

"What?"

"Have you eaten supper yet? It's too hot to cook. I was thinking pizza and would rather not eat it all myself."

"Let me get this straight. Are you asking me to dinner?"

"Oh for pity's sake, it's just pizza."

"Okay, pizza but I buy."

"No way, you're mowing the lawn. I'll buy the pizza."

He followed her up the back stairs that led into the hall across from the dining area. Taking a menu from where it hung on the refrigerator, Caitlin picked up the phone. Her thumb was poised to dial when she looked up with a serious expression.

"What do you like on your pizza?"

"No anchovies." He was rewarded with a giggle. "Almost anything. Except broccoli."

"How do you feel about pineapples?"

"They're great in a fruit salad."

"Not on pizza, huh? How about pepperoni?"

"Can't go wrong with pepperoni."

After calling in their order Caitlin picked up her purse and reached for her keys. He covered them with his hand.

"You buy, I'll fly." He glanced out the window. "If you don't mind my truck."

"I told you before, it's a nice truck."

"Yes, but you were being polite."

"I'm always polite. But I do like your truck."

They walked out together and he opened the truck door for her. She returned his smile and fiddled with the radio as soon as he turned the key. Before he could comment, country music filled the air. Caitlin adjusted the volume so they could still have a conversation. The handheld scanner on Sean's hip beeped loudly. He glanced down, scowling as he turned a knob to silence the report. Looking back up, he smiled.

"Weather alert," he said. "It's gonna rain tonight."

"Oh good, something different." Her dry comment pushed aside his thoughts about the weather. She pointed to the scanner. "Are you on call?"

"I'm always on call. That's what 'paid on call fire fighter' means."

"Even when you're coaching a baseball game?"

"Baseball isn't the most important thing in the world." He paused long enough for her to smile. "But it's pretty close to the top of the list."

Caitlin rolled her eyes. Sean chuckled.

"So, what do you do at a fire?"

"I put them out, ideally."

"Well, duh." She drew out the last word, sounding just like his teenage cousins. "Is it dangerous?"

"Sometimes. That's why we train and practice. And follow the rules, don't take unnecessary risks."

"There's no such thing as a necessary risk."

"Risk is a part of life, the part that keeps it exciting."

She didn't reply. Silence filled the truck cab as Sean pulled up in front of Eastside Pizza. Caitlin wasn't a risk-taker. Was that why she didn't date in high school? Could also explain why she had such a hard time trusting him. Although, today she seemed to have no problem. Because she'd taken time to get to know him? Maybe her confidence had been boosted by Scott Bartlett's approval.

That thought reminded him of the conversation he'd had with Bartlett last week. While working on Caitlin's car, Bartlett stopped by to chat. Sean got the distinct impression it was not a spontaneous visit. After a few desultory comments about lug nuts, Scott casually said, "You seem to be spending a lot of time with Caitlin." Thankfully the lug nuts required focus and Sean got away with nothing more than a grunt in response. Bartlett then went on to comment on how Caitlin wasn't much of a social person but if Sean were to ask her out, Scott was certain she'd say yes.

At the time, the conversation seemed odd and more than a little awkward. Now he recalled Caitlin saying that Scott Bartlett was more like a brother than just a friend. Even more brotherly than her actual brother. And Sean knew for a fact that Janelle Bartlett loved playing matchmaker. Janelle might have suggested Scott push Sean and Caitlin together. Or maybe, as Caitlin's best friends, Janelle and Scott knew something Sean didn't, perhaps something even Caitlin didn't realize.

The question now was did Sean want to ask Caitlin out?

FOURTEEN

Insane. That was the only explanation. She had to be absolutely, unequivocally, irrefutably crazy. What other explanation could there be for accepting a date with Sean Taggart? To a barn dance, no less. As inexperienced as Caitlin was regarding dating, she knew even less about dancing.

Unfortunately, Janelle was delighted with the whole idea. Caitlin stared into her coffee while Janelle gushed about how wonderful Sean was and the fun they'd have at the dance. Sudden silence yanked Caitlin's focus back to her best friend. Janelle eyeballed her as if trying to decipher the meaning of life.

"We've been friends for over ten years," Janelle spoke softly. "I'd like to think we're close. Please tell me why you won't date."

Caitlin dropped her gaze back to the coffee mug. She'd never voiced this belief, this fear. Would Janelle understand?

"Suppose we went out a few times then fell in love. We'd get married of course, maybe even have kids. Then one day Sean wakes up and realizes he doesn't love me anymore."

"You're afraid of a divorce like your parents'?"

"Yes and no." She darted a glance at Janelle and took courage from her sympathetic expression. "If we're truly in love there'd be no divorce. But how could I know? Look at all the bad choices my mother has made. I couldn't possibly do better."

Janelle was thoughtful for quite some time. At last she commented. "I thought you church people had it all worked out. You know, trust in God, that sort of stuff. Seems like this is one of those times you need a God. Do you still believe?"

"Sure I do, but how can I know for certain I'm choosing what He wants?"

"What makes you think scorning marriage is what God wants?"

Caitlin frowned. She'd always thought not marrying, therefore not dating, meant not going against God's will. Was she wrong?

"I can't believe you are giving me advice about my faith."

"Who'd've thunk, huh? Guess all those years of you trying to convert me, something must've sunk in." Janelle paused, smiling. "You know, Sean believes in God, too."

"Some guys will do anything to get the girl." Adam had. He'd even attended church.

"Do you honestly think Sean has spent his entire life going to church and being a nice guy just to get some girl, sometime, to fall in love so he can use her?"

"When you put it that way it does sound ridiculous." She tried to smile but it wouldn't stick. "Still, nobody could be that perfect."

"So go out with him, find out what horrible traits he's keeping hidden."

* * *

Caitlin curled up in the recliner with her Bible. Outside it was raining again. The world was gray and muted. Water streamed down the window. It was odd weather for central New England, as if nature were as out of sorts as Caitlin.

For a while she skimmed aimlessly through the Bible. She'd read every verse that had anything to say about marriage. Today she kept coming back to Genesis 2:24: *"for this reason a man will leave his father and mother and be united to his wife, and they will become one."*

Fear chilled Caitlin. On the one hand, the idea was romantic, joining with the man she loved and becoming one. On the other hand, what if the guy wasn't what at first he seemed to be? She'd get her heart broken, or worse. If only there was a way to tell if Sean was the nice guy he appeared to be or actually a slimy creep like Adam.

Caitlin bowed her head. "Lord, please forgive me. I've been trying to figure this out on my own. But I need to lean on you. Please show me the right path. Help me choose correctly."

Turning to a bookmarked page, she read the verse from last Sunday's service, Luke 6:45. *"The good man brings good things out of the good stored up in his heart, and the evil man brings evil things out of the evil stored up in his heart. For out of the overflow of his heart his mouth speaks."*

A good man was good. Seemed too simple. Comparing Sean and Adam, she saw the wisdom. What did she really know about Adam? Nothing about his past. Of course, now she knew he was cunning, in a sinister way. Willing to pretend righteousness to trick her into a compromising situation. Very like the devil.

He'd attended church with her, occasionally. And Bible study just about every Monday evening. When they started going out for coffee afterwards, he expressed an interest in Jesus that had seemed genuine.

For years, Janelle had harped on her about dating. It didn't have to be about marriage. So she said yes when Adam had asked her to dinner. Even then he still acted like a nice guy, just a friend who enjoyed her company. It wasn't until moving day drew close that he had changed. She should've broken it off with him the first time he showed a possessive streak. It probably didn't matter when she rebuffed him, though. By that time, what happened was going to happen.

Sean was the complete opposite of Adam. He was kind, except for that one instance when they'd butted heads. Even then, though, he hadn't been cruel, merely blunt. Caitlin had been the unkind one. She couldn't imagine him trying to force himself on her.

Closing her eyes, she recalled how it had felt when he took her hand gently between his. She felt again the soft, tender caress of his finger tracing the outline of her palm. Saw the fear and concern in his eyes as he smothered her burning sweatshirt, saving her from worse burns.

She spread a blank sheet of paper on her desk and drew two large overlapping circles like the Venn diagrams her students used, to help figure out if she could trust Sean. Labeling one circle 'Sean' and the other 'Adam,' she jotted the traits of each man in their respective circle. Traits common to both went into the space where the circles overlapped. After she finished, she picked up the sheet of paper to study the results.

Nothing but negative, unattractive characteristics filled Adam's circle, while Sean's contained only desirable attributes. As expected. She already knew that Sean was compassionate, caring and considerate. His behavior showed he was truly Christian, as opposed to Adam who had gone through the motions but didn't really believe.

Her gaze drifted to the traits listed in the overlapping section. She sucked in a breath, gut tightening. Their similarities were the traits that frightened her most about Adam. Both men were confident, almost cocky. And strong enough to get what they wanted regardless of her wishes. Sean was authoritarian, but at least not as domineering as Adam. They had both been pushy and tried to control her actions.

Would Sean try to compromise her the way Adam had? Even if she managed to fend him off, the damage would be catastrophic. Her heart would be trampled, ground to dust. Because, despite her fears, she liked Sean. He held a power over her that Adam had never wielded.

* * *

Friday evening Caitlin sat outside on the deck. Closing her eyes, she pictured Sean standing beside her. She could even smell his clean, soapy scent. This had never happened before. She'd never day dreamed about anyone. A mosquito stabbed her. She slapped it, killing the bug and leaving a red handprint on her arm. She missed Sean, even though she'd just seen him on Tuesday. How had he wormed his way into her life so completely? She hadn't even been nice to him in the beginning.

Another mosquito bit her other arm. A third buzzed her ear. Time to go in. She enjoyed talking with Sean. It was nice being rescued, though she could do without the experience of getting burned. Still, it seemed beyond coincidental that Sean conveniently turned up each time, just at the moment she needed help. That sensation of being watched?—maybe Sean was spying on her, stalking her.

The incident with the grill was her fault but then he'd released her from the church basement, arriving in time so she didn't have to spend the night or longer. When he called after she went to the ER, it was as if he'd known she'd just gotten home. And the flat tire—sure, it was his mother who offered his service as a taxi, but Sean volunteered to fix the tire. He could've been the one to fiddle with the valve thingy, knowing his parents would "make" him come get her.

Then he makes a surprise visit and rescues her from a dead mower and overgrown lawn. He called it dumb luck. Was it? If only there was a way to know for sure that he was as good a man as he seemed.

"The good man brings good things out of the good stored up in his heart..."

She filled the tub, intending to take a nice, soothing bubble bath. As the bubbles mounted, she bowed her head. "Lord, I want to do what's right with you. Please help me to know if I can trust Sean. Show me for certain that he is a good man, or reveal his evil ways before it's too late."

Steam filled the room. She sank into the tub and closed her eyes. Moments later, a low rumble of thunder announced tonight's rain. She waited until the distant booms drew closer before getting out of the bath.

Wrapped in her robe, she sat in the living room working on a crossword puzzle. The storm grew loud but ultimately passed without much more than a heavy downpour. Good thing she didn't have a dog to take out for a walk. Her eyelids drooped and she fell asleep, dreaming of big black dogs barking in the rainy night. When she went out to quiet the animals, cold rain chilled her. She woke shivering.

Outside the rain had ended. Water dripped loudly from the trees. Headlights panned across the living room wall. Curiously the light disappeared although no car passed. She stared out the picture window for several minutes, waiting, but no car reappeared. Giving up on the crossword puzzle, she set it aside and rose, retying her robe. Shutting off the table lamp made the night outside seem slightly brighter. The moon peeked around clouds, casting beams like a weak flashlight.

Suddenly and quite clearly a face peered around the maple tree, about ten feet from the house. Just as quickly, it disappeared. An icy chill ran through Caitlin. Her heart beat double time. She froze, afraid and uncertain. Had she really seen someone?

A shrill ring sliced through the silence.

With a yelp she dashed from the room to answer the kitchen phone. Crouching beside the refrigerator where no one could see her from any window, she answered with a soft hello.

"Caitlin? Did I wake you?"

Sean. Of course, she was in a moment of need and here he was. Maybe not in person but…or maybe he was here physically.

"No, I'm fine." She concentrated on sounding alert and chipper. "Why do you ask?"

"You sounded sleepy." Was he disappointed? "Everything okay after that storm?"

"Peachy."

"I called to see if you'd like to have dinner with me before the dance tomorrow."

"Ah, sure," she hesitated, an idea forming. "Listen, I'm kinda in the middle of something. Can I call you back in a couple of minutes?"

"All right," He definitely sounded let down, confused. "Do you need my number?"

She wrote it down. What a great way to catch Sean spying. After hanging up, she would wait a few minutes then call him. If it was his cell phone, she'd hear it ringing outside. If it was a landline across town, he'd be caught when he didn't answer.

What if Sean had the cell phone set to vibrate instead of ringing?

Hands shaking, Caitlin dialed the phone. *Please answer, please answer.* A male voice greeted her. "Scott, oh thank the Lord."

"Cait? Why are you whispering?"

"Can you come over? Right away. I need your help."

"Be there in two minutes."

Thank you, God, for giving me a best friend who lives less than half a mile away.

True to his word, Scott arrived within minutes. She pulled him through the front door into the dark entry hall.

"What's going on?"

"I saw someone out there," she whispered, pointing to the side yard.

His demeanor changed. "Stay here, lock the door behind me, and give me that."

Taking the big flashlight from her hands, Scott left. He hesitated on the top step until she bolted the door. Then he was gone.

He rapped sharply on the door when he returned. "Cait, it's me."

"You were gone forever." She cringed as he flicked a light switch, flooding the hall with brightness. "Did you see anyone?"

"No, but there was definitely a car over by the dairy barn. How well did you see this person? Could you describe him to the police?"

She shook her head. "I saw a face peer around the tree. Probably a white man, his face seemed luminous in the dark. I didn't see anything more."

"No sense calling the cops now. But I'm uncomfortable leaving you here alone."

"That makes two of us."

"Pack an overnight bag. You can stay in the guest room."

On the short drive to the Bartletts' house, Caitlin remembered Sean. She'd promised to call him right back. Oh well, she could call from the safety of Janelle's kitchen. With eyes closed, she tried to recall details of the face she saw. It couldn't have been Sean, he always made her feel safe, secure. Could she be such a poor judge of character?

Janelle gushed sympathy. Scott disappeared into the family room to resume watching the baseball game. Caitlin sat with Janelle in the kitchen, sipping hot cocoa.

"Cocoa always makes me feel better." She still trembled.

"It's the boys' favorite comfort food, too." Suddenly Janelle grasped her hand. "Oh, Caitlin, you must have been terrified. I'm glad we live so close."

"Me too. Scott's going to talk to Eric Coffey in the morning. They'll look around in the daylight, see if they can find anything more."

"Nice to have friends in the police department." Janelle's lips curved gently. "You're all set if you have a burglar or a house fire."

She chuckled. Speaking of fires... "I need to make a call."

Janelle brought over the cordless phone while Caitlin dug out the scrap of paper with Sean's number on it. The other woman glanced over her shoulder.

"Sean, at this hour?"

"It's only nine. He called right when this prowler thing happened. I promised to call back."

"You told him and he didn't rush over?"

She shook her head, dialing the phone. "Didn't tell him," she whispered.

"What're you doing calling me in the middle of the game?" Sean answered.

"I'm sorry. I told you I'd call back."

"Caitlin?"

"Who'd you think this was?"

"Well, the caller ID says Scott Bartlett."

"Oh," she glanced across the table. "I'm over here with Janelle."

"Tell him," Janelle whispered. Caitlin mouthed *no* as Sean began talking again.

"Ah yes, she's a sports widow. Nice of you to keep her company."

"Yes, she is nice company. Anyway, what were you saying about dinner?"

There was a long pause. Downstairs, Scott yelled. Sean grunted, obviously involved in watching the game but trying hard not to show it. Finally he spoke.

"Huh? Oh, dinner. Would you like to have dinner with me tomorrow before the game?"

"I think you mean before the dance. I gather the Sox aren't doing so well at the moment."

Another gap of silence. "Sorry, I'm trying not to watch. Honest. Hold on a second." Sound on the other end muffled for a moment. "I'm back. TV's off now."

"You didn't have to shut it off on my account."

"I did if we're going to have a coherent conversation. But let's be quick."

"You called me first, remember?"

"The game was just starting then. What took so long?"

"You called right before I had to leave to come over here." She pulled her hand back as Janelle slapped at it.

"Tell him," Janelle urged.

"Is that Janelle? Say hi for me."

"Sean says hello." Covering the mouthpiece she whispered, "I'm not telling him."

"Okay then, dinner tomorrow. I can pick you up about five. Should I bring the car?"

She couldn't help laughing. "No, the truck is fine. Go back to the game now."

"Thanks, I'll see you later."

Janelle scowled. "Why didn't you tell him the truth? Shame on you, you're supposed to be setting a good example for me."

"I didn't lie." But she had. *A lie of omission is still a lie. Lord, please forgive me.*

"You let him think you're visiting me." Janelle's eyes narrowed with suspicion. "Did you think it was Sean outside your house?"

Caitlin's cheeks grew warm.

"You did! I hope you see how wrong you are. How could he be home watching the game, talking to you on the phone and be prowling around outside your house at the same time?"

"Maybe he wasn't at home. He could have called from a cell phone."

"You said the phone rang at the same time as you saw the prowler. Did he look like he was on the phone?"

"No," she was forced to concede. "Well, at least that perfection is showing some tarnish. Sean's as bad as Scott when it comes to watching sports."

"Just think, Scott willingly missed the beginning of tonight's game and you're only friends. I'll bet Sean would give up a whole game for you."

"Maybe, once. So long as it wasn't a play-off or World Series game."

"Or the Super Bowl."

FIFTEEN

"Most likely, your visitor was some kid using the barn for a drug deal." Eric closed a small notebook. "This house has been empty until a few weeks ago. Probably simple curiosity led to this guy checking out the lights."

Caitlin looked at Scott. "What about the car tracks you saw."

He shrugged. "I showed them to Eric. In the daylight, it looks like someone turned around. Nothing sinister."

Eric nodded, confirming the belief. "If it'll help put you at ease, I'll do a walkthrough of the house and make sure things are secure."

She nodded.

Scott fished keys out of his pocket. "I got things to do before tonight. I'll leave you in Eric's capable hands." He gave her arm a squeeze and strode out the door.

"Might as well start here, at the front door." Eric examined the locks then moved to check each window throughout the house before returning to the kitchen. "If anything else happens, or you think of any details that might be helpful, you call me."

"Thank you for being such a good friend."

They walked to the front door. Eric paused, his hand on the doorknob. "I hear you've got a date tonight."

She nodded. "Did Scott tell you?"

"He mentioned you're going to the dance with Tag." His expression grew serious. "You be careful with him, Caitlin. He seems like a great guy. But I heard things about when he was away at college. Walked out on his fiancé, broke her heart. I don't want to see you get hurt."

* * *

Four forty-five. Caitlin stared at her image in the full-length mirror. The outfit was dressed-up simple: a georgette blouse with ruffled front and three-quarter sleeves to be warm in the evening but cool for dancing, topping a crinkled-cotton ankle length skirt. The paisley print blouse picked up the dark rose color of the skirt. It all came together pleasingly, especially with her brown hair brushed back from her face and lying over her shoulder.

"Here, these sandals will do nicely." Janelle stood back from Caitlin's closet. "The heels will make you much closer to Sean's height."

Caitlin eyed the sandals. She'd bought them in a moment of weakness, unable to resist the ankle-wrap straps. But she'd only worn them twice. The two-inch cork heels made her feel unstable, like she might tumble at each step.

"Put them on, that's an order."

"Yes ma'am." She grinned. "Thanks for your help, Janelle. I had no idea what to wear."

"Of course not, you don't have any practice dating. I'd better go now, though. Sean will be here soon and I need to get ready myself."

"I owe you big time." Caitlin hugged her friend. *Unless this turns out as badly as I fear.* Eric's warning this morning only served to confuse her already tangled emotions.

Janelle laughed. "Relax and have fun."

Caitlin grimaced and put on the sandals. Rising, she picked up her purse and shawl and walked carefully to the front room. As she reached the kitchen the phone rang. She jumped, letting out a little yelp. *Silly girl, it's just the phone.*

The phone rang again.

She picked up the kitchen extension.

"Caitlin, honey, it's Mom."

Like I don't recognize your voice. "Hi, Mom. How are you?"

"I get by." A predictable answer. "The question is how're you? Are you okay out there all by yourself?"

"I'm fine Mom. The house is in perfect working order."

"Don't you get lonely? Especially at night? Nights are always the loneliest."

"I have friends. And a television."

"You need a husband."

Caitlin rolled her eyes. "No, I don't need a husband or a boyfriend. Neither do you."

"Don't you start with that tone, young lady. I've been around a lot longer than you and I can say from experience, being alone is no fun."

"Mom, if you'd spend less time worrying about being Mrs. Somebody you could actually find out how to be Irene."

"I've been Irene for over fifty years. It's about time you realize the horrible future ahead if you don't find a husband."

Caitlin sighed. It wasn't worth fighting about. Her mother was never going to change and would never admit that Caitlin might be right.

"I saw Dad." This usually stopped her mother's rants about getting a husband.

"Did he help you move like he said he would?"

"Yes, he actually did."

A light tap on the door caught Caitlin's attention. She glanced around the kitchen doorframe. Sean stood on the front step. Covering the phone she called, "Come on in, Sean."

"Sean," her mother latched onto the name. "Is that a boy or a girl?"

"A man." She swept her gaze over him. He wore brown slacks and a navy blue button-down shirt. His hair was still damp and curlier than normal. He raised an eyebrow, giving her a puzzled look as he nodded toward the phone. Caitlin smiled. Definitely a man.

"Do you have a date?" Excitement filled Mom's voice.

"Mom, I gotta go." She hesitated, needing to tell Mom about her father's news. Now wasn't the right time. "I'll call you tomorrow. There's something we need to talk about."

"If it's about your father and Linda, I already know."

"You do? James told you, didn't he? You aren't upset?" Out of the corner of her eye she saw Sean shift uncomfortably.

"Why would I be upset?"

"Maybe because he moved on and is starting a new family."

"Oh honey, they just bought a house—did you say new family?"

"They bought a house? James didn't tell you Linda's pregnant?"

"No," Mom's voice quavered. "When is she due?"

"The end of November. Oh Mom, I'm sorry. I wanted to tell you in a nicer way."

"Don't be upset. I...I'm happy for them. You should be too." Mom's voice steadied.

I'm thrilled. Her gaze went again to Sean standing in the living room. He looked out the window, probably trying not to listen. There was no way to not hear her.

"I'll still call you tomorrow."

"Okay, but not too early. Gary likes to sleep late on Sundays."

The words were like fingernails on a blackboard. Gary, the latest in a long line of losers. Mom took them in like some people rescue stray animals. This one at least had a job.

"I'll call you after church." Wouldn't it be nice if the hint inspired Mom to go back to church? Fat chance. Caitlin felt a twinge of guilt–she shouldn't be so judgmental. With a final goodbye, she hung up the phone.

Turning, she caught Sean's eye. "Sorry about that."

He shrugged. "No need to apologize."

"It's not right to air dirty laundry in public."

"Sounds like something your grandmother would say."

She laughed despite herself. "You don't need to hear how messed up my family is."

"They're just people. Besides, I'm going out with you not them."

Going out with you. Caitlin felt ill. Sean seemed like a great guy, and oh boy was he attractive. What was she going to do when the inevitable happened?

"Caitlin? I'm trying to be nice. Why do you look like you want to cry?"

"Because you are a nice guy." She tried to smile with trembling lips.

"*Phwew,*" Sean breathed an exaggerated sigh. "Pressure's off. I can be my usual idiot self and you'll be happy."

She laughed. "Hold on there, let's not get carried away."

"Ah, see, I knew there'd be a catch." His lips crooked upward, making her laugh more. He glanced at his watch. "We better get going before the pub fills up."

"Where are you taking me?" Moving slowly toward the door, she felt more comfortable with each step in the high heels.

"Claudia's. It's a pub-style restaurant a block over from the fire station." He cupped her elbow as they went down the front steps. "I'm not so sure the truck was a good idea after all."

She dropped her gaze, uncomfortable under his appraising eye. "I can manage, it's not a tight skirt."

"It's a pretty skirt. You make it beautiful."

Her cheeks felt quite warm now. "You look nice, too. Blue is a good color for you."

"Brings out my eyes, so I've been told."

"Oh, by who?" She settled into the seat.

He smiled and winked, walking around to get in the driver's seat. "By hordes of admiring women. Most of whom I'm related to."

"That bad, eh?"

"When you consider the fact my family has lived in this area for over two hundred years, it's easy to understand how I can be related to so many people around here."

"You must have met non-relatives at college."

"Yes, I did."

Suddenly he went quiet, withdrawn. He kept his gaze on the road. She hadn't meant to delve into his past. Now that the chance arrived, she wanted to find out the truth. Eric's words gnawed at her. She needed to know.

"Were you serious?"

"Very," Sean answered wistfully. "But then she had ideas about our future that turned out to be entirely different than what I had in mind."

"I'm sorry."

He shrugged. "Don't be, I'm not. We could've made a big mistake, instead Melissa went her way, I went mine. She married a stockbroker. I hear they're quite happy."

"And you? Have you ever..." she hesitated.

He shot a quick glance her way. "Been serious with anyone else? No. Once, almost, but she changed my mind."

"*She* changed *your* mind?"

"She thought I had potential. I was like a piece of clay waiting to be molded into a beautiful, expensive, work of art." He glanced at her, raising one eyebrow. "I like being a plain old lump of clay. And I definitely didn't want to be molded into something I'm not."

"So, you're a lump of clay with idiot tendencies, who gets caught up in watching sports. And you're probably an adrenaline junkie—that's why you're on the fire department."

"Ouch."

"Am I right?"

"Too close for comfort." He winked again. "Here's Claudia's. Looks like a full house."

The parking lot was packed. Sean managed to find a space not too far from the door. Walking to the entrance, his hand rested in the small of her back. Warmth radiated from his touch, tingling her senses.

Despite all the cars outside there were quite a few empty tables. The hostess, who turned out to be a cousin of Sean's, seated them on the terrace in a fairly secluded corner. Caitlin suspected he had planned it.

"So now you know all about me. I want to know all about you," Sean prompted.

"There's nothing to tell. You already know about my childhood. And my worst traits."

"Yet I'm still here. Tell me more." He picked up a menu. "What do you like to eat?"

She looked at her menu. "Burgers are okay, I like a good steak on the grill, and chicken is always an excellent choice."

"Is there anything you don't like?"

"Loads." She laughed. "I'm not fond of fish."

"You don't like it at all?"

"Not much, but it's healthy so I try to have a serving once a week."

"Interesting. Do you always do what's good for you even if you don't like it?"

"Well, mostly." She decided it was better not to tell him she was on this date because Janelle thought it would be good for her. They ordered.

Caitlin told him about her brother, James, serving in the Navy and expecting his first child. "He's excited," she told him. "Anxious to get home, a little worried about not being there when the baby comes."

"Will your parents go down to visit?"

"I guess. Mom will definitely, she adores James. My father?" she shrugged, "I don't know what he'll do now that he's got his own baby on the way."

"So I heard, sorry. Are you looking forward to being a big sister?"

"No," she answered quickly. "Linda, my father's wife, is okay I suppose. I'm happy for them, I guess. It's, well…oh it's too complicated."

"He's being the husband, and now father, that he should've been with his first family?"

Unwanted tears pricked her eyes. "Now you're the one getting too close for comfort."

"He's just a regular person, ya know, and maybe he's trying to get it right this time."

A tear dripped onto her plate. "Sure, take his side, everyone always does." She pushed her half-eaten meal aside.

Trying to look anywhere but at Sean's face, and not wanting anyone else to see her crying, Caitlin focused on his hands.

"I'm sorry, Caitlin," he spoke softly. "I guess that was the idiot in me, speaking without considering your feelings."

She sniffled. "So you aren't perfect after all."

He chuckled. "No, I'm not perfect at all. But I'm flattered that you think I am." After a short pause he continued. "I hope you can forgive me. Especially since odds are I'll do it again, and again."

He was honest, she'd give him that. And maybe he wasn't perfect but wasn't that one of her complaints anyway? She took a deep breath and looked up.

"All right, I'll forgive you this time. If you're going to be my friend, though, you have to take my side when it comes to my parents."

"*Because* we're friends," he paused, smiling, "I'm gonna be honest with you. But we can argue about that later. Here comes Randy, so smile."

"Why? Are you trying to prove something to him?"

"Yeah, that he's not your type."

"Since you put it that way," she forced a cheerful grin.

"Not like that, you look psychotic."

"Thanks." She quirked her lips downward to emphasize the sarcasm in her tone then gave him a genuine smile.

Randy stopped at the table. "You two seem to be getting along well. " He gave Sean a nod and a lewd wink Caitlin probably wasn't supposed to see. Turning to her, Randy offered, "I got that mower fixed up. I can come by in the morning with it if you'd like."

"I'll pick it up for her," Sean interjected. "If that's okay with you, Caitlin?"

"That would be nice, thank you."

"Suit yourself." Randy moved on to the bar.

Sean frowned, until Caitlin made a silly face at Randy's back. Then he laughed and signaled the waitress.

"The dance doesn't start until eight," he told Caitlin as they headed for the truck. "But I have to finish the preparations."

"I don't mind." She smiled, feeling relaxed. "I like it up there, it's peaceful."

"It was peaceful the night you were there because it was a weeknight in May. Tonight it's a summer Saturday night. Not so peaceful at High Peak Campground now."

SIXTEEN

From the outside, the large barn was impressive. Inside, it was beautiful. The Rec room in front was decorated with streamers and colorful tablecloths. Margaret Taggart filled punch bowls while Tina, a high school girl working part time at the campground, set out stacks of plastic cups. Upstairs was purely amazing. Sean left Caitlin in the company of his father and headed off to make sure the DJ was all set and ready for the night. Patrick Taggart clearly enjoyed entertaining Caitlin.

"This floor is specially constructed for occasions such as this," he explained. "Now folks pay good money for floating dance floors. We've had ours almost one hundred years."

Stepping gingerly onto the polished surface, Caitlin felt the slight springiness in the floor.

"The secret is the triple layer of pine boards laid at right angles. Gives the floor a gentleness, makes it easy to dance the night away."

"Wasn't this a working farm a hundred years ago?"

"Mostly, but this family's always been big on celebrating, be it weddings, births, or just the seasons. My granddad, Sean's great-grandpa, decided we needed this floor. The loft would still be packed with bales of hay come fall."

"Wouldn't that damage the parquet floor?" She studied the beautiful polished floor.

"Well, the parquet floor you see here is only about ten years old."

"It looks beautiful."

"We don't store hay up here anymore." His eyes sparkled. "Used to line the walls with bales for people to sit on but got too many complaints."

"Too low?"

"Too itchy." He laughed and she joined in.

"Hey Dad," Sean yelled. "Could you bring up that fifty foot cord?"

Giving her a peck on the cheek, Patrick headed off to get the extension cord. Caitlin chose a chair in the corner near the stairs, intending to spend the evening watching. From here she would also be able to easily slip downstairs for refreshments. Although she expected Sean to fight her decision to sit all night, it was his father who besieged her first. He persuaded her to dance by offering to let her stand on his feet. She didn't, of course, but how could she turn him down after such an offer?

Scott was the biggest surprise. To Caitlin's astonishment, Scott could dance quite well. He tried to cajole her into dancing with him, but only half-heartedly.

"I'd feel awkward dancing with you anyway." He plunked into the chair beside her. "After all, you're like a sister. Who wants to dance with their sister?"

"You don't have to shudder when you say that."

"The DJ promised a nice slow song next. Time for you to dance with your date." He nodded at Sean who was crossing the room. "Need me to stick around and defend your honor?"

She slapped his arm softly. "Get lost. I have a brother and he's less of a nuisance."

Before he could protest, Janelle materialized, dragging him away. Sean glanced briefly at the departing couple before claiming the seat beside Caitlin.

"I know you didn't want to dance tonight, but would you maybe reconsider and join me out on the floor?" His usual confidence was tempered with shy eagerness.

"Didn't you see me with your dad? He'll probably need to go to the doctor for those mangled toes." She hated dashing Sean's hopes but the idea of dancing with him scared her.

Music began to play. He smiled, overlooking her objection. "And it's even a country song. You have to dance now." Grasping her hands, he pulled her to her feet. "Don't panic, all you have to do is sway."

Although terrified, Caitlin followed Sean onto the dance floor. He stayed close to the corner, away from the center of attention. As Tracy Byrd's voice crooned 'Keeper of the Stars', Sean took her right hand in his left, placing his other hand on the small of her back. Hard as she tried, she could not follow his lead. After the first verse, and several missteps that surely were painful, she leaned closer and spoke into his ear.

"This isn't swaying."

He smiled, leaning down to speak in her ear. "Would you prefer to dance like them?"

She glanced at the teenage couple he'd indicated. The young girl draped over her partner like a clingy shirt, her head nestled into his shoulder. The boy's hands rested slightly below her waistline. Caitlin turned back to Sean, head shaking negatively.

"That's too suggestive." She shot a look at the pair again. "In fact, aren't they a bit young to be dancing like that, regardless of the music or company?"

"Yup," he agreed. "If I held you that close I'm not sure I could maintain self-control. No way that boy'll keep a lid on his hormones."

A few seconds passed. He did nothing.

"Shouldn't we do something? Break them apart?" Caitlin glanced again at the Velcroed couple.

"This isn't school, ya know." His lips quirked. "Relax. That's my cousin Ashley, and her chaperone is about to handle the situation."

Randy Henderson appeared, barely excusing himself as he pushed past dancing couples. Caitlin had never seen him with such a serious expression. Ashley was oblivious until her uncle placed a hand on her shoulder, while at the same time physically removing her partner's hands from her backside.

"Ashley Marie Henderson," Randy growled, loud enough for Caitlin to overhear. "I warned you about dancin' like this. Now, say goodnight to Roger. He won't be able to dance with you anymore tonight."

"Uncle Randy," the young girl whined. "You got no right—"

"I have every right. Be glad your father isn't here..."

The rest of their argument was lost as they moved toward the exit. Sean chuckled. Caitlin found herself smiling, too. Being a teenage girl was no picnic and having to chaperone one must be even harder.

"You're dancing perfectly now." Sean's breath tickled her ear.

It was true, she was indeed moving in perfect sync with him. Distraction took away the handicap of inhibition, allowing her body to move with effortless rhythm. It was heady, exciting and scary all at once.

When the song ended they stayed close a moment longer.

Caitlin felt faint. As Sean stepped away she grasped his arm, steadying herself.

"You okay?"

"It's these shoes." She felt bad for fibbing, though it was difficult walking in these heels.

"How about sitting out a few songs to catch your breath. Then would you like to try another dance?"

She nodded. She'd never felt so exhilarated. More than anything she wanted to feel Sean's arms around her again, holding her close, conveying a disconcerting mix of safety and attraction.

Oh this was much worse than she feared.

Coward!

Not tonight. Tonight she was going to let go and enjoy. Nothing inappropriate could possibly happen here on the dance floor.

Maybe not inappropriate but something was definitely happening. The next time Sean asked, Caitlin didn't hesitate to get up and dance. When the DJ played a block of slow songs they stayed on the floor for the whole set.

And no one else asked her to dance, although she noticed several other couples switching dance partners occasionally. People were beginning to drift away, heading home, before another man approached them.

"Tag," Officer Eric Coffey nodded his head in greeting. "May I have this dance?"

She realized Eric was asking her. Sean shrugged and turned away to speak with someone else. Fine, if Sean didn't care who she danced with, why should she? Turning to Eric, she smiled warmly.

Eric looked different out of uniform. Caitlin remembered him as a scrawny kid in high school. He certainly wasn't anymore. The pullover shirt stretched taut across the muscles of his chest and upper arms. The same height as her, he still managed to convey a commanding presence. His close-cropped hair reminded her of the Marines who worked with her brother.

Eric's smile was warm, pleasant, his arm around her waist gripping her close but not tight. His hold was as intimate as Sean's had been yet Caitlin felt none of the exhilaration. They moved slowly, edging away from the remaining people. When they were nearly alone, Eric spoke.

"I talked the Chief into having a cruiser drive by your place this evening and once during the graveyard shift." He spoke in his clipped, official voice.

She'd nearly forgotten about the events of last night. "Did you find out something? Do you think the prowler might return?"

"No," his voice softened. "The cruiser is just a precaution. If there is a prowler, it'll probably scare him off for good."

"Thank you." Caitlin didn't feel particularly thankful. Worried was a better description. Her expression must've reflected her emotions.

"Don't worry, Caitlin," Eric squeezed her hand with uncharacteristic empathy. "I've got it all under control."

They danced their way back toward Sean.

"You be careful," Eric nodded toward Sean. "Remember what I told you."

As Eric stepped away, Scott swooped in, wrapping an arm around her waist, lifting her off her feet. They spun around several times before he set her down.

"Couldn't resist," Scott laughed. "I'll probably never get another chance to dance with you."

"Not like that you won't!"

"Goodnight, Cait." Scott kissed her cheek and disappeared downstairs.

"He's rather exuberant," Sean observed.

Caitlin was startled. She looked quickly at Sean. "Did you serve alcohol tonight? He's not supposed to drink, you know."

"No, we didn't serve alcohol. That, my dear Caitlin, is what your best friend looks like when he's having a good time."

"Does he whoop and holler like that when he's at a fire."

"Sometimes," he grinned broadly. "But not because it's fun. Then it's because he's focused on putting the fire out and there's a real sense of accomplishment when we succeed."

She shuddered, a chill running down her spine. "I'd rather not think about that."

"Then let's think about getting you home in time for church."

"It's not that late, is it?" She glanced around, realizing everyone else was gone.

"Nearly midnight."

As they drove through the darkness her worry grew into anxiety. Eric's conversation replayed in her mind and no matter how hard she tried otherwise, her imagination kicked into overdrive. By the time the headlights illuminated her house she sat immobile in the truck, dreading the empty house, stomach queasy. Unwanted tears pooled in the corners of her eyes.

"I hope you had a good time tonight." Sean's hopeful confidence pushed the door closed on her agitation. Nightmare scenarios reached desperate tentacles around the barrier, eroding her composure.

She nodded, then remembering the darkness she whispered, "Yes, I did."

"What's wrong?" He turned on the dome light. "Are you crying?"

Her throat tightened, blocking the words she tried to speak. Concepts of what might happen if the prowler returned paraded through her thoughts. Almost as upsetting was how it would sound to Sean when she confessed.

"Well, I was going to ask for a kiss goodnight but if the prospect scares you to tears I promise not to push." Lighthearted humor didn't hide his disappointment.

"It's not you." Attempted laughter turned to a choking sob. Taking gasping breaths, she tried to calm down. Hysterics would not help. Calm pushed at the fear, now that they were talking and the prospect of being alone was delayed. "I had a prowler last night."

"What? When?"

"It was right when you called." She flinched at the anger that leaped into his eyes. "I'm sorry I didn't tell you. I called Scott."

Sean was silent long enough to worry her. He stared straight ahead, speaking slowly as if controlling his words. "I understand. I wish you had trusted me. But you're accustomed to relying on Scott and he's closer anyway."

Turning to look at her, he smiled reassuringly. "You did good, calling Scott."

"I should've trusted you," she demurred. "You're right about Scott and Janelle being closer. Scott got here in about two minutes."

"And I would've taken at least fifteen." He nodded, anger replaced by concern. "Tell me everything. Is this what Eric was talking to you about?"

She nodded and told him the details of last night's incident. "I'd managed to put the whole episode out of my mind until Eric brought it up again."

"Does Eric think the prowler will come back?"

"He's says no, but I'm not so sure." She sniffled. Sean offered a box of tissues from behind the seat.

"So you're scared to be alone in the house." He paused, weighing the options. "Do you want me to stay tonight? If you're worried about impropriety you could come back to my house. There's a nice guest room."

She thought a moment. "If I stay at your house, I won't know if the prowler came back."

"And you'd be as frightened tomorrow night. I'll stay if it will ease your fear."

"No, you can't do that." She smiled to lessen the rejection. Taking a deep breath, she finished with the logical conclusion. "I need to face my fears, myself. And I won't be alone, will I? I have the Lord as my protector."

He nodded. "His rod and staff will protect you. You're right, this is your house and you shouldn't be afraid to live here. And we need to put our trust in God. But I'm going to park behind the tractor shed and keep an eye on things."

"That's not relying on God." She bit back the angry *I don't need a babysitter*, mostly because she was grateful for the offer.

"What d'ya think happens when you ask God for protection?" When she scowled, he continued. "Could be I'm an instrument of God in this instance and I'm meant to watch out for you."

"Sounds like a perfect excuse for letting you into my home, late at night when there's no one else around to stop whatever might happen." She regretted the accusation in her tone. He stared out the front windshield, jaw clenched. "I'm sorry, that wasn't fair."

"It's hurtful." At last he looked at her. "I'm not that guy, the one who made you hate men. I like you, Caitlin. I'm not going to spoil what could be a good thing by taking advantage of you."

She glanced at her hands, ashamed. "You're right, you aren't Adam. I can trust you."

"Good. But I do think you're right about my not staying in the house for the night. With the truck out of sight your reputation should be safe." He got out, coming around to her side of the truck. Opening the door, he smiled and offered her a hand down. "First, I'm going to make sure the house is secure. Don't want you getting sick with fear. That would make for a very unpleasant goodnight kiss."

Her lips twitched as the tension let up. "You're pretty sure of yourself. What if I don't want to kiss you?"

Putting a hand to his chest he staggered. "Oh, I'm wounded. Here I am being your knight in shining armor and you shoot me down."

"Okay, fine, I'll give you a kiss befitting a knight." She kissed his cheek. "Thank you, kind sir, for coming to my rescue."

Wrapping his arms around her, Sean pulled her against him. "Open the door," he commanded huskily, "and I'll give you a kiss befitting a damsel in distress."

Fear leapt in her again. Not only was he much too strong to fend off, she wasn't sure she wanted to. Putting a hand against his chest she pushed weakly, half-heartedly. He stepped back immediately. She was almost disappointed.

The house was dark, the light over the kitchen sink throwing a faint glow into the hall. As her eyes acclimated to the dimness, she found the light switches and flicked the whole row. Light flooded the hallway and living room.

Sean grasped her hand, lightly kissing the back of her fingers. "I'm not going to kiss you until you aren't scared of me anymore."

She turned away, worried he'd see the truth in her eyes. As nervous as she was about him, it was her own emotions and reactions that were frightening. He locked the front door, moving past her to check each room. He made sure every window was locked, and not only locked the basement door but first went down to be sure the garage was secure as well. At last he returned to the kitchen.

"I'm going to help myself to some of your coffee. Would you like a cup?"

Peering around the corner she saw him making himself at home. He grabbed two mugs when she accepted his offer. "But make mine decaf, please," she added, reaching for the box of single serve coffee cups. He shooed her away.

"I'm making the coffee. Sit down."

"Yes, sir." They both smiled.

"Tell me, Caitlin," he spoke while waiting for the coffee to brew. "Do you have reason to be afraid of me?"

She sucked in a sharp breath. "You've never behaved badly."

One corner of his mouth lifted slowly. "That's not exactly

what I meant. There's someone in your past. Did he do something to you?"

She stared, heat rising slowly up her neck, across her cheeks. This was no girlish blush. This was outright embarrassment. She couldn't talk to him about such things. She turned away.

"That's what I thought."

"Nothing happened." Inexplicably, she felt defensive.

"But he wanted it to happen."

Caitlin risked a glance. Sean stirred milk into the coffee, paying her no attention.

"You don't have to tell me anything, but I have to ask. Is he why you don't date?"

Their eyes met briefly as she accepted the mug he handed her. His eyes looked troubled. She wondered what he saw in hers. "No, he's not the reason. He's an example of why it was a good decision."

Sean nodded, sipping the hot coffee. "So, uh, how insistent did he get?"

"My roommate came home before anything happened." She actually smiled. "I think her boyfriend intimidated Adam."

Sean cocked his head. "Are you worried that there's no one here to intimidate me?"

Everything inside her came to a standstill. Her heart stopped beating, blood stopped flowing, her lungs stopped breathing. For a moment the earth stopped rotating. The edges of her vision blurred. Was she frightened Sean would take advantage of her? Or terrified he would think she was the type who'd want that?

Reality snapped back into place dizzyingly. He watched her closely, a frown deepening on his face. She found her voice. "I don't think you'll need to be intimidated. I honestly believe you can be trusted."

"That's nice to hear." His frown softened. "All the same, I'll leave and you will lock the door. Understand?"

It was a command. She didn't understand his tone. Of course she'd lock the door. He wasn't questioning her safety sensibility, it was a warning. She nodded uncertainly.

"Good." He stood, put their mugs in the sink before turning back to face her again. "You should go to bed now, get some sleep."

Edginess jittered across her nerves, thoughts jumbling. The

Lord would keep her safe. She was safe. Sean was safe. God had brought Sean here to protect her. She relaxed.

"Thank you. For understanding and for watching out for me."

His smile was strained, as if there were things he'd like to say but held back. "Go to bed now, Caitlin."

She should be irritated, being treated like a child but his tension was palpable. His voice had taken on a gruffness she'd never heard before. Her own nerves were unsettled. It was unfair, expecting him to sleep in his truck while keeping an eye on her house. Even briefly considering letting him stay in the guest room flipped her stomach right over and sent a chill of apprehension through her mind.

Slowly she turned away, reaching to close the door and mumbling goodnight. He grabbed her arm, pulling her around to face him.

"I want you to know that you are the most beautiful and attractive woman I have ever met." His eyes held hers. Slowly he lowered his head, bringing his lips down on hers. He kissed her softly, tenderly, with restrained passion.

She swayed, putting hands on his shoulders, fingers curling handfuls of shirt. Everything inside her softened, the icy wall protecting her heart melted. He wrapped an arm around her, pulling her closer. His other hand twined in her hair as the kiss deepened. She was drowning, drifting into nirvana.

And then it was over. He moved away, holding her arms to stabilize her. She felt as if part of her was gone. His steeled jaw warred with the smoldering emotion in his eyes.

He gave her one last admonishing look. "Don't trust me, Caitlin."

SEVENTEEN

Sean waited in the circle of light outside the front door until he heard the deadbolt slide into place. With the glare in his eyes he couldn't see Caitlin looking out the sidelite window but knew she was there. Every fiber of his being vibrated with awareness of her presence. He rolled his eyes heavenward. *Why, Lord? Why did I kiss her now?*

He hadn't planned on it. Had planned not to, in fact. Made a promise to wait until she was ready. She was guarded, afraid of men in general. He needed to go slow. So why'd he just kiss her? He could still feel the soft touch of her lips on his. He groaned. *Lord, please give me strength.*

And she trusts me. He snickered. Thank you, Lord, for strong locks. Not that he'd take advantage of Caitlin, or any woman for that matter. Still, her eyes held an assurance that contradicted earlier wariness. As if her faith in him outweighed all her doubts and suspicions of other men. After the kiss, he could've suggested staying with her in the house and she'd have said yes. Much as he'd like to believe in his honest, steadfast devotion to God, he was still flesh and blood. A man, with a man's weaknesses. And there could be no denying both Caitlin's femininity and her attractiveness. And the way she responded to his kiss…Sean groaned again.

He stepped into the darkness, heading for his truck. Probably he was being too hard on himself. He was quite capable of being a good boy. It's what he did best, according to his family and friends. Still, being alone in the house with her would be sheer torture. Better to be out here, uncomfortable enough to keep vigilant. Her virtue was safer locked up indoors but her life was more than secure in his hands.

Headlights panned across the yard. He tensed, forgetting all concerns about the kiss. The vehicle slowed to an idle roll. When it stopped altogether, he steeled himself for confrontation, adrenaline tingling along his nerves. The driver stepped out of the truck without cutting the engine. He was a bulky shadow, approaching the house cautiously but not furtively. Sean moved to meet him as the moon broke free of a cloud.

"Tag, that you?"

Breath left Sean's lungs in a loud exhale. "Geez, Eric, you scared me. Thought you might be Caitlin's prowler."

Eric Coffey laughed. "I thought the same about you. What're you doing here?"

"I just found out about last night's episode." He stepped closer to Coffey, keeping his voice low in the late night. "I'm gonna hang around, keep an eye on things for tonight."

Coffey nodded to the house. "Caitlin know you're doing it?"

"Yeah, don't want her calling the cops on me in the middle of the night."

Eric snorted. "Cruiser will be nearby, I saw to that. There's no need for you to hang around. If you're that worried, I can park over there and watch out for Caitlin."

"No, I'll do it. You've got a family of your own to take care of."

"Protect and serve, that's my job." Coffey chuckled. "Well, alright, if you're sure, I'll leave you to it."

"'Preciate the offer." Sean slapped Eric lightly on the back as the other man turned to leave. "Gotta prove my worthiness to my woman, right?"

Coffey grunted. "Women don't appreciate all we do for them."

Sean *hmph-ed*. "Probably not."

He waited for Coffey to drive away then moved his truck across the street. Parked beside the tractor shed, he wasn't completely out of sight but it'd take a determined, keen eye to discern the dark blue truck from the deep night shadows. If anyone did spot it, it would likely be taken as just more farm equipment. Wasn't as if his truck was unique.

If Eric Coffey was right and the prowler had been kids or even a drug dealer, Caitlin being home would be enough to scare them away for good. They'd go looking for someplace truly abandoned and secluded. With an increase in police presence, the deal would be sealed. Suppose, however, the prowler was someone else. A peeping tom wouldn't be scared off by the cruiser coming by a couple times tonight, and Caitlin's presence would be the thing that would draw him back. Likewise, a burglar might not be put off by the meager police presence, though he'd wait until Caitlin wasn't home before breaking in. Probably.

Rolling down the windows a few inches helped Sean hear anyone approaching. Warm night air caressed his face. Mosquitoes got in, too, but without a light not many would be attracted. The insects never bothered him, anyway. He wasn't sweet enough to draw flies. He smiled, settling his back into the crook between the seat and door, stretching his legs across the bench seat. Peepers made a pleasant backdrop to the soft night. He closed his eyes, willing his hearing to remain alert.

Caitlin, ah there was something worth dreaming about. He was glad, now, for Dad's lecture about putting effort into a relationship. Not that he had a relationship with Caitlin. Not yet, but he could see it happening, feel good about the possibilities. She'd let him past her carefully constructed defenses. Some of them, at least. He'd caught her off guard with that kiss. Still, she hadn't pushed him away.

Though he hadn't dated seriously since his disastrous relationship with Melissa, he knew how to kiss a girl. It was something a guy didn't forget. Like riding a bike. And he knew when a girl enjoyed the kiss. Caitlin had definitely enjoyed. He hoped to repeat the experience soon. Yet the attraction wasn't purely physical. He'd talked more with her in the short time they'd been acquainted than he had with all his dates over the last ten years combined. He even turned off a Sox game to give her his undivided attention. When had he even thought about doing such an outrageous thing in the past?

Never.

* * *

Gravel crunched, stealthy footsteps revealed. Instantly alert, Sean sat still, listening. The sound drifted from across the street. Someone was in Caitlin's driveway. Squinting, he saw a shadowy figure moving in front of the house.

Sean swung his legs off the seat and reached up to shut off the dome light before cautiously opening the truck door. He slipped out of the cab and closed the door with an almost inaudible click. He moved swiftly and silently across the street. A maple tree near the driveway provided cover as he surveyed the dooryard. The prowler slipped around the far corner of the house. Sean followed.

After circling the house without seeing the prowler again,

Sean was forced to admit he'd lost his prey. Obviously the intruder realized he was present. It was entirely possible, even likely, the prowler had slipped off into the shrubs, doubling back around and thus escaping. But had he left? Sean took a few more minutes exploring the idea, searching the landscape alongside the house. Too bad he hadn't thought to grab the flashlight from his truck.

Reluctantly he conceded defeat. The intruder had slipped away. No need for stealth now. He stood in the bright light at the front door, scanning the scene. In the movies, the guy standing in broad view always got shot. Or stabbed, or otherwise made dead. A ridiculous notion. This wasn't a movie. Still, he moved out of the light. As soon as his eyes adjusted to darkness once more, he spotted a shadowy form darting across the corner of the cornfield. Before Sean could react, an engine rumbled and a car sped away.

A glance back at the house showed Caitlin had slept through the whole episode. Sean was certain she'd have every light in the place turned on, as well as the outdoor floodlights, if she even suspected the prowler had returned. But the house was dark, asleep. No need to wake her. Now that the prowler knew he'd been spotted, Sean felt confident there'd be no further visits tonight. Maybe not ever again.

The truck was a black mass in the shadows, even the chrome grill didn't reflect any light. He opened the door, climbed in, and settled back into sleeping position. It wasn't at all comfortable but he'd manage. There were only a couple hours until dawn.

* * *

Caitlin fell asleep thinking about Sean. The possibility of kissing him had worried her a little. Needlessly. The moment their lips met, her body responded. If the world had moved, she wouldn't have noticed. Nothing existed beyond Sean. It was scary, how easy it would've been to get lost in his embrace. If he hadn't left, would she have had the strength to send him away? What did he mean about not trusting him? She'd never felt safer than when she was with him. Maybe he didn't trust himself, but he'd had the will power to leave.

She dreamed about that kiss, feeling the warmth of his lips on hers, the strength of his arms as he held her close. When sunlight invaded her sleep, dancing bright patterns on the inside of her eyelids, she resisted. Just a few more minutes in the dream, safe in his arms. Sitting up slowly, she glanced at the clock. Already after eight—she never slept this late. Forget church, she'd never make it on time. Summer services were at nine-thirty. She sighed. *Forgive me, Lord.* Some time in personal bible study later today would have to suffice.

She wondered if Sean was still here. He probably woke up much earlier, possibly as soon as the sun climbed over the edge of the lake. Disappointment filled her. It would've been nice, sharing breakfast with him. On the flipside, he hadn't gotten her up during the night so the prowler must not have returned. It was over, things could go back to normal. Well, almost normal. Her life would never be the same after last night's kiss.

Murmuring voices seeped into the room. An electric current of fear coursed over her skin. She'd locked the front door. Breath rushed out of her lungs. The voices must be outside, carrying through an open window. Maybe Sean was still here. Excited, looking forward to seeing him again, she bounced out of bed, quickly pulling on jeans and a shirt.

Suddenly Scott spoke, from down the hall. Not outside. "Relax, I know what I'm doing."

What was he doing here? Sean's response came from further away but definitely inside the house. "I don't think Caitlin's gonna appreciate this at all."

Scott laughed as a knock sounded on her bedroom door. "Wake up sleepy head, you've got company." He knocked again, louder.

She pulled the door open and yanked him into the room. "What are you doing here?"

He leaned down and kissed her cheek. "Good morning to you, too."

She frowned.

"Drove by first thing this morning, saw Tag's truck. I got curious, came back and he was still here. So I invited myself in."

"How did you get in?" She crossed her arms on her chest, tapping one foot.

He dangled a key from his index finger. "You gave me the key, remember."

"For emergencies." Sickening dread weighed down her stomach. Was this an emergency?

"You've got company." He ignored her annoyance.

"You aren't company."

"Sean is." Scott winked. "We aren't who I was referring to, anyhow."

"Who else is here?" The lead weight in her belly started pressing on her heart and lungs, making breathing difficult.

He smiled softly, almost tenderly, cupping her face with his hand then ruffling her hair. She felt her world tilt. Scott was only gentle to her when something was really wrong. Muscles in her throat tightened.

"Come on, we're in the kitchen." He strolled away. "Janelle's making coffee.

Something was wrong. Terribly wrong. She trudged down the hall, trepidation dragging at her feet. Foreboding pulled in the sides of her vision. It'd be like her parents to call Scott, have him and Janelle deliver bad news. Tragedy was the only explanation for Scott letting himself into her house, for Janelle's presence as well. And it had to be James. Who else was in harms' way on a daily basis?

Scott sauntered into the kitchen, going straight for Janelle. Caitlin shuffled into the room, pausing to take note of all present. Sean sat at the breakfast bar, staring into his coffee mug. Eric Coffey sat across from him. Sean pushed his drink aside as she ambled in.

"Hey, sweetie." Janelle's gentle maternal tone did nothing to assuage Caitlin's anxiety. "Want some coffee?" She set a cup on the countertop in front of Caitlin.

Sean looked up then, his gaze locking with hers. She searched his expression, hoping for a clue about what was going on but winding up more uneasy. He smiled but the warmth didn't reach his eyes. Today his blue eyes were icier than she'd ever seen them. Hardened steel.

Caitlin glared at Scott. He must have offended and angered Sean. Probably accused him of all sorts of impropriety. She was surprised Scott tolerated Sean being here. Then again, maybe Sean was mad at her. Irritated that she had actually locked him out last night or displeased with her response to his kiss.

"Sit down, Caitlin." Eric Coffey spoke with gruff tenderness.

This wasn't about Sean and Scott. Eric's presence meant this was about something more serious. She sat, stomach rolling over. The room grew unnaturally bright and blurry. *Oh please God, please don't let it be James.*

"We have some important matters to discuss," Eric said.

Cold rushed down Caitlin's cheeks as the blood drained from her face. Darkness pressed at the edges of her vision. Her shaky legs gave way and she sank into the bar stool Janelle offered, hardly aware of doing so. "It's James, isn't it?" she whispered.

Warmth enveloped her hand as Sean grasped it firmly, his thumb gently caressing her wrist. She looked up and met his gaze.

"This has nothing to do with James," he reassured gently. "As far as any of us knows, your brother is perfectly safe and on his way home."

"Thank you, Lord." She closed her eyes, relief bringing tears.

He moved closer, putting arms around her, resting her head on his shoulder. She wasn't crying but his comfort felt good. He still smelled of sandalwood and leather. She inhaled the scent, peace washing through her with each breath.

"She always does this with her brother," Scott said quietly from across the room. For once his tone wasn't scornful or teasing.

Enjoying Sean's closeness as long as possible, Caitlin tried to explain. "Most of the time I can pretend James just has a high tech job and that he goes on a lot of business trips. It usually works. Deep down, though, I know his life is in danger every time he's deployed. And I'm terrified that one day someone is going to come tell me he's been killed. So when it almost happens but then turns out that he's okay, well it's kinda like almost being in a car accident."

She glanced up at Sean. He smiled.

"Hmm," Sean's eyes held a smile even while his expression remained serious. "When I'm nearly in an accident I don't cry."

"Men, what do they know?" Janelle admonished.

"We know enough to humor you." Scott winced when his wife slapped him. "I mean, we know when to admit you're right."

Caitlin reluctantly pushed away from Sean. This wasn't about James being killed. How bad could it be? Sean sat back on his own stool as Eric picked up where he left off.

"This is about your prowler, Caitlin."

Her eyes snapped to Sean's face, fear freezing her relief. "Did he come back last night?"

"Yes." His eyes hardened once more.

"Why didn't you wake me?" She narrowed her eyes, battling confusion and suspicion.

"You needed rest. He left and stayed away. I'd have woken you if there was any danger."

"So now he's scared off for good?"

Sean shook his head but Eric spoke. "Unfortunately it looks like you have a stalker."

Caitlin sucked in a sharp breath, movie plots running through her mind. Women who were stalked ended up dead. "You're overreacting."

"Cait, he showed up after the cruiser. He's watching everything about you," Scott stated.

Caitlin stared. Eric Coffey nodded, confirming what Scott said. She spent twenty-eight safe years not dating. Then she gives in to Adam. It wasn't fair, the first guy she goes out with —and they weren't even really dating—turns out to be insane and stalks her. Unless someone else had staged all of this. Sean knew about the police drive-bys because she'd told him. Would he do that, just to kiss her? To have her fall into his arms last night? But if he'd staged it all, wouldn't he have jumped on her offer to stay in the house? She shook her head. It just didn't add up.

She turned to Sean. "Did you see this alleged stalker?"

"Yes. He slipped away when I tried to catch him." His eyes met her challenge.

Convenient. Caitlin frowned, thinking again about the notes. The first two arrived after she'd butted heads with him. The last one didn't fit that equation but perhaps it was a product of his twisted sense of humor. Maybe he was trying to scare her into turning to him for comfort.

He even went so far as to warn her not to trust him. Satan blending truth with deception, making the lie believable. No way would she fall for it. The anger in his eyes, was it because he recognized her skepticism?

The memory of his kiss intruded on her thoughts. She turned her gaze away. All of his actions imparted the sensation of safety. His embrace and gently compelling lips were nothing like the hard demand of Adam's out-of-control passion. Sean said he wouldn't hurt her. She had believed him when he said it. She still believed him.

She looked at Scott then turned back to face Eric. "Are you just trying to scare me?"

"I'm here because of evidence," Eric said. "I assure you

someone was here last night. He parked over by the cornfield and was in your yard. There are tire tracks and footprints to back this up. These two aren't pulling an elaborate practical joke."

Sean sat back, crossing his arms on his chest. The steeliness flashed in his eyes. "Tell us about your friend Adam."

She met his stare without flinching. What she had told him was personal, intimate information and now he wanted to share it.

"Caitlin," Eric interjected, "you suspected Marci of leaving those notes but now Tag has been able to tell me a little about this Adam character. I need to know more about him if I'm going to help you."

"What notes?" Scott asked. "Has someone been threatening you?"

She glared at him. "I don't need your protection."

"You were happy for my help Friday night. In the middle of the game."

She dropped her gaze. She had been happy for his protection in the past. Did he have to bring up the fact she'd interrupted the game? Oaf. He was as bad as her father.

Sean leaned forward, capturing her attention. "You didn't mention these notes last night."

"Because I didn't know who was leaving them. For all I knew, they had nothing to do with the prowler. They still might not be connected."

"I have no doubt they're connected," Eric said.

Sean took her hands. "I understand that you don't want him," he nodded toward Scott, "acting like a possessive big brother. My interest isn't brotherly."

Heat flared in her cheeks. She watched his thumb make lazy circles across the back of her hand. His kiss wasn't brotherly, that's for sure. Was he already looking for a physical commitment she wasn't willing to make?

Eric cleared his throat. "You've already given me a statement, Tag. The description you provided is vague but at least it's something. In any case, I don't see that you're needed any further."

Sean's grip on her hands tightened. "I have every right to be here. I promised to protect her and that's what I'm gonna do. I don't care what anyone says."

"You didn't do a very good job of it last night." Eric leaned across the bar counter. "You were right there and he still got away."

Dropping her hands, Sean turned and leaned toward Eric. "Your brilliant idea of having the cruiser drive by wouldn't have stopped him from breaking in and harming her."

"Hey, can we keep focused here?" Scott waved a hand between the two men. "I'd like to find out about this Adam so *I* can figure out how to protect Caitlin."

"I'm not your responsibility, Scott." All this male posturing was ridiculous. She turned to Sean and pointed at Eric. "It's Eric's job to uphold the law, which means he has a duty to go after stalkers. You have no duty or responsibility in this matter."

"You made me responsible last night."

How dare he make such an insinuation? Now they would all think he'd stayed the night with her, inside the house not out in his truck. *I knew this was a mistake.* She should've stayed as far away from him as possible.

"You're no better than Adam." The words slipped out on a soft breath.

He heard. She could tell by his reaction, stony eyes narrowing, fury glinting on the cutting edge of his dagger gaze. A jaw muscle flexed. He stood, knocking over the bar stool, and stomped out of the room.

Caitlin looked to Janelle for support but found her friend glaring at her.

"That was uncalled for," Janelle admonished. "And the meanest thing I've ever heard you say." She crossed the room, righted the stool and sat down. She waved Eric Coffey away.

Taking Caitlin's hand, Janelle spoke with increasing stridency. "There was someone else out there last night. You need to listen to these guys, help them find this stalker. You need to let someone help you, too. Scott is my husband, Caitlin. Get your own knight in shining armor."

Caitlin stared, stunned. There was love in Janelle's expression but her tone said *back off.* Janelle was tired of sharing Scott's affection. Shame washed over Caitlin.

"I'm sorry for all those times I borrowed Scott," she whispered. "About Sean, though..."

Janelle softened. "He cares about you, can't you see that?" She smoothed hair away from Caitlin's forehead. "Why didn't you ever tell me about Adam?"

Tears stung her eyes. She'd told Sean but not Janelle. It seemed she couldn't do anything right. Now they'd all abandon her, and she deserved it. Her lip trembled. She bit down on it.

Janelle glanced around the room. "Could you two leave us alone for a minute?"

Scott and Eric scrambled for the door. "Let Janelle deal with the waterworks," Scott said as he headed into the living room. Eric laughed.

Caitlin took a deep breath. "I'm so sorry, Janelle. I've been a terrible friend."

"No you haven't. You always keep things to yourself that you think I'll worry about." She smiled when Caitlin raised an eyebrow. "I'm a mother, Cait, I can sense these things. Now, tell me about Adam."

EIGHTEEN

"I met Adam about a year ago. Just after getting laid off." Caitlin stared over Janelle's shoulder, focused on the memories.

Adam had started attending her church. He was personable though distant. She assumed he was shy about his fledgling faith. She invited him to Bible study and he eagerly accepted.

"After a few weeks, I could tell he was struggling with what we were reading." Caitlin met Janelle's gaze. "He asked if I'd like to go out for coffee. We discussed the passages from Bible study."

It became a weekly routine. Adam's faith seemed to be growing. A friendship developed though Caitlin wasn't attracted to him romantically. Their conversations stayed within the confines of Bible study until she got the job in Naultag.

"That week, when we went for coffee," she told Janelle, "I was too excited not to share the news. It was the first time we'd really talked about our personal lives. He knew I was an out of work teacher, because others in our study group mentioned it. I didn't know anything about what he did for work."

"You dated a guy without knowing anything about him?" Janelle sat back, leaning against the counter. "Oh, I do wish you'd called me."

Caitlin gave her a half-smile. "Don't forget I had Chondra to advise me." Her roommate considered herself Caitlin's city guardian, because, she said, Caitlin had no street smarts at all.

Janelle returned her smile. "I always did like Chondra. She must've lectured you."

"Going out for coffee each week wasn't really dating." Caitlin rolled her eyes when Janelle frowned. "It was an extension of Bible study. Others in our group came with us."

"So when did you date him?"

"When I found out I'd gotten a new teaching job. He wanted to celebrate with me. We spent the next Saturday afternoon strolling the shoreline, getting to know each other. Then he took me to the Red Rock Bistro."

"So you got to know him?"

She nodded and then shook her head. "I thought so. He was nice, a gentleman. He said he worked in a boring office job, just a pencil pusher. He'd been married once. Alimony ate up most of his paycheck. He'd first come to church looking for forgiveness for his past."

Janelle nodded. "He said all the right things."

"Exactly." Caitlin nodded. "We went on a couple more dates and each time he was the same—a nice, boring man. He even looked average. Then, in May, he changed." He started holding her hand wherever they went. Keeping his arm around her whenever possible. He ordered for her at restaurants. "I should've broken it off then. But I thought maybe he was just having a hard time with the fact I would be moving in a few weeks."

"Did he kiss you?"

"Not up to that point. The first time he tried, I turned my head and got a peck on the cheek. He grumbled but let it go. The next time, I didn't give him the opportunity, and made sure to stress that we were just friends."

Then came their last date. She'd pushed the details into the recesses of her mind, hoping the memories would go away. Talking to Janelle brought them back, fresh as if it all happened the day before. The trapped feeling filled her. Once more his arms pinned her against him. Her lips felt bruised again with the memory of his hard, crushing kiss.

"Did he...I mean...were you able to escape?"

Caitlin nodded. "Chondra and Phillip came home. Adam left, but later came back and sat in his car across from the house. Chondra called the police, but Adam took off before they came."

"Did you file a report?"

"No. What was I supposed to say? Officer, my boyfriend tried to kiss me." She frowned. "I was ashamed. I certainly wasn't going to compound it by filing a foolish complaint."

Janelle shook her head. She took Caitlin's hands again. "Honey, it wouldn't have been a foolish complaint. He didn't just kiss you, and the fact your roommate stopped him doesn't take away his intent."

Caitlin grimaced. "You watch way too much television."

"Maybe, but you know I'm right about this. At least now you're going to talk to Eric and do something about this creep."

Janelle rose and went out of the room.

Eric Coffey returned, looking ill at ease. Scott joined him. A moment later the front door opened and closed as Janelle left the house.

"Not exactly police work by the book, eh?" Scott chuckled, nudging Eric with an elbow. "Bet you didn't know the Ice Princess could be so fiery."

"I am surprised, yes." Something like humor moved in Eric's eyes.

"You thought of me as an ice princess, too?"

"Caitlin," Eric smiled, "every guy in high school thought of you that way. We all took it personal when you wouldn't date any of us."

"If I say I'm sorry now, is it too little too late?"

Eric laughed. "You're sweet, Caitlin. I always knew that about you. The truth is, I met someone else and she's all I could ever ask for in a wife."

"Wow, Coffey, you're a real sap."

"Shut up, Bartlett. I know you feel the same way about Janelle."

"Yeah, well you don't hear me spouting all that drivel."

"Scott," Caitlin reprimanded. "I think that's so romantic."

"I swear all women are romantics and can't see the truth about guys." Scott paused. "Well, not you Cait."

She scowled. "Thanks, I think."

"Are you two done?" Eric asked. "I'd like you tell me about Adam. Why did you suspect he might be leaving you menacing notes?"

She glanced at Scott before giving Eric a watered-down glazed over version of what she'd just told Janelle. Scott clearly suspected what she wasn't saying. His eyes narrowed, jaw muscles bulging.

"If I get my hands on this guy—"

"You'll let me take care of him. Don't make things worse." Eric opened his notepad. "Caitlin, I need you to tell me about Adam. Start with full name and physical description."

"Adam Massey. He's kind of average looking."

Eric frowned. "Average? Can you get more specific?"

"He has short black hair, always perfectly groomed. Smoky blue eyes. I've never seen him with any facial hair. He's just a little taller than me. Not fat, not thin." Caitlin told Eric everything she knew about Adam. "Oh, and he has a slight Southern accent, like he grew up in the South but has been away for a long time."

Eric made more notes. "At what point did your relationship begin?"

"He asked if I could recommend a church."

"A sure-fire way to get your attention," Scott scoffed.

"I've never preached to you, have I?" She frowned.

Scott shook his head. "No, but I didn't mean that as a complaint. I meant Adam used a tactic he was certain would work."

"But you don't know anything more about him?" Eric probed.

"He said he worked for Raytheon. Seemed to know a lot about computers." Remembering that last night in her apartment, she flushed. "He looks nerdy because of the way he dresses, but Adam is definitely not a weakling."

Eric shifted, bouncing his pen against the notebook. "Okay, that'll do for a start. Now we'll show you the bit of evidence that convinced me this situation is serious."

Eric led her outside, Scott followed and Janelle joined them in the yard. Cupping her elbow, Eric steered Caitlin toward Sean's truck. Why was the truck parked in the dooryard and not across the street by the tractor shed?

"You did a good job on that description," Eric said. "Don't you worry, I'm going to take care of this for you."

"Thank you, Eric." She smiled. "It's nice, having a friend to lean on. Figuratively, of course."

Eric draped an arm across her shoulders, giving her a hug. "You can lean on me for real, too, kiddo. Any time you need me, just call."

"That's sweet." She kissed his cheek. Her smile faded when they reached the truck. She gasped, a lead weight hitting bottom in her stomach. Scratched into the paint on the driver's side were the words *She's Mine*. Her legs weakened. Eric's arm around her shoulders steadied her.

"I found it," Scott stated. His expression was grim. "I was curious about Tag's truck being here. Figured on giving you a hard time. Instead I saw this. Tag hadn't noticed it, he was still half asleep."

"He was probably tired from staying up watching out for

Caitlin," Janelle spoke for the first time since rejoining them.

Caitlin wanted to be annoyed with Janelle. Instead, tears blurred her vision as she gazed at her best friend's frown. *Oh dear Lord, what have I done?* She finally found one of the good guys and promptly shot him down. What an exceptionally poor judge of character. She glanced at Eric. He frowned until meeting her gaze. Then he smiled softly, dropping his arm and moving aside. "Glad to help. I'll make sure this guy doesn't harm you."

"I appreciate that." She placed a hand on Eric's arm, squeezing gently.

"At this point, the most I can do is have him picked up for questioning. We'll need Tag's truck as evidence, too. I'll send the flatbed down for it." He strode to the cruiser.

"You have unfinished business." Janelle pointed to the tractor shed across the street.

* * *

The shed interior seemed gloomy to Caitlin. Sunlight struggled to filter through small windows yellowed with dust and age. Sean worked on a piece of equipment. He looked up as she entered, holding her gaze for a split second before turning his back.

"I'm sorry." Her soft words echoed in the open space. "You have every right to be angry with me, and I wouldn't blame you if you never wanted to speak to me again."

Sean grunted. Was that in response to her or because of whatever he was doing? Stepping deeper into the shadows, eyes gradually adjusting, she recognized the big field mower, sitting behind the tractor.

"I was wrong to accuse you of being anything like Adam."

At last he turned around. Grease smeared his face and his hands were black. At least he'd had the sense to strip off the blue dress shirt before getting grease on it, too.

"Why didn't you tell me about the notes? You claimed to trust me."

"I did. I do." Little daggers of guilt etched her gut.

"You told Eric about them, but not me." He took a stepped toward her. "You hung up on me in order to call Scott. I would've been here in a flash."

She broke eye contact. "I know. You're always there just when I need help."

"So you thought I was watching you. Did you think I wrote

those notes? Why? I've never been anything but nice to you."

"I couldn't believe it was just dumb luck how you kept turning up at all the right moments. And you seemed too perfect..."

He stared at her. What was he thinking?

"You forgot to say I still live with Mommy and Daddy."

"Your parents live in Florida, they just stay with you during the summer."

Obviously taken aback, he took a long moment before shaking his head and going back to the mower. But he started talking while he worked. "Did you really suspect I wrote those notes? What do they say, anyway?"

She edged over to the workbench, careful to avoid greasy machinery. An overturned five-gallon pail became a seat. Elbows leaning on her knees, Caitlin told Sean about the notes.

He snorted. "To be honest, when I first met you I thought you didn't belong here."

"I grew up here, where else do I belong?"

He sat up, regarding her with dimpled cheeks. "Think about that day, Caitlin. You wore a pretty blue dress and sandals that sparkled. You were all poised and polished. Nothing like the spitfire you really are."

She slapped her hands on her knees. "I am not a spitfire."

"Right, I meant pigheaded and stubbornly independent." His grin broadened.

She returned his smile. "I like the sound of spitfire better."

"Me too. You've got moxie, my grandfather would say." He went back to greasing the equipment. "Why didn't you call Eric right away?"

"I was avoiding Marci. Then I didn't want to implicate you."

"Well, I'm glad you did go to the authorities. I still wish you had trusted me."

"I'm sorry."

"You really think I'm too perfect?" He glanced up, lips twitching as if fighting a smile.

"Sometimes." Her lips slowly curled upward. "What are you doing?"

With another grunt the mower shifted and he stood up. "Getting ready to hay the fields."

"Today?" She stood up, too.

"It's gotta be done while the sun's shining." Moving to the

workbench, he searched around until finding a rag. He wiped his hands and came to stand before her. "Randy will probably be here early this afternoon to get started. I'm helping him out a little."

"Why are you so grimy?"

"It's a dirt floor in here, or hadn't you noticed? Plus I greased some fittings."

He stepped toward her. She dodged quickly. "No way are you touching me with those hands. And look at your shirt. Yuk!"

"Aw, it's only grease. It'll wash out. Most of it. Maybe."

"Good thing it's just a t-shirt." She snatched the blue silk shirt when he reached for it. "Don't touch, you'll ruin it." She mirrored his smile.

They walked to the house, close enough their arms almost touched. Without the high-heeled sandals, Caitlin was a good six inches shorter than Sean. He was the right height to rest her head on his shoulder. Which she would be happy to do when he wasn't covered in grease.

Approaching the truck, he tensed, steering her around the passenger side.

"I'm sorry about your truck," she whispered. He slanted a glance at her, anger in his expression.

"We're in this together now," he said. "Last night this became my problem, too."

"You could walk away, stay out of my life, and be perfectly safe."

Sean grasped her hand and Caitlin didn't protest. When he turned to look at her, his eyes were full of warmth once more. "I can't walk away, Caitlin. I hope you understand that."

She hid her eyes from his gaze. It held a different kind of possessiveness than Adam's. Adam's eyes spoke only of taking whatever he wanted. Sean's said he'd do anything for her.

"I'm glad to hear you say it."

Slowly he lowered his head, pausing before their lips touched. She leaned into him, closing the gap. His lips were soft and warm, passionate and inviting. When he moved away she stood frozen, eyes closed. He cupped her face in his hands, lightly kissing the tip of her nose. She opened her eyes.

"Okay?"

She smiled and nodded. "More than okay."

NINETEEN

"What are we going to tell your parents?"

"The truth." Sean grinned crookedly. "We've fallen madly in love and are running away to get married."

Caitlin giggled. "Ain't gonna happen, farm boy." She smiled to let him know she was playing along. "Seriously, what will they say?"

"They like you. Having you in the house for a few days won't be a problem at all."

"What about your truck, won't they wonder?" Eric Coffey had taken Sean's truck to his garage for safekeeping, in case it was needed as evidence. Now they were driving Caitlin's car to the campground.

"They think I spend too much time and money on it now as it is. No need to worry them with the details."

She kept quiet a moment. The danger might be greater than Sean acknowledged. "At the Asparagus Festival, I saw Adam."

He glanced sharply at her, refocusing on the road before speaking. "That's what scared you enough to back into the grill. Why didn't you say something then?"

"When I looked again, he was gone. I fooled myself into believing the first note was a cruel joke and seeing Adam was the result of not enough sleep and too much stress." Her left hand lay palm up on her lap. The burn was hardly noticeable. "Later, after Marci locked the basement door, I was certain she had left that first note."

"Did you say anything to Eric about Marci?"

"I did." She was still at a loss as to how Eric could track down Adam with the meager information she knew. "I'm worried that Adam recognized your truck and will come after you at the campground."

"Thing is, I don't drive a unique truck. At least I didn't until someone carved a personal greeting into the door." He laughed but she sensed his anger. It was her fault. His truck would be fine if she hadn't allowed him to stay. "Besides, it's not like you're in witness protection or anything. The idea is to have you around people all the time. Especially at night. And your house isn't safe."

He looked away. Probably because they were turning into his driveway. Still, considering the words and his body language, his comment last night was puzzling.

"Sean?" She waited as he drove around the back of the barn, out of sight from the road. "Why did you tell me not to trust you?"

"I try my best to be a gentleman with you. It's not always easy but for the most part I think I've succeeded. However, being alone with you in that house all night, well," he coughed. "It was tempting. I wasn't sure you could trust me."

He glanced at her quickly. She said nothing, too stunned.

"I liked that outfit you wore last night." He changed the subject.

"Thank you," she found her voice. "You wouldn't have preferred a shorter skirt?"

Shrugging, tension left his body. "Leaving something to the imagination is attractive." His gaze swept her from head to toe. Today she wore a sleeveless t-shirt and shorts. Her hair was gathered in a ponytail. He winked and she blushed. "I like this outfit, too. You have beautiful legs."

"I bet the grease smudge on my face is extra attractive." He'd left a handprint after kissing her this morning.

"It's mostly gone. Makes you look like a farm girl."

"Because I am. I was born and raised on a farm. Well, spent most of my life there anyway." She hoped her look was hard, piercing. "And don't you forget that, farm boy."

He laughed. "You've got spunk, that's for sure."

"Yeah, when I'm not scared witless."

With her suitcase in hand, he headed for the house. She snatched up a small duffle bag and hurried after him. Inside, he showed her to the guest room, pointing out other rooms along the way.

"The bath is at the end of the hall there." He nodded his head to the right then indicated the room directly to the left of the stairs. "Master bedroom here, my parents are in the room opposite, and this is the guest room."

It was a moderate space, neither large nor confining. A comforter in tranquil turquoise and cream tones covered the full size bed, which was centered between two windows opposite the door. Matching curtains hung at the windows. The hardwood floor was bare but for a plush runner along each side of the bed.

"Feel free to use the dresser and closet. You can relax and read in the chair over there."

"It's a nice room. The décor is perfect."

"Amazing what you can get from a catalog. I didn't even have to coordinate it."

"Not good with decorating? Didn't you take Home Ec in school?"

"Ha ha." He made a face. "I don't know the difference between a pillow case and a sham. Women wear skirts, what does a bed need one for? Clean and neat is good enough for me."

"Typical guy."

"And don't you forget it." He tweaked her nose. "Mom and Dad being here is about your only security in this house."

Caitlin looked around the room. "The chair would be effective."

"Hmm, it might work."

He winked. A nervous thrill shot through her. On the one hand, he was obviously attracted to her. On the other was the fear he might act on that attraction.

"Think you can find your way around downstairs? Mom's probably in the kitchen. I'm going to find Dad and catch up on what's been happening here."

He left. As if expecting her to make herself at home. Well, for the next few days this would be home. She set about unpacking, using both the dresser and the closet as suggested. The last item unpacked was the fire department baseball cap Sean had given her this morning. She wasn't sure she wanted him to know how special it was to her. Looking around, she placed it on the small table beside the reading chair. She'd be able to see it from almost anywhere in the room.

Out of place and feeling useless, she wandered into the kitchen.

"Hello Caitlin," Margaret Taggart greeted warmly. "Come, make yourself to home. From what Sean told us, you'll be staying here for a few days at least."

Caitlin drifted to the counter where the other woman was making a salad. Carrots lay waiting to be chopped while cucumbers were being sliced. A quick glance found a knife and cutting board.

She set to work on the carrots. After several minutes working in companionable silence she spoke.

"I'm grateful for your hospitality."

Margaret gave her a sly smile. "It's been a long time since Sean cared for a girl."

Caitlin wondered if he ever brought the others home to visit. On second thought, the less she knew the better she'd feel.

* * *

After supper, Sean took Caitlin outside. Tonight he sat on the porch swing and she happily sat beside him. Pushing off with one foot he set the swing into gentle motion.

"How about a ghost story?" He draped an arm across her shoulders.

"A scary one?"

"No. Sometimes we make up some scary tales, for around the bonfire. I thought I'd tell you about Becky."

"I remember your Dad hinted at an interesting story about Becky."

"Yes, well, he usually comes up with the scary versions. I'd prefer to tell you about the real Becky." He looked into the night, pushing the swing into motion when it slowed.

"There's no such thing as ghosts."

He reflected her smile. "People in the past, even Christians, have believed otherwise. My great grandparents believed Becky was a real specter haunting this farm. We use their *sightings* as the basis of our campfire stories."

"Who was she?"

"Becky was my great-great-great-grandmother. The legend is that she met my great-great-great-grandfather just before the Civil War. They were deeply in love. He joined up to defend the Union and was killed at Gettysburg on the same day his son was born."

"That's terrible."

"Becky took the news badly, too. She became gravely ill and moved back here to be with her family. Shortly after, she died."

"How sad." The words flowed on her exhaled breath.

"Her spirit never left, so the legend goes. Some say she stayed to watch over her infant son. When he was grown and had children of his own, she watched over them."

How awful to lose the man she loved. It made sense that Becky might die of a broken heart and also that she would want to stay here, watching over her son. Thinking about how Becky must have felt, Caitlin's own heart ached. Still, people couldn't decide to hang around to watch over future generations. That was God's job.

"Do you believe she's still here?"

He glanced down at her before looking off into the night. "When I was little, I believed she was my guardian angel. Becky's son was named John Tomas Taggart. My name, Sean, is an Irish version of John."

"Are you Sean Thomas Taggart?"

He nodded. "And I look a lot like him."

"But people don't become guardian angels."

"I know that now. As a kid, the idea of great grandparent watching over me helped get through all the childhood traumas. You know, like being afraid of the dark."

She snickered. "You aren't afraid of the dark. Are you?"

"When you were three years old, weren't you?" Sean lifted her hand to his lips, kissing it lightly. "No guardian angel stopped me from rolling the tractor, or breaking my arm when I fell out of a tree. Becky didn't help when I dislocated my shoulder. I learned quickly not to rely on an angel to save me from stupidity."

She *hmphed* and thought about the bonehead stunts Scott was still prone to despite his supposed maturity. "I don't want to know any more details."

He laughed. "Yeah, I guess you've got an idea, what with being friends with Scott."

"Men," she rolled her eyes and shook her head in mock disapproval. "So what made your great grandparents believe Becky was a real ghost?"

"Oh, the usual. Unexplained footsteps, especially in the barn. A light breeze indoors when all the windows are closed. They claimed Becky made her presence known with the scent of lavender."

"That's all? Not very scary."

"We embellish for the campers. Dad is a gifted story teller."

* * *

A piercing alarm woke Caitlin. She sat up, listening to the shrill beeps repeating rapidly. When the irritating tones stopped she heard a muffled voice. Sean moved around in the room next door. Curious, she opened her door, peeking out in time to see both of the other bedroom doors open. Sean stepped into the hall, still tucking a t-shirt into his jeans.

"What is it?" she asked.

"Structure fire on South Street. I gotta go." He kissed her, calling out as he rushed down the stairs, "Take care of her, Dad."

She looked to his father. Margaret stood behind him, tying her robe.

"House fire," Patrick explained. "Could be any structure, of course, but on South Street it's mostly houses."

"Oh dear," Margaret responded as she came to the door. "We'd best pray, then. Caitlin, will you join us?"

Bowing their heads, Patrick spoke. "Lord, please watch over all the boys as they fight this fire. Guide their actions and keep them safe. And if there are any people inside the building please help them to escape or to be rescued. Amen."

Silently Caitlin added, *Lord please keep Sean safe, and Scott too.*

"You may as well go back to bed, dear," Patrick suggested. "It'll be hours before Sean comes home."

Sean's parents returned to their room, closing the door. Caitlin remained in the hall, staring at the master bedroom. Finally she went back to bed but wasn't able to sleep. Every movie she'd ever seen where a firefighter was injured or killed kept replaying in her head.

When the alarm first sounded it was a few minutes after two in the morning. At two forty-five, she gave up on sleep and went to the window. The room faced the right direction to see South Street, except Town Hill block the view. At three thirty, she crept downstairs and turned on the television. Channel 4 had a Worcester bureau and often flew their news helicopter out this far. All she could find were old movies and an infomercial.

An hour later, too keyed up with worry, she shut off the Abbott & Costello movie. Returning upstairs, she tried to read. Failing that, she set the book aside and picked up the fire department cap. Absently she traced a finger over the Maltese cross emblem, resting her head against the back of the chair.

When Margaret knocked on the door, Caitlin was startled to discover it was nearly seven. She'd fallen asleep sitting in the chair, holding onto the hat. Setting it back on the table, she went downstairs.

The morning news did have a brief story about the fire. She walked into the living room in time to hear the reporter say that soon after fire trucks arrived on scene the house had become fully engulfed. A video showed flames emerging from windows, hungrily licking at the building.

"There is one unconfirmed fatality," the reporter stated, "believed to be an occupant of the house. Also, shortly after the first firefighters entered the house an explosion rocked the building. No word yet on injuries to firefighters."

Margaret prayed again. Caitlin stared at the newscast, numb. Were firefighters inside the house when the explosion occurred? Was Sean? She feared the dead person wasn't an occupant but a firefighter.

"Caitlin?" Margaret interrupted. "Would you like breakfast?"

"No thank you."

"Orange juice, at least?"

"Or coffee?" Patrick added.

"How can you think about food? Aren't you worried?"

"Of course we are, that's why we pray." Patrick spoke matter-of-factly, sitting down at the table to sip his coffee.

"What Patrick means is that we must trust in God's will but we do ask for Him to protect all the boys. Besides, Sean's been a fireman for a long time." At least she seemed to understand Caitlin's anxiety.

"You're telling me that he has experience and you trust his skills?"

"Yes, to a certain extent. And remember, I lived through Patrick being in Vietnam." She laid a gentle hand on Caitlin's arm. "It's like Isaiah says, do not fear for God is with you. And," she further paraphrased, "God will uphold Sean in his right hand."

Caitlin studied the older woman. Put into that context, this fire could hardly be more than a blip on the radar screen of concern. Nevertheless, she had no appetite and continued to worry. While Sean's parents went about breakfast, she remained seated in the living room praying. *Lord, I know I need to trust that you are watching over Sean. Bring me your peace.*

She yawned. In the other room, Sean's parents chatted pleasantly. The aroma of bacon and buttered toast made her queasy. A dull ache lurked behind her eyes, proof she hadn't slept enough. She trudged upstairs, hesitating in the hall. The door to Sean's room stood open. A soft breeze carried the scent of lavender. It was easy to understand why someone might imagine a spirit haunted the house.

The large master bedroom held dark cherry furniture and a color scheme of blues and greens. Windows on the three outside walls flooded the space with light. Along the fourth wall was a walk-in closet. A king size, unmade bed took up one end of the room while the other held a desk and filing cabinet. Caitlin was drawn in that direction, where a number of framed certificates hung on the wall.

The phone rang, echoing loudly in the empty hallway. A moment later Patrick called up that the call was for Caitlin. She picked up the extension in the hall with a tentative hello.

"Hey, how're you holding out?"

"Janelle! Did you see the news?"

"Don't let it get to you."

"This is exactly what I was afraid of. You got me involved with this guy and I think I'm falling for him."

"That's terrible," Janelle mocked. "Next you'll be telling me that he's falling for you, too. Oh, the horror."

"I'm serious. You know it's only a matter of time before it all falls apart."

"You're getting way ahead of yourself. It's the fear talking."

"I can't help it. What if Sean never comes back?"

"Oh, sweetie, you gotta relax. These guys have loads of training. They watch out for each other. And Sean's been on the department over ten years. He helped train Scott. They aren't gung-ho thrill seekers, Caitlin. They're careful and never take unnecessary risks."

"But the news—"

"Just wants a sensational headline. Listen, I called to let you know not to expect Sean back anytime soon."

"You have heard something." Dread plummeted to the bottom of Caitlin's empty stomach.

"We have a scanner," Janelle reminded. "The fire is pretty much out but now there's mop up and initial investigating. Plus equipment to take care of. It'll be hours before the guys go home."

"Sounds so involved for a group of volunteers."

"They perform all the same tasks as paid firefighters. A fire doesn't care if the person putting it out is paid or not."

"Wow, you know about all this?"

"Knowledge is the best defense against that anxiety you're

feeling. Plus it helps keep my marriage together. Scott dances, I learn about firefighting."

"Seems like work."

"It's worth it."

When the call ended Caitlin wandered back into the master bedroom. The lavender aroma had vanished. Now the air was scented with Sean's aftershave. Breathing deeply, she drank in the mix of leather, wood, basil and moss. Keeping busy might take her mind of worrying. She moved to make the bed. Fluffing a pillow surrounded her again with the scent of Sean. She buried her face in the fabric, memories of Saturday night floating through her mind.

She sank onto the bed. What was she to do? It was too late to not become involved. Too late to not care for Sean. Maybe this was love, but was it true love? The kind of love that could stand the tests of time. How could she possibly know? She flung backward and smothered herself with the pillow. After a moment she rolled onto her side, catching her breath.

When she opened her eyes the room was darker. The sun had moved to the other side of the house. She must have fallen asleep. She sat up, disorientation fading quickly, and looked for a clock—already half-past twelve.

A door opened and closed downstairs. Voices murmured, boots thudded on the stairs. A bolt of fear shot through her followed by a rush of shame. She didn't belong in here. She had to get out before someone caught her.

Sean made it to the bedroom door first. He stopped, staring silently. No smile, no frown. No apparent reaction at all. It was unnerving. At last he spoke.

"What are you doing in here?"

I was worried and wanted to feel closer to you. No, she couldn't admit that. Telling him she'd fallen asleep while making his bed would sound foolish. Maybe she should tell him how she had invaded his privacy and read all his achievement certificates.

"Cat got your tongue?" He frowned. "It doesn't matter. I need to change so if you don't mind, I'd like to get into my own room."

He stepped back, allowing her to leave. The door closed with a bang. She flinched. A faint smell of burned wood wafted in the air. She sighed. Well, Sean was alive anyway. Pausing at the bottom of the steps she heard him walk down the hall. A moment later the shower came on. She grimaced, realizing the fire had come home with him, the smell of smoke clinging to his hair and clothing.

"Caitlin," Margaret called. "Come, eat something."

Tuna fish sandwiches were stacked on a platter in the center of the kitchen table. Caitlin helped herself to one and also a handful of potato chips. Patrick came in and grabbed a sandwich. When footsteps shuffled across the floor above, Caitlin glanced up. Margaret surprised her when she spoke.

"He'll probably shower at least twice. Says the smell of smoke won't wash out." Margaret shrugged. "I remember when Patrick first went overseas." The topic shift confused Caitlin. "The first few days I was so listless. We'd only been married a few weeks. I'd lay in bed for hours, too despondent to get up. Sometimes if I smelled his aftershave I felt like he was still there with me."

"Silly female." Patrick winked.

"Patrick," his wife admonished. "I happen to know you kept one of my scented lace hankies with you." Turning back to Caitlin she went on. "You've no experience with family going off into danger, do you?"

"My brother is in the Navy. I know he's in harm's way most of the time. Usually I don't think about what might be happening to him." She grimaced now with the thoughts.

"I suppose that's an effective defense against anxiety. So is holding close something belonging to the person you care about."

She'd been spotted, probably while she slept. "Seems silly, and inappropriate."

"Perhaps, but it's not as if Sean was in there with you."

Caitlin nearly choked.

"Margaret, don't tease the girl like that."

The older woman gave Caitlin a wink and an impish smile. "Puts it all in perspective, doesn't it." She got up to pour more lemonade.

Sean came into the room a moment later. His hair was still wet, lying flat on top of his head, curling at the nape of his neck. He wore clean jeans and a moss green t-shirt screen-printed with the campground logo. Passing the table without notice, he took a bundle of dirty clothing to the washer.

Returning with boots in hand, he sat and put them on. "I've gotta go snake a toilet," he announced to the room.

"Not before you eat," his mother scolded.

"I'm not hungry."

"Nonsense, you haven't eaten since last night." She slid the plate of sandwiches to him.

With a resigned sigh, he picked one up. Meeting Caitlin's gaze, he rolled his eyes, muttering, "Mothers." Caitlin giggled.

"I heard that young man. Someone's got to make sure you take care of yourself. Here, take this glass of lemonade."

Twisting to reach behind him, Sean grimaced silently.

"Did you get hurt?" Fear leaped in Caitlin.

"I'm fine. I don't want to talk about it."

"We saw on the news…" She stopped as Patrick shook his head.

Sean finished his sandwich quickly, draining the glass of lemonade. Standing, he looked around the room, anywhere but at Caitlin, eyes finally focusing on something behind her.

"I'll be down on Juniper Trail if anyone calls." He left without acknowledging her.

Margaret made *tch-tch* sounds and cleared the table. Patrick studied Caitlin.

"Let him be a bit," he advised. "Takes Sean time to let go, especially after a real bad fire." He rose, giving his wife a knowing glance. "Guess I'll go help him."

* * *

Stepping out for some fresh air a few minutes later, Caitlin leaned on the porch rail. It was unusually hot for early June. A soft breeze stirred the air, giving the day a drowsy pleasantness. The scents and sounds of summer floated on the breeze: the fragrance of nearby magnolia flowers, a chickadee calling for the bird feeder to be filled, the gentle murmur of voices. Suddenly Sean's voice carried clearly to her.

"Leave it be Dad. I can't talk to her, that's final."

Caitlin froze, stunned. That sounded like a lot more than winding down from a rough fire scene. He sounded downright angry. A sob pushed its way out of her throat. What happened to the man she thought was too perfect? All that kindness and consideration, had it vanished? Maybe it was all phony, put on to lure her to him.

Fine, if he didn't want to talk to her, two could play that game.

TWENTY

Sean glared at his father. He thought the argument was over. Hadn't he said he didn't want to talk about it, any of it?

"Son, you need to talk to Caitlin."

"Leave it be, Dad," Sean snarled. "I can't talk to her, that's final."

Dad shook his head. "Boy, if that's the way you feel then let me leave you with this. That girl is falling in love with you, but she can just as easily fall out of love. If you don't open up to her she's got no reason to believe you love her."

The elder Taggart left. Heart sinking, Sean watched him go. Dad was probably right. Caitlin hadn't even wanted anything to do with him in the beginning. Then she thought he was spying on her or something. Yeah, he'd convinced her to trust him but why should she keep trusting him if he wouldn't share things with her? Yet he couldn't talk to her, that's for sure. She went to pieces when it turned out her brother was okay. How could he tell her that he had been inside that house during the explosion? That he'd come close to serious injury. She'd freak out.

The rest of it...no, he couldn't even think about that old man. He sure as shootin' wasn't going to talk about it. Not with anyone.

Not even with God.

A few hours later he returned to the house. The clogged drain was more complicated than he'd hoped. The mess he made was almost worse than leaving the toilet plugged. By the time he'd cleared the pipe and cleaned the restroom, he was drenched in sweat and Lord only knew what else. He rinsed the worst of it off his hands with a garden hose but now he needed another shower.

A short hall beside the upstairs bath led to the ell and the business office. Heading for the shower, Sean heard Mom and Caitlin talking. He deposited clean clothes in the bath and peeked into the office. Caitlin sat in front of the computer, keying numbers and explaining what she was doing. Mom watched closely until she spotted him.

"You look a sight," Mom exclaimed.

He waved at his leaf-covered jeans. "Poison ivy, keep clear."

Mom smiled, Caitlin frowned. She hadn't spared him more than a fleeting glimpse when he came into the room. Oh boy, she was not happy. Had he been that curt? Thinking back to when he first came home, he thought perhaps he should try talking to her. He gave his mom a little nod and she took the hint, excusing herself to get drinks. He moved across the wide room, standing near Caitlin. She kept working.

"Mom talk you into doing the bookkeeping?"

At least she glanced up to respond. "I offered to give her a few tips. It's what I do, you know, teach math."

Ooh, chilly. But not frigid. "That's kind of you." He was rewarded with a smile, although it did seem forced. "Look, I'm sorry if I was brusque with you when I came home."

"You had every right to question me."

"I was surprised to see you in my room, but it's not as if I have some deep, dark secret in there." The comment was meant to be humorous but it came out lame. He hadn't even chipped the ice. "Well, just wanted you to know I'm not upset about it. I'm sorry for snapping."

She looked up with a piercing, ice dagger gaze. "I don't want to talk about it."

With her back turned, he got the impression he no longer existed as far as she was concerned. A taste of his own medicine, that's what it was. Did she think this would get him to talk to her about the fire? If she expected him to beg forgiveness, she was wrong.

* * *

Caitlin avoided Sean for the rest of the day. Margaret and Patrick shared meaningful glances but didn't interfere. Dinner was subdued, quiet, but not entirely awkward. After the meal Sean went to bed. Even as angry with him as she was, Caitlin conceded he must be exhausted. She retired early, too, sitting up with a book for a short time before crawling into bed.

She lay awake, staring at the ceiling. How could she possibly care for a man who wouldn't talk to her about the important events in his life? She'd seen him out there, talking to those other firefighters. Men. He'd talked to Scott, too. Being a mere woman, she wasn't worthy of hearing about something as manly as firefighting. So, it turns out Sean was a chauvinist. Just like her father.

The next morning Sean was up and out of the house long before she woke. She spent a few hours helping Margaret with the bookkeeping. In the afternoon Patrick bravely tried to teach her how to drive the old John Deere. After popping the clutch and stalling out several times, she confessed an inability to drive anything but an automatic transmission.

The atmosphere at dinner tonight was tense. Margaret and Patrick tried to engage both Caitlin and Sean in conversation. Sean grunted most responses. Caitlin stared at her plate, pushing peas around with her fork. A knock at the front door came as a relief.

"Caitlin," Patrick called from the front hall. "You have company."

Sean glanced up, a plate halfway into the dishwasher. She turned away. Let him wonder who was calling on her at this hour. He didn't have any right to know. Not anymore. Her shoulders sagged as she headed for the parlor. She longed for him to be at her side, providing support and security. She wanted to lean on him. He'd made it clear he couldn't lean on her. How could she trust him if he wouldn't trust her?

Eric Coffey stood in the center of the parlor. He smiled as she entered, stepping close to take her hands. He said nothing for a moment as his eyes swept her face.

"Are you doing okay?" he asked.

She forced a smile. "Never better. Did you find out anything?"

"You have dark circles under your eyes, Caitlin. I told you not to worry, I'd take care of everything." He steered her to the sofa and sat beside her.

"The alarm woke her last night." Sean stepped into the room. His rigid jaw and narrowed eyes matched the tense, arms-crossed stance he took.

"I'd forgotten about the fire. You okay?" Eric looked at Sean, leaning back in the sofa.

"Just dandy."

"Holly took good care of you as usual." A knowing smile lifted the edges of Eric's mouth.

Sean maintained his hostile pose. "You didn't come here out of concern for me. Did you find out anything about this Adam character?"

Eric shook his head, turning to focus on Caitlin. "Nothing useful. Raytheon has no record of Adam Massey in their Massachusetts locations. Lynn PD has your roommate's complaint on file but nothing that might help locate the suspect."

Sean shifted. Caitlin glanced at him. Why did he look like he wanted to throw Eric out of the house? And just who was Holly? She *took care* of Sean *as usual*. Was he already involved with someone? A woman he was willing to let into his firefighting life? When Sean caught her eye, Caitlin turned away hastily and swiveled to face Eric.

"If there's something you need to do, don't let me stop you." Eric crossed his arms, matching Sean's attitude. "This really only concerns Caitlin."

"I seem to recall it was my truck this joker defaced."

She slanted a look at him. Was he just angry about his truck? Didn't he care about her anymore? She looked down at her hands. Wasn't that the point of giving Sean the cold shoulder treatment? To chase him away before any more damage was inflicted on her heart. She bit her lip. Once Eric had enough information to track down Adam, she'd leave here. Someone must know something. Who, though? She tried to remember if Adam had been friendly with anyone else in their Bible study. A picture flashed in her memory and she gasped.

"I saw him at the bank once. He was in line behind me."

"That's good, Caitlin." Eric got out his notebook and wrote down the name of the bank. "Do you remember if he was making a deposit or a withdrawal? Maybe he had a paycheck?"

She shook her head. "I don't know. He said hello, we chatted about church and I left."

"I can work with this." He patted her hand. "We have a description out to all the area departments. I'm sure he'll be spotted soon."

"Thank you, Eric. I appreciate all the work you're putting in to help me."

Sean snorted. She kept her eyes focused on Eric. Let Sean act like a barbarian. She didn't care anymore. She stood and walked with Eric to the door.

"I talked to Marci again." Eric hesitated before opening the door. "She's got her mind made up that you shouldn't be teaching here. I'm sorry."

"Please don't cause trouble in your marriage over me."

"I needed to be sure she had nothing to do with those notes." He frowned. "I gotta confess, Caitlin. I lied when I said Marci was all I could want in a wife. Things were good at first, but lately she's been irrational."

"I'm sorry to hear that." Was he trying to excuse his wife's behavior?

"Just don't blame yourself for the problems in my marriage. Frankly, I'm worried about her. I'm thinking of getting medical help. Maybe therapy will bring back the woman I married."

"I'll pray for you, both of you."

Eric stepped outside and she shut the door behind him. When she turned, Sean stood in the parlor entrance, arms still crossed. The hostility eased as his face smoothed into a blank expression. He still didn't look very friendly. She tried to brush past him on the way back to the kitchen.

"The dishes are done. You don't need to keep helping my parents."

"I like your parents. At least they talk to me."

"Maybe I'd talk to you, too, if you didn't shut me out."

"You shut yourself out."

"What?" He dropped his arms. "I apologized for snapping and you turned your back."

"I'm not looking for an apology. I wanted you to talk with me." Her voice wavered with uninvited emotion.

"I am talking to you."

"No, you're speaking *at* me but you aren't talking *with* me. Obviously you don't want to share important events." She stared into his eyes, daring him to contradict. He stared back, fists clenching and unclenching. "This is exactly why I didn't want anything to do with you in the first place."

He pulled back as if slapped. She pressed her lips together, afraid more damaging words might escape. Silence lay heavy between them. Finally she spoke the thought she'd been fighting all day.

"I think it would be better for everyone if I went to stay in Groton."

"Groton?" He swallowed once, twice, his next words smoother. "With your sister-in-law?"

"Yes. I'll be safe, they live in Navy housing. You won't have to talk to me anymore."

She left the room as calmly as possible, keeping her back rigid and straight to fend off sobs. Mr. and Mrs. Taggart didn't deserve this tension in the house. The further away from Sean she got the better off everyone would be.

Once behind the closed guest room door she burst into tears.

Sean knocked a few minutes later. In a gravelly whisper he pleaded, "Caitlin, please come out and talk to me."

She covered her head with a pillow. He asked a second time then the house was silent.

* * *

Sean watched Caitlin stomp up the stairs, feeling sick to his stomach. She was leaving. That was it. Their relationship was over before it truly began.

She wouldn't open her door. Though he knew it wasn't locked, because there was no lock, he didn't go inside. Instead he went for a long walk, ending up in the barn.

What was he going to do? To get Caitlin to stay he had to talk about things he didn't want to share. He didn't even want to think about some of it himself. Surely it was unfair to present those images to her.

Yet how could he let her go? She probably would be safe. Although, since she didn't know what Adam did for a living there was no way of knowing where he could turn up. Could Sean use that to keep her here? *Lord, what should I do?* He waited, honestly expecting to hear an answer. What he heard wasn't what he'd hoped for. *Confess your fears, seek forgiveness.*

No, he would not beg Caitlin to forgive him.

* * *

It didn't take long to pack her things in the morning. When she turned to leave Sean was standing in the doorway. Arms hanging straight at his sides, he blocked her exit without menace.

"Please don't go."

"I have to. You don't care for me and I can't care for you."

"How can you say that?"

"You won't talk to me about the things that count."

"I do care for you, Caitlin."

"You say that now. But you won't talk to me about that fire. What else will you hide from me? You'll come home late one night.

Where were you, I'll ask. I don't want to talk about it, you'll say. Okay, dear." She narrowed her eyes. "Whose lipstick is that? I don't want to talk about it. My mother put up with that for way too long."

"I would never do that."

"You won't tell me about the things that matter now. How can I believe that you won't do those other things?" Caitlin folded her arms across her chest. She should confront him about Holly but somehow those words just wouldn't come out. Sean just stood there staring. How could he respond? He was basically an honest person so he wouldn't outright lie. His silence confirmed her belief.

"May I have my keys please?" She held out a hand.

"No."

"Sean, this isn't going to work. You can't force me to stay."

"I'll never force you to do anything. But I can't let you drive off alone. Someone is stalking you and we have no idea where he is or exactly what his intentions are." He gaze seemed focused on a point somewhere behind her, as if he couldn't stand to make eye contact. "If I keep your car, maybe this creep won't realize you've gone to Connecticut."

She sighed. He was right about that. It hurt, though, that he could talk about it in such a detached, rational way. As if he'd already let her go. "And what if Adam tries to do something more drastic to you? I don't want to put your parents at risk."

That brought his gaze back to her face. Not that she felt better with that icy glare focused on her. Sean crossed his arms, a muscle flexing in his jaw. Finally, he spoke again, continuing the pattern of ignoring things she'd said that he didn't like. "I'll drive you home. And then to Groton. Unless you've made other arrangements."

"That won't be necessary." She hadn't made any arrangements. Debbie, her sister-in-law, didn't even know she was coming. It was a two-hour drive she had no desire to make with him.

"Okay, but I don't leave until Scott shows up."

He assumed Scott would show up. And now she had no way to get in touch with him without Sean knowing. She'd have to wing it.

The house seemed foreboding, not welcoming. She unlocked the door, aware of Sean standing close behind her. He insisted on checking the whole house to be sure no one had broken in. Surprisingly he chose to leave her alone after that. She watched him crossing the street to examine the cornfield. Taking advantage, she called her sister-in-law. Debbie was thrilled with the idea of company.

Next she called Janelle. Scott would be out at a job site somewhere. She'd work out the details with Janelle.

"What are you running away for?"

Okay, first she had to make Janelle understand. After a few attempts at trying to explain, she gave up. "Please Janelle, let me take care of myself this time. I need to be away from here, away from Sean."

"For how long?"

"A week, probably. Even if this stalking thing isn't settled by then I'm coming home."

"Then what?"

"I'll have a security system installed. I'll get a dog. But I'm not giving up my life."

At last Janelle conceded. They decided Caitlin should wait at Janelle's house so Sean could leave. Scott would then take her to Connecticut in the evening, when he got home from work. Sean didn't like the idea of leaving her alone with Janelle. He reluctantly agreed when both women pointed out it was no different than Caitlin being left with his mother. Besides, he'd have her car so Adam would think she was still at the campground.

When he left, Caitlin turned away, refusing to watch him go. Janelle stood at the window.

"I can't believe he left. Just like that."

"It's over Janelle."

"Can't be, it never started."

Yes it had. Caitlin kept that thought private. Sean was so perfect. Hadn't she warned Janelle that sooner or later the real Sean would be revealed and then he wouldn't seem so wonderful? Oh how she wished to be wrong.

Throughout the afternoon she moped. She couldn't help herself. At one point Janelle tried talking to her, but she wasn't ready for that.

"Have you done that prayer thing you always do?" Janelle challenged.

Caitlin flopped down on the couch, burying her face in a

throw pillow, crying. Because she had prayed. She'd been praying since Sean left for that fire. And no matter how she prayed, what she said, the answer was always the same. If Sean wouldn't talk to her then she had to let him go.

TWENTY ONE

After leaving Caitlin, Sean drove around aimlessly. He didn't want to talk, especially to anyone he knew. About anything at all. Driving down Meetinghouse Road, he decided he wasn't ready to go home either. The church bell tolled the hour, three loud clangs scolding him: *Sean, Sean, Sean.*

Frowning, he made an abrupt turn onto Indian Rock Road. Rising and falling like a roller coaster, Indian Rock steadily climbed upward to crest at the top of Town Hill. The first settlement had been here, chosen for the panoramic view that was at once beautiful and defensible. Just before reaching the top, he turned onto a dirt fire road. Three hundred years ago this had been part of the original Bay Path, the road leading to the Boston Bay area. Even one hundred years ago it was still commonly used. Now it was abandoned, kept clear and passable only as a fire road access into Willow Brook Wildlife Management Area.

He drove carefully along the road. A sudden jolt reminded him that he wasn't driving his truck. About five hundred feet in, he came to a small, two-story colonial house. A large clear area in front of the dilapidated building served as an unofficial parking lot for hunters and fishermen using the wildlife area. He parked Caitlin's car close to the fire road, unsure of getting back out over the rough terrain of what once was a front yard.

This house had belonged to his great-great-great grandparents. Becky lived here for a short while with her husband, Tomas. People claimed the house was haunted but Sean knew better. Even if ghosts were real, Becky would prefer to haunt the house where her parents had lived, where Sean now lived. There she'd been happy. There she met and fell in love with Tomas. She gave birth to her son in that big farmhouse and, later, after she died, he was raised there by her family.

All this Sean knew about Becky because she left behind journals and letters. He knew more about a woman who died over a century ago than he did about Caitlin.

Sinking to the ground beside the front door, he leaned against the fading building, gazing upwards. Blue sky peeked through the canopy of trees, fluffy clouds floated lazily across the vast expanse of the heavens. Boston ivy, planted over one hundred years ago, thrived as it dug roots into the rotting clapboards. On either side of the front entry wildflowers grew as if in a planned garden—red and yellow columbine, blue bellflowers, and pink bleeding hearts. At the edge of the wood, partridgeberries and bunchberries crept along the humus, mingling their pink and white flowers. Scattered amongst the trees, mountain laurels were beginning to bloom. Closing his eyes, listening to the woodland sounds, Sean tried to let the peacefulness fill him. A single cricket chirping was a reminder of his own loneliness.

"Dear Lord," he prayed, "help me please. I need to fix this. Is it your will that Caitlin and I part ways?"

He waited, hoping for an answer. If only a voice from heaven would reach his ears. Once more, as last night, the answer came from within: *confess and seek forgiveness.* This time he understood. Perhaps it was the voice of his conscience but it was also a heavenly answer. It wasn't to Caitlin he needed to confess or her forgiveness he must seek, though that would come later. No, it was God to whom he must turn.

Lord, please forgive my stubborn pride. I come to you now to confess the fear which has kept us apart and to beseech you to forgive me.

He continued praying, talking to the Lord about all the things he didn't want to share or even face privately. Were the events at the fire scene his fault? Had his choices cost the life of the homeowner? If Sean had done what his partner, Richie, wanted to do—go out a window—they would've been out of the house before the explosion. Yet that side of the house was already engulfed. Getting a ladder to the second floor window would have been risky. But was the hall their best choice?

It was long dark before Sean returned home. Giving him a reproachful glance, neither of his parents spoke, for which he was grateful. Dad had been right about the consequences of not talking to Caitlin. She couldn't be falling out of love. Sean wouldn't accept that. *I can't care for you,* she had said, not, *I don't care for you.* There was hope.

Now all he had to do was tell her how wrong he'd been. To beg her forgiveness if that's what it took. Glancing at the clock he knew she was already in Groton. Ten o'clock at night wasn't a good time to call a stranger. Caitlin's sister-in-law probably wouldn't appreciate his sense of urgency.

Plus, he didn't know the phone number.

* * *

The next morning Sean slipped into the office while his mother cleared the breakfast dishes. Using an online phone directory he searched for J Harrington in the Groton area, getting six promising leads. Between various chores and duties, he called each of the phone numbers. And struck out six times.

What if the phone number was unlisted? Perhaps it was in James' wife's name. All at once he realized he didn't even know Caitlin's sister-in-law's name. A new online search using Harrington, no first name or initial, came up with sixty hits. He needed help. He dismissed his first thought immediately. Caitlin would never forgive him for involving her mother, even if she forgave him everything else. Irene Harrington would have to be saved as his last resort. Janelle came to mind next. She'd encouraged Caitlin to go out with him to begin with so she might help now. Then again, Janelle might hate him. And she was Scott's wife. Sean groaned. Bartlett would be making his life a nightmare if he didn't talk to Caitlin soon.

And above all else, talking to her took precedence. He realized now he hadn't wanted to talk to her because he hadn't wanted to talk to God. He'd been a world-class fool. If only he could find her to tell her that.

How many Harringtons could possibly be serving at that Naval base?

How do you tactfully go about inquiring without sounding like an idiot, or a threat?

He came back to Janelle. It was a risk he'd have to take. At least maybe if Scott knew he was trying he'd back off.

"Hey, Tag, you home?" Scott called through the screen door.

Sean cringed. Perfect timing, hopefully. Going to the back door, he let Scott into the kitchen. Scott was smiling. Must be a good sign. A Cheshire cat grin, but a smile nonetheless.

"How ya doin'?" Scott amiably slapped his bad shoulder.

Sean grunted. "Still a bit sore, but thanks for asking."

"That all that's bothering you?"

"I'm trying Scott, give me credit for that."

"Good, I'll cut you some slack, for now. Meanwhile, I'm on a mission to find chicken."

Chicken. Sean groaned inwardly. The Father's Day barbeque was Saturday and he was committed to helping. He wouldn't be able to see Caitlin until afterwards. Assuming he could find her and she'd want to see him.

"Nice little neighborhood down there where James lives." Scott chatted casually while they loaded his truck, as if reading Sean's mind. "Good for Caitlin to be there, too. Safer than anywhere up here."

Safer from who, Sean wondered. Finally he gave in and took the obvious bait. "Do you know how I can get in touch with her?"

The tailgate slammed shut. "Maybe. Don't know how she feels about it, though. Want me to pass on a message?"

Fat chance he'd spill his guts to Bartlett. "Tell her I'd like to talk."

* * *

The following morning Sean was miserable. He'd honestly hoped to hear from Caitlin. Surely Bartlett had talked to her by now. Maybe she really never wanted to speak to him again. To make matters worse it rained most of the day. Although the forecast called for clearing by mid-morning, business at High Peak Campground was slow. If this weather pattern of weekend rain kept up, his finances would have a serious crunch. Saturday dawned gray and dreary. The rain did stop, but the sun was reluctant to shine. Despite the weather, the chicken barbeque was on.

Firemen starting fires—the irony was not lost on them. With much good-natured ribbing the grills were lighted and soon the mouth-watering aroma of flame-broiled chicken filled the lot behind the fire station. By noon the line of waiting people was quite long. The first batch of chicken ready was welcomed with cheers. The line dwindled quickly. Soon all ticket holders had been served and the cooks sat down to enjoy meals of their own. Sean wasn't particularly hungry. He was slinking away behind everyone when Janelle grabbed him. She pulled him to a nearby table, pushing him into a chair.

"You look awful."

He raised an eyebrow but couldn't bring himself to give her a witty reply.

"You are miserable, aren't you?"

"Janelle, I'm not in the mood to chat. I think you'd be better off finding other company."

She studied him another minute. "Scott is trying to help. I want to be clear about that."

"Did he give Caitlin my message?"

"Yes." She sighed. "Cait either doesn't believe you'll talk or she isn't trusting Scott."

"Why wouldn't she trust Scott?"

"She's positive there's some sort of male conspiracy going on. She's miserable. I've never known Caitlin to be this upset. And since she blames me for getting you two together in the first place, I'm going to try to help."

"Will she listen to you?"

"Are you kidding? Right now, she trusts me less than Scott. No, I can't help that way."

Sean rubbed his forehead and pinched the bridge of his nose. "Then how?"

"With this," she offered a piece of paper.

Cautiously he took the paper, glancing at it. "A phone number?"

"Debbie would like you to call." She paused, taking in his confusion. "Caitlin's sister-in-law, that's her number."

He stared at the paper. Here was proof of angels watching over him. He felt giddy. Of course, Caitlin probably still wouldn't talk to him but that didn't matter. Not at this moment, anyway.

* * *

The phone rang five times before being answered. Sean glanced at the clock, hoping he wasn't interrupting dinner.

"Debbie? This is Sean Taggart. Janelle said—"

"Sean! Oh I'm so glad you called." At least someone was excited to hear from him. "Hold on a minute." Debbie's voice muffled, though he could hear her calling Caitlin. After a moment Debbie came back on the line. "Are you still there? Oh, good. She'll be just a minute. Don't go anywhere."

He chuckled. "I don't plan on it."

It seemed like much longer than a minute. Uncertainty raked through his stomach. At last there was a click on the other end and Caitlin's voice filled his head. She sounded gruff. She'd been crying.

"Caitlin," his voice caught in his throat, "I'm so sorry." On the other end she was silent. "Please believe me. I was wrong. I can't tell you how sorry I am." Silence. "Caitlin?"

"Please don't do this," she pleaded quietly.

"I'm not your father, Caitlin. I will never, ever be unfaithful to you. And I promise I'll never keep something from you again." Why wouldn't she respond? Although, the dead tone of her voice was barely better than the silence. "I'll tell you anything you want to know."

"You're only making this more difficult." The sound of her sobs abruptly ended with a clattering that hurt his ear.

"Sean?" Debbie's voice came back on the line. "Are you still there?"

"Yes." The word nearly stuck in his dry mouth.

"Try calling again, either later this evening or tomorrow morning. I'm a hopeless romantic, I know. Still, I'd bet my first born child that she loves you."

"Debbie, you are truly an angel."

She laughed. "No, I'm just trying to stop all this crying."

"Can I come down there? Do you think she'd see me?"

"I think that's a wonderful idea."

* * *

"Please Debbie," Caitlin pleaded. "I don't want to go out in public."

Debbie took up a chastising maternal pose. "You can be mad at Sean and even refuse to speak with him, but I'm not letting you turn your back to God."

Caitlin looked down at the fire department ball cap in her hands. She'd been toying with it off and on since Sean called, as if rubbing salt in a wound to remind herself not to trust him. "I can worship from here."

"But you won't." Debbie smiled, easing the harshness. She took the hat, waving it for emphasis. "As soon as I leave you'll curl up on the sofa and cry yourself back to sleep. No more. Either you talk to Sean, and I mean really talk, or you get on with life."

Caitlin's eyes followed the waving cap. "Please don't make me go out in public. I look awful."

"Yes you do, but it's nothing a good hot shower and a bit of makeup can't fix."

Reluctantly Caitlin trudged off to take a shower. Afterwards, the baseball cap had disappeared. She sipped coffee. Ah, that feels better. Until she thought about Sean. Then her stomach roiled, curdling the cream in her coffee. *Guess it's good Debbie hid that hat.*

"I love your hair." Debbie patiently braided it. "You know, when we first met I thought you were a cold fish."

"I have that effect on people."

"The better I knew James, the more I learned about your family. I sympathized with you. It's nice, now, to see you do have feelings."

"Thanks," Caitlin responded dryly. "I'm glad someone thinks this feeling is nice."

"You know what I mean, silly. There, done."

Caitlin looked over her shoulder into the mirror Debbie held. "Pretty. Thank you."

"We need to leave now, if we're going to be on time for service."

The Shepherd of the Sea Chapel was a short drive away. There were quite a few cars outside. Even so they had no trouble finding a space to park. Inside, they went straight to Debbie's customary pew without stopping to greet anyone. Waiting for service to begin, Caitlin's thoughts drifted back to Sean. She needed to do what was right, not what made her pride feel better. Prayer hadn't changed her decision, though. If he wouldn't talk to her now there was no way to trust he'd talk to her later, when it was more critical. She had to end their relationship.

He promised to talk. At least, that's what he'd said last night on the phone. Was she wrong, not giving him a chance? She might be letting hurt feelings keep him away. She could wall herself up again, hide behind an icy façade protecting her heart. It was the safe course of action.

Was it the right course?

Chaplain Oakes' voice cut through the fog of uncertainty surrounding her thoughts. "Please turn with me now to 1 Corinthians chapter thirteen. I'll read verses four through seven in a moment. But first, I'd like you to think about your earthly fathers."

The pastor paused a moment, letting each parishioner gather thoughts of their parent. He smiled. "My dad was a wonderful man. Of course, it wasn't until I was a father myself that I could fully understand how wonderful. Even so, he often had occasion to lose patience with me as I have struggled to keep mine with my children."

A smattering of laughter supported his sentiment. Caitlin smiled, too. Being a teacher had given her a healthy respect for the difficulties of raising children.

"Now, as I read these familiar passages I'd like you to think about your earthly father in contrast to your Heavenly Father. We, as children of God, often give the Lord good reason to be angered or lose his patience. Yet He sent us his Son, and we are all saved by the sacrifice of Jesus. As you go about celebrating Father's Day today, think about how loving our Heavenly Father is"

Chaplain Oakes turned to his Bible, glancing at the congregation to be sure all were ready for the reading. In those few seconds of waiting, Caitlin bowed her head. *Lord, I haven't ever thought of my dad as loving. Please forgive my selfish feelings. Even if those feelings are the product of my parents' bad marriage and their nasty behavior during the divorce. I'm an adult now, please help me to let go of the bitterness.*

Lifting her head, she smiled. A sense of peace and calm filled her. Forgiving her father had nothing to do with the issue of what to do about Sean. Still, letting go of the pettiness left her feeling light, closer to God and able to follow whatever path He chose for her. Chaplain Oakes began reading.

"'Love is patient, love is kind. It does not envy, it does not boast, it is not proud. It is not rude, it is not self-seeking, it is not easily angered, it keeps no record of wrongs. Love does not delight in evil but rejoices with the truth. It always protects, always trusts, always hopes, always perseveres.'"

The minister raised his eyes, allowing a moment of silence to accentuate the depth of the verses. When he spoke once more, Caitlin wasn't listening. Her thoughts spiraled around Sean and the topic of perfect love. Maybe forgiving her father did have something to do with Sean. She'd finally admitted to holding a grudge against Jack Harrington. She held onto the bitter hurt Sean had caused for the same reason. Refusing to let him apologize meant she could shut him out, avoid disappointment.

On the other hand, even if he apologized this time nothing guaranteed there'd be no next time. Was it a risk she was willing to take? The fact was, Sean couldn't be perfect. And that was okay, because Jesus was and no matter what happened with Sean, she would always have the love of her Heavenly Father.

* * *

"I'd like to speak with the chaplain." Debbie informed Caitlin at the end of service. "He'll be baptizing the baby and I like to keep him up to date on things."

Caitlin smiled. For the first time in a week she felt at peace. Somehow God would make this all work out for the best. Tomorrow she might be crying again but today she'd enjoy the beauty of God's love.

"I'll wait outside if that's okay."

"Are you sure? Would you like a cup of coffee, maybe a donut?" Debbie glanced around. "Most everyone will be in the social hall. I'm not sure you should stand outside alone."

"I'll be okay. This is a Naval base. How could Adam harm me here?"

Debbie cocked her head to the side, frowning. "We aren't actually *on base*." She made quotation marks with her fingers. "Anyone can come to this chapel."

Sun streamed through the glass wall behind the pulpit, flooding the sanctuary with light. The wood paneling glowed. It was impossible to believe evil could exist in the same space as this chapel.

"I'll go over to stand near the doors to the social hall."

"All right."

Caitlin watched Debbie waddle up the sloping hallway before walking to the chapel exit. Even with the abundance of natural light indoors, her eyes blinked rapidly in the brightness outdoors.

"Hello Caitlin."

The smooth, smug voice sent a chill down her spine. How could he be here? Turning slowly, she faced him.

"Hello Adam."

TWENTY TWO

Caitlin faced Adam, trying to project a calmness she didn't feel. "What a surprise to see you here."

"I'm sure. Why are you hiding from me?"

He was still the urbane, relatively attractive man she'd met a year ago, clean-shaven, wearing slacks and dress shirt, hair perfect and unmoved even by the slight breeze. Today he wasn't even pretending to be nice. Lips curled in a sneer, his eyes the color of storm clouds. It gave him an unappealing, deranged look.

"I came to visit my sister-in-law. Why should I hide from you?"

"Don't play innocent, Caitlin. I've been watching you. I know what a hypocrite you are, pretending to be all high-and-mighty pure, not interested in a relationship with any man. Ha, what a farce."

Forcing her smile to remain steady, Caitlin held his gaze as long as she could. Inside, she felt like a quivering puddle of grape jelly. Of course he knew about Sean, and was definitely taking it personally. The words carved into Sean's truck weren't a spur of the moment, petty act of jealousy.

Adam's gaze swept the area. "I see you've come to your senses and dumped that buffoon. Obviously he couldn't compare to me."

"No comparison at all." Completely true.

"Let's you and I go someplace and celebrate our reunion." He grasped her arm, propelling her along with him as he headed toward the far end of the parking area. "Now, now, don't struggle. I don't want to hurt you."

This can't be happening, it can't be real. She looked around at the half dozen people outside, most fellowshipping some walking to their cars. Going about their business oblivious to the kidnapping happening right under their noses. A furtive glance at Adam showed why. His face was the picture of pleasantness and he kept close enough to her that anyone would think they were walking

179

arm in arm.

"Let go of me!" She screamed. "Leave me alone."

Panic erased his smile. "Shut up, you tramp."

It was too late. People looked their way, second guessing their amiability. Still no one seemed inclined to come to her aid. How loud did she have to scream?

"Adam, you're hurting me. Help!"

He slapped her, the impact snapping her head sideways, but the pain was worth it. Two men broke off their conversation and headed toward her. As they came closer, she recognized one as her brother's neighbor. Seeing their determination, Adam let go of her and bolted across the parking area. One of the men took off after Adam. "Hey, you there," he called. "Stop where you are." Adam ignored him. The second man, her brother's neighbor, gently took her arm.

"Are you all right, ma'am?"

Caitlin gazed into caring eyes then turned to scan the parking lot again. Was Adam really gone? And how had he found her here? A tremor started in her arms, hands shaking. Her legs wobbled. The world took on an unnatural brightness even as darkness squeezed the edges of her vision. Her rescuer's arm came around her shoulders and he spoke soothing words.

"Deep breath, let it out slow. You're okay now." He searched her face. "You look familiar."

She gave him a trembling smile. "I'm Chief Harrington's sister. You live down the street from him. Lieutenant Field, right? James says you're the head doctor." She covered her mouth. Hadn't she caused enough problems without getting James in trouble too?

"Don't worry, Miss Harrington." Lieutenant Field smiled. "It's a joke he's shared with me. I'm the top dog in my office, and I'm a psychologist."

"So James thinks he's being clever?" She returned his smile.

"That's right. I prefer the title doctor, but you may call me Jeff. You're staying with Debbie, aren't you?"

His companion returned and indicated that he'd had no luck catching the assailant. All at once the small group of onlookers parted and Sean skidded to a halt. Amazement ground her thoughts to a standstill. The numbness broke with a jolt as she realized he'd come to rescue her, once again.

"What's wrong? Are you okay?" Those wonderful blue eyes searched her up and down.

"What are you doing here?" Her tears struggled to return.

"Is this the man who assaulted you, Miss Harrington?"

Turning to look at Jeff Field, Caitlin blinked several times to regain focus. Her mind filled with Sean. Why was he here? Was it a sign from God, and if so was it a good sign?

"No, he's," she hesitated, avoiding Sean's gaze. "He's a friend." Keeping her gaze turned away from Sean, Caitlin addressed the other two men. "Thank you for coming to my aid."

"I'd also like to know what happened." Jeff waved an arm toward the chapel. "Let's go inside and contact the police."

The Naval officers flanked Caitlin with Sean trailing behind. Debbie was alarmed when she saw the group. Chaplain Oakes suggested everyone move to his office. Jeff Field sat with Caitlin while his friend called the police before leaving. Debbie, despite admonishments from all, went to fetch coffee.

"We should probably wait for the police, so you don't have to go over this twice, Caitlin." Jeff Fields took control of the situation. "Someone should be here quickly. I want to be clear on one thing. Did this—Adam you said is his name?—did he injure or harm you in any way?"

Instinctively her hand went to where Adam had gripped tightly. "I may have a bruise, but that's all."

Jeff reached for her sleeve. "May I?" Nodding, she helped him push up the material. "Oh, yeah, I'd say that's gonna bruise."

The deep red impression on her arm already showed signs of discoloring. Glancing back up at Jeff, she wrinkled her nose in distaste. He smiled, eyes shifting to look behind her.

"And who's your friend here?"

She flushed. His tone and expression made it clear he assumed that Sean was more than a friend. She still wasn't sure what to make of Sean's presence here today.

"This is Sean Taggart. He's familiar with the situation with Adam, too." Risking a glance over her shoulder, she saw Sean standing with his arms crossed over his chest. All those things he said last night, did he mean them? Right now he looked as closed-up as he had a week ago.

When a female police officer arrived, she addressed her attention to Jeff. "What've you got here, sir?"

"We waited for you before going over it." Jeff turned. "Caitlin, are you ready? Please tell Officer Talbot what happened."

Carefully, Caitlin recounted everything, trying to remember details. Sean interjected to add explanations. A short silence punctuated the end of her statement. A hand landed softly on Caitlin's shoulder, startling her. Sean squeezed gently, silent encouragement and comfort. Her emotions jumbled up again. Closing her eyes, taking a deep breath, she focused on the matter at hand and reopened her eyes.

"He was wearing a short sleeve khaki shirt and black pants."

Jeff glanced quickly at Officer Talbot. Taking Caitlin's hand, Jeff gently rubbed the back in a calming gesture. "Think carefully. Are you certain? Did he have any insignia?"

Again she closed her eyes, trying to picture Adam, but no other details stood out. She met Jeff's gaze. "I don't remember any insignia of any kind, so probably it wasn't a real uniform."

Jeff nodded. "Very good, Chief Harrington would be proud of you. Your description sounds like a summer uniform, however, he may have just been trying to look the part, blend in."

"We'll comb the area as best we can, relying more on the suspect's physical description than clothing. I'll alert area law enforcement, as well." Officer Talbot turned to Caitlin. "It might be a good idea for you to stay put here for a few days. Perhaps it will help us catch this guy."

Debbie cleared their coffee cups. Caitlin watched her leave. "I can't do this to Debbie. I can't put her at risk."

Jeff shook his head. "I'd like to say she's perfectly safe with plenty of protective and watchful eyes. But I never would've expected something like this to happen here at the chapel."

"For the next few days I can arrange for increased security in your neighborhood," Officer Talbot offered.

Glancing at the police woman, Jeff nodded. "Good. Will you stay, Caitlin?"

She hesitated for another moment. "I guess, if that's best. What if you don't find him? Will you be able to keep Debbie safe?"

Sean squeezed her shoulder again. "Then you come home, Caitlin. Scott can arrange a place for you to be safe."

Scott? He wasn't offering or even suggesting he'd take care of her himself? So he hadn't meant those things last night. He made a promise he had no intention of keeping. Dipping her head, Caitlin hid her eyes from everyone.

"Please stay a day or two, Caitlin," Jeff requested. "Give us a chance. And pray we catch him. After Tuesday, if the police here haven't found this guy then you're probably better off at home, on familiar ground."

"I agree," Officer Talbot closed her notepad and left.

Caitlin exhaled slowly. How could they possibly hope to catch Adam? He was too good at disappearing. Sometimes he seemed more like a phantom than a real person.

* * *

Sean helped Debbie out of the car then walked behind them into the house, striding with his arms at his sides, not touching Caitlin. She chastised herself for wanting him to hold her. She'd seen the way he stood in the chapel, still closemouthed. He wasn't any better than her father no matter how much he denied it. Her earlier resolve to bask in the Lord's love and let Him take care of everything vanished.

Debbie went right upstairs. Out of habit, Caitlin shuffled to the parlor, sat on the sofa and hugged a pillow. More than anything she wanted to lie down and cry but there was no way she would let Sean see the effect he had on her. He'd come to say she was right and it was over. That must be why he wouldn't come near her now. Edging uneasily into the room, he hesitated at the sofa before moving to the recliner. When she dared meet his gaze, the tenderness in his eyes surprised her.

"I've never been so scared in my life." His voice was soft but gravelly. "If anything had happened to you..." As her tears flowed unchecked, Sean dragged his hands over his face. "I meant every word I said last night, Caitlin. Do you believe me?"

She wanted to believe him, oh how she wanted to. Yet how could she trust him? She pressed the pillow to her mouth to muffle the sob that escaped her lips.

"I was wrong, not talking to you. It's inexcusable but I'm begging you to forgive me."

Her weeping increased as she buried her head in the pillow. *Don't look at him. Don't look and this won't be so hard. Oh Lord, please make it better.*

"Caitlin, I was injured at that fire."

"I know," she squeaked.

"I didn't want you to worry the next time a call went out. But that's not what I didn't want to talk about."

He was telling her. Like he promised. She peeked over the edge of the pillow.

"All I'm asking is that you listen to me. If when I'm done you still don't want anything to do with me, I'll leave. If it's what you want I'll never bother you again."

The force of Sean's statement brought her head up. Slowly she sat straight, taking in his expression—a sheen of moisture in pleading eyes, a jaw muscle twitched. His clasped hands, fingers laced together, pressed against his mouth as if he'd said too much but feared it wasn't enough. Okay, she'd give him a chance. Just one.

"What didn't you want to talk about?"

"You know the man who lived in that house, Donald Prescott, died?" He waited for her to nod. "I was the one who found him, and I'm pretty sure he was still alive."

His voice grew quieter, more tentative. With each sentence he laid himself open, became vulnerable. This man she thought of as strong and confident was slowly revealed as someone with weaknesses and insecurities. Human.

"He was breathing, I'm almost certain. The fire was encroaching rapidly, we had to move fast to get out alive. My partner, Richie, wanted to go through the window. We would've had to cross the room and already the fire was coming through the wall. The hallway leading to the stairs was mostly clear. Only a bit of smoke stood between us and safety in that direction."

"You chose the stairs?"

"Getting a ladder to that window would've been dicey. The flames were on that side of the building. I knew with fire coming through the adjacent wall that the next room was engulfed. There was a chance opening the window would feed the fire. At least, that's what I thought."

For a moment Caitlin pictured what he described, fire leaping across the room to consume all three people. She shuddered. It was good Sean knew what he was talking about.

"I carried Mr. Prescott. Richie led the way. We almost made it out." He stopped, searching her face as if uncertain how much detail to tell. She trembled, afraid to hear what happened, how he was injured. Yet he was here, all in one piece, so it couldn't be too bad.

When he didn't continue, she prompted, "What happened?"

"The whole house gave a big shudder and wood started falling." Seeing her confusion, he clarified. "There was an oxygen cylinder, apparently at Mr. Prescott's bedside. It exploded."

"Was that when you got hurt?"

"Yeah. I don't remember much after the initial boom. Something knocked me down. Next thing, Richie's yelling and my PASS device is screeching."

Sucking in a breath, she forgot to let it out. His lips formed a tentative smile. "I'm still alive," he said softly and she breathed out again.

"Later I found out part of a wall smacked into me, knocked me down. I ended up fairly well covered with debris. Mr. Prescott was thrown clear of the rubble and Richie carried him the rest of the way outside."

"And you? How did you get out?"

"They tried carefully removing the debris but the blast had fueled the fire to the point we all needed to get clear immediately. So Scott yanked me out. That's what popped my shoulder."

"Did you have to go to the hospital?"

"Nah." He shook his head, grinning. "It dislocates now and then. Hasn't in years but it's not such a big deal. One of the EMT's popped it back into joint and I'm good as new."

She shuddered again. A chill ran down her spine. The visual images his words evoked—particularly Sean buried in a burning house—were too disturbing to think about.

"I don't like fires."

"Me either." His dimples deepened.

Warmth washed over Caitlin, a sense of contentment that Sean wasn't holding anything back. Or was he? There was still one thing, one name, she really needed to know about. She stared at her hands. "Who is Holly?"

"What? Why would you ask about Holly?" Surprise spiked Sean's voice up an octave. Caitlin closed her eyes, held her breath. At last, Sean spoke again. "Oh, yeah, Coffey mentioned her. Is that why you left? Did you think there's something between me and Holly?"

Now his tone held a barely contained chuckle. Caitlin snuck a peek at him through her lashes. He wore a big grin, shaking his head as if having just heard the most unbelievable story. Her jaw clenched as angry heat replaced earlier contentment. How dare he make fun of her fears? Raising her head, Caitlin speared Sean with her gaze.

"What was I supposed to think? You wouldn't talk to me, about anything. And you still haven't answered my question. Are you hiding something?"

He gave a short bark of a laugh, cutoff perhaps by the glare with which she pinned him. Abruptly, Sean wiped a hand over his face, wiping away the smile, and blew out a short breath. He cleared his throat, looking fidgety. Guilty.

"I'm sorry, Caitlin. I shouldn't laugh." Leaning forward, elbows resting on his knees, hands clasped, he met her stare with a gaze full of compassion. "Of course you have no idea what to think about Holly. Well, you can relax. She's one of the town's EMTs— an actual nurse, really. She doesn't respond to every fire, of course, but she's popped my shoulder back in on several occasions. The chief likes her because she usually gives me a lecture for not going to the hospital. I like her because even with the lecture, she lets me not go."

Caitlin sat back. He *likes* Holly. What was that supposed to mean? She crossed her arms, maintaining the cold glare. He reached for her hand but she scooted away, just out of reach.

"Please, Caitlin," he edged forward in the chair, settling a hand on her knee. "I meant it, I'll never be unfaithful. And I may have trouble talking about some things but I'll always be honest with you. I promise." He exhaled long, slow. "Holly is a friend and nothing more."

"No? Why not tell me about her sooner, then?"

"Well, for one thing, you and I weren't exactly communicating." He raised an eyebrow and Caitlin couldn't squelch the grin tugging on her lips. "Plus, I didn't want you worrying which meant I couldn't tell you the extent of my injury. If it'll help, as soon as we go home I'll take you to meet Holly. You'll like her—she treats me like a child."

"That sounds good." Caitlin let the grin bloom into a wide smile. After a moment, something he'd said at the start popped into her thoughts. "You said the injury wasn't what you were keeping from me."

He took a deep breath, as if preparing to plunge into turbid waters. "Mr. Prescott was dead when Richie got him outside. Being thrown half-way across the house was the final straw."

"So why does that upset you? I mean, it's sad and tragic but there must be more to it."

"The fire moved too rapidly. I should've realized it was an oxygen-saturated environment. If I had shut down the tank valve, things might not have gone haywire. If we'd gone out the window, Mr. Prescott might still be alive."

"But he might not have lived. It was a tough decision, possibly with no good answer."

"I failed, Caitlin. There's no way around that."

"How can you say that? You got out alive. Mr. Prescott's obituary said he had emphysema. He probably would've died either way."

"I didn't save him, that's how I failed." His gaze became hard. "I'm not a firefighter for the thrills. You think I'm an adrenaline junkie but I'm not. I hate fires. With every fiber of my being I despise fires. I do what I do to help people. And I didn't help Mr. Prescott. I failed."

There must be something she could say to help bring him peace. "The fire didn't spread to other houses. So you helped those people."

"I sat in the ambulance, watching everyone else fight the fire."

"Well, what if you did smash the window and the fire rushed into the room. You all could've been killed. Or the explosion may have been worse, injuring a bystander."

Sean sighed. "I was so wrong, Caitlin. So very wrong. Can you ever forgive me?"

"You didn't kill that man, Sean." Her mouth snapped shut. It was the first time in days that she'd said his name without crying.

"I was wrong not to tell you about this. I couldn't face you because I didn't want to face God. I still believe I caused Donald Prescott's death. It's something I'll have to live with. When I finally 'fessed up to the Lord I realized what a fool I was."

"You're not perfect."

"No, I'm not even close."

"You're pretty close." She flashed a smile then ducked her head. "I have issues with keeping secrets. My father is a great one for secrets, and for making promises he never keeps. Well, almost never." With her mind and emotions settled once more, she remembered she'd forgiven Jack.

"I don't know any other words to use. I care about you, Caitlin. A lot. From the first time we met I haven't been able to get you out of my head. I know this is something I have to work at, convincing you to trust in my promise. All I ask is that you give me a chance."

A chance, exactly what she'd decided to give him. And hadn't she already accepted the fact that Sean couldn't be perfect, only God was perfect? Love keeps no records of wrongs. Who was she to contradict scripture? Sean stood, holding his right arm stiffly.

"Does it still hurt?"

"Yeah, it's pretty sore. Like I said, I've popped my shoulder a few times over the years. Never had a wall drop on me before. Got a real nasty bruise. Wanna see?"

She shook her head no but whispered yes.

He unbuttoned his shirt and gingerly slid it off, revealing a wide bruise that stretched across his shoulder blades in the ugliest shade of puke green and putrid yellow. She touched the edges, pulling back sharply when he winced.

"I strictly forbid you to ever get hurt again."

"Yes ma'am." Looking over his left shoulder he winked.

Impulsively, Caitlin brushed her lips over the bruise. "A kiss to make it better."

Sean turned, dropping his shirt and wrapping an arm around her waist. He pulled her close. She looked up, meeting his mouth with her own. His hand caressed across her shoulders, fingers sliding beneath braided hair as he cupped her head. Caitlin molded to him, palms flat on his warm, bare chest. She went limp, barely aware of his grip tightening, holding her up. When at last the kiss ended, Sean kept his arm around her. She leaned on his strength as he spoke softly.

"Now that's a kiss to make it better."

TWENTY THREE

"You can come home any time. Adam isn't in Connecticut," Scott announced when Sean answered the phone on Monday.

"How do you know?" It was mid-afternoon and all had been quiet at Debbie's. No Adam sightings or any suspicious activity.

"Eric had a break-in this morning."

"Coffey? He's a cop."

"Yeah, you'd think that'd be a deterrent but not with our boy," Scott said dryly.

"Was anyone hurt?"

"No, Marci was out shopping and the kids were at school. Coffey was on duty."

"How do you know it was Adam?"

"Pretty obvious." Scott cleared his throat nervously. "You're gonna need a new truck."

Closing his eyes, Sean groaned. "Why?"

"Well for starters, Adam slashed the tires, cut your seats to ribbons, smashed the windows, and took a sledgehammer to the side panels."

"That's to start with?" Sean cringed at the image.

"Drove a screwdriver through the gas tank, repeatedly. Punctured the radiator, and ripped the tail pipe off. There's not much left of the engine. Well that's not true. All of it was in the garage but most of it wasn't in your truck." Scott snickered. "I think Adam's mad at you."

"Ya think?" Sean took a deep breath and let it out slowly. "Has Dave finished the security system at Caitlin's?"

"Says he'll be done by this evening."

"I guess if Adam's up there another safe night here wouldn't be a bad idea."

"Sounds pretty good. Ah," Scott hesitated a moment. "Do you want me to see about someone keeping an eye on your folks tonight?"

Oh, Lord, please keep them safe and out of this. "I'd appreciate that."

"They're probably not in any danger. You're the one Adam wants dead. And make no mistake about it, that's what he wants. He's not out to just hurt you and he's done with trying to scare you off."

* * *

Caitlin stared at the keypad, listening as Dave Montigue, the security expert Sean had hired, explained the procedure once more.

"All right now, think you've got it?" The older man turned to her. She nodded. "Good, show me. Arm the system."

Punching the required codes, Caitlin went through the process of arming, then disarming the system. An electronic rendition of "Fur Elise" began playing. She grabbed the cell phone clipped to her pocket and grumbled hello.

"Hey, it works from here!"

"Hi, Scott. Where are you?"

"Up at High Peak. Put Tag on."

She squinted, looking across the yard to the shed where Sean should be. She couldn't see him. "Call his phone if you want to talk to him."

"Ooh, touchy. Is he even there?"

Scott's lighthearted tone irritated her. He probably loves this. Caitlin with a security system and cell phone, Scott's dream come true. Mentally she kicked herself for being so critical and negative. This wasn't Scott's fault.

"Hel-lo, Cait? Is Tag there?"

"Yes," she sighed. "But he's across the street and I'm still busy with the alarm."

"Okay, I'll call his phone."

Caitlin clipped the phone back onto her pocket. "I hate these things."

"I hear ya. My work depends on 'em though."

"Apparently my life does." She made a face and Dave smiled, patting her hand.

"Let's hope it doesn't come to that. The Naultag PD had thrown out a pretty thick net. Eric Coffey's determined to get this guy."

Dave, Caitlin had learned, was a retired state trooper. He still hung out with area cops and knew what he was talking about. Since retiring he'd run a successful security business, mostly installing alarms in all the new houses in the area. Caitlin trusted his advice.

"Listen," Dave spoke in a paternal tone. "If you get into trouble away from the house, head straight for the State Police Academy. Don't take trouble to Sean's doorstep. Those troopers at the academy barracks are well equipped to make sure you're safe."

"Thanks Dave, I'll remember that." She smiled. He knew the places she'd be traveling to on a regular basis. Most, like the grocery store, were public and reached by heavily trafficked roads. Her one vulnerability would be visiting Sean, because no matter how she approached the campground she'd have to travel lonely back roads.

"Might be best if you didn't go out there at all," Dave added.

"I refuse to give up my life."

Dave shrugged. "Sean would be more than happy to come here instead."

Caitlin looked away, glancing again at the shed. "Sean's the one Adam wants to hurt. He's in more danger than I am."

Dave scrutinized her expression until she shuffled uncomfortably. "This Adam wants Sean out of the picture, no doubt of that. Make no mistakes though, young lady. Adam may not kill you outright but he certainly intends to do bodily harm."

The icy hand of fear squeezed Caitlin's heart. She fought the sensation of helplessness. Adam would not harm either of them. She trusted the Lord's protection. Still, it was frightening to think the extent one man could negatively affect so many people.

"Just be careful." Dave squeezed her hand.

She kissed his cheek. "You're a sweetheart, Dave. I'll be extra careful, okay."

Dave left. Outside, she heard him yell to Sean. "Tag, your turn. Let's discuss personal security."

She snickered. Sean was set against changing his lifestyle because of Adam. Well, she had to get a cell phone the least Sean could do was make a few minor changes to his routine. From the front entryway she could see across the street. The corn in the field was stretching, the ground barely visible between each row. Sean had been working on the tractor. His silhouette filled the shed doorway as he waited for Dave to cross the road.

Closer to the house the vegetable garden showed signs of neglect. The weeds were growing quite well and even from here she could see the tomatoes needed to be staked. She'd planted a border of marigolds in Gram's memory and now they needed deadheading. Only a few bright yellow pompoms showed amongst the brown, gone-by flowers. And the lawn—no, she wasn't even going to think about the lawn. The house was almost as badly neglected. Thankfully she'd closed all the windows before leaving, preventing dust from settling indoors. Even so the rooms needed vacuuming and dusting. And airing out. Not today, though. It was too hot to think about housework. Besides, they still needed to get something for Sean to drive. She wanted her car back.

When Sean came inside after talking with Dave, he looked downright grumpy. Caitlin felt a stab of guilt for thinking Sean should make changes. After all, he wouldn't even be in this situation if it wasn't for her.

"I'm sorry."

Sean drained a glass of ice water before responding. "Why, because it's finally hot outside?"

"About all the hassles."

"You're the one with a new electronic fortress."

"Well, then, I'm sorry about your truck."

Crossing the room, Sean planted a kiss on her forehead. "If you need a reason to be sorry, then I accept your apology. Now let's go get me a new truck."

He watched closely as she armed the security system. "Changed your password yet?"

"Yup."

"Do I get to know it?"

"I haven't decided." She smiled coyly. "You did tell me not to trust you."

"Oh, you are funny." He frowned.

"You're grumpy. What did Dave say to you?"

"Nothing."

"Oh, took him twenty minutes to say nothing?"

"Okay, okay," He grinned despite his grouchiness. "Nothing I didn't already know."

"Ah," she nodded. He opened the car door for her. "Can you really afford to buy a new truck and pay for my security system?"

"I'm not buying a new truck, I'm renting one. And in a few days I'll rent a different one. I'll keep changing every few days until we find Adam."

"See, that is a lot of hassle."

"You're worth it."

At the Ford dealership, Sean chose an Explorer. "Black, something completely different."

Caitlin laughed. "I have noticed blue seems to be a theme for you."

"Maybe next I'll get one of the convertible Mustangs."

"We don't rent those, Tag," the salesman said. "Perhaps you'd like to buy one?"

Sean looked at her, raising an eyebrow in question. She shook her head negatively. "Sorry, Steve. I'm beginning to suspect I've got me a pick-up girl." He winked at her.

* * *

Caitlin dived off the dock, swimming a few yards out and then back to shore. She was content to sit with Janelle, plunking their lawn chairs down at the edge of the water. At this time of day there was little boating traffic and the water was still but for small ripples made by the breeze. Lazily splashing at the gentle waves, Caitlin watched Sean swim.

Slicing obliquely into the water, he disappeared, surfacing far out in the lake. Shading her eyes, she watched as he swam out a good distance before turning back. He pulled himself up onto the end of the dock, flopping onto his back to catch his breath. With the sun sinking behind her it was easy to study Sean as he stretched out. His legs draped over the end of the dock, feet gently swishing the water below. Sunlight sparkled in droplets of water along his flat abdomen. He could sunburn out there with no sunscreen. His arms showed a clear demarcation where his shirtsleeves normally ended, the skin on his lower arms deeply tanned.

After a moment Sean put an arm under his head, rolling slightly to look across at her. Their eyes met and held. He had told her that she was the most beautiful woman he'd ever met. Could she find the courage to tell him that he was the most attractive man that she'd ever met?

Unexpectedly Scott shot up out of the lake on the far side of the dock, dumping a pail of water on Sean's stomach. Sean came to his feet instantly, only to have the twins open fire with their water guns. Ducking the water streams, Sean leapt into the lake, piercing the surface cleanly. The water smoothed quickly, showing no sign of his passage.

When he didn't come up for air, Caitlin sat straighter,

watching with growing concern. Minutes ticked by. Scott swam around to her side of the dock. The boys moved to the end, searching the lake. Fear gripped Caitlin. Was the lake deep enough for Sean's dive? If he struck bottom and was injured surely his body would have surfaced. A chill slithered down her spine.

"How long could he possibly hold his breath?"

"Not this long." Janelle also scanned the lake surface. Suddenly she snickered, shushing Caitlin's concern. "Wait a minute," she whispered.

Then Caitlin saw Sean. Fear evaporated in light of his cleverness. A slight stirring of water showed as he moved out from under the dock. Abruptly, Scott jerked under the water, spluttering as he resurfaced. Sean was already charging the dock, hands thrust out, sending a massive wave splashing over the boys.

Sean disappeared again, but Scott had caught on. They set about a game of splash and dunk, with the twins cheering equally for both men. In the end it was clear neither had won. Scott crawled onto the dock, tapping water out of his ears. Sean swam slowly to shore, rolling his shoulders as he came out of the water. His wet hair lay flat in a long shag on his neck, until he shook his head, then the curls sprang to life. Flinging himself onto the sand beside Caitlin, he lay back with a groan.

"I'm gonna regret that."

"Poor baby," Caitlin teased. "Want me to kiss it and make it better?"

Sean sat up. "Yes, I do."

Deliberately she came out of the chair and walked around behind him. She gave his shoulder the lightest kiss. "There, all better."

He caught her ankle as she moved away. "It didn't work. Try again."

Glancing at Janelle, Caitlin found no sympathy. Looking back to Sean, she tried appealing to him with her eyes. Using his free hand, he tapped his lips. His other hand moved up her leg, pushing the back of her knee.

"Stop it," she warned. "I'll fall over and hurt you."

He gave another tug on her leg and down she went, arms out to brace herself. He caught her deftly, falling gently back onto the sand. Their eyes met. His were full of humor.

"You're incorrigible."

"Guilty. Now kiss me."

* * *

"You have to go home now, Cait." Scott said. "You too, Tag. I need to go to bed."

Caitlin stirred sleepily. They sat on the deck, overlooking the lake. Stars filled the black sky overhead, reflecting in blurry streaks on the water below. Sean's arms wrapped around her as she lay back against him.

"Make him go away," Caitlin mumbled.

"I wish I could." Sean kissed the top of her head. "But he's right, it is getting late."

Reluctantly she pushed off the chaise lounge, shivering at the sudden loss of Sean's warmth. Groaning, Sean stood and rubbed her arms. She tilted her head to look up at him.

"Does your shoulder hurt?"

"Just stiff from sitting so long. It'll be okay. I'll follow you home to make sure you're safe."

"What about you?"

"I'll call when I get home."

Walking out to their cars, Caitlin was struck by a feeling of dread. Not truly fear or even worry. Just a sense that this might be their last happy day together.

TWENTY FOUR

Sean expected to be busy all day but they'd made plans for him to come over for dinner. Caitlin spent the morning weeding the vegetable garden. In the afternoon, she tackled the house. Dusting, vacuuming, mopping, even washing the windows. By four-thirty the place was spotless. Pushing the vacuum aside, she sank into the recliner with a satisfied and exhausted sigh. Only a few minutes passed when a car pull into the yard. Sean must've gotten away early. She bounced up to greet him at the door. A police car sat behind hers, Eric Coffey strolling casually toward her.

"Oh, hi Eric." She tried to keep the disappointment out of her voice, opening the door to let him in. "What brings you here?"

Eric smiled warmly, brushing by her. His eyes went to the security system key pad, studying it for some minutes before responding to her question. "I wanted to be sure you were doing okay. Heard about what happened in Connecticut."

"And I heard about your break-in. Sorry for causing you so much trouble."

He waved off her concern. "Not your fault. I see you had an alarm installed. Smart move. Looks like a good system."

"Sean's friend Dave Montigue put it in. You must know Dave."

"Sure, we all do. He's the best at what he does." Eric shifted, eyeing the living room windows. "Looks like Dave's got you covered."

"I hope so. Would you like a drink? You must be hot in that uniform." She moved toward the kitchen. "Sean'll be here soon. I'm sure he'd love to touch base with you."

When she turned around, soda in hand, Eric wore a frown. Catching her eye, he smiled brightly, thanking her for the drink.

"I haven't talked to Tag personally about the truck yet. How angry is he?"

Caitlin shrugged. "Hard to tell. I think he doesn't want me to worry more than he's upset about the truck."

Eric nodded, digesting her words. "You two are getting pretty close."

"I guess so," she hedged, a little uncomfortable. Talking about their relationship was difficult enough with close friends. It felt awkward with a casual acquaintance like Eric. Tires crunched on the gravel driveway. "Here's Sean now."

Sean was almost running when she opened the door. She smiled and his pace slowed. Coming up the steps he kissed her quick before turning his gaze to Eric.

"Got scared there for a second. Everything okay?"

"Just having a drink with Caitlin." Eric lifted the soda can. "I should get back to work."

Caitlin walked Eric out while Sean went to get himself a drink. At his car Eric paused, glancing back at the house and placing a hand on her arm. "Be careful, Caitlin."

"I will, Eric. Thanks for checking on me."

She watch him leave, puzzled. There was something different about Eric's voice today, or maybe it was his general attitude. His parting caution made her worry that perhaps Eric also felt the futility of their search for Adam. Hopefully he wasn't giving up. Sean came up behind her. She gave him a bright smile before voicing her thoughts.

"That was strange."

"Why? Eric's being a good cop."

"He wanted to talk to you about the truck, but then he didn't once you got here."

"Guys don't like to chat with each other about their feelings. And that's all there'd be to talk about. How I feel about my truck being trashed and how he feels about having his garage broken into."

"I suppose." She peered around him. "Did you get the propane tank?"

"Yes ma'am." He retrieved the small gas tank from the back of the Explorer. "Let's do some grilling."

* * *

"What was that you prayed?" They were nearly done eating when Caitlin's curiosity finally got the best of her. "When you said grace, I didn't understand a word of it."

"Ah," Sean smiled. "You didn't ask so I thought perhaps you did understand."

"I'm asking now."

His smile broadened as he chucked her under the chin. "You're pretty when you pout."

"I'm not pouting." She tried to spear him with an angry stare. He laughed, not the reaction she was going for.

"Yes you are. Relax, I'll tell you what I said." He took a long drink of lemonade. At last he lowered the empty glass. "It's Irish. About the only Gaelic I know. *Beannaigh sinn , a Thiarna , do na do bronntanais a bhfuil muid ar tí é a fháil ó do rath, trí Chríost ár dTiarna. Amen.*"

The words sounded poetic. All frustration at his teasing evaporated as she listened to the words rolling off his tongue. "What does it mean?"

"Bless us, O Lord, for these your gifts which we are about to receive from your bounty through Christ our Lord. Amen."

"You don't know any more Gaelic?"

Sean shook his head. "My grandfather taught me that when I was a little boy."

"Did he speak much Gaelic?"

"Not much. Snippets here and there, sometimes whole phrases like that prayer."

"Was your grandfather from Ireland? Did he teach Gaelic?"

"No, he was a farmer from right here in Naultag. He learned from my grandmother. She was an Irish girl, I mean really Irish not Irish-American. They met during the second world war."

Caitlin smiled. "So you're Irish-Irish-American."

"Guess you could say I'm very Irish-American. My great-grandfather married a girl from Ireland, too. And my great-great-great-grandfather, Tomas, had been in America only a few months when he met Becky."

"You know your family heritage quite well."

"You should see the family tree in our Bible. It goes on for pages." Cocking his head, he considered her for a moment. "What about you?"

"I never knew my great-grandparents. Gram and Grampa didn't talk much about their deceased relatives. I do know the Baxters moved to this area around the turn of the last century."

"How about the Harringtons?"

Caitlin half shrugged. "My father's parents disapproved of my mother, said she ruined him. They had very little to do with us."

"Just holidays and special occasions?"

She stared past Sean. "No, not even holidays. My father would sometimes try to get them to talk to me. Grandfather Harrington occasionally spoke. I think he was trying, maybe. My grandmother never spoke directly to me. She called me 'that impertinent little brat.'" Laughing lightly, her eyes settled on his. "At least she noticed me. I'm sure I was quite impertinent."

Sean smiled. "What about your brother? Did they talk to him?"

"Nope, he was the reason for my father's ruination. Grandmother's words," she added. "When James was referred to, he was called by names I'd rather not repeat. Mom, too. For a supposed well-bred, upper crust type, my grandmother knew some pretty crude language."

"That's too bad," Sean said sadly.

"Don't feel sorry for me. I never knew them, really. And I had Gram and Grampa Baxter. They more than made up for the Harringtons."

She slapped at a mosquito and tried to smile nonchalantly. Another mosquito buzzed her ear. Smacking a hand against her head brought on a momentary headache. She grimaced.

"You better get inside." He brushed yet another mosquito off her arm. "You're too sweet."

He carried a stack of plates to the sink while Caitlin brought in their glasses. She stared out the window as the basin filled with hot soapy water. Slowly her eyes focused on movement. A red sedan pulled into her yard. Would Adam be so bold?

"Sean?"

"I heard." He placed the salad dressing in the fridge then moved to the hall. "It's okay."

She recognized the man approaching as one of the men Sean spoke to the day after that fire. Worry unsettled her stomach. Scott told her Sean wasn't in trouble. Was this man here to confirm Sean's belief that Mr. Prescott's death was his fault? What would happen to Sean?

"Hello, Chief." Sean held the door open. "Come on in."

"You're a hard man to find these days, Tag." The Chief smiled warmly, turning to Caitlin. "And this must be Miss Harrington."

"Just Caitlin," she said. Sean looked at her quizzically. Her nervousness must be showing clearly. His smile was soft, gentle and reassuring.

Caitlin eyed the older man. His weathered face was crinkled with care and laughter. He wasn't much taller than her but a good deal heavier, with a round paunch overhanging his belt. He bore the air of one used to command and friendliness. His warm smile was infectious.

"It's nice to meet you, Chief." She took his outstretched hand. It was rough, calloused, the hand of a working man.

"*They* call me Chief." He nodded his head at Sean, indicating all the firefighters. "You may call me Darin."

She liked this man. He was flirting, but harmlessly. And he had a manner about him, an undercurrent of confidence maybe, that said he watched over his men. Anyone looking to keep Sean safe was okay in her book.

"Tag, I've got something to discuss." Darin held up a sheet of paper, one eyebrow raised, tilting his head toward Caitlin.

She frowned slightly. Perhaps she was wrong. All these men were the same—secretive. Sean took in her disapproving look and grinned. He waved an arm at the living room.

"Anything you need to say to me, Chief, can be said in front of Caitlin." Glancing at her again he added, "We don't keep secrets."

"Good man." Darin slapped him lightly on the back. "Took you're time coming 'round." He leaned close to Caitlin. "He's a bit thick-headed at times."

She giggled. "Only at times?"

"Hey, I heard that." Sean glared playfully. "She's just as stubborn."

"A match made in heaven." Darin chuckled. "I think you'll both like this."

Sean took the proffered paper, reading it deliberately as he sank onto the sofa. At last he glanced up and handed her the page. He explained as she looked it over.

"The autopsy shows Donald Prescott died of heart failure. Before the fire started."

"The fire didn't kill him?" Caitlin looked from one man to the other. The chief nodded.

"I thought he was breathing." Sean turned to Darin.

"You wanted him to be alive. No one enjoys finding dead

bodies. You have a natural rescue instinct."

Mirth bubbled in Caitlin. She'd seen that instinct in action on numerous occasions.

"So I rescued a dead man," Sean said dryly.

"Better than thinking you caused his death."

Sean looked up sharply. "How'd you know that?"

The chief's lips curved slowly. "You shut up tighter than a clam when something's bothering you. Now, if some*one* bothers you, you get right in their face."

He turned to Caitlin, wearing a stern look. "You remember that now, miss. If he clams up there's something eatin' him."

"He's not allowed to clam up. Never again, right?" She eyed Sean.

"Yes ma'am." Sean ducked his head in mock submission.

Darin chuckled again, rising to leave. "He will, but don't you let him get away with it."

"Shouldn't you be on my side?"

"She's much prettier than you, Tag," the chief said by way of explanation. He took her hand. "It was good to meet you, Caitlin. I hope we'll be seeing more of you."

They stood in the door and watched him leave. Sean dropped an arm around her shoulders. His hand on her arm gently squeezed and he fairly bounced on his toes. He was giddy. Good news looked better on him than anything she'd ever seen him wear.

TWENTY FIVE

When the house phone rang Thursday morning, Caitlin answered it absently.

"Caitlin," Eric Coffey spoke on the other end. "I've got some interesting information about this Adam character. I'd like to share it with you and Tag."

"That's great, Eric. Do you have a lead on where he is?" Her heart raced with hope.

"A pretty good idea. Listen, I'm over near High Peak. Why don't you swing over here and I can talk to both of you at once?"

"Okay. Let Sean know I'm heading out right now."

Grabbing her keys and purse, Caitlin sprinted out the door, almost forgetting to set the alarm. Maybe this stalking nightmare would be over soon. She drove down Maple Street to Route 9, sticking to main roads as long as possible. Before reaching Lake Road, she noticed a big black truck behind her. It rushed up to loom over her bumper then backed off slightly, still technically tailgating. *It's just an impatient driver, no need to be afraid.* But when she turned onto Lake Road, the truck followed and her nervousness grew.

Making a quick decision, she circled around to Main Street and headed for the center of town. *Don't take trouble to anyone else's doorstep,* Dave Montigue had told her. It was wise advice. So she drove to the police station, located on the ground floor of the town hall.

The small parking area beside the police department entrance was empty. Suddenly she remembered the rest of Dave's advice and understood—go to the State Police Academy, he'd told her. Because Naultag's police force was small and apt to be out of the station, patrolling the town. At the academy there would always be troopers on hand.

The black pick-up drove by as she turned around in the police station parking lot. She tried to remember how to get to the State Police Academy from the center of Naultag. Finally deciding on her best option, she drove up Main Street, turning onto Summer. A block later the black truck was once again on her tail.

All the way down Summer Street the truck stayed at a respectable distance. Still she had no doubt it was in fact following her. Accelerating slightly, the car hurtled around the tight curve onto Menameset Road. Caitlin increased her speed, driving as fast as she thought she could handle on the twisting road. It wasn't much farther to the academy. Besides, if she got pulled over for speeding then at least she'd be with a cop, which would chase Adam away.

She thought the pick-up was gone, or at least out distanced, when suddenly it reappeared. He came up to her in a rush, filling her rearview mirror with chrome grill. He loomed there a moment before hitting her bumper. She jerked, barely keeping the car steady. Heart racing, she fumbled with her purse until the cell phone tumbled out. The truck dropped back and she had time to flip open the phone and push 9-1-1. As the operator answered the truck rammed again. Caitlin yelped. He dropped back, not quite so far this time.

"Ma'am?" the operator called through the phone. "Are you all right?"

"No, he's trying to kill me."

"Where are you?" The voice remained calm.

"Menameset Road, almost to the State Police Academy."

"I'm sending help at once. What is your name?"

This time when the truck hit, he stayed there. She heard his engine revving deeply and knew it was much more powerful than her little economy car. He began pushing her. Abandoning the phone without disconnecting, she struggled to maintain control. Should she try the brakes? A glance in her mirror only showed the gleaming grill, looking like a menacing shark ready to bite. Nope, brakes wouldn't work. That truck was too much bigger.

Abruptly he backed off again, playing cat and mouse. Coming out of a shallow dip in the road, she spotted the academy on the horizon off to her left. She hit the gas, hoping this short but steep hill would give her a slight advantage. At the top the road curved slowly right. She barreled on, now driving on the wrong side of the road. Once more the truck gained on her.

He hit the corner of her trunk, sending her careening out of control and off the road. The shoulder dipped and, as she pushed both feet down on the brake pedal, the car slid on its' undercarriage like a toboggan on gravel.

A tree rushed to greet her. She screamed.

* * *

"Sean, you have company." His mother's voice squawked over the intercom.

He looked out the office window, hoping to see Caitlin's car. Instead, a red truck with Bartlett Construction stenciled in tan on the door parked in front of Dave Montigue's black and gray utility truck.

When Scott and Dave came into the office from with the store below, Sean directed them into the conference room. He waited for one of them to start the conversation.

"Heard an interesting rumor," Scott began.

"I don't care much for rumor." Sean scowled.

"You'll care about this one. Remember how Eric said Marci was out shopping when the break-in occurred? Well, Marci filed for divorce last week and on Saturday she left."

"Saturday? You'd think Eric would've noticed." Sean leaned forward, intrigued.

"She took the kids and moved into her sister's place. Says she caught Eric cheating."

"Coffey? She caught him?"

Scott shrugged. "I guess she's suspected it for a while because he'd go away, supposedly for business, almost every weekend. Then she found out it wasn't police business."

Sean shook his head sadly. "They should try to work it out not throw away eight years of marriage."

After hearing the rumor, Janelle called Marci, Scott explained. Apparently Marci confronted Coffey, accused him of having an affair with Caitlin. Sean remembered the afternoon of the Asparagus Festival. Marci had locked Caitlin in the church basement. Now he understood why. Janelle said Marci complained that Eric constantly talks about Caitlin. She'd even found a scrapbook with newspaper clippings of stories about Caitlin, going back as far as high school.

"Scott called me," Dave piped up. "I agreed it was worth checking into."

"Because, how would this Adam guy know where to find your truck?" Scott added.

Dave continued. "Until the middle of last month, Eric Coffey hadn't worked a weekend shift in over a year. Plus he often called in sick when scheduled for either Monday night or Tuesday morning."

"Are you suggesting…" Sean grasped the implication. "Wait a minute. The descriptions are way off. Coffey's short, barely the same height as Caitlin. She said Adam is taller than her by a couple inches. And the hair—Adam's is jet black and medium length whereas Coffey has brown hair which he keeps buzzed off."

"The eyes are different, too."

"Right, thanks Dave."

"I'm not trying to help you, Tag." Dave opened a file folder, revealing various printouts and note pages. "Good elevating shoes can add up to four inches to a man's height and look like ordinary shoes."

He showed Sean a printout from a website picturing several styles of such shoes.

"With enough money, an excellent quality wig can look real. Especially when worn over a nearly bald head. Maybe if Caitlin had been physically attracted to Adam and ran her fingers through his hair she might have thought it felt different. Maybe not."

Another page showed a number of different hairstyles, all of them wigs.

"And eye color is about the easiest thing to change, with contact lenses. All these things can be obtained on-line."

"It all fits, Tag, when you look at this from the right angle." Scott slapped his hand on the conference table.

Sean thought about it carefully. Eric Coffey was willing to believe in a prowler even before being presented with evidence. Eric knew when the police cruiser would be driving by. In fact, Eric always knew where Caitlin was, until she went to Connecticut.

Why would Eric offer to investigate? To throw off suspicion, perhaps. Having failed to win her affections as Adam, was Coffey trying to gain gratitude by rescuing Caitlin? Losing his wife and seeing Caitlin slipping away yet again, it was reasonable to think the man would snap and take out his frustrations on Sean's truck. After destroying it on Saturday he went in search of Caitlin. And when that failed, Eric blamed the truck on Adam. Made sense.

Dave added his last thoughts, confirming some of what Sean was now thinking. "As Adam he struck out, again. It could be that he thought to scare Caitlin and then come to her rescue. She'd have to love him then."

"I was thinking that myself." After a pause Sean shook his head. "It would never have worked, though."

"Coffey doesn't understand that." Scott leaned forward emphasizing his words. "It was always about him. He never bothered to figure out anything about Caitlin."

Silence filled the room as Sean accepted what they were telling him as truth. At last he spoke. "What now?"

"Now Eric wants you dead," Dave informed him. "And he's in a position to get what he wants. We need to collect proof, legal evidence and have him arrested. In the meantime, you need to consider ramping up your personal security."

"What about Caitlin?"

"I'm not sure." Dave sighed, frustrated. "They have profilers to figure out guys like this, ya know. What I can say with certainty is that you and Caitlin are the talk of the town. A lot of people saw you together at that dance—including Coffey. He's can't be happy about it at all. If he thinks she'll love him instead, we have time. But I don't think even a sick mind could believe Caitlin is going break it off with you as long as you're alive."

Sean sat back in the chair, a thrill shooting through him. Caitlin was probably in love with him. His heart beat a little faster then the jubilation crashed down, overshadowed by the certainty that he was a marked man. If Coffey really was Adam, and the evidence pointed to that being true...

Dave nodded grimly. "It's bad. You have to die now. He might feel the same about her."

Picking up the phone, Sean dialed Caitlin's house. His insides were in a knot and getting more knotted with each ring. He started counting. At ten rings he hung up and dialed her cell phone. Busy.

Scott's phone rang. Glancing at the caller ID he answered without stepping away. "Hi honey...When?...Don't panic, I'm sure it's kids drag racing." He glanced at Sean. "Busy for how long?...I'm with Dave now, we'll take care of everything...Janelle, don't worry...Yes, I'll call you back."

Dave was looking at a text message on his phone when Scott ended his call. "Your wife heard it on the scanner?"

Scott nodded. "Is it her?"

"Is what who? You mean Caitlin, don't you?" Sean was on his

feet, ready for action. Scott's handheld scanner toned, the sharp shrill followed by several beeps. The sound was echoed distantly by Sean's radio in the other room. Ordinarily it was a call to action. This time, the alarm froze him in place.

"Sit down, Sean," Dave ordered. "The State Police are already on scene. I'll get the details." He dialed his phone, moving well away from them.

"What scene?" Sean felt ill. Whenever Dave used his first name he knew it was serious.

"Car accident," Scott had turned his scanner off. Apparently, Janelle had already supplied enough information for him to answer. "Near the academy, small gray car."

Sean's head dropped. *Dear Lord, please don't take her away from me.* Realizing how selfish that sounded, he added, *Lord, please protect Caitlin and keep her safe.*

Dave returned. "Her car, yes," he confirmed. "But she's not in it. On the bright side, there's no sign of significant blood loss and it appears the car hit the tree at a reduced speed."

Sean was already on the stairs, barely hearing Dave's words and only just registering the fact that the other two were following him.

* * *

Caitlin groaned. Everything hurt. Where was she? There was a grating sound, metal on metal. Slowly her eyes opened. It didn't help much. She was surrounded by whiteness.

"Caitlin, are you okay?"

It all came back in a rush. She was in her car and this thing around her was an airbag. Already it was beginning to deflate. Her chest ached as she gasped great gulps of air.

"Eric?" Her voice cracked. She tasted blood. Her lower lip was swelling and her nose felt like she'd been punched.

Eric pushed past the airbag. "Are you hurt?"

"Oh Eric, I'm so happy to see you." She didn't even try to stop the tears. "He was trying to kill me."

"I know," Eric said remorsefully. "I'm so sorry."

Eric Coffey slid an arm around her, gently easing her toward the open door. When her arms were free she flung them around his neck, burying her face against him, crying. Terror and relief mixed in the flood.

"It's okay now." Eric stroked her hair. "I'm here now. You're safe."

Gradually his words sank in through her sobs. His voice was soft, soothing, wrapping her in calm. He caressed her hair and rubbed her back as he spoke tender words of comfort.

"I'll take care of you now. Everything will be okay."

There was nothing wrong with the words. It was more the way he said them, breathing softly in her ear. Suddenly she was aware of how closely Eric held her, pressing her against his chest. Her sobs subsided. Eric lifted her, scooping her out of the car. He carried her easily and for the first time she noticed how muscular he was. He continued speaking compassionately in her ear. She didn't move, afraid to see where they were going. Something felt wrong.

"Here's my truck," he told her. "Let's get you inside now, honey."

Slowly she turned her head. Did he call her honey? Catching sight of his face, she inhaled sharply. He was gazing upon her in utter adoration. Before she could react further, Eric kissed her. It was a quick, hard kiss with none of the loving feel of Sean's kisses. Her split lip felt further bruised.

"In you go." He slid her into the truck. "Buckle up now, *dahlin'*."

She was too stunned to protest. What was happening? The seat belt stretched across her with a click. He kissed her again, smiling. It wasn't a happy or joyful smile. It was lascivious. And his voice...when had Eric ever drawled like that? Something cold went around her ankle followed by a short series of clicking noises.

"A little insurance." Eric's odious smile was disturbing. "Can't have you jumping out while I'm driving."

Turning her eyes away from him, she finally noticed his truck—a big black pick-up. The one that ran her off the road. Paralysis gripped her, made her senseless, robbed her of speech and action alike. *Think, Caitlin, think.* She forced herself not to shut down.

"Where are we going?" she whispered at last.

"Someplace safe, honey."

"What's happening here?"

He laughed, a bitter, sardonic sound. "You still don't know? Oh, dear sweet Caitlin."

Tears flowed anew. Closing her eyes, she began praying. *Lord,*

I don't understand what's going on. Please let everything be okay.

Wiggling her foot, she realized the series of clicks had been the sound of handcuffs closing. She was a prisoner, chained to the seat. How could anything ever be okay again?

* * *

Sean stared at the car sitting on the flatbed. Dave said it hit with reduced speed, even so the front end was accordion pleated. He'd seen worse, much worse, but this was Caitlin's car. He could almost picture her lifeless body pinned behind the airbag.

"You can see here where she applied the brakes," a state trooper told Dave. "Braking like that, plus the fact her car bottomed out going over the shoulder edge probably saved her life."

Probably. Sean didn't want to hear probabilities. He wanted to hear that they knew something, like where Caitlin was. Even deflated and crumpled the airbag looked ominous with its reddish brown streak of blood.

Dave came over, patting Sean's back paternally. "Airbags pack a punch, you know that."

"I know." He sighed. "It was probably a bloody nose. That doesn't change the fact that it's her blood. Worse, I know about the bruised ribs and breastbone. Her legs could be broken. Just because there's no blood, except that little bit on the airbag, doesn't mean Caitlin isn't badly injured." He groaned. "Where is she, Dave?"

The other man eyed him closely. "Wish I could tell you, Sean. Really wish I could."

Scott hustled over. "You hear about Coffey? He's AWOL."

"Is that why the Staties rolled on this?"

"Well, that and the fact she's about a quarter of a mile from the academy. When Caitlin called 9-1-1 they were closest and it made sense to send a car to investigate."

"Who's here from town?"

"Tom Jacobs was first on scene. He was over on the other side of town." Scott waved a hand, vaguely indicating the various police officers near the crash scene. "When dispatch couldn't raise Coffey, Jacobs got the call. Chief Masiello got here right before us."

"He's coordinating with State Police," Dave added, looking over at the chief of police talking with the state trooper in charge.

Scott nodded. "They've issued a warrant for Coffey's arrest. And I heard someone say Cait left her phone on and 9-1-1 has a recording of Eric taking her out of the car."

"Caitlin still doesn't know Eric's the one who's been stalking her." Dave shook his head. "I hope she keeps her cool when she figures it out."

TWENTY SIX

The scanner squawked with another description of the truck.

"Well, looks like your boyfriend is brighter than I thought." Eric sneered.

Caitlin kept her face turned away from him. Tears trickled from her eyes and she brushed them away. He drove the truck along yet another back road, much like the others they'd been traversing since leaving the accident scene. Trees overhung the road, some reaching out to scrape at the side of the truck.

Eric used to be gentle and caring. As he drove, his behavior flipped wildly from the tenderness he'd shown when he first rescued her to angry, sardonic outbursts. His tone reminded her of someone. Of course his voice was familiar. They'd known each other since ninth grade. Her gut churned. At the edge of memory the truth lurked. She tried to focus but thinking made her headache worse.

"Where are we?" she asked in a subdued voice.

"Half-way between your place and his. I found the perfect little hideaway. You're going to love it." His caustic laugh sliced through her pounding head.

"You know what I'd love, Eric? If you'd tell me what's going on." She held her breath. How angry would her boldness make him?

"You're so naïve, Caitlin."

He slowed the truck, turning onto what appeared to be a logging road. Scrub brush scratched at them as they passed. The town had changed a lot in the past ten years but she recognized this trail.

"This leads to Devil's Elbow Road."

"Very good, A+ for the teacher."

A throbbing ache started at the nape of her neck and settled behind her eyes. She closed them, hoping against hope it was all a nightmare. Praying that when she opened them again none of this would be happening.

"I warned you, Caitlin. Men and women can't be just friends."

She stilled. Eric was Adam? It couldn't be. His appearance was too different to ever have made the connection. Though his voice always stirred a memory, she had dismissed it because they were friends. She was wrong. She opened her eyes. This nightmare was far worse than she ever imagined.

"You should never have been friendly with Taggart. Now I know you aren't such a pure and good girl."

Suddenly Eric slammed on the brakes. She hurtled forward and stopped short as the seat belt tightened. That hurt. The airbag in her car had bruised her breastbone and ribs. A whirring sounded above, growing louder and then slowly droning into the distance as a helicopter passed overhead.

"Lucky for us it's still daylight." Eric chuckled. "They'd have spotted the headlights even with these thick trees."

After waiting a moment, they moved forward again. The truck inched carefully over the shallow drainage ditch that separated the trail from Devil's Elbow Road. This was the far end, away from the few houses and not far from the old stone bridge that had been built over three hundred years ago. In the early days of the original settlement this was an important thoroughfare. After several Indian attacks, the settlement was abandoned and when people returned to the area they built new roads.

Eric pulled the truck to the side of the road just before the bridge. The structure was wide enough for the truck, and to the best of Caitlin's knowledge it was still maintained so should hold the truck's weight as well. Why stop here? There weren't any houses around. Perhaps this hideaway of Eric's was actually a glade in the woods.

"Your new love nest is over the bridge," Eric instructed, as if reading her confusion. "Come, let me show you."

He unlocked the cuff around her ankle but before she could even contemplate running he snapped another onto her wrist, holding the other end like a leash.

"Great thing about being a cop." Eric smiled smugly. "I can get just about anything and no one questions it. Handcuffs? Sure, of course you need an extra pair or two. Handgun? What caliber would you like, Officer Coffey?"

She shuddered. He laughed.

"Demolition explosives," he continued taunting, "for a joint training exercise with the fire department? Of course, no problem Officer Coffey."

She began to hyperventilate. Explosives, what was Eric planning to do? *Calm down. Keep your wits about you.* Somehow she had to find a way to escape. Hysteria would hold her captive as effectively as the handcuffs. Taking a long breath elicited an involuntary wince. Oh man, her ribs hurt. She sucked in as much air as possible, slowly letting it out of her lungs.

The road on the western side of the bridge was a dirt lane. It went steadily uphill before leveling off as it passed through a small clearing. Through the trees the sinking sun highlighted a grassy meadow. Even short gasps hurt, as did her legs which were also bruised in the crash. Eric slowed as they climbed, incongruously considerate of her discomfort even while he verbally badgered her.

Vaguely Caitlin remembered this part of town. There was a house in the clearing, a modest two story colonial building. An old shed had long ago fallen in, bittersweet vines and poison ivy covering the remains. People said the house was haunted. High school kids often dared each other to go inside. She stared at the faded façade, noting rotted wood even from this distance.

"Isn't it beautiful?" The sarcasm in Eric's voice was unmistakable. "The great part is who owns this place. What irony, to die in your family's ancestral home." He took note of her confusion. "You are dense, woman. What did I ever see in you?"

His exasperation vanished with a leering snicker. "Except a great body, of course."

She whimpered. Nothing that was happening made her think things might turn out okay. One minute he was her rescuer, the next he's making lewd and suggestive comments. And clearly he intended to kill someone—she was the most likely candidate. Pushing open the door, he pulled her into the house. The interior was dark. Boards covered broken windows. The door looked to have been nailed shut at one time as well. Affecting an attitude of a real estate agent, Eric showed her around the house.

"Downstairs we have a spacious kitchen and dining area, and over here a parlor. The bedrooms are upstairs." He winked, steering her in the direction of the dilapidated stairs.

She planted her feet, refusing to move even when he tugged on the handcuff. He glanced back, laughing menacingly as he yanked harder. She jerked off balance and stumbled against him.

Holding her close, Eric searched her expression.

"Why can't you love me, Caitlin? If you say you love me and not him, I'll let you go."

She had no doubt he was lying. He'd never let her go. She stared back, tears in her eyes and determination in her heart. Disgusted, Eric pushed her away.

"Hypocritical tramp."

"I am not a tramp." She couldn't help arguing, defending herself, even though it only made him more agitated.

He dragged her to the large fireplace in the parlor. Shoving her into the wide firebox, he clipped the free end of the handcuff to an andiron.

"You forget, I've been watching you," he growled. "That maggot spent the night with you after two dates."

"He did not!" She met his disdain with a raised chin.

He snorted. "Come on, Caitlin, I was there. That night and the next morning. And so was Taggart. You expect me to believe he stayed outside all night? He was right there in your kitchen and you were still in bed. Slut." He spat the insult, glowering.

She dropped her gaze, head bowing. "We did not sleep together. Not then, not ever."

"Right, and I suppose you're going to tell me he slept on the sofa in Connecticut."

"Yes, he did." She stopped herself from adding that unlike Eric, Sean was a gentleman. It probably wouldn't help. "Why, Eric? Why are you doing this? Why invent Adam?"

He was busy with something near the front door. When he finished, he systematically poured gasoline over the floorboards. He seemed to have some sort of a design in mind, tracing an invisible pattern with the noxious liquid. As he shook out the last few drops, he replied.

"You should've gone to the prom with me, Caitlin. We'd have been a wonderful couple."

"But you have Marci now, and your children." She kept her voice calm and soothing.

"She was always second best. And a nag." Rage made his face livid. "Don't even get me started on those brats. I wouldn't have married that whore if she hadn't gotten herself knocked-up. Entrapment, that's what it was."

Got herself knocked-up? It would be foolish to point out that it took two people to get pregnant. Eric obviously felt he was blameless. Even if he didn't love Marci, surely he must care for his own children. Yet he spoke as if they weren't his kids, his flesh and blood. Had Caitlin truly made him insane simply because she wouldn't date him? The pulsing pain in her head jumped up a notch. Gas fumes gave her a queasy feeling and aggravated her breathing difficulties.

"Why Adam, you ask." Eric spoke more calmly after venting his fury about Marci. "Isn't it obvious? You'd recognize me. Adam is tall, dark and handsome, just what all you girls like."

All at once she had a horrific revelation. The only boy she did anything with in high school was Scott. They never dated. In fact, she used to fix Scott up on dates. But they were always together. He'd reached his full height of six three by senior year. And though Scott's hair wasn't jet black like Adam's, it was dark nonetheless. Eric, as Adam, was trying to be Scott. He thought that was what she would be attracted to. She'd never been attracted to Scott. It made this whole thing doubly worse.

"We could've had a great love affair, Caitlin. But you still thought you were too good for me. Or maybe you already had a thing for Taggart?" Eric's acerbic voice drew her attention.

"I didn't even meet Sean until after moving back here."

As soon as she said it she knew it was a mistake. Maybe it confirmed her disdain for Eric, or punctuated the fact she fell in love with Sean so quickly. Whatever the reason, Eric was incensed. He stormed around the old house, making adjustments to little devices placed here and there. She couldn't quite see what he was doing. His final work was devoted to the doorway into the parlor. Carefully he threaded tubing into the gap beneath the threshold, the intricacy slowing his irate actions. Satisfied, he gently replaced the molding and stood.

Ever play paintball?" Adjusting the contraption standing in the corner, he calmly conversed as if he hadn't just kidnapped her. "Wonderful sport, so like real warfare. In fact, the military uses paintball mortars similar to this." He patted the two-inch PVC tube device. "Of course, their mortars spray paint and cover a considerably larger area than I need worry about."

A deep thumping in the distance grew louder. Her heart leaped. The helicopter was coming back. Surely they'd see the truck this time. The aircraft came over low enough to cast a shadow across the open door. Eric didn't seem the least bit concerned. He looked pleased and grew calmer. He smiled, giving the mortar one more check.

"All I need is coverage in this room. And it won't be firing paint balls, either."

Looking closely at the paintball mortar, Caitlin realized what Eric had been doing. James had taught her enough about weapons to know the device was triggered by compressed gas. Paintball participants used a handheld push-button trigger attached to a length of hose. Eric had probably jerry-rigged the trigger, using the doorsill as a pressure plate.

Apparently amused with himself, he went out of sight, circling the downstairs. He stopped at each window. At last he came back to the fireplace. Back to her. He wore a deranged smile again.

"Time to make a memory." He pulled a cell phone out of his pocket. Flipping it open he pointed it toward her. "Smile, baby, this one's for your lover."

"He's not—" the phone clicked.

"Aw, now you weren't smiling." He took several more pictures before closing the phone. "Thank you, you've been a lovely model." Crossing the short distance between them, he unlocked the handcuff from the andiron, yanked her out of the fireplace and snarled, "Let's go."

At the parlor entrance he carefully directed her to step over the threshold, confirming her suspicions. "Don't want a premature triggering incident," he sneered. Caitlin's heart stopped a moment as the implication finally made sense to her fear-numbed mind. He'd rigged the house with explosives. Her sharp intake of breath caught Eric's attention.

"I've prepared an outstandingly spectacular welcome for lover boy," he scoffed. "When he goes into that house to rescue you— BOOM!"

She flinched, glancing back as they left the house. Tears blurred her eyes. She stumbled.

"Oh don't fret sweetheart. The explosion won't kill him. In fact it'll hardly be more than a little firecracker." A breath escaped her. Eric laughed. "Yup, he'll be fine after that initial explosion. Fine enough to go searching for you. By the time he realizes you aren't in there, all those little charges will have started such a fire that he can't possibly escape. I made sure, even added a back-up."

Oh no, please Lord, no. "How…" she faltered. "How do you know he'll come?"

"Because you're going to call him."

They were back at the truck. Absently he cuffed her to the side mirror as he pulled the phone out again. "I'm going to send these lovely pictures to lover boy. He'll recognize the house right away. After all, he still owns it. I'm sure the Staties could see my truck on that last fly over, they'll send a cruiser to check it out. By the time a car makes it down here, we'll be gone. Well, I will be anyway."

With another sinister laugh Eric dialed the phone and pressed it to her ear. It rang three times. When Sean answered, she felt weak, unable to speak. Impatiently Sean again said hello.

"Oh Sean," a sob choked her words.

"Caitlin? Caitlin, where are you? Has he hurt you?"

"Sean don't—" The phone whisked away.

"Hello, Taggart," Eric's voice dripped with disdain. "I've sent you an interesting e-mail."

"Don't come Sean! I'm not there!"

Eric closed the phone, ending the call before Caitlin finished crying out. His eyes narrowed, jaw line tensing.

"That wasn't nice." He forced the words out between bared teeth. Brusquely he took the handcuff off the mirror. He twisted her arms behind her and cuffed her wrists together. Grabbing a backpack, he pushed her down the road, away from the bridge. A short distance away, he shoved her into the undergrowth beside the road.

Surreal images, unnaturally bright and crisp assaulted her mind. Low-bush blueberries lined the roadside, white bell-shaped flowers promising an abundance of fruit later in the summer. As they moved uphill, away from the marshy area, the drier ground was carpeted with wintergreen and princess pine. And everywhere poison ivy clung to trees or snaked across open spaces in search of new places to root.

A little bit off the road were the remains of an old root cellar. Eric gagged her, forced her into the cellar hole then shackled her legs. Light framed him as he stood looking down into the blackness at her. An unexpected tenderness softened his features. He rummaged in the backpack until he found a towel and a flashlight. He folded the towel and, using the light to see, placed it under her head as a pillow. He backed out of the cramped space and closed the flimsy door.

"I'm sorry, Caitlin, you can't have the flashlight. Someone might spot you too soon."

Too soon—what did that mean? His behavior was confusing. It was as if he couldn't decide her ultimate fate, torn between obsessive love and the need to punish her for loving another.

He moved around outside for a few more minutes. Thuds and scrapes hinted that he covered the door with branches. Then a hush settled on the woods. A low rumble reached her ears as the truck started and drove away. The sounds of woodland life rushed to fill the ensuing silence.

She closed her eyes and wept. *Lord, please don't let Sean go into that house. Keep him safe, Lord. Oh please keep him safe.*

* * *

Sean stared at the computer, concentrating on the details of the room shown in the picture. He tried avoiding looking at Caitlin. Every time his eyes strayed to her face his stomach lurched. She looked terrified. Scanning the details of the fireplace, scrutinizing the andirons, stabilized his raw emotions. The photo could be of almost any colonial home. He let his eyes drop to the next thumbnail picture. He inhaled sharply and clicked on the file to enlarge the image. He should've started with this photo showing a portion of the house exterior.

"I know this house." Excitement shoved aside the helplessness.

"Are you sure?" Dave Montigue leaned over his shoulder, hopeful.

"Positive, Dave. I haven't been inside in a long while but I recognize this door." He tapped the computer screen. "I was there last week."

"Where?" Scott leaned over his other shoulder.

"Becky's house." He looked at their puzzled faces. "My great-great-great-grandmother. We donated most of the furnishings to museums but the house is still standing. Mostly."

"Again I ask, where?"

"Devil's Elbow Road."

"The devil house belongs to your family?" Scott's voice held a hint of awe.

"Scott," Sean smiled benignly. "It's not haunted."

"Oh, I know that." His off-hand dismissal made Sean chuckle. "Becky haunts this house."

"Ha ha, very funny." Scott looked closely at him. "You serious?"

"Of course not." Sean rose, reaching to shut down the computer "We need to get over there and save Caitlin."

"Whoa there, big fella," Dave put a hand firmly against Sean's chest, stopping him. "You can't rush into that house. Eric Coffey is a well-trained cop. You don't think he left Caitlin there so you could waltz right in and be the big hero, do you?"

"Well," he faltered. "What else can I do?"

"First, we take a closer look at these pictures. Second, we coordinate with law enforcement." Dave moved back to the computer. He scrolled quickly through the thumbnail images and chose one that looked promising. Clicking on it, he enlarged it to fill the screen.

"Okay, here we've got a good shot showing part of the perimeter. Let's examine it and the one of the front door." He glanced around the room. "That printer work? We'll start with a printed copy for each of us. Anything looks suspicious, zoom in on screen here."

Sean took one picture, Scott the other while Dave called his contacts. The State Police were working closely with the town police, who were still shocked that one of their own was doing this. Snapping the phone shut, Dave turned back to the other two.

"Got help coming and a team is going to do a preliminary check at the house. Easy, Tag. No one goes in until we're sure it's safe."

They stared at the pictures then looked closer. Sean was the first to notice something. Calling Dave over, he pointed it out. Dave studied the printed photo then went to the computer, zooming in on an area near the door latch. The wire was clearly seen.

"He rigged the door." Scott was disgusted. "Figure it's explosives?"

Dave grunted, staring at the screen. "Too easy for that."

"What d'ya mean, too easy? Took me five minutes to spot that."

"Because it's a photo in an email. We'd have spotted that wire right away on scene. It's red, for crying out loud." Dave made a backhand slapping motion.

"So we spot it quick. Why's that important?" Sean itched to go get Caitlin.

"Exactly—why?" Dave shook his head. "Coffey's no idiot but he might be banking on you thinking he is."

Footsteps sounded on the stairs as a State Trooper appeared. Dave recognized the man, introducing him as Bob Zelinsky. He was accompanied by Naultag's chief of police, Ed Masiello.

"Tag," Ed slapped his back, a grim expression on his face. "Sure wish this wasn't one of my men. You know we're doing everything possible to apprehend Eric Coffey."

"I know, Ed, and no one blames you. Coffey's been foolin' us all."

"So what've you got?" Bob Zelinsky asked. Dave showed the pictures to both policemen.

"Coffey called you?" Bob looked to Sean. "He had to expect you to recognize the house."

"We aren't dealing with your average run of the mill whacko here," Chief Masiello stated.

Trooper Zelinsky nodded. "Eric Coffey has had extensive training, a lot of it up at the academy. Including courses in explosives, incendiaries, and weapons. This could be a red herring, meant to slow us down and buy him time to escape."

"On the other hand, we can't assume the wire is bogus. We should assume it does trip some sort of explosive device," Dave advised.

"We need to call the bomb squad," Scott said with a mix of dread and excitement.

"Yes, we need a hazardous device unit on site. They can determine what's in there and how best to deal with it." Zelinsky said.

"Look at this photo here." Dave pointed. "Notice this blur? Zoom in and now what does it look like?"

"A beam of light, a ray of sunshine?" Ed Masiello speculated.

"I don't think so. The windows in that house are all boarded up. Plus, it's horizontal."

"Very good, Tag." Dave said. "Some sort of infra-red trip device, I'm guessing."

"So he's got the whole place rigged to go sky-high if we try to go in?"

"Can't say for sure, Scott," Zelinsky stated. "We'll have to wait for a bomb technician to figure out what type of explosive we're dealing with."

"What about Caitlin?" Ghastly images filled Sean's imagination.

"Every precaution will be taken to safeguard life." Zelinsky smiled sympathetically. "Sean, we've all got wives, girlfriends, sisters, someone we wouldn't want in this situation. No one is going to do anything to jeopardize Caitlin. That means we'll keep a tight leash on you."

* * *

Amazing, how sound really does carry through the ground. Caitlin noticed it quickly as she lay with only a towel between her ear and the dirt. When Eric drove his truck away she actually felt it. Unfortunately she also felt something crawling up her bare leg. It had to be a spider. Shaking her leg had no effect, probably because she couldn't move her legs much. She'd scream if it wasn't for the duct tape covering her mouth.

Dear Lord, please make the spider go away.

She giggled mentally. *Spiders, I'm praying about spiders. I've completely lost my mind.* She focused, trying to think of some way out of this situation.

Maybe if she turned around she could push her way through whatever covered the opening. She started wriggling, scrunching and stretching, slowly turning to face the opposite direction. Bits of light filtered through the broken wood door. It was more like a fading patch of lesser darkness, but it was enough to show her the way out.

Moving like this hurt her already battered body. Bruises on her shins cried out every time she bumped them. She had a full-blown headache and her muscles were starting to cramp. But she'd managed to turn 180 degrees and now faced the exit. As she lay catching her breath another vehicle rumbled out on the road. Was Eric returning? She strained to hear better. No, whoever it was drove by without stopping.

Sean? Her breath caught. She had to get out, warn him. Pushing her feet against the dirt floor, she ignored her sore muscles and barked shins and rammed a shoulder against the door. The wood was stronger than it appeared, or she was weaker than she thought. After several tries a gratifying crack signaled success. She collapsed, breathless and with a painful shoulder. As her breathing slowed, returning to normal, her eyes drooped and she felt herself sliding into exhausted oblivion.

Sometime later, heavy rumbling shook the ground, waking her with a start. This sound felt different than the earlier vehicles, heavier than Eric's truck. Listening closely she heard the rhythmic knocking of diesel engines.

Fire trucks! It was starting. She was too late.

TWENTY SEVEN

"It's a timer."

Sean groaned. "How long?"

The bomb disposal technician frowned. "I can disarm the device, but it's gonna be tight."

"Let's just go in. You said they're small charges. How much damage could they cause?" Sean started pacing again.

"Tag," Chief Sminski placed a hand on his shoulder, halting him. "They're incendiary charges. Look at that house. You'd be engulfed in flames before you ever found Caitlin."

"I know my way around in there, Chief." Sean pointed to the house. "The parlor, where the pictures were taken, isn't far from the door."

"And if she's not still there? Which she most likely won't be," Dave cautioned.

Sean studied the house. They were right, of course. Still, he couldn't chance running out of time. Let the trooper keep working on disposal, he had another idea.

"Okay, Chief, I concede your point." Sean chose to overlook Dave's objections. "Now, how about I go in an upstairs window? I doubt he set charges up there."

"We can't be sure." Dave edged closer to Sean.

"The stairs are falling apart. He'd have to be insane to go up there." Sean scowled at Dave, aware the older man planned to restrain him if he moved toward the house.

"And you think Coffey isn't insane? Besides, if the stairs are in such bad shape how will you get down them?"

"It's the only way. I have to do it." Sean moved away from Dave, focusing on the chief.

"No." Darin's hard eyes bored into Sean.

The two men stared hard at each other. Sean seriously considered acting on his plan regardless of approval. Out of the corner of his eye he saw Dave edge closer again.

"Don't make me cuff you, Sean," Dave warned quietly. "We'll

use desperate measures only when the situation becomes desperate. Understand?"

"And if anyone goes in, it will be Richie and Web. They're in gear, you aren't." The chief's tone held no room for negotiation.

Sean slowly turned to look to where the other firefighters stood waiting, prepared for the worst. Then he glanced at the bomb technician. *Trust in the Lord with all your heart and lean not on your own understanding.* He exhaled slowly, realizing the wisdom of Proverbs 3:5-6. The rest of the sentence humbled him, and gave him the courage to wait. *In all your ways acknowledge him, and he will make your paths straight.*

Okay, Lord, we'll do this your way. Please give me strength to remain patient and the wisdom to know when to act.

"All right, I'll wait a little longer." Relief flashed on the others' faces.

Long slow minutes ticked by. Town and state police cars, fire apparatus, an ambulance, and several personal cars filled the immediate area. Down the hill, near the old stone bridge, the forestry truck and a second ambulance waited along with more police vehicles. They were prepared for every eventuality—a fire that might get out of control and cause injuries as well as the possibility of apprehending Eric Coffey.

Darin's radio crackled a transmission. Sean ignored it, seeing the bomb technician carefully open the door, thoroughly checking the entrance before giving an all clear signal. Sean rushed forward, all his earlier resolve to wait on the Lord vanishing in an instant. Darin yelled something that he didn't hear.

Inside, the house was dark, darker than the twilight outside. Sean took a moment to let his eyes adjust then went straight to the parlor.

"Tag, wait!" Scott called. "It's a trap."

* * *

Switching to her other shoulder, Caitlin renewed her attack on the exit. Desperation and fear drove her, lending her strength. She had to warn Sean. An old nail ripped into her. She cried out, the sound trapped in her throat. No time for pain. Moving back to the first shoulder she slammed against the splintering wood. The old, rotted door gave way. Losing balance, she slid back into the cellar. Root tendrils snagged and raked at her bare skin. The entry slope wasn't steep and she slipped barely twelve inches before stopping.

She fought the panic welling up at the sensation of sliding into dark oblivion.

Her lungs burned with the effort of breathing. She struggled upwards once more. Only a few branches blocked the way now. It was dark outside. Had she actually broken out of the root cellar? She crashed through the last of the branches and fell to the ground. Far above black shadows moved gracefully in the wind, revealing glimpses of a moon partially shrouded by clouds. She was out.

The noise of breaking out drew the attention of nearby firefighters. She heard voices. Above the others she recognized Randy's. He called out to someone as men tried to locate the source of the noise. And then her magnificent view of the sky was gone, blocked by a large dark shadow. She tried to smile. The duct tape kept her lips firmly in place.

"Hey, Graeme, get over here and bring a light," Randy bellowed.

He tossed aside branches. Caitlin could make out his form bending low, looking right at her and seeming not to see her. She tried to speak. The sound came out as a moan. Randy inhaled sharply. An engine rumbled to life and the loud *beep-beep-beep* of a truck backing up filled the air. As she struggled to sit up, light flooded the woods, searing her eyes. She stopped moving, no longer able to see which way to go.

"It's Caitlin!"

Randy's hand cupped her face and he spoke softly to her. "We've got you now, Caitlin. Everything's gonna be okay."

"Greg," a different voice yelled from the blinding light. "Radio the chief. Caitlin is down here. Make sure he understands. She is not in that house."

"Gotcha," a response filtered through the trees.

Hands lifted her. Pain, everywhere pain. She fought against the branches tangled around her legs. The rescue effort halted as arms cradled her. Randy's voice spoke gently in her ear, an imploring command. "Stop trying to help, Caitlin. Let us get you clear."

Slowly her eyes focused on his face. He smiled a sweet smile that she'd remember for the rest of her life. He lifted her carefully and looked her over.

"Gonna have to take you to the truck to get bolt cutters. Sorry for the delay."

She wanted to smile, to tell him it didn't matter because Sean knew she wasn't in that house. Everything was okay now that Sean was safe. But she couldn't open her mouth to say anything. Instead she laid her head on Randy's shoulder, closing her eyes as tears of relief slipped silently between her lashes.

When they reached the vehicles, John Graeme found bolt cutters to free her.

"I can do you one better." Tom Jacobs held up a key. "Let's get you out of these cuffs, Caitlin, and then Jay and Al can check you out. You look pretty banged up."

When her hands and legs were free, Randy cautiously set her feet on the ground. She staggered, catching herself by gripping his arm, then stood firm. He touched the side of her face, gazing into her eyes with a tender sorrow.

"I'm real sorry for this, Caitlin. Please don't hold it against me." He ripped the tape off.

She shrieked.

"That hurt." She eased the complaint by kissing his cheek. "Is Sean really okay?"

His eyes shifted, looking over her head. She turned, seeing the two EMT's approach. Tom Jacobs shook his head. The movement caught her eye. His expression was grim.

"Don't you worry about Sean," Randy said. "We need to take care of you."

She pushed him away and looked up the hill. The glow she'd assumed was work lights suddenly took on an ominous tint. As they all watched, flames shot up into the night sky.

"Sean!" She screamed. Paralyzed only momentarily, she started to run and was brought up short against Randy's arm around her middle.

"No, Caitlin. I can't let you go up there. If anything happened to you, Tag would never forgive me."

She struggled, kicking her legs when he lifted her off the ground. Randy held her firmly, refusing to let go even when she twisted and slapped him. At last her fury spent what little energy she had left. She sagged, a limp rag doll in Randy's arms. He turned her into his shoulder and she wept.

* * *

"Tag, wait. It's a trap!"

Sean hesitated, momentum carrying him forward another step.

226

He heard a *fwhoop* and instinctively threw himself to the floor. Above him and across the room something softly exploded, the concussion pressing him into the floorboards.

He glanced up cautiously. The dim light filtering in through the front door highlighted a shower of burning particles falling like stardust, followed by puffs of white smoke. Phosphorus. Memory dredged up a course on incendiary devices. *Infernal machines.* White phosphorus caused deep, painful burns to any area of exposed skin. He rolled into a ball, tucked his head against his chest and shielded it with his arms.

Face down, he waited for the deadly rain, praying his t-shirt would be enough protection for his back. All the while he had one dominant thought—Caitlin. She'd be burned alive and it was his fault.

Then the burning particles reached him, burrowing into his bare arms. He cried out involuntarily at the pain. At the same time the phosphorus particles ignited the house. This close to the floor, he smelled the gasoline soaked wood. Flames leaped up, danced across the floor, raced up walls. Heat blistered all around him. His shirt and jeans might be sufficient protection from the phosphorus but not the fire. In seconds the shirt began to melt and would soon burst into flame from the high temperature. The denim jeans wouldn't last much longer. He needed to get out but couldn't risk uncovering his head. Which way was he facing? If he crawled forward, would he be going toward safety or further into danger? He coughed in the smoke and fumes.

Boots thudded across the floor. All at once a rescue blanket covered him. He relaxed mentally as the surrounding air temperature dropped slightly. Muffled voices called to each other above him then a masked face peered under the blanket.

"Can you walk?" Richie Grimes shouted. He looked like something from a sci-fi movie. Was this how victims saw him? It was almost as terrifying as the fire. Richie called again, voice raised to carry through the breathing apparatus. "Tag?"

Sean nodded. Richie recited instructions. "Keep covered, move fast, follow me."

It was like any other fire except that Sean was the victim and not in turnout gear. Richie always led the way out. Sean held the aluminized blanket over his head even though his arms were in agony. As soon as they were outside, EMT's rushed to take over.

Richie took the rescue blanket back, tossing it aside as he and Web went to join the fire suppression efforts. Then Scott was in Sean's face.

"What in the name of all that's holy were you thinking? You have no protective gear, you can't go charging into a building like that. You could've been killed."

"That's enough, Bartlett," the chief interrupted. "Let Holly cut Tag's shirt off before more damage is done."

Sean dutifully lifted his arms to allow paramedic Holly Parker to cut away his shirt. She carefully eased it off. It stuck in a few spots, eliciting a wince as it tugged on his skin. He sucked in a sharp breath as cold water bathed over his back allowing Holly to pull the material away. Holly methodically checked for signs that phosphorus had penetrated the shirt or jeans. His pants had not yet succumbed to the flaming heat. He'd gotten out in the nick of time. After a moment Holly ordered him to lie down on a stretcher.

At last the shock wore off and he sat back up, glaring at Scott.

"I had to go in. Caitlin is in there." His voice caught. He glanced at the house, fully involved now. Caitlin was dead.

Scott deflated, but only a little. "No, Tag, she isn't in there. That's what we were all yelling, if you had opened your ears." He shook his head sadly. "I've never seen you act so foolish."

"Back off," Darin growled with a smile. "He's in love and that makes even level-headed guys like Tag do some truly senseless things."

"Yeah, well what am I gonna tell Cait about this? She's never going to forgive me."

"I'm a big boy, Scott. I can tell her myself and take the consequences."

Holly placed a hand on Sean's chest, pushing gently. "Okay, big boy, lay back down. This is gonna to hurt. A lot."

Sean eased back onto the stretcher. "You have a wonderful bedside manner, Holly."

"Tell me that later, Tag, after I've removed these imbedded particles."

Holly's partner, Stan, applied saline soaked dressings to burns along Sean's left arm. Holly covered the burns on his right then began carefully extracting pieces of phosphorus. She'd been honest. It hurt. A lot. Gritting his teeth and closing his eyes, Sean tried to shut out the pain.

Caitlin wasn't in the house. They must know where she is. His eyes flew open as he started to rise. Stan pushed him back down. Someone snickered. Turning his head he saw Dave talking with Scott as they watched the procedure.

"Finally realized what you forgot to ask?" Dave snickered again.

"Where?" Sean spoke through a clenched jaw.

"She was in that old root cellar down passed the bridge. Randy's with her, says she's beside herself worrying about you." Dave's tone became gentle, humor gone for the moment.

"Is she—" Sean winced again, jaw tensing as his eyes closed tight.

"Sorry, Tag." Holly dropped the particle in a bucket and covered the burn with a fresh saline soaked gauze pad.

"Caitlin's okay," Dave reassured. "Some minor cuts and bruises. We'll let her ride in the ambulance with you, if that's okay with Holly."

"We've got LifeFlight coming for Tag," Stan responded, allowing Holly to concentrate. "Have someone bring Caitlin up here. We can drive her to the hospital."

Holly switched sides. Sean opened his eyes, taking advantage of the brief respite. "I want to see her. I need to see her."

"Can't you give him something for pain?" Scott grimaced as he watched the procedure. "Morphine maybe?"

"No morphine," Sean hissed through clenched teeth.

"As I recall, morphine makes Tag lose his cookies," Holly said.

Sean smiled despite the pain. The one time he let EMS take him to the ER, Holly had been the one to give him morphine. And she was the one who took the brunt of his reaction.

Holly removed another piece of phosphorus. "Don't worry about Tag, he's taking it like a man." She smiled when he cracked open one teary eye to glare up at her. "Trust me, Scott, we've all been waiting to strap Sean to a stretcher and force him to take medical treatment."

Dave found a radio and called Randy. Sean heard chuckling as Dave expressed half-hearted sympathy. Then a long quiet. When Dave spoke again his voice took on a paternal tone.

"Don't cry, honey. I'll let you talk to him in a minute. I'm not lying to you. He's fine."

Holly finished her work. "I think that's all. We'll keep you covered until you get to the ER." She nodded to Dave. He held a radio to Sean's ear.

"Are you really okay?" Caitlin was still crying.

Sean glanced at his arms. "I'll be fine. You come up here so I can see you before they whisk me away."

There was a long pause. Randy must've explained about LifeFlight coming for him. "Why do they need to fly you?"

"Doctors and EMT's are always overly cautious. Caitlin, it's going to be okay."

Another lengthy pause. "Randy's having the ambulance down here drive me up."

"Can't wait to see you."

The transmission ended. Sean trembled. He felt shaky and weak with relief. Adrenaline let down. Stan put an intravenous catheter into the back of Sean's hand. Sean watched with mild disinterest as the drip line was attached and Stan adjusted the fluid flow. Holly pulled a blanket over his bare torso. He smiled gratefully. She smiled back and ruffled his hair.

"How's my bedside manner now?"

"Better. Those fluids are cold."

"That's because you're still hot." Holly looked up into the purple blackness of the night sky. "Your ride will be here soon. They'll land in the field next door, so we'll have to drive over to meet them."

She and Stan prepared to roll the stretcher into the waiting ambulance.

Sean protested. "We have to wait for Caitlin."

"You can't wait, Tag. You have extensive third degree burns on your arms. Time is of the essence."

"Please wait," he pleaded.

"We can wait near the landing zone. Once LifeFlight is ready you have to leave."

* * *

The pain subsided. It didn't mean anything. Third degree burns were insensate and the pain had mostly been from the phosphorus burning through his flesh. Feeling better now only meant the particles had all been extinguished or removed.

None of it mattered. Not the pain, not what it was going to

take to recover. All that mattered was that Caitlin was safe. They knew who was stalking her and soon the cops would catch Eric Coffey. The nightmare was over. Sean let his eyelids droop. *Thank you Lord, for taking care of both of us.* Probably would've been easier, at least on him, if he'd left control of the situation in the Lord's hands. A private laugh shook his shoulders.

"What could you possibly be laughing about?" Holly chided.

Opening his eyes, Sean smiled up at Holly. She sat beside him, monitoring the IV drip. They'd worked together at innumerable rescues over the past ten years. He didn't care much for hospitals and usually declined medical treatment, still he knew Holly was more than competent. A nurse by training, she was the town's best paramedic. He relaxed in her care.

"Laughing at my own stupidity," he admitted.

"You were foolish, I'll agree." Holly shook her head. "Wouldn't call it laughable, though. Have to admit I was scared they'd bring out a charred lump."

"It'd take more than a little fire to bring me down, Holly." He winked.

"You're not Superman, Tag."

"I know, I know. They keep telling me I have to listen to you medical people. After today I'll be a better patient."

"*Huhn.* Not likely." She patted his shoulder. "Just get better."

Through the open rear doors of the ambulance he watched the fire. The building was well involved. Fellow firefighters used master streams and ladder pipes in a defensive attack, to drown the fire. At least the surrounding woodland hadn't caught fire as well. What a shame, losing Becky's house like this. Ah well, it was slated to be demolished in the near future anyway. It had become a danger, particularly to all the kids who continued breaking in to look for ghosts.

The front radio squawked. Stan responded then looked back at them. "Time to go."

Where was Caitlin? It shouldn't take more than a couple of minutes to drive up the hill.

"Please Holly," Sean beseeched as she closed the doors. "Two more minutes."

She came back to his side, testing the straps holding him to the stretcher. "You're as bad as my kids," she scolded gently. "Be a good boy now and I'll give you a lollipop."

"Can tell your husband is a pediatrician."

The ambulance inched past the police and fire vehicles that surrounded the area. Flashing red and blue strobes faded, blocked by trees as the rig drew closer to Indian Rock Road. A short drive on the paved road and they would turn into the field where the blue and white EC135 helicopter waited. Stan halted the ambulance at the end of the fire road. They sat idling a moment longer than seemed normal.

"Why aren't we turning?" Holly looked quizzically at Sean.

The truck crawled forward, as if under its own power. As she rose to check what was going on the truck came to a jolting stop. She staggered, managed to keep upright for a minute then fell ungracefully onto the floor. Her personal radio crackled to life.

"Holly, I know you're in there." Eric Coffey's voice filled the rear of the truck. "Stan had it coming, Holly. He's been flirting with Marci for years."

Holly's eyes widened with fright. She stared at Sean for a long moment before scrambling to look into the front. She drew back quickly, lost balance again and sat abruptly on the bench. Her breath came in short, rapid gasps, all blood drained from her face.

"He's dead," she whispered.

"Holly?" Eric radioed again. "This has nothing to do with you. Step out now and you'll be fine."

Holly's eyes slowly focused on Sean. "Stan's dead. He killed Stan."

With a grimace, Sean yanked the catheter out of the back of his hand then reached down to release the straps that kept him from falling off the stretcher while in transit. Pushing the sheet aside, he swung his legs over the side of the stretcher. Holly began to shake. He grasped her arms.

"Get out now, Holly." Eric sounded irritated. "I don't want to hurt you. This is between me and Taggart."

"He killed Stan." Holly's eyes filled with tears.

"Get out now before he kills you too." Sean gently pushed her toward the rear doors. "Tell Caitlin I love her."

Holly fell out of the ambulance. She recovered quickly, not even brushing herself off before running back down the fire road. Sean watched until she was swallowed by the night. Then he lifted the two-way radio he'd taken from her.

"All right, Coffey, it's just you and me now." Somewhere deep inside a voice reminded him that he was unarmed and there was no telling how much firepower Coffey had.

"Why don't you step outside, face this like a man."

"Right, so you can shoot me? I'm not stupid."

"You fell for my little surprise in that house." Laughter cackled on the radio. "Tell me, are phosphorus burns as painful as they say?"

Sean didn't bother responding. He had to find some way to stop Coffey, preferably without getting killed. His eyes went to the front cab. Cautiously he looked in at Stan. A small clean hole showed where the bullet pierced Stan's right temple. A glance out the windshield explained the abrupt stop earlier. The front of the ambulance rested against a large old maple tree. The engine was still running. He ducked back into the rear.

Okay, so Coffey was on the right side of the road. Maybe Sean could get out onto the left side. At least that way he wouldn't be trapped if Coffey decided to storm the truck. He moved to the rear corner. Both doors hung wide open. He'd have to move fast, swinging down and around the door before Coffey could react.

Hopefully.

Only one problem. His arms hurt again now that the wet dressings had fallen off. Holly must have missed some phosphorus particles. With a renewed oxygen supply, the chemical reignited.

Burn a hole in my arm or get one drilled into my brain? Easy choice. Sean leaned forward, prepared to jump.

A bullet whined off the corner of the other door. He ducked rapidly back inside. The window—Coffey could see what Sean was doing. He'd have to go out low, and without illumination. He punched out the overhead light. Dumb move. He swore softly, cradling his lacerated fist. A superficial inspection showed shallow scratches, nothing serious. This wound wouldn't kill him but Coffey might. Sean dove out and under the door and rolled quickly to get the truck body between himself and Coffey.

Another bullet burrowed into the ground beside Sean as he rolled. A third shot missed completely as Coffey cried out sharply and began swearing.

"What'd I ever see in you?" Coffey bellowed. "You're just like my wife, the whore." He cursed all women his accusations getting progressively more abusive in tone.

The implication of the words hit Sean hard. Caitlin was with

Eric. *Oh Lord,* Sean closed his eyes, praying fervently. *Please keep her safe. Don't let her do anything rash.*

The shouting stopped abruptly. Even the helicopter ceased to make noise. In the eerie silence, Coffey's voice carried clearly through the night air. "I'll be back for you." His growl held ominous portent of Caitlin's doom. Unless Sean did something and soon.

He closed his eyes briefly, taking a deep breath to prepare for action. *Run, Caitlin* his mind implored. *Lord, give her strength to escape.* Coffey crashed loudly through the brush on the roadside. Fear tingled Sean's nerve endings. Could he sprint to the trees fast enough? If Coffey followed, Caitlin could get away. If Coffey didn't follow, he might turn on her.

Sirens and strobe lights drew closer, coming from the fire scene. Holly had made it to safety and alerted the others. Sean watched for a split second, thinking. Yes, he'd head into the trees, slow enough to draw Coffey away from Caitlin. It should give the authorities time to act.

He shoved himself to his feet and dashed toward a large maple near the road edge. Coffey screamed obscenities from behind him. Then something hot bit into Sean's leg. He stumbled. Sharp stinging burned his thigh. The pain spread like fiery poison. His jaw clenched as he focused on moving. The tree was only a few yards away now. Each step took more concentration.

Blood flowed unchecked, a warm stream running down his leg. He stumbled again, going down on his knees. The world tilted. The blood loss was finally more than his body could take. His brain was shutting down all unnecessary functions, like the ability to keep running.

"Move it, Taggart," Sean growled, searching for a last surge of strength.

Coffey laughed. He stood about ten feet away. Sean pushed, raising himself off one knee before collapsing again.

"Sweet revenge." Coffey advanced, pointing a handgun. "She would've loved me but you had to ruin it. Now I'm gonna get rid of you once and for all."

TWENTY EIGHT

Eric knocked out the two EMTs who were to drive Caitlin to meet Sean then handcuffed her once more and slapped another strip of tape over her mouth. Climbing the hill in the dark had been tiring. Caitlin's breaths came in short, rapid gasps long before they reached the top. Her lungs burned and ribs ached with each excruciating breath. Her shoulder throbbed where the nail had stabbed into it and her headache hadn't gone away. She stumbled. Eric hauled her upright and continued moving. The trek hadn't bothered him at all.

The fire cast a warm glow on the various apparatus encircling the old house. Eric paused for a moment. Flames stretched skyward. Sparks glittered in the darkness. Streams of water cascaded into the blaze. The scene had a deadly beauty. Above, a deep purring hum built into a soul-thumping whir. LifeFlight. Caitlin's stomach lurched. How badly was Sean really hurt? Eric growled unintelligibly and tugged her into motion. He kept to the edge of the meadow where tall grass, weeds and shrubs hid them in the darkness. No one noticed their passage.

At last they stopped. Eric released her and she collapsed onto the ground. The faint light of the moon revealed his cache of supplies. He hefted a sleek, black rifle, complete with scope and sound suppressor. She inhaled sharply.

"I thought the house would get him." He loaded the rifle. "He went in there with no gear. Those other firemen saved his worthless hide. Still, that phosphorus should've done a number on him."

She didn't want to know what he meant but Eric elaborated regardless. Boasting about his plans, talking about maiming and eventually killing Sean seemed to bring a small measure of calmness to Eric's actions. How sick he must be that such sickening atrocities were soothing.

"He was supposed to die. Then, if you were repentant

enough, I could come back for you when everyone was gone." He poked the rifle at her. Caitlin scrambled back against the stone wall. "This is your fault. But I'll give you one more chance. Just gotta take care of this loose string." He waved the gun in the general direction of the house. "Then we'll hop a flight outta here, just you and I."

He lifted the rifle and sighted through the scope. "Don't know why I should forgive you." Lowering the weapon, he looked at her. "You're just like that no good, two-timin' whore I married. She's been cheatin' on me for years."

It was all about sex with him, and if Marci didn't want him then she must be sleeping with someone else. He muttered a few more lewd descriptions of his wife. Caitlin wanted to point out that he despised his wife so why should he care what Marci did. The tape over her mouth stopped the words. Good thing. It would be foolish to further anger him now. She blocked out his words for a short while by focusing on the loud *thump-thump* of LifeFlight.

The ambulance stopped before turning onto the paved road. Eric growled angry accusations. He lifted the rifle to his shoulder and fired a shot before she realized what was happening. With an agitated gut she watched as the ambulance rolled slowly across the paved road, veering almost imperceptibly downhill before jarring to a halt.

Her scream was muffled and muddled by the tape covering her mouth. He killed Sean. Just like that. She hadn't done anything to stop him. Eric's voice cut through her anguish as he radioed Holly, warning her to leave the ambulance. Guilty relief flooded Caitlin as she realized Sean was still alive. For now. If only she could find a way to stop Eric. *Lord, please help, please keep Sean safe.*

Eric fired another shot. Even though the gun had a silencer Caitlin heard it, a soft noise of air being forcefully displaced. The suppressor was meant to deaden sound, especially from a distance. Involuntarily her eyes opened. A shadow moved inside the ambulance then the light went out. Renewed hope leapt in Caitlin.

Eric was engrossed in revenge. Hesitantly she raised her hands, finding the edge of the Duct tape. Taking a deep breath and holding it, she ripped the tape off. Her eyes watered, a moan escaping her lungs. Eric didn't notice. He got ready to shoot again. The gun fired. Caitlin rushed him, tackled him to the ground as another shot went into the night sky. Then she sank her teeth into his wrist.

Howling in pain, Eric backhanded Caitlin, knocking her across the small clearing. The blow sent a blinding flash of pain through her head. She lost balance and fell, more pain coursing through battered muscles. Eric let out a string of cusses, condemning her and all women. Throwing the rifle aside, he pulled the pistol from the holster on his hip.

"I'll be back for you," he snarled, hopping the stone wall and stomping across the road.

Caitlin crawled to the rifle. James had taught her to shoot and though she didn't enjoy it he did say she was reasonably good. Then again, he was her brother and a qualified marksman, so he was probably bragging about his skills as a teacher. The gun wasn't heavy, just cumbersome. But handcuffed and with her shoulder injured there was no way she'd be able to hold the weapon steady. Awkwardly she rested the barrel on the stones and looked through the scope. Night vision, cool.

Except it showed all too clearly what was happening. She watched Eric shoot Sean, saw Sean stumble and go down.

She had to do something.

It wasn't easy, keeping the gun steady and squeezing the trigger. She wedged the barrel between two rocks, wriggling until it pointed roughly at Eric's upper body. She didn't necessarily even have to hit him, just distract him. Get him away from Sean.

One shot, and make it good. Be quick about it, too. Satisfied she wouldn't accidentally hit Sean, Caitlin closed her eyes, mumbled a quick prayer and squeezed her fingers.

The rifle butt kicked back into her shoulder, softer than she'd expected but it still knocked her off kilter. When she looked through the scope again, strobe lights nearly blinded her. Emergency vehicles sped toward the scene. Abandoning the gun, she scrambled over the wall, running as fast as she could.

Eric had fled. Police cars appeared on Indian Rock Road as well. Eric was as good as caught.

Caitlin didn't care.

Sean lay prone on the ground, his back to her. She knelt, reaching with trembling hands toward him. Her heart stilled and her breath caught. As her fingers lightly touched his bare shoulder, he jerked as if shocked. His upper torso twisted, eyes searching, desperately seeking hers. Air whooshed out of her lungs. He was alive! Tears stung her eyes.

"Caitlin," he rasped.

"Where are you hit?" Her voice sounded strange, timid and frightened.

He rolled onto his back, reaching out to grasp her hands. Something slimy slicked his palm. Bile rose in her throat as she realized blood covered his hands. She didn't have time to think about it. With surprising strength for a man she supposed was dying, Sean pulled Caitlin, guiding her hands to his thigh. The moment her palms settled on his leg, she forgot about his bloodied hands. The world became preternaturally bright and the edges of her vision drew in sharply.

"Don't faint on me." His husky plea steadied her. "Press down, firmly."

"I can't." Her words caught in a sob. There was so much blood.

"Apply pressure, Caitlin." His voice was a little stronger. "Now. And don't stop because you think it's hurting me."

It obviously did hurt. She pressed on the wound and he groaned. The sound rumbled low in his chest and she imagined he was grinding his teeth, trying not to show the pain. She cried freely, pressed down firmly and prayed for EMS to hurry up and get there. Sean gave her a weak smile, lying back with another strained groan. His body went slack. Only the rise and fall of his chest reassured that he still lived.

Gunshots rang out somewhere in the trees. Caitlin shuddered, hoping Eric hadn't taken another life. Then a second ambulance pulled up next to them and two men jumped out of the van. Caitlin recognized Jay and Al, the EMTs who'd checked her over earlier.

"What've we got here, Caitlin?" Jay Hatcher crouched beside her, grasping Sean's wrist and glancing at his watch.

"Gunshot, heavy bleeding." Sean gritted his teeth.

"I'm talking to Caitlin, Tag. You lay there and be a good patient for a change."

Sean grumbled. Jay quickly assessed his overall condition before focusing on the gunshot wound. Placing a reassuring hand on Caitlin's arm, Jay spoke quietly. "He's upset about having to go to the hospital."

Sean's growl morphed into a groan as Jay pressed on Caitlin's hands. "Keep the pressure steady." He left, returning quickly with supplies and his partner.

"Here's the plan," Jay told her. "First we deal with this bleeding. Then while I finish up here, you and Al are going to recover those burns."

Her eyes followed Jay's gesture. In the light that now bathed the area, the burns on Sean's arms were revealed. Her gaze slid to meet Sean's. His eyes were glassy, slightly unfocused. A breath caught in her throat as tears welled in her eyes.

"Hold on, Caitlin," Jay soothed. "We can get him through this." She turned to look at Jay. "That's a good girl. Focus on saving him."

Jay deftly cut Sean's jeans down the length of his leg and above the wound. "Ease up slowly," he directed her. She lifted her hands and he carefully peeled the fabric away. Swiftly he slapped gauze pads onto the leg, bandaging to reassert pressure. Turning away, her gaze fell on Sean's face once more. Eyelids drooped as he struggled to stay conscious. He smiled in an effort to offer her comfort. "I'll be okay," his strained voice was almost too quiet to hear. His eyes closed. She watched the slow rise and fall of his chest.

"Tag, you naughty boy," Al scolded playfully. "You pulled out your IV. Holly's gonna be mad at you."

Sean grunted but didn't open his eyes.

"Hold this." Al handed Caitlin a fluid bag. "As soon as Jay is ready, we'll get Tag onto a stretcher." He leaned close to Sean's face, speaking sympathetically. "How're your arms, Tag? Any burning sensation?"

"Some." His eyes fluttered open. "Think I could get a blanket?"

"Sure. Here, Caitlin, hold one side and I'll get the other."

"I can't." She jingled her wrists. "It's the fluid bag or the blanket."

"Oh, geez, more cuffs. Okay, keep the bag." Al stood, shaking out the lightweight blanket and draping it across Sean's upper body. Then he grabbed a radio off his belt. "Tom, you out there? We need your keys again."

Al returned with a bottle of saline for irrigation and gauze pads. Setting them aside, he and Jay carefully moved Sean onto the stretcher, pulling it up to full height for working comfort.

"Okay, we can hang that bag now." Al took the fluid bag

from her, and for a moment Caitlin had nothing to do but worry. The burns on Sean's arms were tiny craters of raw flesh. They looked more frightening than the gunshot wound.

"Talk to him, Caitlin." Jay spoke at her shoulder, giving her arm a reassuring squeeze. "Let Sean know you're still here. Give him a reason to fight."

She stared at Jay, eyes widening. A reason to fight...that could only mean one thing. The muscles in her neck and chest constricted, cutting off speech and breath. Jay took a moment to focus on her, grasping each of her arms, drawing her away from the stretcher.

"Tag can get through this, just give him a reason. Don't let him see how scared you are or he'll worry himself to death over you." He held her gaze for a long moment. "You have to be the strong one now, Caitlin."

"Okay." Her voice betrayed her uncertainty.

"Deep breath, in through the nose, out through the mouth." Jay watched her closely. "Good girl. Ready to be strong?"

Lifting her chin and squaring her shoulders, Caitlin nodded.

Sean's eyes were open when she stepped back to the stretcher. Seeing her, he visibly relaxed. "I'm sorry Caitlin," he whispered. "I broke a promise."

The burns were far worse than he'd let on but it wasn't something she'd hold against him. "What promise?"

"To never get hurt again."

She choked on a laugh. He was serious and it was so ridiculous. "I fully expected you to get hurt again. You didn't break any promise."

He let out a breath of relief, smiling faintly. He was losing the battle to stay conscious.

"Don't you die on me, Sean Taggart, or I'll never speak to you again."

"Yes ma'am," he answered hoarsely, eyes closed.

She leaned close and whispered in his ear. "I love you."

He didn't respond. She looked desperately to Jay, panic rising in her again.

"It's okay, he's weak and exhausted. I'm sure he heard you." Jay moved to the end of the gurney. "We've done what we can here. Time to get him on board LifeFlight."

"Can I go with him?"

They loaded the stretcher into their ambulance before Jay answered. "I think it's best you don't fly with him."

"Is he going to die?"

He put his hands on her shoulders. "I don't think so, but they will have a lot of work to do and there's no extra room in there."

Jay helped her into the back of the ambulance, climbing in to sit beside her. She kept her eyes on Sean for the short ride, holding his hand while praying silently. The team from LifeFlight met them when the ambulance came to a halt. They spoke briefly with Jay, glancing over at her once. She ignored them all, focusing on Sean. Bowing her head, she prayed fervently, ending with a plea, "Please don't die."

A hand covered hers, startling her. She glanced up into the doctor's gentle smile and relaxed. He was a young man, probably only a few years older than her. He swiftly checked the IV line, bag of fluid and bandages, exuding a confidence that filled Caitlin with hope. Satisfied with his cursory examination of Sean, the doctor turned to her.

"We'll take him from here." He smiled compassionately, carefully removing Sean's hand from her grip. Placing his hand on the side of her face, his thumb gently pulled down her lower lid and his examining gaze searched her eyes.

"Had a bit of a bad day yourself, eh?"

She nodded, unwilling to trust her voice. The doctor's hand dropped away from her face. He patted her knee before standing to leave. Her hands reached again for Sean.

"Uh-uh," the doctor stopped her. "My turn now." He nodded and Jay carefully slid the stretcher out of the ambulance. "We're very good at what we do, but you need to let us do it."

Caitlin stood. She wasn't leaving Sean now. A sudden sensation of weightlessness came over her. She swayed slightly and put out her hands to steady herself. The doctor caught them. He frowned when the handcuffs clinked. The gentle smile returned quickly as he helped Caitlin down from the truck. To her immense gratitude, he cupped her elbow and let her walk alongside Sean until they reached the helicopter. Handing Caitlin off to Al, the doctor climbed aboard the aircraft accompanied by his nurse and Jay. Jay exited a moment later, calling out a thank you. He led Caitlin away, back toward the ambulance.

The Eurocopter's rear door closed. The rotor blades whined

and picked up speed. The sound of doom. It was more than Caitlin could take. The tears she'd held back while focused on Sean broke free. Jay pulled her into a comforting embrace, cradling her head against the downdraft of the helicopter lifting off. The deep reverberations seemed to go on forever as the helicopter raced to save a life. Caitlin's legs buckled a moment before Jay realized she was collapsing. He eased her down to sit on the ground.

Blue strobes flashed behind them as Tom Jacobs arrived in his police cruiser. Scott sprang out of the car before it stopped rolling.

"Caitlin!" He skidded on the grass, dropping to his knees beside her. "Are you okay? I think I've lost ten years of my life worrying about you."

She looked up at him. "That's what brothers are for."

"Then I don't want to be your brother any more. Let James worry about you like this." He smiled warmly when she giggled. "Janelle will kill me if anything happens to you."

Tom unlocked the handcuffs and helped Caitlin to stand. She burrowed close against Scott. He wrapped an arm around her shoulders. This was one of those rare moments in their friendship when she allowed him to be the overbearing protector. For the time, she didn't have the strength to protest. Jay waved at the ambulance and both men propelled her in that direction.

"You definitely need to go to the ER." Jay smiled. "How about a first class ride? And you can sleep on the way."

"I'm not going to sleep until I know Sean is all right."

"I was afraid you'd say that."

A sharp pain alerted her to his meaning. She glanced down at the syringe in her arm.

"Now onto the stretcher you go." Jay helped Scott ease her down. A sheet was tucked under her arms, straps pulled across to secure her.

Already she felt woozy. She searched frantically for Scott. At last he swam into view, speaking incoherently. He smiled and patted her hand. Sleep claimed her.

TWENTY NINE

Sean's arms ached. There were pains in places he had no reason to hurt. He must be in the hospital. The phosphorus burns had stopped bothering him when the wet dressings were reapplied. So doctors must've been at work, debriding and flushing and all that stuff meant to heal.

By comparison, his leg didn't hurt much. Sean hoped that didn't mean it'd been amputated. He was quite fond of having two legs.

He opened his eyes slowly, focusing on the room. Turning his head, he became aware of the only thing that mattered—Caitlin. She slept right here next to him, in a chair at his bedside. His gaze roved from her face, down the length of her body and back to her face. She was so beautiful. She wore blue scrubs, feet curled up in the chair, hands pillowing her head. Her soft brown hair brushed back from her face to drape gracefully over her shoulder.

Sean, on the other hand, probably looked only slightly better than something the cat dragged in. Maybe worse. Both his arms were wrapped in bandages. His leg was bandaged too—unless that was the ghost sensations of an amputee. Tubes ran into and out of him, some in places he'd rather not think about. And this hospital gown—even if he could get out of bed he didn't want Caitlin to see him in a dress.

Looking in the other direction revealed a large window of blackness. Was it still night or night again? Closer to his bedside was a large monitor with colorful lines and numeric readouts. It reminded him of the multi-parameter vital signs monitor that had been in his father's ICU room last year. There was an ECG reading with its regular pattern of peaks and valleys, a blood pressure reading, heart rate, respiration, blood gasses. When he turned back again, Caitlin was awake. She sat up, hazel eyes watering. Puffy redness gave away hours of crying. She also had a black eye and her nose was swollen slightly. But she smiled and he'd never seen her more radiant.

"Hi." His voice came out in a raspy squeak. He cleared his throat and grimaced.

"You were intubated. Your throat will be irritated for a bit."

"Was I out long enough for you to become a nurse?" Speaking at barely above a whisper seemed to help, though his voice still came out as a croak.

She chuckled and helped him drink some water. "Almost, but no. The nurses here are wonderful and explain everything to me. I'm a quick learner."

Pushing a button on the side of the bed, she sat down and watched him. He didn't ask what she'd done. He knew she'd pressed the call button for the nurse. As the door opened Caitlin spoke again.

"Everyone, and I do mean everyone, told me how much you hate hospitals and what a horrible patient you are."

"Maybe," he grumbled. The water felt soothing. He sipped some more.

"You never told me about all the other times you've been injured."

"Not that many." He scowled at the nurse as she studied his vital signs. "Nothing serious."

"Not in the last few years, anyway."

Sean groaned. "You've been talking to my parents."

"Yes I have. And it's a good thing you've learned to be more careful. I don't think I could survive anything like this ever again."

The nurse reached for the bed sheet. "Ah-hem," He nodded toward Caitlin.

The nurse laughed. "Caitlin, would you mind stepping out of the room?"

"No problem, Meghan." Caitlin leaned over and kissed his forehead. "Behave yourself."

Nurse Meghan pulled back the sheet, checking his bandages and catheters. Hesitantly he looked down at his toes. Hallelujah—two feet! Wiggling them both confirmed each leg was still attached.

"I'll report to your doctor," Meghan said. "I'm fairly certain we'll be able to take the urinary catheter out right away."

"Sounds painful."

She smiled. Great, now he was sure it would hurt. He opened his mouth to protest more when Caitlin returned. His jaw snapped shut.

"One of the nurses will be back with something for your pain." Caitlin said.

"How much of my, uh, conditions are you aware of?"

She laughed lightly. "It's all just basic biology, Sean."

"No, it's my biology and I'd like to think I still have some dignity."

"Relax, you're very dignified. I know in a clinical sense what's going on, that's all."

Sean breathed a sigh. "So how long has it been?"

"Thirty-two hours, forty-six minutes since you first came out of the fire." Her lower lip trembled. "I was so afraid of losing you."

"I'm here now." Pain shot up his arms when he tried to reach for her. "I wish I could hold you."

"Me too." She sniffled. "But I'd rather you get better, and quickly." Caitlin held his hand where it rested on the bed.

"Nice shiner. Was your nose broken?" He said after several silent minutes.

"Apparently not really. You'd think that would be a yes it is or no it isn't kind of condition."

"I understand completely. Badly banged up but not actually broken."

"I guess that's what the doctor said. A lot like my ribs. They're not broken, either, but knowing that doesn't help them feel any better." She made a face. He smiled.

"Does it hurt to breathe?" She shook her head. "Good. That would be a bad thing."

"Had your fair share of cracked ribs, eh?"

He ducked his head guiltily. "More than my mother knows about."

"Mmm, yes, I've gathered you haven't always been forthcoming about your injuries." She smiled coyly. "I also spoke at length with Jay and Holly." He rolled his eyes and groaned. She laughed. "Actually, I think I understand. However, while I do expect that you will get hurt again, you are ordered to accept all medical treatments recommended."

"Jay once tried to send me to the ER for a splinter."

"It was a three inch metal shaving. And you did end up seeing a doctor about it."

"I'm not going to win, am I? At least I get to see you smile." He hesitated, not wanting to dampen the mood. Still, there were questions he needed to ask and they almost certainly would wipe away her smile. "I was afraid of losing you, too."

Her smile dimmed. At the same time her grip on his hand tightened. He squeezed back.

"Do you know what happened? With Coffey, I mean."

She dropped her gaze. Her grip loosened as she tried to withdraw. He held on firmly, not letting her slip away. After a few seconds of half-hearted struggling, her hand relaxed in his. Her answer came in a quiet voice.

"Eric gave up."

"Really?" That seemed too easy. After years of obsessing over Caitlin, planning his way back into her life and then months of plotting revenge, giving up didn't feel like something Eric Coffey would do.

"They had him surrounded. I guess Eric figured it was all over." Tears slid silently down her face. "He shot himself."

Not surprising. It was the only solution that let Coffey be in complete control. And a cop in prison...well, death might be preferable. "It's probably better that way." Sean offered, thinking she cried simply for the lost life. "Coffey was obviously miserable being alive."

Her sobs increased. Pulling away, she covered her face with her hands, muffling the sound of weeping. Ignoring the pain, he reached and managed to grasp her wrist. He tugged at it. She leaned into him, rested her head on his chest and kept crying. At least at this angle he could stroke her back relatively painlessly.

"What's wrong, Caitlin?" She should be relieved to have the nightmare over, but these weren't tears of relief.

"I made Eric that way."

"Oh, no Caitlin, no. He made himself that way. You didn't date anyone in school. None of those other guys went insane."

After a long moment, she whispered, "Maybe."

When the tension in her shoulders relaxed, he knew she'd accepted the truth of his words. Their silence returned. It was the comfortable quiet of two people happy just to be near each other. Her tears subsided. She kept her head resting against him. He ceased stroking her back, his arm draped across her. He laid his head back, closed his eyes and sank into their closeness.

The door opened, breaking the spell. He frowned. Caitlin sat up, wiping at her teary eyes, and smiled shyly up at him. The intruder smiled broadly, his attire giving away his profession even before he spoke.

"Good morning," the doctor intoned. His amused gaze went to Caitlin. "And how is our patient today?"

"He seems in high spirits, Dr. Ben."

"Only for you, sweetheart," Sean qualified.

"Ah, well, I didn't expect you to be happy to see me." Dr. Ben chuckled. "EMS tells me you are not an easy patient."

Sean rolled his eyes, grumbling under his breath. So he refused medical attention on occasion. Okay, all the time. That didn't make him a bad patient. Did it? Besides, they weren't serious injuries.

"Caitlin, why don't you go out with Mr. and Mrs. Taggart. I'll be out shortly." When she left, the doctor turned and formally introduced himself to Sean. Then he set about examining Sean's arms and leg, all the while detailing the course of treatments planned. They discussed skin grafts, proper nutrition, exercise, and probable length of stay in the hospital. Sean groaned.

"Two weeks, and that's on best behavior." Ben waggled a finger at him, giving away his suspicion that Sean would be staying longer. "Now, I think you will like your first assigned exercise. How do your arms feel?"

He lifted his right arm. "Much better."

"Good. You must tell the nurse of any discomfort. Despite what you believe, it is not my goal to keep you in pain."

"That's my exercise?"

Ben laughed. "No, your exercise is to hug Caitlin. At least two or three times an hour, until we come get you for surgery. Think you can handle that?"

"Yes sir."

* * *

"You have to eat, Sean."

"I'm not hungry."

Caitlin gave up. "You're such a grump today. Do your arms hurt?"

"No, and my leg is fine too." He kept his face turned away.

"Have you been doing your exercises?" She overlooked the obvious fact that he was avoiding her. She had to choose her battles.

"You'd know if you were here." He finally looked at her. His eyes narrowed. "What's with the shirt?"

She glanced down at the navy blue shirt with its EMS emblem on the left breast. A larger Star of Life covered the back. "Jay gave it to me."

"And why are other men giving you gifts?" His eyes filled with accusations.

She rose and gathered the food tray. "If you can't be civil then the nurses can deal with you."

She turned to go, trying to swallow her tears. This surliness was normal. Dr. Ben and the nurses had warned about it and other psychological stages to be expected. That didn't make it any easier to deal with.

"I'm sorry Caitlin." He waited until she was at the door. It was the furthest he'd pushed her so far.

She hunched her shoulders and turned back to face him. "I love you, Sean Taggart, but you are pushing my buttons."

His head drooped. Finally he repeated his apology. "I'm sorry."

"It's only been ten days. What're you going to be like after a month?"

"I just want it to be over." He leaned back against the chair, eyes closed.

She inhaled deeply, let the breath out slowly. "You're frustrated. You'll feel better when you can do things yourself again."

"Hmph." He didn't open his eyes. "Where were you today?"

"I told you, at school." She moved back into the room, setting the tray on his bedside table.

"In July?" Sean opened his eyes, watching her intently.

"New teachers have to go in early for orientation and stuff." She played with the food on the tray. It was true about new teachers going in earlier, but not a month and a half early. She'd been in a meeting with Arlene Millis, the school superintendent. The question of her higher salary had become a moot issue when Eric Coffey killed himself. Marci Coffey's veiled hatred had turned to public accusations. The woman clung to the belief that Caitlin and Eric had been having an affair. She made a formal complaint to the school committee, claiming it was Caitlin's fault that Eric became psychologically unstable. Concerns about her job were more than Sean needed to deal with right now. He needed to focus strictly on getting whole again. She felt awful keeping secrets from him. When she glanced up and met his gaze, the suspicion in his eyes twisted her gut.

"So when did you see Jay?"

She sighed. "He came to see you yesterday. Remember? The shirt is a peace offering, an apology."

"Apologizing for what?"

"For stabbing me with a syringe full of sedative." She rubbed her arm, remembering.

Unexpectedly, Sean smiled. "Jay did that? Accidentally?"

"No, not accidentally." Despite the fact it was at her expense, she was happy to see his good humor returning.

"You should have a fire department shirt."

"I have three. Richie and Web brought me one when they came in, because they figured they should bring something and you're not the flower type."

"Who else gave you one?" His demanding tone softened.

"Stand up." She waited until he was on his feet. "Randy came in with Jay and had to counter the EMS shirt."

"That's two." He smiled again.

"Walk to the door." When he was half-way there, she went on. "The chief of course wanted to make sure I know I'm part of the department family. Walk back."

Sean crossed the room, faster this time. "I know what you're doing."

"As long as it works." She smiled. "I have a State Police Academy ball cap and sweatshirt, too. Know who from?"

He wrapped his arms around her. "Dave gave them to you. I knew about that gift."

"Know what Scott gave me?" She smiled coyly.

He grunted. "The yellow roses out at the nurses' station."

"Are you jealous of Scott?"

"Only that he knows you so well."

"He's got a few years head start but I think you'll do much better in the long run." She stepped back, forcing him to pull her closer. "Your arms seem to be healing well."

"I have my slave driver girlfriend to thank for that."

"So, I've gotten all these gifts from everyone else. What are you going to give me?"

"This," ducking his head, he kissed her. His lips moved on

hers, soft and tender at first, insistently passionate in the end. "And I'd better be the only one giving you that gift," he whispered huskily.

"The only one ever."

* * *

Sean watched through half-lidded eyes as Caitlin crossed the room. She thought he was sleeping, stretched out on the recliner. In fact he had been dozing. When she stole into the room he came out of the half-sleep state. It happened all the time. Whenever she was near he was acutely aware of her presence. Not that he let on about it.

For more than four weeks she'd been his nurse. First in the hospital, now at home. Dr. Ben had said Caitlin was determined Sean would live, and that was that. He thought he'd relish having Caitlin nurse him back to health, and at first he had. Now...he still liked it—oh yes, no doubting that—but there was something else nagging at his conscience.

She tiptoed past again, this time on her way upstairs. She'd been working in the camp store and now would be heading for the office.

When he came home from the hospital, Caitlin began spending all her time at High Peak. She gave up her summer of leisure so that she could help his parents as well as play nursemaid. Almost every morning at eight she arrived and didn't leave until eight or nine at night. She helped out in the store and office, took a hand at cleaning the facilities and pools, even occasionally mowing the house lawn.

She deserved so much better.

Sean shifted in the chair, trying to get comfortable. It wasn't his cramped muscles that made him uncomfortable. What made him uneasy was mostly his mind. He wanted to be out working, hated having to rest in the middle of the day. Chafed at the slower pace his healing arms demanded.

In the beginning he'd been relegated to office work—ordering supplies, taking reservations, checking guests in and out. Then they let him feed the goats and chickens. But Caitlin wouldn't let him clean the animal pens or restrooms, for fear of infection. Today he'd been allowed to use the walk-behind mower. He could probably mow with the big John Deere except that it lacked power steering. And if he did drive the tractor, he'd have to admit to being able to drive a car. Would Caitlin stick around if he didn't need her?

Caitlin fell in love with a strong, capable, hard-working man. Now she was doing much of his work for him. She didn't complain, always had a smile for him. Still, Sean saw how tired she was at the end of each day.

She deserved so much more.

Several times last week she hadn't come to the campground until after five in the evening. She claimed she had to be at the school. Maybe it was true. No one talked to him about her teaching job, not even his parents. Whenever he brought up the subject of Arlene Millis or Marci Coffey conversation strained. Something had happened. Why wouldn't Caitlin tell him?

This morning, she told him she'd be gone all day tomorrow. "I have to take a fire safety course," she explained. "Can you believe Scott is teaching it?" She had laughed.

That was supposed to be his workshop. He'd planned it out to the *nth* degree back in April. They hadn't even let him know about his replacement. The only one to blame for that was himself. He couldn't obey orders. Didn't have the sense to not charge into a burning building wearing nothing but his street clothes. Even a rookie wouldn't be that stupid.

He dozed off again. The clock on the mantle read four when voices in the kitchen woke him. Randy's baritone elicited a tinkling laugh from Caitlin. Sean rose slowly from the recliner and moved on silent footsteps toward the door.

"See you tomorrow, then," Randy said. "I'll just peek in on Tag before I go."

Sean stepped into the room. Caitlin sat at the table, across from Scott. As he watched, she turned her face up to accept a kiss on the cheek from Randy. She smiled. Anger and resentment flared inside Sean. He clenched a fist and glared at his cousin.

"Are you going somewhere together tomorrow?"

They turned, startled and looking guilty. Caitlin started to get up. Randy pushed her back into the chair. "Stay and talk to Scott. I can show myself out," he said.

Sean kept his glare trained on Randy. The younger man crossed the room as if he had no cares in the world. Reckless, irresponsible, jerk.

"Lighten up, Sean," Randy muttered when he got closer. He

went by, forcing Sean to turn toward the hall. "She loves you, Tag. You've got no cause to be jealous of anyone."

Randy continued down the hall and let himself out the front door. Sean stared after him. Were his emotions that easy to read?

"Hey, Tag," Scott called. "Did you hear we got approval for the new LaFrance?"

Slowly, Sean turned back to the kitchen. Caitlin smiled at him.

"Come sit and talk with us," she said.

She looked happy sitting there talking to Scott. The dark circles under her eyes weren't so noticeable. She was full of energy. Not like when she spent time with him. Bartlett met his gaze. *What were you thinking?* The words reverberated in his head.

"I'm tired. Think I'll go upstairs to lie down." As he hobbled down the hall, part of their conversation carried to him.

"...reached a decision yet?" Scott's voice was hushed, hard to hear clearly. "Are you staying or leaving?"

Sean's step faltered. He grabbed the railing of the stairs. It felt like he'd been sucker punched in the gut. Caitlin was thinking of leaving? It was his fault. Because of his stupidity she had given up her life. Because he'd acted foolishly, Caitlin was stuck loving a weak, useless, hideous man.

He should let her go. She deserved so much more, she deserved better. If he was any kind of a real man, he would send Caitlin away so she could find someone to love who could give her all she deserved. Someone who could take care of her.

Dear Lord, give me the strength to do the right thing.

Sean's eyes burned, stinging with tears he fought to control. Caitlin deserved a better man than him but he just couldn't let her go. He was too much of a coward. The thought of life without her was a great, empty blackness, painful to touch.

THIRTY

Physically, Sean seemed to be doing quite well. Emotionally...Caitlin wasn't sure if anything was wrong or if she was just being critical. He had refused to go to any functions or get-togethers with the fire department. Whenever Scott visited, Sean clammed up or, more typically, disappeared. He barely spoke to Randy. He wouldn't even go near the grill.

"Understandable," Dr. Ben had told her, reassuringly patting her arm. "Sean was high on life when survival became certain. Now all the hard work lies ahead. Naturally he's questioning. How did this happen? Is it worth the effort to recover? Do you think less of him?"

Did Sean blame her for what had happened to him? Maybe he no longer thought she was worth all the trouble he'd been through but just didn't know how to tell her. Seeing her every day was just a reminder of what she'd put him through.

Later, Caitlin tried again to draw Sean out.

"My class reunion is this weekend." She glanced quickly at him. He stared out the passenger window. "Would you like to go with me?"

He continued to stare silently out the window for several minutes. "If you want me to, I'll go."

The truth was she didn't want to go. Eric Coffey was still the hottest topic of conversation. Marci still blamed Caitlin. It didn't help that she felt guilty, as if it truly was her fault Eric had snapped. Whenever the school committee requested a meeting, she jumped to do their bidding. She needed to prove to everyone that she was worth keeping on staff. Going to the class reunion would be good PR, something she really should do whether or not it was enjoyable.

Regret gnawed at her as they drove in silence. She hadn't shared with Sean that for now, at least, Superintendent Arlene Millis had decided to keep Caitlin on a probationary basis. He had enough to worry about. Wasn't that the excuse he'd used for not talking to her about the fire and Mr. Prescott's death? Was that only two months ago? She was such a hypocrite.

Sean spent the rest of the week working around the campground. His overall attitude and demeanor seemed to improve with the increase in workload. Except in regards to Caitlin. He took over the mowing and many other physical labor tasks—except for driving the tractor. She derived a bit of perverse satisfaction knowing he couldn't manhandle the old John Deere any better than she could, though that would soon change.

Her days were taken up with school. Even with all the professional development days, she still helped at the campground. She could fit in time to work on the bookkeeping. If only it was so easy to find a way to work in time to talk to Sean. He deserved to know what was going on, with her job and with Marci Coffey.

* * *

Friday evening after dinner, Caitlin decided it was time to tell Sean about the school. Maybe if she opened up to him, he'd reciprocate. It wasn't so much that he wouldn't talk to her, although he said little. More bothersome was that he never looked directly at her. Sometimes she'd catch him staring when he didn't think she was looking. But he never made eye contact.

"It's a beautiful night," Caitlin opened. "Would you like to sit outside for massage therapy?"

Sean shrugged, another typical response. Margaret had suggested that maybe Caitlin needed a break from being a nursemaid. Caitlin had objected, said she didn't need a break from Sean, but maybe she did. His lack of emotion was irritating.

She faced the porch chairs, sitting opposite Sean and taking one of his arms in both of her hands. Gently she massaged his forearm, moving slowly upward. He stared out at the sky where stars began to appear. Saying nothing. As usual. Once upon a time touching him like this elicited a definite reaction. She tried to smile at the memory. Instead hot tears stung her eyes. Sean's counselor had warned her to expect bouts of depression. This wasn't what she'd expected. He was perfectly normal with his parents. He slept fine, at least so he claimed. Work was something he enjoyed, like before.

No, this wasn't so much depression as rejection. Sean rejecting Caitlin. She brushed away a tear, not that he would have noticed it in any case. Changing arms, she tried to talk to Sean.

"School will be starting soon."

"You'll be going back to work, then?" He spoke in the dull, lifeless tone he usually affected when talking with her.

"I'm on a kind of probation." She waited but he didn't ask why. "Marci Coffey almost convinced them to let me go."

"Marci blames you." His tone was matter of fact. Did he blame her, too?

"I can see her point. Blaming me, I mean. At least Arlene Millis is willing to give me a chance." Her hands stilled, wrapped around his arm.

His eyes flickered, his gaze going to her face for a fraction of a second. "So you won't be around during the day anymore."

Her breath caught. Would he miss her? But he didn't say anything more. She let go of his arm. It thudded softly against the Adirondack chair. He didn't react. Didn't he feel anything? Even an angry outburst would be better than this apathy.

"Are you glad I won't be here to nag you? Am I driving you insane? Maybe I just have that effect on people." She stood, arms straight at her side, fists clenched, nails digging into her palms. "If you prefer, I'll leave you alone."

Still he kept silent and didn't look at her. She closed her eyes, fighting for control. *Lord, what more can I do? If Sean doesn't love me I need to know. Please help me to do the right thing.* She waited, willing her breathing to become normal. And then the answer was clear. She was afraid to confront Sean, afraid to hear him confirm her worst fears. But she needed to give her fear over to the Lord.

"If you don't love me, Sean, I wish you'd just say so." Pain squeezed her heart. "I don't want to be a thorn in your side."

The silence became a wall. She opened her eyes and looked to Sean. He hunched his shoulders and his head drooped. No sound came from him. She gnawed at the inside of her lip, holding back tears. Maybe he wasn't sure, just needed time. Or perhaps he didn't want to say it to her face. Didn't want to deal with her crying.

"I'm leaving now." She kept her voice as steady as possible. "I won't be back tomorrow unless you really want me here."

He said nothing. Didn't move or even acknowledged her exit. A hollow, aching chasm opened in her heart, a black hole sucking in her life force, suffocating her being. It was all her fault. She shouldn't have kept secrets from him, no matter how good the intention. Plus, he'd gotten burned and then shot because of her.

She'd really messed up his life. Just like she ruined Eric's. Tears blurred her vision, making the drive home more difficult.

Lord, what now? I didn't want to fall in love but that seemed like your plan. Was I wrong? Is this Satan's trickery? Or your way of letting me know I need to stay away from men?

A nice heavenly *hmph* would've been reassuring at this point. But there was no response at all. Maybe she hadn't asked the right questions.

She trudged into the empty house focused on God, trying to see what He wanted her to do next. She'd been so afraid to love and now she was terrified of losing that love. Where did it all go wrong?

The glowing red numbers on the alarm clock showed midnight when she finally came up with the answer. She was letting fear control her. First it was the fear of making bad choices, of repeating her parents' mistakes. Fear of being abandoned. Now it was the fear of losing Sean, of being alone for the rest of her life. But she wasn't alone. She was never alone. Jesus was there for her whenever she needed guidance. The Lord knew what she needed and He would never abandon her. The Holy Spirit was with her day and night. She need not fear.

Sure, losing Sean was painful. It would take time to adjust, to accept this as God's will. But she would adjust, she could go on. The Lord would fill her heart, make her whole again. And she wouldn't hold a grudge. Not that she could ever hate Sean, in any case. No matter his feelings for her, she would always love him.

A yawn cracked her jaw. Her eyelids kept trying to stick shut. Peace settled in her heart, it was time to rest. First she prayed. *Lord please help me to accept your will, even if it isn't what I want. And please be with Sean, help him to follow the path you choose for him.*

* * *

Sean lay in the dark, alone on the big bed in a cavernously empty room. Hard to believe only months earlier he'd dreamed of sharing this bed with Caitlin. How wonderful to be able to hold her in his arms all night, feeling the softness of her hair, inhaling her scent, listening to her heartbeat. Wrapping his arms around her, knowing she'd never leave.

He shifted restlessly. He'd never hold Caitlin like that. The dream was dead, gone in a fiery funeral pyre. He gave in to the self-pity, tears sliding soundlessly down his cheeks as he thought of all he'd never share with Caitlin.

In the beginning Caitlin seemed loving. She doted on him in the hospital, trying to ensure his full recovery. Gradually he noticed signs that she was falling out of love with him. All those gifts from other men. Time spent with others, as if avoiding Sean. When Scott or Randy visited, she always had a smile for them, and a hug. The first time he saw Caitlin hug Randy something inside him snapped. Like a blood vessel in his head had popped.

And she'd been keeping things from him. Marci Coffey had accused her publicly and put Caitlin's job in jeopardy. She should've come to him. They could've faced it together. But she didn't trust him. No longer felt he had the strength to support her.

Because he didn't.

Caitlin had every right to look elsewhere for love. He was too weak. A sniveling coward. She deserved more, better. It hurt, but it was the truth. He couldn't face his fellow firefighters, knowing they'd ridicule his stupidity for going into that house. They'd laugh at him. Especially if anyone found out he couldn't even bring himself to light the gas grill. How could any of them understand? It wasn't the flames, it was that soft little explosion when the gas first ignited. And he wasn't frightened. The sound didn't trigger some sort of posttraumatic stress episode. That little *fhwumph* was a reminder of his idiotic recklessness. It mocked him, laughed at how he'd lost Caitlin.

He was such a coward.

And now it was so much worse. Caitlin deserved better than him. More, she deserved to know what he thought. The least he could do was let her know that he'd let her go.

He rolled onto his other side and punched the pillow in an effort to get comfortable. Here was another example that he was a spineless loser. He couldn't tell Caitlin anything. He dreaded life without her, hated the life he was forcing her to live, but was truly horrified of what her reaction would be if he did talk to her. He was terrified she would confirm all his suspicions that she didn't love him anymore and stayed only out of pity. He groaned. *Lord, what am I supposed to do? I'm so scared. How can Caitlin possibly love such a coward?* He closed his eyes, exhausted by all the doubt.

Do you love Caitlin?

Of course I do. *Then maybe you should tell her that.* But what if she says she doesn't love me? *Wouldn't it be better to know?*

He opened his eyes, groggily staring at the alarm clock. He'd nodded off and slept about an hour without realizing he wasn't awake. Had he really conversed with God in his dream? He tried to remember details but only the words remained in his memory. Would it be better to know whether or not Caitlin loved him?

Lord, please give me strength to do what's right.

* * *

The morning dawned with bright promise. Caitlin glared at the apricot globe peaking over the treetops. Traitorous weather. It should be rainy or at least gloomy, to match her mood. It was all well and good to decide something in the middle of the night, when the brain grasps at any answer to hasten sleep. Now, in the light of day, her doubt and fear returned.

Every day for almost two months, she was on the road to Sean's by seven-thirty in the morning. Today she dragged out each step of her morning ritual. She stayed in the shower until all the hot water was gone. Shivering, she dressed slowly before shuffling down the hall to the kitchen. She stared out the window while waiting for coffee to brew.

Walking around the yard, down to the dairy barn, across to the cornfield and back to the house didn't use up as much time as she'd hoped. The kitchen clock alleged the time to be a little after nine. She eyeballed the clock. The second hand ticked faithfully. Suspiciously, the phone was silent. She edged over and lifted the receiver. The dial tone buzzed. It was working fine.

Sean was keeping his silence even without being present. It should've made her angry, and strengthened her resolve to move on without him. Instead it deepened her sorrow. Her heart felt like it pumped thick sludge. Energy was nonexistent. It was as if gravity had multiplied and she no longer had the power to lift her legs and walk. One day, maybe, she'd look back and see how the Lord got her through this. In the future she'd be a better Christian, dedicated to serving God. But for now the sense of loss was too great to bear.

She plodded through the house. Everything reminded her of Sean. The living room where she'd first shared her love of math. The stairs to the basement garage, where he rescued her from the lawn tractor. The front door where he first kissed her.

Nausea tossed her stomach. She collapsed on the hall floor, and abandoned herself to the tears, crying until all strength left her.

The hardwood floor felt cold against her hot, tear soaked face.

What was she to do? How could she go on without Sean? *Oh dear Lord, please take the pain away, make the hurt stop.* Bring him back to me. She couldn't pray that, though. More than anything she wanted Sean to love her but she didn't want him in her life if that meant he would be miserable. She couldn't force him to love her.

"Oh Sean." She wept again.

A knock sounded at the door. She ignored it. The screen door groaned opened. Footsteps came hesitantly down the hall. She turned her face into the flooring, shielding her eyes with her arms. The heavy tread could only be boots, had to be a man. It was Scott, coming to joke with her until she felt better. Maybe a crazed killer had come to end this pain. As if she could be so lucky.

"Caitlin?"

It wasn't Scott or a crazed killer.

It was Sean.

Her stomach flopped again. Sean, here. Why? How much more hurt could he inflict? A keening moan escaped from her. She curled into a ball, keeping her eyes covered. If only she could disappear. Poof, no more pain, no more Caitlin.

"I'm sorry, Caitlin." His voice was husky with emotion. "I...I" he stammered. "I don't think you're nagging me."

Her sobs faltered.

"I don't want to be alone."

Did he only want company, not her? "Do you love me?"

"More than life," he whispered. "So much it hurts."

"Then why won't you look at me? Why don't you talk to me?" She risked a glance up. Head bowed, his shoulders rounded and drooped as if under a heavy weight. A sheen of moisture on his cheeks.

"It hurts, Caitlin." His voice cracked. "How could you love me? No one could love me. Not now." He slumped against the wall sliding slowly to the floor, hands covering his face. "It hurts so much, loving you."

She crawled to him and placed a hand on his knee. "Why couldn't I love you?"

"I didn't protect you." He brushed away her attempt to uncover his face. "I can't even take care of myself. How could I take care of you? You deserve a better man. I'm a coward, a failure."

"You're not a coward or a failure. You are the bravest man I know."

He was silent for so long she thought he would never respond. When he did, she had to strain to hear him.

"I'm afraid to talk to you. Because you think I'm something I'm not. I'm so scared..."

"Oh, Sean." A sob caught in her voice. "Then it's me who failed. I never wanted you to be afraid to talk to me."

She pushed herself up and sat beside him. "You are the bravest, handsomest, most wonderful man I have ever or will ever know."

He shook his head and fingered his sleeve. "I'm none of those. Not anymore. Not ever."

"Look at me, Sean Taggart." Putting a hand on his stubbly cheek, she forced him to turn. "I love you. I will always love you. Some silly little scars aren't going to stop me loving you. Whatever else is scaring you, we can face it together."

He looked away and for a dreadful moment she feared he would reject her.

"Do you really love me?" Hope lilted his voice.

"Yes, oh yes, yes, yes! No matter what."

"Even if I never go back to the fire department?"

"Even if."

"What if I do go back?"

"I'll still love you. No matter what."

His head turned slowly, eyes bright with tears. "No matter what, always and forever?"

"Till death do us part." She paused. "And even after that."

His arms went around her and he buried his face in her hair, weeping unabashedly. Caitlin cried with him.

"I love you, Caitlin Harrington." Taking a deep breath, he added, "There, I said it."

"It's about time. I can't remember the last time you said it. I was beginning to think maybe you didn't love me anymore."

His mouth came back to hers. She turned to warm Jell-O under the heat of his passion. When his lips moved to her neck, she placed a hand on his chest and pushed him away. It took a moment to catch her breath.

"I think you'd better stop that." Heat flamed her face.

He chuckled nervously. "Maybe some space would be a good

idea."

"That would be wise." She slid out of his arms, scooting a few feet away. "This better?"

"Do you still love me?"

"Yes!"

"Then this is better." He smiled, let his legs relax and leaned back with his eyes closed. "I'm exhausted. Can you drive me home?"

"How'd you get here?"

"Hitched a ride with Randy."

"I'll drive today but I think it's time you got back behind the wheel."

He gave her a sheepish smile. "The physical therapist told me weeks ago I could drive."

"Then why...?"

"I was afraid you'd leave me if I didn't need you anymore. I mean to drive and stuff."

"You're as messed up as I am," she said dryly. "We deserve each other."

"My thoughts exactly."

He stared at the ceiling, mumbling. "Can't get away in the summer. Fall won't work either, 'cause of school starting. I don't think I can wait until spring vacation."

"What are you talking about?"

"Getting married. You want to be able to take a honeymoon right, and celebrate our anniversary every year."

"Are you proposing to me?"

"Can't just yet—no ring. Give me a day or two to figure this all out."

"No, you ask me now. The ring can wait."

"Yes ma'am." He winked. "You're such the romantic."

"Sean," she warned.

Shoving a foot against the floor, he twisted and knelt before her on one knee. "Caitlin Marie Harrington, will you marry me?"

"Yes, Sean Thomas Taggart, I will."

"When?"

"The sooner the better." She smiled at his surprise. "I don't want you to worry anymore about me leaving."

They thought about it awhile. Finally she made a suggestion. "I could live with a long weekend for a honeymoon. Columbus

Day is a three day weekend for school."

"By October things get pretty slow and quiet at the campground."

"Do you think that's too soon?"

"Seems like more than enough time for whatever plans have to be made."

"With Janelle and your mother together we won't have to do a thing." She chuckled.

"Don't leave out your mother." His index finger pushed the corners of her frown up. "Maybe she wasn't the best parent, but she's your mother. And you are her only daughter."

She grabbed his hand. "She's going to be shocked that I'm getting married. We may have to sedate her, she'll be so ecstatic."

He smiled and leaned in for another kiss. She snuggled against him. His heartbeat thumped under her cheek. She closed her eyes. This was where she belonged.

After a length of comfortable quiet, his voice rumbled in his chest. "We could probably still make it to your class reunion."

"No thank you." She glanced up. He averted his eyes but not before she saw his sadness. "I don't feel like talking about Eric Coffey anymore."

"Oh." He hesitated. "I figured you didn't want to be seen in public with me."

He gestured at his arms, encased in full-length elastic garments meant to prevent excessive scarring. At home he wore short sleeve shirts for comfort. When they had to go out to doctor appointments, he put on long sleeve shirts. She hadn't thought much about that behavior until now.

She opened her mouth to tell him there were people much worse off. That some burns on his arms were nothing compared to people with facial burns. But those words would only hurt. She snapped her mouth closed again. Right now Sean felt he had it the worst. Later he could figure out the truth. Still, people always notice anything different. And they stare. It didn't matter that his wounds, though severe, were on the low end of the disfigurement scale. He was uncomfortable in the public eye. It wasn't so different from her reason for not wanting to attend the reunion. In her case, people not only stared and whispered behind her back, they said things to her face. She understood Sean's reluctance to go out in public and his need for reassurance.

"It's your hair. Everyone's admiring those adorable curls." She combed her fingers through the hair at the nape of his neck.

He grabbed her wrist. "Keep it up and we'll be back at that line you don't want to cross."

"Yet," she smiled

THIRTY ONE

The little orchard at High Peak campground was a perfect backdrop for the wedding. A few stray apples still clung to nearly bare branches. The day was a perfect example of Indian summer, warm with a crisp edge to the breeze.

"I can't believe how well this dress fits you."

"Thanks, Janelle. Apparently you think I'm chunky."

"No, I wore this when I was nineteen. I'm jealous that you're still this thin." She circled Caitlin one more time, adjusting the train on the wedding dress.

Janelle held the train as Caitlin moved to the window. Below, in the orchard, Sean talked with Scott and Randy. All three men wore tuxedos yet looked laid back as they chatted. What a difference eight weeks made. Finally and completely assured of her love, Sean was once again the man Caitlin first fell in love with. Confident, compassionate, strong. Loving.

How could she have ever doubted him? He glanced at the house and smiled. A kind of tickling flip-flop sensation fluttered inside. She put a hand on her stomach. Caitlin turned to face Janelle, who dropped her gaze.

"I have a confession." Janelle twisted the sleeve of her dress. "When you stopped talking to Sean, I prayed."

"You did? Why?"

Janelle smiled. "Because you needed it, didn't you?"

"But you don't pray. I mean, I've never known you to pray."

"I don't talk about it, that's all. Anyway, it worked, so maybe I'll make a habit of it."

"I hope so." Caitlin smiled warmly. Nothing could top marrying Sean, but this confession made the day more wonderful. "And maybe you could come to church with me. With us, I mean. Ooh, that sounds weird."

"Nervous?" Janelle grasped her hand, giving it a squeeze. "Relax, enjoy the day. It's only a ceremony. Nothing will change about either one of you."

Caitlin started to say she wasn't worried about Sean changing. A light tap on the door stopped her. James stepped into the room, resplendent in his dark dress uniform. This was the first time Caitlin had seen him in it since he made Chief Petty Officer.

He spotted Caitlin and gave a low whistle of approval. "You look gorgeous."

"Thank you." Warmth filled her. They weren't as close as some siblings but they shared a history that bonded them firmly. His approval of Sean meant more to Caitlin than anyone else's. James made a circle motion with one finger and she twirled slowly. Janelle scrambled to keep the train from tangling. James crossed the room and kissed Caitlin.

"Sean's one lucky guy." James nodded his head toward the door. "They're ready for you down there."

He moved away, crossing the room to where Debbie sat nursing their baby.

"I'll be down in a few moments," Debbie told them.

Jack Harrington waited at the bottom of the stairs. He wore a simple dark suit that she knew from experience was an expensive designer label. He was a handsome man. She had his brown hair and hazel eyes. Today it felt good to have her father's features. Under his approving gaze she felt like a little girl.

"Hi," she spoke softly.

"You look beautiful, princess."

Tears prickled her eyes. He hadn't called her princess since she was five years old. He held out his arm.

"Come, there's a young man waiting for you."

They walked arm in arm out the front door and across the driveway toward the orchard, stopping at the corner of the barn. In another minute or two Sean would see her in the wedding gown. She glanced down, admiring the dress. A simple A-line gown with a sweetheart neckline, the ivory satin delicately embroidered with gold thread, it definitely made an elegant statement. The herringbone back was laced tightly, accentuating her curves. The butterflies started up in her belly again.

The musical prelude played. She took a deep breath. Janelle and Debbie went around the corner. Their mid-length dresses swished softly. The wedding march began. Caitlin progressed in a slow stately promenade. All heads turned to watch but she only saw Sean. He looked more wonderful than she ever could. The tuxedo was a smoky black with a platinum vest and Windsor tie. The dark colors accentuated his blonde hair and blue eyes. He stood with hands clasped in front, eyes riveted on her.

As she drew closer, he smiled and dimples bracketed his face. A nervous thrill rippled through her. She returned his smile. Then they stood side by side facing the minister. Her heart beat faster. Emotion choked her breathing. When her father placed her hand in Sean's, tears rolled down her cheeks.

When at last the ceremony was over, Sean cupped her face in his hands, brushing away tears with his thumbs. Their eyes held for what felt like an eternity. Slowly he lowered his head until their lips met. The kiss began soft and tender. His lips caressed hers, moving with a building passion. When it ended, he held her close, shielding her tears.

Someone whistled, breaking the spell. Caitlin giggled, wiping away tears as they turned to face their guests as Mr. and Mrs. Sean Taggart.

The reception was memorable for the number of times glassware rang out as firemen egged-on Sean's campaign to constantly kiss Caitlin. She didn't mind. Twilight settled over the hill. Along the length of the hayloft, strings of small lights gave the area a candlelit glow. The overhead lights dimmed as Sean led Caitlin out onto the dance floor.

Taking her into his arms, he whispered, "I love you Caitlin Marie Taggart."

The music started—'Keeper of the Stars.' She pressed into Sean.

"I'll love you till death do us part," she said. "And even after that."

She turned her face up and met his kiss.

EPILOGUE

All these pretty girls and they were either married or related to him. Didn't Sean have any single female friends? Randy leaned a shoulder against the wall, eyeballing the wedding guests. At the far end of the loft, a DJ was getting ready for the first dance. Caitlin would look radiant in Sean's arms. Bartlett would take to the floor with his wife. Traditionally, Randy would be expected to dance with the bridesmaid he'd been paired with, and he would, for propriety's sake. But then he'd let Debbie's husband take over.

So who would Randy dance with? He hadn't brought a date. Odd. In the last ten years, he could count on one hand the number of social functions he'd attended without a date. And none involved dancing. What was the sense of going to a party unless he had someone to dance with? There was something seriously wrong with him—not just today, but since June. Since rescuing Caitlin from that root cellar.

Crossing his arms, Randy examined that thought. Something happened that night and over the course of the following weeks. Finding Caitlin, extracting her from the brush and branches covering the root cellar then carrying her to the safety of the waiting ambulance, had made him feel like a hero. He didn't often rescue people at fire scenes. Generally he was tasked with fighting the flames and he was not part of the SAR team. The sense of saving the day, playing the hero, was just the tip of the problem, though.

Caitlin's grateful kiss on the cheek had not tumbled his heart, drawing him into a forbidden love. No, though he liked Caitlin. She wasn't the cold, aloof girl from high school. A great sense of humor, dedication to her profession, and a responsible personality all made her perfect for Sean. They were the kind of couple you read about in fairy tales. They'd each been willing to risk their lives for the other.

Watching them now, laughing with some of the other guests, the niggling twinge dug at Randy once more. It wasn't Caitlin that had him feeling this way. It was seeing how much she loved Sean, how happy his cousin was with her love. At that moment, Sean leaned down and kissed his new wife, their embrace lingering a little longer than a mere sweet caress. Fellow firefighters whooped and whistled. Randy turned away and ambled toward the stairs.

A decade of dating since high school and not one single woman ever made him feel the way Sean obviously felt about Caitlin. Which was just as well, now that he thought about it. He wasn't exactly husband material. To be tied to one woman for the rest of his life...a shudder shook his shoulders. Besides, a woman would have to be crazy to want to spend her life with him. An adrenaline junkie, he loved taking risks and making them payoff. Routine was the death knell of life. He was better off single. Free to do as he pleased.

"Uncle Randy," a young voice called. Randy turned to see his niece Julia waving from the barn doorway. She ran out, apparently set on stopping him from leaving. Despite his gloomy thoughts, a smile lifted Randy's lips.

"What's up, Jules?" He swept her up, swinging in an arcing circle as Julia laughed. She was by far his favorite niece. Setting her back on her feet, he tweaked her nose and waited for her to speak.

"It's time for the bouquet and garter toss. You gotta be there, Uncle Randy, 'cause you're single." Hands plunked on her hips, Jules reminded him of his mother.

"I'm not interested in that, Jules. Someone else should be catching the garter."

"Uh-uh." Julia grabbed his hand and dragged him back to the barn.

Overpowering an eleven year old would be easy but he loved her too much to resist. It was just a silly tradition, anyway. He could purposely not catch the garter and even if he did, it wouldn't mean anything. Everyone in Naultag knew he was a womanizing booze hound. Women might enjoy going out on dates with him, but none would want to get serious. He intended to keep it that way, too.

The single females gathered for the bouquet toss and Randy saw a flaw in his plan to avoid catching the garter. His oldest niece, Ashley, jostled around all the other ladies as Caitlin stood with her back to them. The bouquet flew through the air. Ashley leaped and nabbed the flowers. People laughed and cheered. Unfortunately,

Randy knew what would happen next.

Sure enough, Ashley's date—Roger—lined up with the other single men, jockeying to find the most strategic location for catching the garter. That kid couldn't keep a lid on his hormones, or his hands off Ashley. If Roger was the garter recipient, he'd be more than happy to slide his paws a little too far up Ashley's leg. All in the guise of tradition. Probably something Randy would've done at that age, which only made him dislike Roger all the more.

As he moved into the group of men clustered in front of Sean, Randy caught his cousin's eye. Sean grinned, a kind of knowing smirk. Fine, let him think Randy deserved to be next on the marriage chopping block. Whatever. So long as Roger kept his mitts off Ashley. Sean turned his back on the group, glancing over his shoulder once before tossing the garter blindly. Roger made one of his slam-dunk, lay-up jumps, beaming with a sure fire win. Randy straight-armed him, knocking him aside gracelessly, and snatched the garter out of the air. He was rewarded with a murderous glare from Ashley and a loud chorus of whoops from the fire fighters.

"Yeah, Henderson's next," someone yelled, possibly Richie.

"Who'd be foolish enough to marry him," someone else—Wedge? —sniggered.

Randy turned to face them all, twirling the garter on his index finger and waggling eyebrows at the crowd. Didn't matter what any of them thought—he was never getting married.

ACKNOWLEGMENT

This book has been a long time in the works. I began it shortly after my son was born and finished the first draft in the "usual" time. Since then, it has undergone a number of rewrites and extensive editing. I joined American Christian Fiction Writers (ACFW) and honed my writing skills. I also met my #1 critique partner, Nike Chillemi, and together we joined a critique group. Scribes207 deserves major kudos in making SHE'S MINE tighter, crisper writing. Nike cracked the whip to keep me going and didn't just nudge but truly shoved me over the finish line when my writing juices seemed to have stopped flowing. My other critique partners were also invaluable: Sally Bayless, your suggestions and constructive criticism helped me chop unnecessary scenes; Emily Reynolds, you helped with the romantic tension; Jean Thompson, Marti Chabot, and Pat Krugel provided the eyes of a reader filtered through the editing eye; Betty Thomason Owens, amongst other things, your help with commas is greatly appreciated.

Growing up, my dad was a volunteer firefighter and an EMT, which is partly why I made Sean a firefighter. Yet, that job has changed a lot since the 1970s and I needed inside help for accuracy. I turned to a local fire chief, Peter Martell, who is also a Paramedic. The information he provided is absolutely correct and up-to-date. Any discrepancies or inaccuracies are strictly my fault; some may be due to regional differences and for some I simply needed literary license to make the story work. It is true, however, that firefighters in this region are no longer "volunteer" per se but are "Call Firefighters" - despite getting a meager payment, these men and women really are volunteers, putting their lives on hold and often in danger to protect their communities. Training requirements for Call Firefighters are the same as for Career Firefighters with the drawback of the Call Firefighters footing most of the cost on their own. Every chance you have, thank a firefighter, EMT/paramedic, police officer and all other EMS workers for their service.

Without fans, people clamoring for this book to *finally* be published, SHE'S MINE would probably still be nothing more than a large file on my computer. Thank you to everyone who read my previous books and continually encouraged me to write more. I know this one is a departure in genre and I hope you will all forgive me anyway. Although the time period is different, the characters face similar challenges in love, friendship and faith journeys.

More than anyone else, my family have supported and encouraged me in this endeavor. My husband was instrumental in the publication of my first novel. Without his uplifting attitude, I never would have had the courage to let the public see my work. Thank you! My children have grown accustomed to my lack of housekeeping skills for which I am grateful. I have been a published author all of my son's life and he seems to take it in stride. My daughter adapted to my writing and now she has become a publishing asset - her Photoshop and artistic skills pulled together my vision for the book cover. I look forward to collaborating with her more in the future. I love my family!!

Saving the best and most important for last, I must give a big shout out to the Lord. He has given me this talent to write, the imagination to think up stories and "what if" situations, and He is solely responsible for this book being in your hands today. I am thankful for a loving God, who sent me (and you) a Savoir that we can be forgiven of our multitude of sins, and who lives within each of us (when we invite Him in), giving us strength to face our daily challenges. I strive each day to lean on His wisdom and to patiently wait on His timing. I'm not always good at it, which makes me all the more grateful for Jesus' sacrifice and God's forgiveness. THANK YOU, LORD!!

Made in the USA
Las Vegas, NV
11 February 2022